Morvenn Vahl
Spear of Faith

Other stories and audio dramas featuring the Adepta Sororitas

THE ROSE IN DARKNESS
Danie Ware

THE ROSE AT WAR
Danie Ware

THE TRIUMPH OF SAINT KATHERINE
Danie Ware

PILGRIMS OF FIRE
Justin D Hill

SISTERS OF BATTLE: THE OMNIBUS
James Swallow

THE BOOK OF MARTYRS
Alec Worley, Phil Kelly & Danie Ware

MARK OF FAITH
Rachel Harrison

CELESTINE: THE LIVING SAINT
Andy Clark

EPHRAEL STERN: THE HERETIC SAINT
David Annandale

Other stories from the Warhammer 40,000 universe

LEVIATHAN
Darius Hinks

• DAWN OF FIRE •

Book 1: AVENGING SON
Guy Haley

Book 2: THE GATE OF BONES
Andy Clark

Book 3: THE WOLFTIME
Gav Thorpe

Book 4: THRONE OF LIGHT
Guy Haley

Book 5: THE IRON KINGDOM
Nick Kyme

Book 6: THE MARTYR'S TOMB
Marc Collins

Book 7: SEA OF SOULS
Chris Wraight

Book 8: HAND OF ABADDON
Nick Kyme

Book 9: THE SILENT KING
Guy Haley

WARHAMMER 40,000

Morvenn Vahl

Spear of Faith

Jude Reid

BLACK LIBRARY

A BLACK LIBRARY PUBLICATION

First published in 2024.
This edition published in Great Britain in 2025 by
Black Library, Games Workshop Ltd., Willow Road,
Nottingham, NG7 2WS, UK.

Represented by: Games Workshop Limited – Irish branch,
Unit 3, Lower Liffey Street, Dublin 1,
D01 K199, Ireland.

10 9 8 7 6 5 4 3 2 1

Produced by Games Workshop in Nottingham.
Cover illustration by Robson Michel.

A CIP record for this book is available from the British Library.

ISBN 13: 978-1-80407-669-9

Printed and bound in the UK.

For Julia and Sofia, with all my love, always.

For more than a hundred centuries the Emperor has sat immobile on the Golden Throne of Earth. He is the Master of Mankind. By the might of his inexhaustible armies a million worlds stand against the dark.

Yet, he is a rotting carcass, the Carrion Lord of the Imperium held in life by marvels from the Dark Age of Technology and the thousand souls sacrificed each day so his may continue to burn.

To be a man in such times is to be one amongst untold billions. It is to live in the cruelest and most bloody regime imaginable. It is to suffer an eternity of carnage and slaughter. It is to have cries of anguish and sorrow drowned by the thirsting laughter of dark gods.

This is a dark and terrible era where you will find little comfort or hope. Forget the power of technology and science. Forget the promise of progress and advancement. Forget any notion of common humanity or compassion.

There is no peace amongst the stars, for in the grim darkness of the far future, there is only war.

Dramatis Personae

The High Lords of Holy Terra

Roboute Guilliman, Lord Regent of the Imperium of Man, Avenging Son of the God-Emperor

Trajann Valoris, captain-general of the Adeptus Custodes

Morvenn Vahl, Abbess Sanctorum of the Adepta Sororitas

Eos Ritira, cardinal of the Ecclesiarchy

Fadix, Grand Master of the Officio Assassinorum

Kadak Mir, Paternoval Envoy

Sisters of the Order of the Argent Shroud

The Living Saint Hestia, leader of the sacred pilgrimage of Saint Athenasia the Martyr

Perdita, Seraphim of the Abbess Sanctorum's honour guard

Ignatia, Celestian Superior of the Abbess Sanctorum's honour guard

Fionnula, Celestian of the Abbess Sanctorum's honour guard, heavy gunner

Kseniya, Celestian of the Abbess Sanctorum's honour guard, augurs specialist

Hiromi, Celestian of the Abbess Sanctorum's honour guard

Zafiya, Celestian of the Abbess Sanctorum's honour guard

Sisters of the Order of Our Martyred Lady

Illuminata, prioress of the Convent Sanctorum

Sujata, palatine assigned to the sacred pilgrimage of Athenasia the Martyr

Aleyna Amarys, Battle Sister assigned to the sacred pilgrimage of Athenasia the Martyr

Sisters of the Order of the Bloody Rose

Elsvieta of Rheins, canoness of the Preceptory of Saint Mina's Hope

Kerem, Sister Superior assigned to the sacred pilgrimage of Athenasia the Martyr

Sisters of the Order of the Valorous Heart

Lucreziana, canoness assigned to the Convent Sanctorum

Rukhsana, Retributor assigned to the sacred pilgrimage of Athenasia the Martyr

Marayd, Retributor assigned to the sacred pilgrimage of Athenasia the Martyr

Sisters of the Order of the Sacred Rose

Kharys, palatine assigned to the Chapterhouse of the Holy Liberator

Sisters of the Orders Minoris

Véronique, Hospitaller Superior of the Order of the Eternal Candle

Carmine, Hospitaller of the Order of the Eternal Candle

Theodosia, Novitiate Pronatus of the Order of the Quill

Crew of the Mars-class battle cruiser *Lux Dominus*

Abram Haraquis, Lord-Captain

Elion Winstet, Voidsman

Black Templars

Armond Montford, known as 'Godshelm', Marshal of the Black Templars forces on Ophelia VII

Aymar Tancret, castellan to Marshal Montford

Balian, Sword Brother to Castellan Tancret

Theobalt, Sword Brother to Castellan Tancret

Jehan, Sword Brother to Castellan Tancret

Tiberias, Techmarine and pilot of the Thunderhawk *Lacessit*

Sibellian, Techmarine and pilot of the Thunderhawk *Dorn's Wrath*

Night Lords

Kol Rakhul, known as the 'Death of Saints'

Brother Merthok, his second

Brother Ostrov, known as 'Skull-taker'

Brother Dmitrev

Brother Yevgeni

Inhabitants of Ophelia VII

Amrek of Malk, mason assigned to the restoration of the shrine-temple at Caelestis

Solana of Malk, mosaicist assigned to the restoration of the shrine-temple at Caelestis

Yulius, penitentium overseer

Tulla, penitentium overseer

Penitent 867

The Mythologie of the Abomination known as the Death of Saints

An excerpt found amongst the papers of Canoness Preceptor Mwyfania after the destruction of the Priory of the Six Miracles.

We are the Order of the Argent Shroud.

We are the bearers of the God-Emperor's light into the darkest of places, the shining spear-point that strikes at the heart of His enemies. Our armour gleams with silver radiance, our weapons swift and sure.

But the brighter the light, the deeper falls the shadow.

And our shadow has a name.

He is Kol Rakhul, and he is the Death of Saints. A fallen legionary of the thrice-damned Night Lords, he has hunted us through the centuries, his hatred written in the blood of our dead, his armour adorned with the skulls of our saints. He burns our shrines, desecrates our cathedra, defaces our effigies in his mission to erase us from existence. His movements cannot be predicted. Attack follows relentless attack until it seems the galaxy entire must burn, then centuries pass without a sign, until all are convinced that his bloody reign has at last been brought to an end.

All are convinced but the Sisters of the Argent Shroud.

We know the truth: always he returns, and death follows in his wake.

Many have sought to bring his atrocities to an end, and all have failed. Even the Blessed Saint Athenasia, who fought him in the first years of his bloody ascension, could not defeat him, though at the moment of her death she dealt him a miraculous blow that wounded him sore and bleeds to this day.

He cannot be defeated.

So long as the Argent Shroud endures, there he will be, for this is our secret and our shame: that Saint Athenasia and the Death of Saints were sister and brother who shared a single womb, two halves of a divided soul, one half filled with holy radiance, the other steeped in foulness and corruption. He is our failures made manifest, the darkness where all our fears take physical form. He is our sin, come to claim us and drag us with him into damnation.

He is the Death of Saints.

And he is here.

Act 1

The Book of Prayer

I

It begins in darkness.

The blade, freshly whetted, ice-cold against her scalp. The stones of Holy Terra, rough and unyielding where she kneels. The fluttering of wings in the chapel's vaulted ceiling. A robe of pearl-white samite, clinging to skin still damp from the sacred font. The heady scent of incense – rose attar, sandalwood, and myrrh – and the solemn tolling of the bell.

Abbess Sanctorum Morvenn Vahl rises to her feet, and only then does she open her eyes. The God-Emperor stares back at her from above the altar, His golden visage stern, His lips pressed tightly shut. Light floods through the glassaic windows, painting the stone pillars of the chapel in patches of blood-red, brilliant white, sun-bright gold. Swinging censers suspended high above her head fill the air with smoke, dark clouds against a darker sky.

These are the rites of faith.

The ancient rituals must be observed, no matter how long and arduous, as sacred as the bolter and the blade, but the stillness makes Morvenn uneasy. On the battlefield she knows her place. There she is a holy warrior, a bringer of death to the enemies of the Imperium, a living paean of praise to the God-Emperor in all His majesty. There His presence is made manifest in the flamer's brilliant light, the thunder of the assault cannons, the screams of the enemy as they lie dying at her hand.

But here in the chapel He is silent.

Morvenn tears her eyes from the statue's face and returns her attention to the task at hand. Beside her on the dais, the towering golden form of the Purgator Mirabilis looms above her, the ancient Paragon warsuit as motionless as a statue. Its right hand is locked around a heavy golden lance; its left ends in a heavy bolter, the ornate golden gunshield marked with the words *Prioris* and *Sanctorum*, honouring the twin bastions of the Adepta Sororitas. It is a relic beyond price, and its might is hers to command.

Before her, her Sisters stand assembled, their faces turned to the God-Emperor in mute adoration, their visible devotion a stark contrast to the eyeless faces of the choir-servitors. An ancient litany rises from the servitors' mechanical throats, the familiar melody rising sweet and plaintive above the layers of polyphony below. The sound is unearthly in its perfection, but all the incense in the chapel cannot mask the distinctive odour of the servitors' flesh: sacred unguents, machine oil and decay.

Two Celestians in silver armour step forward, their helmeted heads bowed in submission. The taller of the two women slides the white samite robe from Morvenn's shoulders, while the second offers the close-fitting bodyglove that will serve as its replacement. Morvenn takes it without a word and slips it on, the close-woven ballistic fabric closing around her like a second skin.

Next, the gambeson. The quilted corselet settles around her shoulders, chest and waist, and a flicker of impatience builds in her. A galaxy of endless war awaits her, but today she is donning her armour for a battle of a different kind. How many times did she watch the sacred rite of armouring as a novitiate, each time imagining how it would feel to stand at the eye of the storm? In those days, Abbess Sanctorum Sabrina had been a saintly figure, as close to the God-Emperor Himself as Morvenn's mind could conceive.

Had Sabrina – had any of her predecessors – felt this same restlessness, the same longing for the cleansing purity of battle, the same burden of responsibility that hangs around her neck like a penitent's yoke? For today, she dons her armour not for war but for the council chamber, to sit amongst the High Lords of Terra and wield words in place of weapons, a duty for which she finds herself ill-inclined and poorly equipped.

All but one of the choir-servitors fall silent, the exquisite polyphony of the martyr's hymn fading to echoes as the soloist's voice rises high and pure. Morvenn closes her eyes and lets the music drown out her thoughts and fill her with holy purpose.

God-Emperor, give me strength to face what is to come.

'*Ave Imperator,*' the Sisters intone.

A cherub flutters onto the dais, a golden vambrace clutched in its chubby hands. Celestian Superior Ignatia takes it and clasps it solemnly around Morvenn's right wrist, her gauntleted fingers securing the fastenings with well-practised dexterity while Fionnula, her second, attends to the left. Couters and rerebraces follow until her arms are adorned in holy armour, ready for what is to come.

'Will you accept the burden of this sacred armour?' Ignatia's voice booms through her helmet's vox-speakers, sonorous in the chapel's sacred air.

'In the God-Emperor's name, I will,' Morvenn replies.

'Will you wield these weapons – the Lance of Illumination and the thrice-blessed heavy bolter Fidelis – as the God-Emperor ordained, with hatred and fury?'

'In the God-Emperor's name, I will.'

The candles flicker, and in the shifting light the Purgator Mirabilis is alive with holy fire.

'Will you lead us to Holy War, that all who stand against us shall perish by the bolter and the blade?'

'In the God-Emperor's name, I will.' A cool breeze drifts across Morvenn's bare scalp, sending a shiver running down her spine.

'Then don this armour and wield these weapons that you may deal death to all enemies of the faith.'

Three small suspensor-platforms rise to form a miniature staircase at the Purgator Mirabilis' feet, their edges embossed with the names of the saints. Their motors whine as Morvenn takes her first step, but the marble platform is steady as though carved from rock. She steps into the command cradle, and the ornately filigreed chestplate closes into position with a familiar and welcome click. The control batons are waiting for her hands, and she locks her gauntlets around them with instant familiarity.

Only the helmet remains.

The cherubim fly upwards, returning to their roost in the cathedrum's lattice of roof-beams. A Sister in the unadorned black robe of the Order of the Holy Ossuary – one of the Orders Pronatus, responsible for the care of the Sisterhood's most sacred relics – offers her a golden helm on a scarlet velvet cushion, the brow wreathed with golden laurels, the eye-lenses dark and unseeing. Morvenn bows her head and readies herself for this final burden, but before the weight settles on her skull the chapel doors fly open, the thud of wood on stone enough to rattle the glassaic windows and send the cherubim fluttering away in mindless consternation. Morvenn's muscles tense, and the warsuit responds to the imminent threat in a smooth series of movements that bring the heavy bolter round to bear and set the Lance of Illumination blazing.

But the threat is not in the doorway.

Standing between the great iron-bound doors, her face crimson and her veil hanging askew, is a novitiate of the Order of Our Martyred Lady. Already Morvenn is striding forward, the vast feet of her warsuit echoing off the stone as she steps down from the dais to the nave.

'Abbess Sanctorum!' The novitiate drops to her knees with a sharp crack of bone against flagstone.

Celestian Superior Ignatia moves forward to stand at Morvenn's side, her hand raised sharply in remonstration. 'Novitiate, you forget yourself.'

The words strike the girl like a blow to the face, turning her cheeks an even deeper shade of scarlet. 'Forgive me.' The young woman's voice is shaking. 'But the news is of the greatest urgency. I was placed under instruction that the message was to be delivered to you in person. Immediately.'

Booted feet echo along the cloister outside. Morvenn knows that sound as well as that of her own breathing: a squad of Battle Sisters in formation, approaching fast.

'You have interrupted a sacred ceremony,' Ignatia begins.

'Let her speak.' Morvenn studies the novitiate. The newcomer is visibly shaking, her hands blanched and bloodless where they grip the skirts of her robe. 'Continue, novitiate. What news is this that cannot wait?'

'Ophelia VII is under attack.'

Visions of the last great battle for Ophelia VII flood Morvenn's mind: the cardinal world ablaze in the blasphemous light spilling from the Great Rift, the white marble cities running with the blood of the faithful, the endless swarm of the Neverborn that for a time had threatened to destroy and enslave all in their path. Before relief had arrived at last in the form of the Black Templars and the primarch Roboute Guilliman's Indomitus Crusade, she had been wholly resigned to death. Every day since has been an unexpected gift from the God-Emperor to be put to use in His service.

But surely that battle is over?

'The Tyrant of Blueflame.' Morvenn spits the name of the Lord of Change like bile. 'Has the abomination returned?'

The novitiate shakes her head, and a wave of relief passes over Morvenn. No matter what threat has come, she tells herself, nothing can be worse than that which we have already endured.

'What then?'

The novitiate speaks four words, and the faint light of Morvenn's hope is snuffed out like an altar candle.

Because what has come to Ophelia VII is worse than she had ever imagined.

II

'Grant us your blessing, holy Sister!'

The pilgrims' demands are unending, and Sister Aleyna Amarys of the Order of Our Martyred Lady has no choice but to ignore them all. Their hands leave smears on her armour, grubby fingerprints on the lining of her robes, the stench of unwashed flesh clinging to them like the stain of sin. The procession has been winding along the Way of the Saints towards the Cathedrum of Athenasia the Martyr for hours already, but the crowd of the faithful grows only thicker with each moment that passes. They line the torchlit bridges that overlook the Holy Way, straining to touch the sacred reliquary that cradles the skull of the blessed saint within its silver confines. They lean from windows, reach across gilded parapets, jostle their way up stairways carved of spiral stone.

When Aleyna looks down over the Way's stone parapet, the architecture of Ophelia VII falls away beneath her in an infinitely complex tangle of bridges, buildings, towers and buttresses; when she looks up, mere slivers of sky are visible between the reaching fingers of the spires, dark as lead, heavy as a curse. The cathedrum sits at the heart of a labyrinth of stone and adamantine wrought in every conceivable dimension, and the stately procession of the saints marks the one true route to its heart.

'Your blessing, holy Sister, I beg you!'

The pleas are without end, their cries mixing with the tolling of Ophelia VII's ever-present bells. Some of those tight-pressed to either side of the Way of the Saints are locals, idol-crafters or parchment-makers for whom this brief pilgrimage might represent the only relief from their labours in years, but the majority are from off-world, the fruits of their life's work exchanged for passage to Ophelia VII in the belly of a voidship. They have come to the cathedrum in the hope of redemption, as though it were something to be bought and sold like a skewer of grox-meat at a market stall.

Aleyna knows better. Redemption is only ever earned in blood.

She is young for a Battle Sister. At the start of the Thirteenth Black Crusade, she was still a novitiate with years of training ahead of her, but the relentless attrition of the war that followed thrust many young Sisters into positions of seniority beyond their years. Had things been different she might still be wearing carapace instead of her gleaming black power armour, her hair still hidden beneath a veil instead of straightened and bleached to an unnatural white, stark against the warm dark brown of her skin.

'My child, Sister! Bless my child!'

The silver reliquary-casket that holds the saint's remains is small enough to be carried by a single pilgrim, but the floating suspensor-platform on which it sits is the size of a Rhino. As well as the relic, the platform bears six members of the Orders Pronatus, robed and hooded, their voices raised in a perpetual chant extolling the saint's virtues. A mission of Sisters from every Order march with it along the Way of the Saints, their armour night-black, gleaming silver, blood-red, purest white. Glittering silver banners streak through the air above them, borne aloft by the greatest miracle yet.

Saint Hestia of the Argent Shroud, radiant, swift and glowing, soars with a dozen of her fellow Seraphim, her eyes ablaze with holy fervour. She is a Living Saint, the God-Emperor's will given physical form, and it is only right that she should have the place of honour above Saint Athenasia's Triumph. In years to come, her remains will be displayed to the faithful in a silvered casket, but today she is a vibrant, living reminder of the God-Emperor's might and grace. The mere sight of her fills Aleyna's heart with a hope almost enough to drive away the bitterness of loss.

Because majestic as the procession is, the war that followed the opening of the Great Rift has taken a heavy toll on each of the Orders. When Aleyna allows herself to regard the procession, it is hard to look beyond the absences where beloved faces used to be. Death in the Emperor's service is a gift much to be desired, but the scale of their recent losses is staggering. It is said that for every Sister who survived the Tyrant of Blueflame's punishing invasion of Ophelia VII, one more was called to the Golden Throne in glory. Whether or not those numbers are true, there is no doubt that the ossuaries of the Convent Sanctorum are every bit as full as the cloisters are empty.

'Sister! I beg you!'

Aleyna spares a glance to the wretch at her side: a man at the front of the crowd, thrusting a squirming infant forward in his outstretched hands. His face and hands are roped with the distinctive burns that mark him as a candlewright, a maker of holy candles to light the halls of the faith. Some of the burns have healed to thick cords of shiny pale skin, others are still raw and weeping. Both he and his child are filthy, the infant's hair a halo of dirty gold, its toothless mouth open as it screams in bewilderment and surprise. The man's gaunt face is full of desperate adoration, an expression Aleyna has seen a thousand times before. It is the kind of fervour that spreads like wildfire through a packed crowd, the kind that begins with prayers and ends in bolter shells.

'Step back.' Aleyna's voice comes through her helmet-vox as a low bark. The pilgrims to either side flinch away, but the father himself is undeterred, pushing his way forward alongside the procession. The infant is purple in the face, its screams of protest muffled by a choking wheeze as pinkish froth forms on its tiny lips. Aleyna is no Hospitaller, but even she knows the stigmata of lung-rot. That, then, is the reason the father is so desperate for her benediction, why he has travelled miles across Ophelia VII's battered surface for a glimpse of the saint's passing. Those with the means to pay will be granted a moment of communion with the saint once she is returned to her resting place – some even permitted to touch the sacred skull-bones with the tip of a cleansed and anointed finger – but not this pathetic family. This man is half-starved, dressed in filthy rags, shoes worn so thin that the outline of the toes beneath is clearly visible through the cheap synthleather.

'I beg you, Sister!'

He is close, now. Too close. One misstep, one stumble, and his desperate pilgrimage will come to its end beneath ranks of marching feet.

'I said, step back.'

This time the force in Aleyna's voice halts the man in his tracks. Tears spring to his bloodshot eyes, tracing two clean lines down his filthy cheeks.

'Please. He is all I have.'

Aleyna does not need to hear more to know the bitter tale: the man's family lost with the opening of the Great Rift or perishing one after another to the war, starvation and pestilence that followed. These people have so little. Would it be so great a sin to give him a little hope in exchange for all that he has lost?

'The God-Emperor's blessing be upon you.' Aleyna touches the tip of her armoured index finger to the child's grubby brow. A man in agricultist's robes gives an envious gasp and makes the aquila across his chest, but the father continues his desperate pursuit, undeterred by the gift he has been given.

'Take him, Sister.' He holds the child out like an offering, and finally Aleyna understands his meaning. 'The plague claimed my wife and my daughters. We have no food, no fuel. I want him to live.'

It would be such an easy thing to take the infant from his father and carry him to the convent. But what then? There are no children in the Convent Sanctorum, nowhere to raise an infant until a ship could be found to bear him to the Schola Progenium. Already the crowd is poised, hungry for an answer she cannot give. To agree would be to open a floodgate of desperation, one that she has neither the right to unleash nor the ability to close.

And the truth of the matter is simple: what use is a boy to the Adepta Sororitas?

'Go to the Hospitallers,' Aleyna says, and the hope in the man's face dies. 'They will give you succour in the God-Emperor's name.'

He nods, but already his attention is turning from Aleyna back to the procession, no doubt seeking another Sister to whom he can make his case. She can hardly blame him. With luck and the Emperor's guidance, the infant will find his way to the Sisters Hospitaller. Without it, the miserable pair of lives will end beneath marching sabatons or crushed between the bodies of their fellow pilgrims. Perhaps that is a kinder fate. Even if the child survives this time, there is always another winter, another plague, another way for death to claim him.

The pilgrim road begins its upward incline towards the cathedrum, its towers and buttresses casting jagged-edged shadows in the flickering torchlight. Aleyna keeps step with her Sisters, offering up a silent prayer of thanks to the Golden Throne. To walk in the presence of not one saint but two is a wonder beyond price, and yet her brief encounter with the man and his coughing child has left the heart beneath her cuirass as heavy as stone. So much has been lost that it will be decades before Ophelia VII is restored to its former glory, and that road is paved with sorrows for the candle-wright and his kind.

A cloud passes across the sun, dulling the glittering banner's shine to leaden grey. A murmur passes through the crowd, a tension building in the air like a gathering storm. A sudden wind stirs the dust around her feet, gusting hard enough that the nearest pilgrim staggers and almost falls. The light takes on the intensity of an eclipse, and she wonders for one giddying instant if this is a miracle, if the God-Emperor is blessing their pilgrimage with a fresh demonstration of His power–

And then the screaming starts.

Panic shoots through the crowd like a bolt of lightning, turning the thoroughfare to a clamouring press of bodies.

Where is the relic?

She searches the space where the suspensor-platform stood a moment before and sees only the frenzied mass of the crowd. Eyes bulge from terrified faces, hands claw at her robes and armour until she finds herself being shoved back and forward like a toy between squabbling children. One blow from her power-armoured fist would put an end to their squabble, but in the moment she is unable to raise her hand to them, caught in a web of indecision of her own weaving. The moment does not last, and an instant later the stock of a bolter flashes through her peripheral vision to slam into the skull of the closest pilgrim, who falls, his bleeding body swallowed immediately by the swarming mass of human panic. She looks round to stare into the helm of a Sister Superior of the Bloody Rose, who acknowledges her presence with the merest of nods.

'My thanks–' Aleyna begins, but the Sister Superior has already turned away, pushing herself through the press of pilgrims as she heads towards the reliquary.

'I have sight of the enemy.' The voice of Saint Hestia is calm as it comes through the helmet-vox, soothing as a draught of clear water, but still her words send a trickle of ice down Aleyna's spine.

'What, and how many?' The answer comes in Palatine Sujata's augmented rasp. When last Aleyna saw her palatine she was at the head of the procession as they began the saint's Triumph, but it has been hours since then, hours since they set off to the tolling of bells and the bright clarion call of the trumpets. Those moments feel like they belong to another life now.

There is a long pause. Then: *'Night Lords. Too many to count. And with them, a flying host of the damned.'*

'Take courage, my Sisters,' the palatine says. *'We are in the God-Emperor's hands.'*

Bolter fire rips through the crowd, far enough away that Aleyna cannot see its target, but close enough to make out the spray of blood rising into the air. Hestia's shadow passes across her, and she shoots a glance to the sky in desperate appeal for guidance and inspiration. Where is the enemy? What must she do?

But the flying figure above her is not that of the saint. The silhouette is wrong, the shoulders too broad, the helmet malformed and crested with monstrous wings, the enamel plating swallowing the light it should have reflected.

God-Emperor, grant me courage.

Fear prickles across her skin. Her gauntlets lock tightly around her bolter, swinging the muzzle upwards. A second shadow crosses the dying sun and then a third, until the sky is black with bodies. A horn sounds overhead, and Saint Hestia soars through the air at impossible speed, her sword blazing and her silver armour glowing from within.

'The reliquary-casket!' Palatine Sujata's voice cuts across the vox. *'Defend the blessed martyr!'*

Bolts of fire streak down from the sky. Aleyna shoves her way towards the heart of the procession, the air darkening as it fills with noxious smoke. Her armour's ceramite plating is resistant to all but the strongest heat, but the luckless pilgrims have no such protection, and their screams are turning to a wall of sound that makes it nigh impossible to concentrate. Where is the reliquary, and where is the enemy? The Way of the Saints is burning, and she has yet to lay eyes on a target.

'Heretics!' Palatine Sujata bellows, her words followed an instant later by a thunderous volley from her bolter. *'Look to the skies! Bring them down!'*

Another torrent of fire streaks through the crowd, the roiling black smoke thick as a crematory plume. A blazing figure lurches through the maelstrom towards her, and she almost fires, her finger stopping a fraction of an inch short of the boltgun's trigger as the figure half-stumbles, half-falls into her. For a moment she is holding the shoulders of one of the pilgrims as the skin peels and blackens from his face, his hair already scorched to ash – then a bolter fires on her left, and the man's head explodes. His corpse drops to the ground and continues to smoulder, rivulets of melting synthcloth searing miniature canals through the charred remains of his skin.

'Sister!'

A vox-amplified voice shatters her reverie, and she turns to find herself gazing into the lenses of a Sabbat-pattern helm, blood-red with a visor of stark skull-white and a golden fleur-de-lys above the brows. It takes a moment before she recognises the Sister

Superior she saw before – though whether 'before' is a matter of seconds, minutes or hours she can no longer be sure.

'We are called to defend the reliquary. Quickly!'

This is not Aleyna's first battle – far from it – but the speed and chaos of whatever assault has begun threatens to shatter her composure. She offers up a prayer, a plea for focus – *in battle, God-Emperor, may I know the sureness of your will* – and manages a hasty nod. The Sister Superior's shot had been a mercy killing, but the speed and nature of the pilgrim's death is still shocking. He had been neither heretic nor enemy, merely one of the faithful caught in an apocalypse of flame and confusion.

'Yes, Sister Superior.'

The other woman is already pushing her way through the crowd, bolt pistol in one hand, chainsword in the other. Aleyna hurries after her, the stifling heat inside her helmet bringing stinging sweat into her eyes and flooding her mouth with salt. And then the world erupts in a fiery conflagration, the force of the explosion lifting her from her feet and hurling her high into the air.

For the space of a breath, Aleyna is weightless, then the earth rises to meet her in a blow that drives the breath from her lungs. She lies blind and stunned, her ears ringing, something sticky running down the right side of her face as sensation slowly returns. Drawing breath is an exercise in agony, and when she inhales, she tastes blood.

Someone is shouting, but her vox – or perhaps her hearing – is too badly damaged to make out who is speaking or what they are saying. Aleyna pushes herself to her knees, releases her helm's neck-seals with a shaking hand and pulls it off. Freed of its stifling confines, she sucks gratefully at the air, rewarded with a lungful of scalding smoke that sends her chest into a painful paroxysm of coughing. Her ears ring like cathedrum bells, her sense of balance knocked askew by the force of the blast.

The explosion has blown a crater forty feet wide in the Way of the Saints. The stone parapet along its western side has been shattered into rubble, leaving only a crumbling edge of broken stone and twisted metal struts that spills away helplessly to the drop beyond. Aleyna struggles to her feet and braces herself against the base of a broken column, trying simultaneously to regain her balance and to make sense of the scene before her. The Way is all but unrecognisable, reduced to a ruin of shattered stonework and broken bodies wreathed in a thick pall of smoke. She picks her way forward, then stops as her sabaton connects with something solid: a Seraphim in silver armour lying face down, her right arm missing at the shoulder, her neck at an angle incompatible with life.

There is no sign of the reliquary.

'Palatine!' Aleyna shouts, but her voice is swallowed by the battle. Where are her commanders? She casts a desperate look around her for someone to take charge of the situation – her palatine, the Sister Superior of the Bloody Rose, even one of the Sisters Pronatus – *anyone* who can give her an order to drive away this uncertainty. 'Palatine Sujata!'

The vox stays silent.

Something moves through the smoke ahead of her – a vast, dark shadow with red eye-lenses blazing like furnaces. One of the Night Lords of whom Saint Hestia spoke, the traitors of the VIII Legion; once the beloved sons of the God-Emperor, now fallen from grace and sworn in service to the Archenemy. Her gut clenches tight with hatred and fear, but with knowledge comes relief. An enemy with a name is something she can fight, something she can hate, something tangible to wash away the confusion that has threatened to overwhelm her.

Aleyna raises her bolter and fires, sending a volley of shells into the ceramite armour where they erupt like Candlemas fireworks. The heretic continues his steady advance. Blue-white lightning crackles between the grotesquely elongated digits of his left hand; in his right, he wields a headsman's power axe, the blade raising sparks where he trails it along the ground. Each time she has fought these horrors before, it has been as one of a unit of her Sisters – never one-on-one, never alone with her ears ringing and barely able to stand.

God-Emperor, grant courage to thy faithful servant.

The heretic strides clear of the smoke, monstrous in all his blasphemous glory. He stands nine feet tall, the iridescent midnight-blue armour smeared with clotted gore. From the viciously spiked armour rack mounted on his shoulders, the rotting faces of the dead stare back at her, some nothing more than skulls, others so fresh they can only have been severed moments before. Light glints on the metal of an augmetic larynx, grotesquely exposed in tattered neck-flesh, and in a moment of horror she recognises the topmost head as that of Palatine Sujata, her right eye gouged from its socket, her bloody mouth hanging open as though in an endless scream of warning.

Aleyna's lungs are full of the smell of carrion, thick and nauseating, the hum of corpse-flies throbbing in her ears like a pulse. Every fibre of her being screams at her to run, but her muscles are locked tight, the entirety of her being held rigid in the dead palatine's one-eyed gaze. *Run,* she hears the dead woman say. *Run, before you suffer my fate.*

But Palatine Sujata would never have uttered those words in life. She would have told Aleyna to *fight.*

'Heretic!' Aleyna's finger tightens on the trigger of her bolter, spraying the blue-and-bronze armour with explosive shells. 'You have no place here!' The air fills with smoke, the smell of burning almost strong enough to mask the rank sweetness of rotting meat, but when it clears, the horror is gone. Has he fallen? Has the barrage of her thrice-blessed boltgun been enough? The answer comes in a flash of lightning, as a clawed hand lashes through the air and tears the bolter from her grip.

'What folly.' The Night Lords Champion shakes his head. 'What misplaced faith, that you should think to stand against me.' The words come out in a heavy growl that scrapes her soul raw, a sound that promises an eternity of torment at the Night Lord's hands.

'Who are you that I should fear you?' she spits.

A deep laugh booms from beneath the winged helmet. 'I am the Death of Saints.'

Aleyna has time to pray for a swift death, a plea that her soul will have found its place by the Golden Throne before her head joins the others on the heretic's trophy rack, and then the black clouds part, and a miracle comes.

Like a streak of blazing silver, Saint Hestia descends on wings of flame, her eyes glowing white-hot, her sword a burning brand directed at the heretic's black heart. He turns, and the impact of his vast fist catches Aleyna across the temple. It is only a glancing blow – the full force of the heretic's strength would surely have shattered her skull – but it is still enough to send her sprawling to the ground with a searing bolt of pain shooting behind her eyes. Through the haze that hangs across her vision like a silver veil, she watches him bring his lightning claw up to parry the saint's power sword, the impact of the two weapons sending a magnesium-white flash into the air. They are figures from a glassaic window, the rising daemon meeting the descending angel, illustrations from a holy script, the saint as bright with holy fire as the Night Lord is dark with corruption.

Saint Hestia's hair is a silver halo around her head. The pistol in her left hand discharges a burst of sacred flame directly into the heretic's face, but instead of the choking miasma of burning flesh, the air fills with the sweetness of holy incense. Radiance pours from her face, the sight so beautiful that it takes what little breath remains from Aleyna's lungs. She struggles to rise, but her aching muscles fail her and all she can do is watch in rapture as the saint raises her blade and swoops down in what surely must be a killing strike.

The Death of Saints moves too fast for Aleyna's eye to follow. In one smooth movement he spins the axe above his head and mag-locks it to the backplate of his armour, seizes her sword hand in his and crushes it into the hilt of her sword.

'Your Corpse-Emperor will not save you.' The Death of Saints leans close to the saint, the lightning claw of his right hand reaching for her face.

'You shall not prevail!' Hestia pulls back, the engines of her winged jump pack screaming in protest, but the force of his grip holds her fast. Slowly, inexorably, he begins to drag her down to earth.

A hand locks around Aleyna's shoulder. 'Sister. We must act. *Now.*'

The Sister of the Bloody Rose is beside her again, her armour gore-smeared and her vestments charred to tatters. She is shoving a slight figure in novitiate's robes ahead of her, the smaller woman's arms wrapped tightly around the saint's silver reliquary. Aleyna stands on shaking legs, and searches the broken earth for her bolter, but it is gone, lost in the smoke and carnage. Instead, she draws her bolt pistol and takes unsteady aim. The two figures – saint and arch-sinner – are so close that she cannot be sure of hitting one without risking the other. She looks to the Sister Superior for instruction and finds her already striding forward with chainsword in hand.

But they are too late.

With a scream of ripping metal, the heretic punches his clawed hand through the plackart of Saint Hestia's armour. Lightning arcs between the claw-tips as they emerge between her shoulder blades, and her head falls back with silver light pouring upwards from her eyes and mouth. For a second the saint hangs suspended, as though caught in the instant of taking flight, until her body goes slack and the radiance fades from her eyes.

The Death of Saints pulls the lightning claw free, and Hestia drops to her knees, her head tilted back, her eyes fixed on the sky in mute appeal. He draws his axe, and in a single smooth movement takes her head from her shoulders.

'...to me!'

Dimly, as though from far away, Aleyna realises that someone is talking to her. A hand in a blood-red gauntlet grabs her by the pauldron and shoves her into the shelter of a half-ruined archway where the novitiate Sister Pronatus is already cowering. The Sister Superior of the Bloody Rose lifts her visor, revealing sweat-streaked olive skin, with a fleur-de-lys tattooed on her left cheek and the right pockmarked with a constellation of tiny scars. Through the smoke, Aleyna watches the Death of Saints lift Hestia's severed head by her silver hair and mount it in the centre of his armour rack.

'Listen to me,' the Sister Superior hisses. 'We have lost one saint already today. We must do all that lies within our power to ensure we do not lose another.'

III

'No,' Morvenn says.

The word echoes across the chamber like the bark of a bolter. Two servo-skulls hang in the empty air, casting a soft reddish glow across the vast gnarlwood table and the eleven seated dignitaries, across the empty chair behind her and the lord regent's vacant throne.

No one speaks.

Morvenn is the only one of the twelve on her feet, and one of only two in armour, towering head and shoulders above all but Trajann Valoris himself. The captain-general of the Adeptus Custodes bears a power spear that is the sibling of the one in the Purgator Mirabilis' right hand, his face hidden behind the golden mask of his plumed helmet. The senate chamber is impossibly large, its black granite walls absorbing more than reflecting the flickering lumen light, but the expressions on the faces of the other High Lords are still clearly visible.

Contempt. Disdain. Hostility.

'No?' The Paternoval Envoy, Kadak Mir, is the first to speak, the single syllable emerging from beneath his velvet hood in a rattling whisper. His seat is to the right of the empty throne, his misshapen body draped in layer upon layer of heavy robes.

Every inch of his flesh from the hands up is hidden from sight, the wrists pale and bony, the fingers somehow too long as they taper towards the pointed nails at their tips. There is something about the Navigator that makes him difficult to look at directly, some subtle sense of wrongness, some *inhumanity*.

Morvenn fixes her glare on the dark recess of the hood. She has no intention of looking away.

'Perhaps the good abbess will be kind enough to expand on her statement,' says Mir.

'I said no, my lords.' Morvenn straightens her back, and the Purgator Mirabilis mirrors her movement with a soft purr of motors. 'No, I decline your offer. No, a nebulous promise of reinforcements to be sent to Ophelia VII "when matters permit" is unacceptable.' She makes no effort to keep the disgust from her voice. 'The threat is now, and my place – and the place of every Sister of Battle not presently engaged – is there. To ask me to stand by while it is under attack is an affront of the highest order.'

The Navigator tilts his shapeless hood to one side. 'To ask us to strip Holy Terra of its defences to protect Ophelia VII from some...' He gives a wheezy laugh, like a dry wind through long-dead bones. 'From some Night Lord's *raid* would seem the greater affront.'

Inside her gauntlets, Morvenn's hands are taut with rage. The assault on the blessed cardinal world is bad enough, but Kadak Mir's sheer obstinate idiocy is a thousand times worse. How can he fail to see the importance of what she is telling him? The time for action has come, and yet he is content to sit in comfort and complacency.

'This is no mere raid.' She turns her glare around the rest of the High Lords, as though understanding was something that could be driven into them with the force of her gaze alone. If only it were so simple.

'No?'

'He is the Death of Saints.'

An expectant silence falls across the room.

Morvenn draws a deep breath, holds it, then exhales to a silent count of five. This meeting has turned to a tangle of words, a morass that sucks at her ankles, slowing her progress, dragging her down. What slaughter has already been inflicted on the cardinal world in the time she has wasted here?

'Should that name mean something to us?' Kadak Mir asks.

'For centuries he has made it his business to hunt the Sisters of the Argent Shroud. His strike cruiser appears without warning, slaughters without mercy, and vanishes without trace. Sometimes he appears again mere months later, other times generations pass before he returns to burn our shrines, to slaughter our Sisters, to trample our cathedra into rubble. But never before has he come to Ophelia VII. We have an opportunity to deal with a threat that has plagued my Order for a thousand years – and you would squander it with your inactivity.'

'I see no reason for such urgency.' Mir shrugs. 'By your own admission, this Death of Saints will return in time.'

'By which point we may all be dust!'

'He certainly bears an impressive title.' The remark comes from Cardinal Ritira, another of the Avenging Son's appointments to the council of High Lords. She is a soft-faced woman, her face creased in an expression of gentle compassion, but Morvenn is not deceived by the mildness of her appearance. No doubt the Ecclesiarch wears a similar expression while she watches the heretical and the heterodox sent to the pyre. 'Is the sobriquet self-styled or awarded by your Order?'

'My Order has nothing for him but his death, and that is long overdue.' Morvenn shakes her head. 'But the title will suffice for its accuracy alone. Shall I recite the names of those slaughtered at his hand? The saints whose severed heads rot on his armour rack? The slain pilgrims? The murdered Sisters, the beheaded novitiates?'

'That will not be necessary, Abbess Sanctorum.' Grand Master Fadix of the Assassinorum extends a placating hand. He is a small man dressed in a plain grey robe, forgettable in every detail other than the way he holds himself, every movement of his body made with careful, deliberate grace. He may look like a simple adept, but if what Morvenn suspects of him is true, he is the deadliest in the room. 'Regardless of the heretic's sins, you must understand the reticence of this council to acquiesce to your wishes. The blessed Abbess Sabrina, your predecessor, was lost on such a warp voyage, and these are unsettled times. The Sisterhood cannot stand to lose another Abbess Sanctorum so soon after your investiture.'

'That is the least of my concerns.' Morvenn makes no effort to curb the volume of her voice. 'Better a short life spent bringing death to the God-Emperor's enemies than a hundred years spent rotting in this chamber.'

'I too have been an instrument of death to the God-Emperor's enemies, Abbess Sanctorum, for all that I serve differently now.' Fadix's voice is conciliatory, but Morvenn is not deceived. He is a viper, and these are a viper's words. 'I understand that this is an emotive issue, and there is much to discuss–'

'Much to discuss?' Morvenn slams her fist down onto the table, sending a web of cracks radiating out across its polished surface. 'You talk, and Ophelia VII burns.'

With a whirring of gears, the Fabricator General of the Adeptus Mechanicus leans across the table, their single augmetic eye telescoping outwards to study her with care.

'Why do you feel such fear, abbess?' There is a musical note to the Fabricator General's voice, the inflections subtly inhuman.

Does any trace of human flesh remain beneath those crimson robes? 'There are many Battle Sisters in the Convent Sanctorum. Surely you do not doubt their abilities?'

Morvenn closes her eyes and entertains the vision of choking the tech-priest to death with their own mechadendrites. She should already be on Ophelia VII with her Sisters, far from this chamber and its politicians. The battlefield is the place the God-Emperor ordained for her, not locked here in this endless struggle for political advantage.

'You have not listened,' she says. 'Or you have listened, but you have failed to understand.'

'My auditory apparatus is not at fault, Abbess Sanctorum, nor are my cogitators, mechanical or organic.' A hand made of interlocking brass joints and digits describes a broad arc through the air. 'No one doubts your valour or denies the sacrifice your Sisters have made. But it can hardly be a surprise that morale has been damaged.'

Morvenn clenches her jaw with teeth-grinding force. 'Morale is not the issue, and this threat is far from trivial.'

'Of course not.' The Navigator, Mir, raises his bony hands in mock placation. 'But not every attack is of planet-shattering proportions. Your own histories are full of such incursions – minor raids, easily driven back into the warp from whence they came.'

'To underestimate the enemy is to court defeat.'

'And to overestimate them is to commit resources we can ill afford to lose to a fool's errand.' The Navigator's arrogance is breath-taking. He tilts his head, and the hood falls away to reveal a smiling, lipless mouth set into maggot-pale flesh.

Morvenn's anger flares white-hot. Her hands tighten on the Purgator's control rods, and the great warsuit lunges half a step closer to the table. The Navigator jerks as though electrocuted, his chair screeching back across the marble floor. She lowers her voice to a growl; it is either that or bellow into the man's face.

'Were you a warrior, Lord Navigator, you would answer for that accusation in blood. Fortunately for you, I have never seen anyone less suited for the battlefield.'

Kadak Mir swallows. 'Your arrogance will be your undoing, Morvenn Vahl.'

Fadix clears his throat. 'My lord Navigator. It is natural that the abbess should wish harm on the enemies of the Imperium, and any threat to the Convent Sanctorum is a threat to the Ecclesiarchy itself.' He turns to her, a smile that is no doubt meant to be reassuring on his forgettable face. 'But it is perhaps worth remembering that your Sisters do not stand alone – the brotherhood of the Black Templars are there to grant any protection they might require.'

'*Protection?*' This time the word comes out without conscious thought, pushed through her lips on a wave of anger. 'My Sisters and I have shed blood alongside the sons of Dorn for centuries. And you would have me ask them for protection?'

Trajann Valoris leans forward. 'Marshal Armond Montford was charged with the defence of Ophelia VII following the Tyrant of the Blueflame's defeat. When last we received word from the sons of Dorn, it was to inform us that he had been gravely wounded in a recent engagement. His Apothecary tells us he will recover in time, but command of their defences has been handed over to Castellan Aymar Tancret. A fine warrior, though he lacks Marshal Montford's long years of command experience.'

'Then with such allies your Sisters will have no need for reinforcements from Holy Terra.' Satisfaction drips from Kadak Mir's voice. 'And I would wager every throne in the treasury that the threat will be dealt with long before reinforcements arrive.'

'You are gambling with sacred ground,' Morvenn says. How

can they be so wilfully blind? 'With the lives of my Sisters. With ancient, irreplaceable relics.'

'I treasure the cardinal world just as you do.' Eos Ritira's voice is full of reproach. 'But the resources with which the God-Emperor blesses us are far from infinite, and you would draw them away from Holy Terra on a voyage of futility.'

'And what say the rest of you?' Morvenn steps back from the table and turns her eyes to the other High Lords. Only the captain-general of the Custodes meets her gaze. The rest seem fascinated with their own hands or with the chamber's dark recesses.

'The Abbess Sanctorum has my support.' Trajann Valoris' booming voice fills the chamber, and Morvenn feels a sudden sense of relief. She needs no mortal approval to know the rightness of her actions, but the captain-general is the one High Lord in this room whose opinion she values. 'The threat to Ophelia VII is grave. We would be fools to ignore it.'

'And if this Death of Saints turns his attention to Holy Terra instead, captain-general?' Kadak Mir waves a pallid hand through the air. 'For all we know, this attack on the cardinal world is nothing more than a decoy to tempt us into weakening our defences.'

And there it is – the real reason for Mir's refusal to grant her aid. A life in politics has made him so soft, so fearful with the desire to protect his own soft underbelly that he would see the galaxy burn rather than expose it. Worse still, the rest of the High Lords – with the exception of Valoris – seem cut from the same flimsy cloth.

She is wasting her time.

'Captain-general, your support means a great deal to me, but the time for words has passed. Unless this council is willing to revise its position, my place is with my Sisters.'

Cardinal Ritira shifts uncomfortably in her seat. 'Perhaps we might put this difficult matter to the vote?'

Fadix raises an eyebrow. 'A show of hands should suffice. All those in favour?'

One golden gauntlet rises into the air. The others – the gloves of the masters of the Astronomican and the Adeptus Astra Telepathica, the hands of the Inquisitorial representative and the rest – stay firmly on the table. Morvenn glares at Cardinal Ritira, but the older woman will not meet her eye.

'Let the record state that the Senatorum Imperialis stands opposed to this course of action.' The satisfaction in Kadak Mir's smile could curdle milk.

'I see where this council's priorities lie.' Morvenn inclines her head in a stiff bow. She releases her warsuit's control batons long enough to clasp her hands across her chest in a white-knuckled aquila. 'I have wasted enough time on words.'

She stalks from the room, and the great double doors clang shut behind her with the solemn toll of a funeral bell.

IV

Penitent number 867 – who still thinks of herself as Lethe Fulmens, despite the fact that she has not heard her name spoken aloud for over a decade – stares up at the cavern's roughly hewn stone roof and imagines the sky beyond it. The greasy yellow air in the mine is thick with the stench of unwashed bodies and human excrement, but the wanderings of her mind take her outside to where the night breeze blows beneath the twinkling lights of far-off stars.

Or so she imagines.

It has become a game of hers, to try and remember the details of her life before, though the boundary between reality and imagination has been eroded to nothing by the long years of her sentence. The memories of the first half of her existence are divided between a two-room hab-unit and the local manufactorum's schola, the days bookended by the catechisms of the faith on waking, and her father's bedtime tales at night. There was a time she could remember every detail of her father's face, but now his memory has been reduced to fragments: the rasp of stubble against her cheek, the smell of fresh sweat and machine oil. Those things meant safety once, but that time is long past.

A whip cracks close to her cheek, breaking her concentration.

She is grateful for the interruption. Remembering her father awakens the memories of what came next. The zealots with their burning brands, the hab-block in flames, the screams of the dying. And moving through the smoke, the women in gleaming silver armour, eerie green lights glowing from the eyeholes in their blank-faced helms. The smell of burning skin and hair lingered in her mind long after the flames had died to ash.

'Attend to your labours, penitent!'

The whip cracks again, and for a moment she considers spitting in the overseer's face. The heavy steel muzzle that holds her jaw shut makes that all but impossible, but it is a pleasant fantasy nonetheless. All the penitent labourers wear the same ill-fitting apparatus across their faces both waking and sleeping, removed only for their single daily meal and for the prayers that follow. Occasionally, when the muzzle is removed and the overseers' attention is elsewhere, she traces the callused scars on her face with her fingertips and wonders what she looks like now – but of course the answer to that is written on the face of every penitent around her. She is filthy and starving.

'Eight hundred and sixty-seven! Do you hear me?'

Lethe nods, letting the weight of the muzzle carry her head downwards as if in submission. She knows Overseer Yulius well and likes nothing of what she knows. He is a burly man, pale-skinned and shaven-headed, with a thick roll of flesh at the nape of his neck that attests to a level of nourishment of which she can only dream. Some of his fellow overseers approach their labours with a grim-faced duty, but this one makes no secret of the pleasure he takes in inflicting torment. The slightest hint of disobedience is met with disproportionate and petty retribution, yet on the few occasions the Holy Sisters come to visit the mines, his manner transforms into one of grovelling obsequiousness. On balance, Lethe prefers his cruelty.

Cruelty is something she understands.

'I said to work!' The whip cracks out again, and this time its tip catches the back of her neck. Sharp pain blossoms across her skin, but she has felt worse before. In a few minutes it will dull to a throbbing ache. In a week, it will be nothing more than another scar. It will pass, just as it always does. A second blow strikes the same spot, and this time an involuntary hiss of pain escapes her lips. 'This labour is the gift of the God-Emperor!' Yulius shouts. 'Through service shall your miserable soul be redeemed!'

Lethe lifts her pickaxe and joins the other penitents labouring at the rock face. For a fleeting moment she wonders how it would feel to bury the blade in the overseer's bare scalp. She would be dead before she had a chance to tug it free – the autoguns and shock mauls of his colleagues would see to that – but the few seconds of satisfaction would be worth it. In her imagination, she brings her pickaxe round again to slam into his left eye socket, sending a glistening pulp of blood and jelly squirting down his cheek.

Instead, the pickaxe meets rock with a jarring impact. Another fragment falls loose, and the stooped and toothless woman who sleeps in the bunk below Lethe's claws rock fragments into a coarse woven sack. The number *874* stencilled on her penitent's robe stands as a reminder of their arrival together on the same crowded ground transport. The woman's name is Evania, and for their first few terrifying nights in the mine she had tried to soothe Lethe's nocturnal distress with gentle words of reassurance. That scant comfort had come to an abrupt end when Overseer Yulius overheard, unlocked Evania's muzzle and smashed the teeth from her mouth with the butt of his shock maul.

After that there were no more whispers.

When a dozen sacks are full of rocks, the penitents will load them into barrows, which in turn will be pushed to the surface by the broken-spirited wretches who can be trusted not to lift their heads and search for the stars. Lethe has long since ceased to wonder what material purpose their labour serves. For all she knows, once the tunnels are excavated to whatever arbitrary extent their captors see fit, they will simply be ordered to reverse the process and fill them in again.

Her pickaxe chips another piece of rock from the wall, and she stoops to place it in Evania's sack. The older woman looks up and for an instant Lethe meets her eyes, but there is no connection there, no shared spark of humanity. It is as though the living spirit was driven from Evania's body along with her teeth, nothing left but a servitor moving by rote as its flesh decays around it. They are all like this, the penitents with whom she shares her imprisonment, their dead eyes windows looking onto deader souls. How long will it be, Lethe wonders, until her own volition is sapped to nothing by exhaustion and cruelty?

Penitent.

The word is an iron chain that weighs her down. Her father taught her the meaning of the word long before it became her existence: *one who repents their sins and seeks atonement.* If only she knew for what sin she must atone, the reason why the Sisters of the Adepta Sororitas came to consign her gentle-voiced father to the pyre and his daughter to endless labour in a lightless pit. She has prayed so often for understanding and for forgiveness, but an answer has never come.

The cavern's dirty yellow lumens flicker. Lethe does not pause in her work, but the crackle of static from the vox-unit clipped to Overseer Yulius' belt draws her attention. She risks a sidelong glance to where he is standing behind her and watches him raise the communicator to his ear. The expression on his face changes as he listens, the usual look of self-righteous satisfaction sliding free like skin sloughing from a rotting corpse.

'Yes, my lord,' he says. 'I will see to it per–'

A klaxon blares through the mine's vox-system, drowning out the overseer's words and setting the hair on the back of Lethe's neck prickling in time with the siren's eerie rise and fall. A murmur passes through the labourers, the sound enough to stir excitement even in their worn-out souls – and the overseer reacts immediately, activating his shock maul and striking Evania where she grovels over her sack. The old woman goes down hard, the sack scattering its useless contents around her as she lies with limbs twitching and blood trickling from beneath her muzzled face.

'All of you! Picks down! Backs to the wall! Now!'

The penitents' equipment hits the floor in a clatter of metal. Lethe puts down her pick with the rest, and pauses, hate burning in the pit of her stomach as though she has swallowed a burning coal. A fist-sized rock lies close to her feet, spilled from Evania's sack. Before she rises, she wraps her fingers around it and withdraws her hand into the sleeve of her robe.

The dull rasp of metal on metal joins the wail of the klaxon. It takes Lethe a moment to realise where the noise is coming from: the great portcullis that separates the upper and lower levels of the mine is descending. The overseer sheathes his shock maul and steps away, his eyes flicking between the huddled penitents and the cavern behind him. He gathers up their equipment and locks it securely away behind the heavy iron grille of the storage alcove.

'Wait here.' His voice is shaking. 'Not a sound, do you understand me?'

Lethe stares back in mute hatred, enjoying every second of

his fear. His footsteps die away, then with an abrupt clang, the grinding of the portcullis stops.

And every light in the cavern goes out.

Under other circumstances, Morvenn thinks, there would be a ceremony: a cathedrum full of cherubim, the servo-choir's voices rising in perfect harmony, ranks of Sisters bearing solemn witness to the departure of the Abbess Sanctorum from Holy Terra into the void. This is better.

Instead, she and the captain-general of the Adeptus Custodes are walking through the drizzle towards her lander on the High Lords' private landing pad. Its engines are running, her entourage already on board, awaiting only her command to bear her to the Imperial Navy battle cruiser waiting in geostationary orbit overhead. Perhaps her fellow High Lords intend the lack of ceremony as a slight, but that is the least of her concerns.

The captain-general has removed his helmet, and with the height granted by her warsuit her eyes are level with his: an experience shared by few outside his brotherhood. Rain flurries around him, glinting silver and crimson in the lander's tail-lumens, beading on the golden armour like tiny round-cut gems. His eyes are narrowed, fixed on some distant point far beyond their immediate surroundings, his thoughts unreadable.

'I need not ask if you remember the last time we spoke together.' She feels the deep vibration of his voice in her lungs like the opening notes of a battle hymn.

'No, captain-general. I have not forgotten.' How could she? The majestic golden lance in the hand of the Purgator Mirabilis stands as a constant reminder of their last meeting: the candlelit darkness of the reliquary at the heart of the Imperial Palace, the sharp scent of ozone catching in her throat as she saw the lance blaze into life for the first time. 'That day we spoke of prophecy. But my trust is in the God-Emperor, not in the words of the dead.'

A smile kindles in Valoris' eyes. 'Indeed. But these are dark times, Abbess Sanctorum, and we must take what guidance we can.'

'And what guidance is that?'

'That a darkness is coming greater than any the Imperium of Man has ever known.'

'The Death of Saints?'

'Perhaps.' A frown passes across the captain-general's brow. 'My brothers have kept the prophecy safe for millennia, so long that even the name of the seer who uttered it is dust. It speaks of the great darkness against which only one light can stand.'

'The Lance of Illumination.'

'In part. But yours is the hand that must wield it, Morvenn Vahl. Yours is the will that must drive out the darkness. If it can be driven back at all.'

Morvenn glances at the spear in her warsuit's hand. 'I do not need prophecies to know where my duty lies.' A duty that would be made considerably easier with your brethren at my side, she thinks, but bites back the sharp words. Valoris has earned her respect, not her scorn. 'Why did you not speak of it to the other High Lords?' she asks instead.

'"A fool dies with his blades still sheathed."' Valoris shakes his head. 'They would have found another reason for inaction.'

He offers her his hand, and she takes it, clasping forearm to forearm. She can feel the power of his grip even through her gauntlet, and he leans close, lowering his voice so that only she can hear. 'The time of that great darkness is close at hand. The threat to Ophelia VII may be greater than any we have yet known.'

'I will not let the Convent Sanctorum fall. Not while I draw breath.'

Valoris nods. 'May your voyage be swift and your wrath sure.' He releases his grip and steps away. 'And may the Lance of Illumination be a beacon to guide you through the dark times to come.'

Morvenn waits. She watches the great golden figure retreat into the rain until he is swallowed up entirely by shadow, until a nervous cough at waist height pulls her attention to the lander pilot at her side.

'Abbess Sanctorum? We await only your command to depart. If you are ready, of course.'

'I am ready.'

She follows the pilot to the rear hatch of the vessel and moves the warsuit inside, placing the spear into its reliquary case at her right hand. The ramp begins its tortuous journey upwards, and she nods to the Celestians of her personal retinue – Fionnula, Kseniya, Hiromi, Zafiya, and Celestian Superior Ignatia – who each make the sign of the aquila in return.

'I was starting to wonder if you had changed your mind, my abbess,' Ignatia says dryly. Had they come from another mouth, Morvenn might have taken the words as a mark of disrespect, but Ignatia is one of the few people in all the Imperium who she considers a friend, one whose honest counsel she values more than all the High Lords' pretty words.

'You should know me better than that, Celestian Superior.'

Ignatia smiles, revealing the metal teeth implanted into her upper jaw, the indirect gift of a Dark Apostle of the Word Bearers who had come within an inch of taking her head from her shoulders. The Heretic Astartes had paid for that insult with his life, though he had sent half a squad of Celestians to the Golden Throne before they had taken him down together.

'I did not wonder for long, my abbess.'

Gravity pulls at them as the lander takes to the air, banks, then speeds upward through the thinning atmosphere. Morvenn leans back in her warsuit and closes her eyes, striving for stillness in her soul and finding none.

The time of the great darkness is close at hand.

Valoris' words echo in her mind, drowning out the growl of the lander's engines, and a shiver runs down her spine that has nothing to do with the cold.

V

The stench of burned flesh clings to Aleyna's skin, her hair, her vestments, the inside of her nose and mouth. When she coughs she brings up thick phlegm flecked with particles of soot, and the sound ricochets off the crypt's bare stone walls. Her bones ache, her head throbs, and some time during their desperate flight her armour seems to have doubled in weight.

The necropolis lies far enough from the scene of the attack that the thunder of bolter fire has faded to a low rumble – though how any living targets possibly remain is beyond Aleyna's imagining – but not so far that they can relax their guard. For all she knows, the Night Lords are in the necropolis already, preysight trained on any heat or sound that might mark the position of survivors. The Sisters and the remaining pilgrims cannot hide here forever, but where else is there for them to go?

From her position by the wall, Aleyna scans the miserable little group. A few dozen pilgrims have survived, huddling close for comfort and for warmth, but she has found only five of her Sisters. At first they had only been three: herself, Sister Superior Kerem of the Bloody Rose, and Theodosia of the Order of the Quill with whom she had borne the reliquary of Saint Athenasia to safety, joined a little time after by two Sisters Retributor of the Valorous Heart. They had found the sole survivor of Saint Hestia's honour guard in the necropolis, the Seraphim staggering blood-soaked and dazed, one wing torn from her jump pack and the silver enamel of her armour blistered away to reveal the dull grey metal beneath. Her name, she had told them, was Perdita, and since then she has said nothing at all.

Footsteps echo down the narrow steps that lead to the crypt. Aleyna's hand flies to her bolt pistol, though the steps are too quick and light to belong to one of the heretics. It is Sister Superior Kerem who appears in the doorway, chainsword in hand as it has been since they abandoned the cathedrum.

'How many?' Sister Retributor Rukhsana asks her.

Kerem shakes her head. 'Too many. A dozen Raptors at least, as many again on groundbikes. And the others.'

'The arch-heretic?'

'Moving amongst them as though the whole world was his to command.' Kerem hawks a mouthful of bloody spit onto the dusty stone floor. 'I saw one group of Traitor Astartes disposing of their dead. At least they were not the only ones to spill blood.'

'Sister Superior – what do we do now?' The question comes from the novitiate Sister Pronatus. She is sitting in the corner with the reliquary on her knees, her arms wrapped tightly around the silver casing.

'We regroup. Assess our situation, our assets and our options. And then we act.' The Sister Superior of the Bloody Rose regards each of them appraisingly. 'In the absence of any who outrank me, I am assuming command.'

A steady drip of liquid falls from the crypt's vaulted roof, adding to the chalky smear of lime staining the ancient flagstones.

'The situation as it stands. The cathedrum and its surrounds have been seized by the heretic Night Lords. They are moving to consolidate their position as we speak. We are vastly outnumbered. A direct assault is impossible.'

'Unwise, perhaps, but not impossible.' Retributor Sister Marayd pushes the fringe of her dark brown bob back from her freckled face. A livid purple bruise covers much of her right cheekbone. Her eye is swollen shut beneath her lacerated brow, but the heavy bolter lying across her lap is pristine.

'Your life is not yours to waste,' Kerem says.

Aleyna glances at the huddled pilgrims, who shy away from her attention like startled birds. A sudden stab of pity takes her below the breastbone. This situation is bad enough in armour with Sisters at her side. How terrible it must be to be defenceless and unarmed in such a situation. She tries to offer a reassuring smile but receives nothing in return.

'If there is hope to be found,' Kerem continues, 'it is in the assets we retain. Six of us, armed and capable of combat, if not a direct assault. Sisters Retributor, your heavy bolters may be the greatest physical weapons we have at our disposal. We have blades and guns. Seraphim Perdita?'

The name hangs in the air, but the Seraphim does not reply. Her bloodied head is bent forward in prayer over clasped hands, the Sister oblivious to all but her desperate communion with the God-Emperor. Aleyna places a hand on her shoulder, then, when Perdita does not react, gently guides her chin upwards so that they are face to face. Perdita's eyes are red-rimmed and unfocused, her cheeks streaked with tears and mottled with bruises.

'Seraphim Sister,' Aleyna says softly. 'We have need of you. For the God-Emperor's sake, will you fight with us?'

Perdita stares back at her, then manages a shaky nod.

'She is with us,' Aleyna says.

Kerem frowns. 'Very well. Then we may count the Seraphim's inferno pistols amongst our assets.'

'I would that we all had her wings,' Marayd says. Aleyna watches for the Seraphim's reaction, but she is as still as a plaster saint and every bit as brittle. What is a Seraphim without her wings, or a member of a saint's honour guard who has failed in her duty? Only death or a place in the Orders Repentia can follow such failure.

'And we have the sacred remains of the Martyred Saint Athenasia.' Kerem motions to the reliquary, though Aleyna notes that she does not mention the novitiate who bears it. 'Such as we are, we are the reliquary's sole guardians. It falls to us to protect the blessed saint's remains, and to see her returned safely to the Convent Sanctorum.'

The novitiate clears her throat. 'If I may speak?'

'Go ahead.'

'I know the identity of the heretic who has attacked the city.' Theodosia's voice is as high and clear as a chapel bell.

Kerem's eyes narrow. 'Will that help us in the fight against him?'

'Perhaps, Sister Superior. His name is Kol Rakhul. It appears many times in the histories of the Argent Shroud. I am sure Seraphim Perdita knows more than I...' Her voice trails off uncertainly.

'Carry on, novitiate,' Kerem says.

'He is the Death of Saints.'

The pilgrims murmur, then fall silent.

'He has been a plague upon the Order of the Argent Shroud for many years. A destroyer of relics, a murderer wherever in the Imperium he goes. And I believe...' She swallows. 'I believe I know why he is here.'

Marayd rolls her eyes. 'Out with it, then.'

'Saint Athenasia was his sister in life,' the novitiate begins. 'She was called to the light just as he was called to darkness. It was her life's mission to destroy him.'

'And she failed?' Marayd asks.

'She dealt him a miraculous blow, more than any have done since. It is said that his axe took the head from her shoulders, but before she fell the divine radiance of the God-Emperor flowed through her, forcing him back.' Theodosia swallows. 'The God-Emperor denied him the saint's head, and in revenge, he has taken the heads of countless saints to mount on his armour rack.'

Theodosia releases the catches on the reliquary case, then swings the lid open. Inside, a jawless human skull sits on a purple velvet cushion, the surface of the bone parchment-yellow with age. Aleyna's breath catches in her throat. It is as though the skull is radiating light, a soft ivory glow that warms the chapel.

'He strikes at the hour of the saint's Triumph. He is here to recover what was denied him centuries ago. I am sure of it.'

Kerem is leaning forward, her eyes narrowed with interest. 'The heretic has had centuries to recover the reliquary, yet only now comes to seek it out. Why?'

'Because we are weak.' The crypt falls silent as Aleyna speaks. 'We are yet to repair what the Tyrant of Blueflame destroyed, yet to rebuild our strength and replace all that we lost.' She chooses her next words with care. 'The Abbess Sanctorum wages her wars across the galaxy. The Sisters of the Orders of the Ebon Chalice and the Sacred Rose are much needed on Holy Terra, and the Argent Shroud must also see to their preceptories close to the Great Rift.' She closes her eyes. 'There can hardly be a more opportune time for this Death of Saints to strike.'

'The Night Lords are thieves and raiders,' Marayd says. 'They are drawn to strike when their enemies are weakest, seeking to sow fear and inspire terror.' She shrugs her armoured shoulders. 'The heretic may find our numbers diminished, but he will find us unbowed.'

'But he will find us all the same.' There is unexpected steel in the novitiate's voice. 'If he is here for the reliquary, then he will not rest until he has found it. To remain here is to seal our fate. And hers.'

A distant rumble shakes the crypt, mortar and rock-dust falling like a flurry of snow. Realisation hits Aleyna like a fist. 'He is tearing down the shrine.'

Kerem looks to the archway that separates the crypt from the necropolis above. 'Then if we are to act, it must be soon.'

'Very well.' Rukhsana stands, straps her heavy bolter to its harness and turns to the Sister Superior. 'We are yours to command. What must we do?'

Kerem looks uncertain, then her resolute expression reasserts itself. 'Something is interfering with the vox.' She casts an uneasy glance to the stone roof above her head. 'I have experienced such happenings before. Often it speaks to the presence of daemonkind, daemon engines, but the cause matters little. Until such time as we can re-establish contact with the wider world, we must consider ourselves alone. The Convent Sanctorum lies eighty miles north as the corvid flies. At a force-march, we can reach it in four days.'

'And them?' Marayd tilts her head towards the pilgrims. 'That hardly strikes me as a pace most of them can sustain.'

'What alternative do we have?' Kerem snaps back.

'The catacombs,' Theodosia says, her eyes bright. 'The crypts beneath the cathedrum connect to passageways that will take us to the Convent Sanctorum without need to cross open ground.'

Aleyna glances between the Sisters, then to the wretched survivors huddled against the far wall. They are a curious mixture: from a shoeless old woman in rags to a nobleman whose soot-stained velvet coat must surely have cost more than the beggar-woman has seen in her lifetime, but the fear and weariness on their faces grants them a curious kinship.

'You would not abandon us, would you, Sisters?' the velvet-clad man says, the mask of a smile plastered onto his face. 'I have been most generous in my offerings over the years. If you would kindly escort me to the Convent Sanctorum, you would find me more generous still.'

Kerem's face twists with revulsion. 'The daughters of the God-Emperor are not mercenaries to be bought and sold.'

The man's hands fly up in immediate supplication. 'Of course not. But as the blessed Sister there just said' – he gestures to Marayd – 'most of these pilgrims are not fit to make such a journey. Surely wisdom dictates that it is folly to sacrifice those who can be saved for the sake of the unsalvageable?'

Aleyna's guts twist. The man's wheedling tone and his cowardice are repulsive, but worse is the fact that he is speaking at least a partial truth.

'Sit down, you fool.' One of the other pilgrims – a young woman with a fall of dyed-blue hair covering half of her otherwise shaven scalp – grabs the man by his velvet sleeve and heaves him to the ground. He opens his mouth to protest, but she delivers a ringing slap across his lips with the flat of her hand, and he subsides into a state of mute outrage. Somewhere at the back of the group, a very young child begins to cry.

'Why do we not use a decoy?' Aleyna asks. Every head in the room swivels to look at her. Her face prickles with a sudden and uncomfortable heat.

'Continue.'

'Yes, Sister Superior.' Aleyna swallows, her mouth suddenly dry. 'The heretics are close at hand. A group of this size will attract attention the moment we leave the crypt, no matter how carefully we move. But we have frag grenades – perhaps not enough to cause significant damage to the enemy, but enough to draw their attention. If a smaller group – even a single Sister – was to set off a series of explosives as a distraction, it might allow the rest to reach the cathedrum undetected and enter its catacombs.' She closes her eyes, offering up a wordless prayer for guidance, then opens them. 'I will gladly do this.'

'Any one of us would do this.' Sister Rukhsana gets to her feet, and for the first time Aleyna notices the blood trickling from beneath her black cuirass. 'Your Order does not grant you precedence in matters of holy martyrdom.'

'Nor does yours.'

The Sister Superior unfastens the strap that binds her leather-bound prayer book to her belt and opens the slender volume. 'God-Emperor and His scribes forgive me.' She tears a blank sheet from the back of the book, rips it into six parts of roughly equal size, discards one and daubs another with a fingerprint of soot from the muzzle of her boltgun. 'Those who volunteer to provide the necessary distraction may draw lots.'

Theodosia opens her mouth, but Kerem forestalls her with an upraised hand. 'No, novitiate. Your duties lie elsewhere.'

Kerem folds each piece of parchment in turn and drops them into Rukhsana's offered helmet. The damp air of the crypt takes on a curious stillness, even the rumble of the shrine's destruction muted by the solemnity of the moment. Only the child's cries continue, hungry and desolate.

One by one, four of the five Sisters Militant draw their lots.

'Seraphim Perdita?'

Without looking up, Perdita reaches out a hand and takes her token. The parchment in Aleyna's hand is warm, heavy with the weight of the future.

'God-Emperor, we give thanks for your guidance.' Kerem nods to each in turn. 'May your will be revealed to us.'

Aleyna holds her breath. She unfolds the ragged-edged scrap without looking and waits, listening to the pounding of blood in her ears, not daring to look, as though the act of doing so will determine the paper's state of being and with it her fate.

The silence breaks. Marayd hisses with frustration, crumples her parchment in her gauntlet, and tosses it to the floor. Rukhsana displays both sides of a blank piece, her mouth set in resignation. Perdita opens her hand, and a blank scrap drifts to the ground like a shed feather.

Two remain.

Even odds: life and death, duty and absolution. Aleyna searches her soul but cannot tell for which outcome she is praying.

'Very well, then, my Sisters.' Kerem's gauntlet is steady as she displays her soot-marked parchment. 'We must prepare for our respective journeys – yours to the Convent Sanctorum.' She smiles, and the expression transforms her scarred features to a mask of radiant beauty. 'And mine, perhaps, to the Golden Throne.'

VI

The Mars-class battle cruiser *Lux Dominus* is a voidborne testament to the power of the Imperium of Man and to the surpassing skill of its tech-priests. Over three miles long from prow to stern, and a little under a fifth of that from port to starboard, it slices through warp and realspace with equal and enviable power. Its hull, rarely glimpsed from outside, bristles with gunports, void lances and hangar bays, but its interior is no less impressive. The passageway outside the chapel is spacious enough for Dreadnoughts to walk two abreast, lit by burning braziers mounted high on wood-panelled walls interspersed with alcoves holding illuminated manuscripts and the relics of the saints.

The sleeping quarters offered to Morvenn at the start of the journey in tribute to her rank are gilded to the point of indecency, the curtains of the four-poster bed embroidered on cloth of gold, the walls hung with heavy silken tapestries. She refused them in favour of a simple pilgrim's cell, causing consternation in the voidship's steward assigned to see to her needs.

'The *Lux Dominus* has carried High Lords, planetary governors, even the blessed brothers of the Adeptus Astartes,' the steward had muttered to her subordinate, in tones clearly not meant for the abbess' ears. 'None has ever made such an outrageous request. Any other High Lord would demand accommodation befitting their station.'

As well as being impudent, the wretched little jobsworth was incorrect – it hardly seemed likely that the lord regent and the captain-general would insist on feather beds and embroidered silkcloth drapes. As for the other High Lords, they could keep their luxuries and pleasures of the flesh. Pampered politicians, every one of them.

'The Abbess Sanctorum prefers a chamber kept free of material distractions, the better to listen for the word of the God-Emperor,' Ignatia had said, and the little man had flushed scarlet to the roots of his hair before abandoning them to their spartan accommodation and its welcome silence.

The voidsmen to either side of the bridge doors snap to attention as Morvenn and her honour guard arrive. A pair of servitors with the mouthpieces of bugles surgically embedded in their jaws blow a wheezy fanfare as the large double doors swing inward to reveal the bridge beyond. It is a solar system in its own right, the crew in perpetual purposeful orbit around the captain seated on the command throne at its centre.

Captain Abram Haraquis is a man of advanced years, his long hair and elegantly braided moustache the same skull-white as his void-pale skin. A thick metal cable connects the back of his skull to the headrest of his command throne, while identical copies in miniature tether each fingertip to panels on the armrests beneath his hands. He is the living soul of the *Lux Dominus*, every stimulus that passes across its hull relayed to his brain in real time. As the abbess and her great warsuit enter the heart of his domain, his meditative manner changes to one of complete alertness, leaving Morvenn with the sense that his mind has abruptly returned from some remote corner of the ship.

'Abbess Sanctorum.' He utters her title with utter solemnity. 'I trust you have suffered no ill effects from our journey?'

'The God-Emperor protects.' Morvenn points at the bridge's viewscreen, where Ophelia's sun is the size of a golden throne piece. 'How far are we from deployment?'

The captain's fingers twitch. 'Four hours out at full burn. I would prepare yourself for double that. More, perhaps, depending–'

'Depending on what?'

'Depending on whether or not you would like to arrive alive.' The captain does nothing to conceal the acerbic note in his voice, and Morvenn hides her smile. The Ecclesiarchy could use more servants willing to speak their mind. 'If the God-Emperor favours us, you and your Sisters should arrive in the Convent Sanctorum in around eight hours.'

Eight hours. A third of a day. It stretches out in front of her like a penitent's sentence.

'That is longer than I had hoped for.'

'An oblique approach should maximise your chance of landing in one piece. Especially given the perils that lie between us and the cardinal world.'

'What perils?' Morvenn is quite sure that the old man is enjoying himself rather too much – the privilege of a consummate expert sharing his expertise with those of lesser knowledge.

Captain Haraquis extends the fingers of his right hand into a fan, turns it palm upward, then closes it into a fist. In response the bridge's viewscreen dims to a faint crimson glow and a hololithic projection composed of a grid of fine green lines springs into life in front of the command throne. The room takes on the atmosphere of a chamber lit by a banked-down fireplace. Ophelia's ancient sun hangs at the centre of the projection, the worlds spinning out around it in a digital orrery, the tiny mote of light that represents the *Lux Dominus* heading towards it with agonising slowness. But whatever perils stand between her and the cardinal world, she cannot make them out.

'What am I missing?'

Haraquis' magnificent moustaches twitch. 'The enemy, Abbess Sanctorum.' He makes another fluid gesture with his right hand, and the projected image closes in on the seventh of Ophelia's planets, the moons in orbit around it forming a miniature orrery of its own.

It takes a moment for Morvenn to follow his line of thought to the obvious conclusion.

'There.' She points, aware of the absurdity of trying to indicate such a tiny object floating in a subjective interpretation of space, but the captain nods like an approving drill-abbot. 'On the dark side of Ophelia VII.'

'Indeed. Long-range augur scans have picked up a strike cruiser in orbit around the cardinal world.'

'Not a vessel of the Black Templars, I take it?'

'Regrettably, no.' The captain's gesture returns the projection to the long view of the system, this time overlaid with a dotted line showing the prospective route of the *Lux Dominus*. 'They are still on the surface, although I regret that all attempts to make contact have failed thus far.'

'What do we know about the enemy's position?'

Captain Haraquis shrugs. 'Our auguries suggest they are holding a geo-stationary orbit some eighty miles north of the Convent Sanctorum.'

'Above the Cathedrum of Athenasia the Martyr. We received reports of the assault there before we departed Holy Terra. I had not expected to find them still there.'

'Regardless, we can use that fact to our advantage. By keeping the planet between us and them, we should be able to avoid the attention of their augurs.'

'And you are sure our presence has not been detected?' Morvenn asks.

'You may have no fear of that.' The captain's long white moustaches twitch again. 'For the simple reason that if it had, we would already be under attack.'

It is almost seven hours before the note of the ship's engines falls, the wall-lumens dim to a dull red, and the vibration of the deck plates changes to a softer, heavier rumble underfoot.

'Entering vox-silence,' the helmswoman says. A hush settles over the vessel, as though even idle conversation might transmit itself through the void and betray their position to the enemy. When Morvenn and her retinue return to the bridge they find the captain rigid in his chair, the lights low and the viewscreen disabled. The hololith of Ophelia VII hangs in front of him, the red dot of the Heretic Space Marines' strike cruiser glowing like a baleful fiery eye on its sunward side.

'You have made good time, captain.'

'I am mindful of the pressing nature of your appointment.' The captain's eyes are closed, only an ever-moving sliver of light and dark between the lids betraying his intense concentration. 'Once we reach orbit, the lander will take you down. I trust all is packed in preparation.'

One of the vessel's cogitator-looms gives a high-pitched chirp, and the atmosphere in the room abruptly changes. The helmswoman straightens and turns in her chair, but from the way the captain sits forward he is already all too aware of what she is about to tell him.

'What is it?' Morvenn casts her eyes around the bridge, aware that something is happening but unable to make sense of what everyone else seems instinctively to understand, as though a conversation is taking place in a language she does not speak. 'Have they seen us?'

At a gesture from the captain, the hololith spins and their field of view lengthens, bringing the largest of Ophelia VII's moons into the display. There is something moving on its dark side, the lines of its silhouette flickering with data-runes as the ship's augurs try to identify what they are detecting.

'Another strike cruiser?'

Haraquis shakes his head, not in disagreement but in frustration. 'Please be patient, Abbess Sanctorum.' He might as well be asking her to fly. Ten breathless seconds pass before he speaks again. 'Not a voidship. We had taken its signal for part of the strike cruiser's own, but it has become separate.'

'A Thunderhawk gunship?'

'Too large for that.'

'And what is it doing?'

'Closing.'

Another alarm sounds. The augur operator turns in his chair, but the captain silences him before he can speak. He already knows what the augur array has detected, Morvenn realises, and from the look of grim anticipation spreading over his face, she thinks she knows what he has just learned.

'Have they detected us?'

The advance of the red dot that represents the Astartes strike cruiser is answer enough.

'Captain. What now?'

'Three options.' The captain speaks briskly, as though this is a training exercise and not a matter of life and death. 'One, attempt to retreat. It will take some hours to alter our trajectory, but with a combination of mines, heavy artillery and interceptors we have a slim chance of reaching the Mandeville point.'

'Unacceptable.'

'That was my assumption, yes. Option two – an attempt to directly engage them – is equally likely to fail. Which leaves us with one remaining possibility. We continue the deployment as planned. Once you are safely on your descent – and I use that word advisedly – the *Lux* will take evasive measures and burn for the Mandeville point. Which will, I regret to inform you, leave you at least temporarily stranded until Naval reinforcements arrive.'

'Then the third is–'

He cuts her off with a wave of his hand, and she falls silent out of sheer surprise. 'Already underway. As you must also be.'

The viewscreen flares into life. The Night Lords strike cruiser is already terrifyingly close, an unearthly silver light emanating from its broadside ports and from the massive glassaic windows above its prow. She has seen the voidships of Chaos Space Marines before, most recently the spiked and blood-smeared abominations that carry the thrice-damned Word Bearers Legion on their eternal crusade of blasphemy, but this is something different: predatory and sleek, almost restrained.

'Macrocannon batteries coming online,' the gunnery lieutenant says. He is a slight man with a shaven head who looks as though he would struggle to withstand a stiff wind, but the weapons at his command are capable of shattering planets. 'Shall I instruct the nova cannon crew to make ready?'

'Not at this range, and not so close to the cardinal world. The Abbess Sanctorum is here to relieve Ophelia VII, not to set its atmosphere ablaze like a votive candle. Divert power to for'ard lance batteries and prepare targeting runes. Interceptors, stand ready for deployment.'

'Aye, lord captain, as you command.'

The bridge lights turn a brighter red, and the chirp of the cogitators dies. Though this is her first Naval battle, Morvenn knows this moment – the long inhalation before the fight begins, the terrible stillness before enemies clash. On the ground, this part would take minutes at most. Here in the void, the terrifying ballet of steel will play out over hours, each order enacted by hundreds of gunnery-serfs and teams of voidsmen as they bend the *Lux Dominus* to their will.

The captain's hands dance across his rune-pads, a virtuoso musician at the keys. 'Continue our course for the deployment point, full burn.' He leans forward in his chair, his pale eyes scanning the image of the heretic strike cruiser with fascination. 'A modified Vanguard class,' he murmurs. 'Type one, unless I am much mistaken, God-Emperor be praised.'

'Where is the God-Emperor's hand in *that* monstrosity?'

The captain's head twitches. 'The type one carries shorter-range weaponry, which buys us time. Were it equipped with a lance battery we would already be close to engagement range.'

'The strike cruiser is changing trajectory, my lord.' The augur operator adjusts the image without looking up from his data-loom. 'Heading for us to intercept, opening its broadside ports.'

The captain's eyes narrow. 'Lance batteries, lock on and prepare to fire.'

Morvenn is no Naval tactician, but she can tell from the atmosphere on the bridge that this is an unexpected development.

'Captain. How long until we are in weapons range?'

'Abbess Sanctorum, if you intend to remain on my bridge I must request that you allow me to concentrate on the task at hand.'

Morvenn nods. There are few men in the Imperium from whom she would accept such a request, but the captain is one of them.

'Lance batteries ready, lord captain,' the gunnery lieutenant says. 'Runes locked. Awaiting your command.'

'Lord captain!' The augur operator's voice is sharp. 'Ports opening on the heretic vessel's side. Multiple energy signals detected, bearing life signs. Boarding craft and Thunderhawks, my lord!'

'Praise be to the God-Emperor for His wrath, which He has placed in our hands,' Haraquis says, his voice ringing out across the bridge. 'For'ard lance battery. Upon my order, in the God-Emperor's name, give fire!'

'Aye, my lord! We hear and obey.'

Nothing happens. Morvenn looks around the bridge, then to her Sisters, who stare back in shared and silent confusion, and then the bridge's viewscreen is lit with glowing crimson light as a lance beam streaks across the void to strike the enemy vessel just above its armoured prow.

'A direct hit, my lord!'

The first blow of this battle has found its mark.

'Enemy craft have launched,' the augur operator reports. 'Two dozen targets already deployed. Thunderhawks inbound, weapons hot.'

'Fury pilots, this is your captain. Deploy immediately. Intercept those Thunderhawks.'

Like birds of prey, the attack craft of the *Lux Dominus* burn across the void. In a battle whose pace is better measured in hours than seconds they move at lightning speed, streaking towards the enemy with lithe, impossible grace, the beams of their weapons turning the void an unearthly emerald.

'Dorsal lance. Give fire.'

The gunnery officer relays the order, and a second coruscating bolt glances from the strike cruiser's hull.

'They are launching torpedoes, captain.'

'Engage countermeasures.'

No matter how many times Morvenn has read of the great Naval engagements of Imperial history, nothing compares to watching it unfold with her own eyes. A moment ago the void was black and still, and now it swarms with points of light, torpedoes meeting torpedoes on intercept courses, fighter craft wheeling and plunging with guns ablaze, the huge beams of the lances burning through everything in their path. Macro-cannon shells explode like solar flares along the strike cruiser's flank, and the heretic vessel returns fire in kind. The corrupted Thunderhawks are appallingly fast as they make strafing runs on the *Lux*'s shield generators and gun turrets, and the Fury Interceptors struggle to match them despite their superior numbers.

'Captain. What is that?' An urgent question forces itself from Morvenn's mouth. Something is approaching through the flaming void – something with folded legs, barbed like a poisonous insectoid ready to strike.

'All hands, brace for impact.' The helmswoman's voice does not waver.

'That, Abbess Sanctorum, is a Dreadclaw. A boarding craft.'

'More of them inbound, my lord.'

A shudder passes through the ship, and the captain shudders along with it. His eyes open to their full extent. 'Abbess Sanctorum. Our time grows short, and with the greatest of respect, your place is not on this bridge. Your place' – he punctuates the words with a jab of his index finger towards the display, to the serene grey-green orb floating far below the unfolding battle – 'is on Ophelia VII, and my duty is to see you safely there. Voidsman Winstet?'

A deck officer who looks barely old enough to shave steps smartly forward and snaps a salute. 'Yes, captain?'

'Escort the Abbess Sanctorum and her Celestians to their lander with all haste.'

'Sir.'

'The rest of my Sisters. They must be informed of this and made ready to deploy.'

He does not look, but his hands dance across the control runes of his command throne. 'You have the vox, Abbess Sanctorum. Be quick.'

'Sisters of the Adepta Sororitas.' Her voice echoes back at her from the ship's vox-casters. 'The *Lux Dominus* is under attack. Report with all haste to the Devourer drop-ship *Aeolis* and deploy immediately for the Convent Sanctorum. I will join you there. The God-Emperor is with you.'

The bridge lurches to the right.

'Impact, captain,' the helmswoman says, with remarkable composure.

'Helm, keep our present course. All hands, stand ready to repel boarders. God-Emperor speed you, Abbess Sanctorum. Light a candle for the *Lux* in the Convent Sanctorum, if you would.'

'I will.'

Outside the bridge, the lumens are dim. Somewhere in the distance someone screams, and a bolter fires. The air already smells faintly of smoke.

'This way, Abbess Sanctorum,' the voidsman says, and breaks into a run.

VII

Aleyna watches from the doorway of the crypt as another explosion tears the night in half. Sounds of battle ring off ancient marble: a boltgun's dull report, a deep voice raised in anger, the distant rasp of a groundbike's engine.

Kerem's distraction is beginning.

Aleyna turns to the crypt's gaping mouth. 'Bring them up.'

The journey ahead of them is daunting. As long as they remain in the necropolis there is the hope of shelter, but once they reach the broad, open expanse of the Way of the Saints, the little refugee column will stand out like a nest of crypt-rats in a canoness' chamber.

The pilgrims stumble up the stone steps into open air. Another thunderous volley of bolter fire ruptures the night – not the disciplined bark of a Godwyn-De'az-pattern weapon in the hands of a Battle Sister, but a wilder, deeper sound – and is followed an instant later by the explosion of a frag grenade. The sound brings a smile to Aleyna's face. Sister Kerem is making good use of the time and explosives available to her.

The two Sisters Retributor flank the little group of survivors, the black of their armour and vestments a stark contrast with Perdita's blistered silver as she stumbles along at the column's rear. The wound on her scalp has clotted to a thick, fist-sized scab, and she is growing drowsier and more withdrawn by the hour. At first Aleyna had thought the Seraphim's silence was the result of shame and grief, but it is becoming clear that her injuries are to blame. Without a Hospitaller they have little option other than to continue, but Aleyna's concern is increasing with every minute that passes.

A chill breeze bites at the exposed flesh of Aleyna's cheeks, her every exhalation pluming like dragon's breath in the icy air. It is not merely the devastation that has made her surroundings unfamiliar, but the darkness itself. In normal times even the dead of night would be lit with the glow of lumens through glassaic, burning braziers, thousands of votive candles. But the lights of faith have been extinguished, and what little illumination remains comes only from the last embers of burning ruins. How far does the devastation go? Aleyna imagines Ophelia VII in darkness without prayer or song, the tolling of its bells silenced forever.

It cannot be so.

It *must* not be so.

She leads them through the shadows of tombs and statues, towards the ghost of the cathedrum's shattered dome and the broken towers that once lined the martyr's way. The scale of the devastation is astonishing, considering the short time since the attack began. Kerem's bolter has fallen silent, which means she is dead, captured or in hiding again. Aleyna murmurs a fervent prayer – *God-Emperor, grant my Sister the blessing of a swift martyrdom when her work is done* – and leads her column through the eastern entrance of an ancient mausoleum, flinching as the pilgrim child gives a piercing wail.

'Keep him quiet,' she whispers, and the father nods. The child whimpers again, as if sensing his father's fear – and Aleyna's.

'If the enemy hears him, they will find us.' The high vaulted ceiling of the mausoleum returns her whisper to her over and over. 'And they will not be merciful.'

'Forgive me, Sister. I will do what I can.'

Aleyna turns away, her face burning. The noise is not the man's fault, nor is it the child's, but silence may prove to be their only defence in the moments to come. If the child cannot be hushed, what dreadful choice will she be forced to make?

Aleyna scans the open ground through the mausoleum's western doorway before she steps outside. The cathedrum is nearer than she had allowed herself to hope, and the way to its door is clear.

'When I give the word, run for the cathedrum's door.'

A cold beam of light pierces the smoky air – not the moon's yellow glow, but the piercing lance of a search-lumen carried on the underside of a low-flying lander. If the heretics are hunting them by air as well as land, then any slim hope is gone. Their bones will lie here unburied, or be taken, nameless, to decorate a heretic's panoply.

The light passes overhead again. In the distance, someone screams, once, then twice, then the sound turns to a drawn-out shriek of agony. A groundbike growls, so close that she can smell the acrid fumes from its exhaust. Another screaming voice joins the first, then an ululating chorus of human voices rises from all sides, the sound laced with hatred and madness.

'Cultists,' Sister Marayd growls. 'Who would serve such masters?'

Aleyna has no answer for that. 'If we are to reach the cathedrum, the time is now.'

She calculates distances. A quarter of a mile will take them to the cathedrum's outer wall, their way concealed by the building's enormous shadow. From there, four flights of stone steps lead to the courtyard before it, and it is then that they must cross open ground to the doors. In those twenty yards they will be visible not only from the air, but also to anyone on the Way of the Saints – but there is no choice, not if they are to survive.

'Go.'

Aleyna breaks into a steady jog. At every moment she expects to see the flames of a Raptor's jump pack or hear the grinding rasp of a chainglaive, but it seems the attention of the Night Lords is elsewhere. She glances back and is relieved to see that the pilgrims are maintaining their rudimentary cohesion, though more through fear than discipline.

They are almost halfway across when a figure erupts from the darkness. Aleyna's finger twitches to her bolt pistol's trigger as a boy of no more than twelve or thirteen sprints towards them, all flashing bare limbs and tattered trailing rags, his eyes rolling like those of a terrified beast. Aleyna steps in front of him, and the boy jigs sideways with a yelp of terror, his bare feet skidding on the hard-packed ground.

'Stop!' Aleyna snaps out a gauntlet and locks it around his shoulder. The boy's feet go out from under him. He sprawls face up and panting, staring up at her in desperation. 'Peace. You are amongst allies.'

'It is coming.' The words leave the boy's mouth in heavy gasps. Even through her gauntlet she can feel how hard he is shaking.

'Get up.' She guides him back to his feet and pushes him forward, waving the group behind to follow her. His bones are light as a bird's. '*Who* is coming?'

'The beast. The beast is coming.'

Aleyna's blood turns cold. 'What have you seen?'

A screech too loud and too harsh for a human throat rips the air in half. The boy falls to his knees and clutches his head.

'No – no!'

'Look!' Marayd shouts, pointing a black gauntlet to the skies over the cathedrum, where a jagged silhouette is soaring across the clouded sky. It shrieks again, and a column of fire gouts from the shadow onto the cathedrum's dome, turning the building to an inferno of orange and gold.

Aleyna's first thought is that it is a fighter craft, but a moment's observation puts paid to that notion. The light of the conflagration illuminates an armoured underbelly, vast scything wings, and a pair of rune-carved talons like those of some monstrous bird of prey. It is larger than a Rhino, larger than an Immolator tank, a great barbed tail behind it and two draconic, razor-mawed heads before.

Heldrake.

It draws one head back to scream again, while the second breathes another torrent of flame at the cathedrum's bell tower, reducing the bell within to molten streams of bronze. The daemon engine plunges down through the flames, talons reaching out to tear the gold adornments from the cathedrum's roof and casting them aside.

'It is destroying the cathedrum.' Rukhsana's voice is suffused with horror. 'We cannot stand by and allow this to happen.'

'But what can we do?' Aleyna points to the hellish fusion of daemon and machine. She has seen such a horror only once before, fighting as a new-made Battle Sister under Palatine Sujata's command. That beast had killed half a combat patrol of Sisters before they had brought it down and cracked its carapace open to find the remains of its pilot curled foetus-like at its rotting heart. 'If we draw its attention–'

But Marayd has already made the decision for her. With a cry, the Retributor raises her heavy bolter and pulls the trigger, sending a deafening burst of shells streaking towards the Heldrake.

'What are you doing?' Aleyna turns and sees half of the pilgrims frozen in terror, the other half either flat on the dirt or falling to their knees in prayer. 'Sister Retributor! You will draw its attention!'

Marayd takes her finger from the trigger long enough for a few words. 'You may be content to stand by and watch the cathedrum torn to the ground without a fight. I am not.'

Whatever reply Aleyna might have had for her is drowned out by gunfire. Any hope that the beast might not hear the sound over the blaze proves to be a futile one, as first one head and then the second snaps around, baleful eyes glowing. The vast wings beat once – twice – as it hovers in the air, then with tail whipping, it dives towards them.

Rukhsana's heavy bolter joins Marayd's, and Aleyna cannot fault her for that. She aims her own weapon at the glowing light deep in the Heldrake's throat, counting the seconds until it is within range. Its vast mouths open to unleash two parallel torrents of flame, the heat setting the night air rippling, filling Aleyna's ears with the roar of the inferno. She draws a scalding breath, knowing with absolute certainty that it will be her last. Let it leave her lips in a prayer.

'God-Emperor, accept this, my final sacrifice–'

And something changes.

Power flows through her like cool water, soothing the burning heat in her lungs, filling her limbs, her throat, her skull, spilling outward from her eyes in a blinding burst of radiance. She is unmade, she is reborn, her soul buffeted like driftwood against a rocky shore, her ears filling with a song of such ineffable sweetness that her only desire is to surrender herself entirely and become part of that sacred choir forever.

It seems that years pass before she finds herself again.

When the world returns, she is kneeling in the shadow of the burning cathedrum, the smell of smoke and ash mingled inextricably with that of incense and roses. Flames burn in the necropolis behind her, but where she kneels the ground is unmarked. Her Sisters are standing around her, the novitiate clasping the reliquary case to her chest, all of them staring fixedly in her direction. She looks down at her hands, and sees smoke coiling from her fingertips, the grey curls carrying the same fragrance as the incense in the air. Her eyes sting as though rubbed with salt.

A lone voice is singing, high and sweet. The sky above them is clear, the Heldrake receding into the distance, and for the first time in years she sees Ophelia's stars.

Seraphim Perdita's song comes to an end, and she limps forward, her face ashen, but her eyes suffused with holy wonder. She extends a shaking hand to help Aleyna to her feet. 'The God-Emperor has saved us,' Perdita says. 'He has sent His miracle.'

'What happened–' Aleyna begins, then falls silent as one by one the Sisters join the pilgrims on their knees.

VIII

In the dim red light of the emergency lumens, the *Lux Dominus* is a tangled labyrinth of passageways and bulkheads. Morvenn has long lost her sense of direction as they sprint for the hangar bay that contains her lander, the long mechanical legs of the Purgator Mirabilis eating up the ground with ease. Her Sisters keep pace with little difficulty, but the scarlet-faced Voidsman Winstet is falling further behind at every turn.

'Which way?' Morvenn waits for Winstet to catch up, Fidelis aimed down the passage to the right while her Sisters cover the left.

'Left,' he gasps.

'How far to the hangar bay?'

Winstet's eyes flick upward, either in mental calculation or accessing data. 'Eight hundred yards, Abbess Sanctorum.'

Half a mile. They are almost there.

The next passageway is already full of smoke. A sudden sharp scream pierces the air to Morvenn's right, and she turns with weapons raised before she realises the noise has come through the ship's ducting. A burst of las-fire follows, then a deep and inhuman laugh laced with corruption and viciousness. Morvenn's anger is a burning coal in her throat, and she swallows it down, banking the heat to a dull glow, ready to blaze once her target comes in sight. The *Lux Dominus* belongs to the God-Emperor, and these invaders are an affront to the Imperial Navy, the Ecclesiarchy and to the Imperial Creed itself. To flee when she should be fighting goes against everything she has been taught, everything for which her Order stands.

But she is not here to save the *Lux Dominus*.

She is here to save Ophelia VII, and she cannot do that if she is lost in the void – and she has no intention of granting Grand Master Fadix the satisfaction of being proven correct.

'Abbess, please. A moment.' Winstet has fallen behind again.

'We cannot afford delay.'

'Of course, abbess. But I must ask you to retrace your steps a little. Our route lies through this hatch.' Winstet turns the wheel set into the bulkhead, and a hatch just wide enough to admit the warsuit swings open.

'I could have blown that open for you,' Fionnula observes, tapping one armoured finger to the stock of her multi-melta. 'Next time, you need only ask.'

Winstet's mouth drops open. 'Celestian Sister, the *Lux Dominus* is a venerable vessel, the captain would not permit–'

Celestian Superior Ignatia pushes her way through the hatch. 'Celestian Fionnula is wasting words on facetious chatter. She has no intention of damaging the vessel. Do you, Sister Celestian?'

'Of course not, Celestian Superior. Not unless the good voidsman asks, at any rate.'

Morvenn has almost crossed through the hatch when something moves in the shadows at the end of the passageway. Her Sisters are through already, but the prickle on the back of her neck tells her that this is an enemy that will not wait. She activates her helmet's preysight and breaks into a run. The passageway resolves into a shimmering tunnel of green and black, a huge figure in spiked armour in the shadows at the end.

'Fiat lux!' She activates the Lance of Illumination and the passageway floods with blue-white light. There is not one heretic but three – all of them wearing skull-face helmets, one horned, one surmounted by a single jutting spike, the third with a gore-soaked crimson plume. Already the teeth of their two-handed chainglaives are caked in a thick layer of clotted gore.

'Morvenn Vahl,' the horned heretic rasps. 'How pleased my lord Rakhul will be when I bring him your head.'

She lets Fidelis answer for her. Shells from the Purgator Mirabilis' heavy bolter rip through the air to punch into the Traitor Space Marine's chestplate. He staggers back, gore spilling over the human skulls that hang from his belt.

'Better than you have failed before,' she says.

The Traitor Space Marine has just long enough to raise his guard before she is on him, a second volley of shells leading the charge. This time he is quicker, and as her lance sweeps round he brings the chainglaive up to parry, deflecting her blow an instant before it would have taken the head from his shoulders.

'Ave Dominus Nox!' he spits.

Morvenn strikes again, her stomach twisting with hatred mixed with a sudden, fierce joy. This creature should have been one of the God-Emperor's beloved sons, and instead he and his brothers have cast aside that greatest of blessings as though it were nothing but a worthless bauble.

A second chainglaive whirrs towards her, this time at the warsuit's left knee joint. She kicks it away with contempt, and rewards the attempt with a bolt-shell aimed at its wielder's skull-faced helmet. It explodes in a shower of metal, bone and brain matter, and she does not pause to see the heretic fall. The Lance of Illumination is feather-light in her hand, the Purgator Mirabilis responding at the speed of thought, her every movement precise, economical and designed for a single purpose.

'You have no place here.'

The wounded heretic is staggering back, and she presses her assault without mercy. Cleansing this place is a sacred duty, and more than that, it is a pleasure.

'No right to walk amongst the God-Emperor's faithful.'

She brings her lance down and his parry comes a moment too late. The power weapon's glowing blade severs his armour at the shoulder in a spray of sizzling ichor, and as the blow's momentum drives him to his knees, she stabs downward in an impaling strike through the dome of the spiked helmet.

'And you will take no heads today.'

Where is the third Chaos Space Marine? Morvenn pulls her spear free of the heretic's sizzling flesh and searches the passageway. The two corpses are already cooling at her feet, and she spares a moment to stamp the warsuit's boot on what remains of the skewered traitor's face with contempt. *Ave Dominus Nox?* If this is what she can expect from the Lords of Night, then perhaps the relief of Ophelia VII will be a simpler matter than she had feared.

A shadow moves in the darkness, resolving into the outline of the last of the infernal trinity, already twenty feet away. She flicks gore from the spear's gleaming haft and raises Fidelis as he ducks around a corner, but her preysight can still perceive his movements through the bulkhead. He is waiting there, though whether in ambush or in terror does not matter. She stalks forward into the darkness without fear. The God-Emperor's light will drive away all shadows.

'Abbess Sanctorum!' Celestian Superior Ignatia's voice comes sharply through her vox-bead. 'Wait – in the God-Emperor's name!'

'What is it?'

'More of them. Kseniya has them on the auspex.' Ignatia motions towards the rest of the honour guard, standing with weapons raised a few yards behind.

'How many?'

'A dozen or more.' Another impact strikes the voidship. 'Blocking our route to the lander.'

Morvenn turns to Winstet. 'Is there another route?'

'To the hangar bay?' The voidsman shakes his head, his eyes wide. 'None that we could traverse in time.'

'The drop-ship, then. Do we have a clear route?'

Kseniya nods. 'For now, at least.'

'Voidsman. Hail the drop-ship immediately.'

'Yes, Holy Sister.' Winstet reaches out to a wall-mounted vox-unit and thumbs its activation catch. 'Drop-ship *Aeolis*, what is your status?' He waits for a slow count of ten before trying again. 'I repeat, *Aeolis*, this is *Lux Dominus*, what is your status?'

No reply.

'I take it they have gone already?' Ignatia asks.

Winstet nods. 'In accordance with the Abbess Sanctorum's orders. Drop-ship *Thallis* is also gone.'

A hiss of frustration escapes Morvenn's lips. 'Alternatives.'

'The salvation pods?' Fionnula asks.

Morvenn glances down at the bulk of her warsuit and scowls. The prospect of abandoning the ancient relic in order to cram herself into an adamantine coffin is not an appealing one.

'Very well,' she begins, then pauses as a memory of the over-attentive steward resurfaces from the depths of her thoughts. 'Voidsman – the *Lux Dominus* has carried Space Marines in the past, is that not so?'

'It is so, abbess–'

'Would *they* have a means of leaving this vessel in such a situation?'

Winstet pauses, brow furrowing in thought. 'I believe so. A cargo delivery pod was modified for that purpose. The captain insists that the *Lux* is prepared for all eventualities – but it has never been used. It would not be comfortable–'

Morvenn rolls her eyes. 'Are all voidfarers so obsessed with bodily comforts as those on board the *Lux Dominus*? Can the delivery pod be programmed to arrive in a set location? The Convent Sanctorum?'

'In principle, but–'

'And is it close by?'

'With the other salvation pods in the aft compartment, but–'

'Then that will be our destination.'

IX

Hunger gnaws in the pit of Lethe's belly, her mouth dust-dry. It is impossible to know how long she has been left in darkness, one hour blending formlessly into the next, bereft of comfort or relief. The whimpering of the penitents comes and goes, each identifiable by the pitch and cadence of their moans. Some cry almost continuously. Others have been silent for hours.

The darkness is absolute. She can sense the presence of her fellow penitents by the heat of their bodies, the rasp of their breath, the damp touch of flesh against flesh, but so far as she can tell, they are all sitting in mute acceptance of their fate. She has no illusions about her chances of survival – if the enforcers have sealed the mine with no intention of returning then they will all starve to death – but already she is making plans to ensure she lives as long as possible. Her time as a penitent has taught her to treat each day of life as a victory. A new day brings a new opportunity, and this change in routine is so strange that it is almost welcome.

A muffled rumble shakes the cavern's roof. It could be gunfire, heavy machinery, falling rubble – any one of a thousand possible deaths. More than once Lethe has allowed herself to speculate that the mine's entrance has already been filled in, and that the noise is the heaping of stone upon stone, but that is a thought she cannot afford to follow to its logical conclusion. The straps that hold her muzzle in place are a more tangible concern, something that can be addressed with a sharp-edged rock and time, and both of those are in abundant supply.

Lethe saws at the synthleather until her fingers ache. The task seems impossible, but at last a strand yields, and she tests what strength remains with a sharp tug forward. This time the leather stretches far enough that she can hook a finger behind it. Another thirty seconds of sawing breaks the strap entirely, and she turns her attention to the second until it too breaks, the muzzle slack enough now that she can open her jaws in a narrow yawn. The air tastes rank and stagnant, but the pleasure of it against her tongue and throat is astonishing. She moves her lips in the attempt to shape words, but finds nothing to say.

The rumble through the rock changes to the grinding whine of metal on stone as the portcullis rises, and a minute later a pair of wavering lumen-beams break the darkness.

'Penitents?' There is an unfamiliar uncertainty in Yulius' voice. Lethe closes her fist around her rock – the third muzzle-strap will have to wait – and creeps along with her back to the wall. The passageway is wide enough that she might pass the overseers without attracting notice, and even if not, she has no intention of submitting to death without a fight. She is not defenceless, either. She is strong and quick, her muscles developed by years of hard labour, she has the element of surprise, and of course she has her rock.

The overseer's lumen-beam plays across the shivering mass of her fellow penitents. Evania lies like a heap of rags on the ground, and as the beam touches her face a sleek, brown-furred body squeals in displeasure before scurrying into the dark. The old woman has only been dead for a few hours, but the mine-rats have already gnawed her face down to the bone.

'All of you.' Overseer Yulius has another guard at his side, a woman Lethe does not recognise. Both are carrying firearms. He motions with his weapon to the huddled penitents. 'Line up, by the wall.'

Lethe creeps another yard along the darkened passageway beyond the lumen's reach. The space is broader here, and the attention of the guards is so firmly on the group of labourers at the end of the tunnel that it seems all too possible to sneak past them – but what then? She tries to remember her first journey into darkness, but the years have taken the clarity from her memory. The portcullis may still be up, but if there are locked doors – and surely no prison-mine was ever created without them – then no matter how quickly she outpaces the overseers, they will catch her in the end.

Lumen-light glints on the ring of keys hanging from the overseer's belt, and her decision is made. The penitents have shuffled into position as ordered, their backs pressed to the stone, eyes wide above the heavy steel muzzles that turn their faces into identical masks. The muzzles are not only to stop the prisoners from speaking. They are also to remove every trace of their individuality. If their guards ever saw them as people, who knows what acts of mercy might follow?

The second of the two guards – a burly woman with closely cropped black hair – stops behind her companion and raises her autogun.

'Now?' she asks.

Lethe takes the word as her signal to act. She launches herself forward, raising the rock high above her head and swinging it round hard into the side of the woman's skull. The overseer turns an instant before the impact strikes her temple and shatters her left eye socket, the force of the blow rupturing her eyeball in a spray of blood and vitreous humour. She staggers, but before she can fall Lethe is on her, ripping the autogun from her hands, spinning it round and slamming the stock into the woman's throat. The overseer drops, wet breaths gurgling through the ruin of her larynx. Lethe fumbles at the woman's belt, her fingers sliding over the cloth of her overalls until they hit the cold metal of the heavy iron clip that secures the keys to her belt. She pulls it free and lunges to her feet, keys in one hand and autogun in the other, and runs.

And the shooting starts. Slugs ricochet from roughly hewn stone, the air fragrant with fyceline and blood. When she looks back, half of the penitents are slumped in a heap at the foot of the wall, but the others are surging forward, heading for the overseer with fists raised to strike. His nerve breaks, and he turns to run, but Lethe is already ahead of him.

Years of mine-work have stripped her of every spare ounce of flesh. The muscles of her legs are pistons, propelling her onwards with all the speed they have been denied for a decade and more. The portcullis is half-open when she reaches it; she ducks beneath its jagged metal points then swerves to follow the passageway up and to the right. The tunnels are alive with movement now, full of shouts and gunshots, and down a side passageway she catches sight of a shadow too large to be wholly human. She dodges another penitent crouching in the centre of the passageway, and almost stops when she sees what the woman is doing. The rock-breaker's mallet in her right hand is rising and falling with well-practised precision onto what was once an overseer's face and now is a wet and bloody mess. A savage grin splits Lethe's face as she sprints on towards the cavern-mouth, the light from outside growing brighter, the air clearer with every step she takes.

Outside the mine, the world has turned to flame. The hulking shadows of giant warriors stalk back and forward through smoke and fire, corralling the newly escaped prisoners as they try to flee. The air smells of wood smoke and freshly spilled blood, the crackle of the flames mingling with the screams echoing in her ears.

Someone slams into her from behind, the weight sending both her and her assailant lurching to the ground in a tangle of limbs and the autogun flying from her grip. She scrambles to her knees and scrabbles to reclaim her weapon, but a hand locks tight around her ankle and drags her back.

'Not so fast, penitent,' Overseer Yulius says.

'Let go!' The words hiss out through her half-closed mouth. She kicks out with her one free foot, and is rewarded by the sensation of her bare heel striking the dome of Yulius' head.

'Bitch! You'll die for that!'

Lethe laughs. The penitentium is burning around them, and still all this fool can think of is maintaining the old order, exerting the last of his authority before it is stripped from him forever. She tries once more to tug herself free, but his grip is locked on like a vice.

But then, why is she trying to get away?

He pulls on her ankle, and this time she yields to the pressure, allowing him to drag her back towards him. There is no sign of his autogun – perhaps knocked from his grasp during their flight, perhaps discarded in his haste to run – but his shock maul is still clipped to his belt. She rolls towards him, tears it free of its clasp, and brings it down unactivated into the side of his face.

His head snaps to the side. A wide gash opens on his cheek, and he snarls with rage. 'Kill you for that, sinner–' he begins, but Lethe has her weight on top of him now, straddling his well-padded chest with her left hand digging into his throat. He manages to spray a glob of dusty spit into her mouth, and in return she activates the shock maul and slams it into the side of his head. His face convulses as the shock passes through him, and she casts the weapon aside, consumed with the desire to feel his skin tear, his flesh rupture, his bones shatter beneath her bare hands. She punches her closed fist into his mouth, rewarded by a snap as his lip bursts and the tooth behind it breaks.

'What sins are these?' A sense of perfect calm is washing through her. This is how the overseers must have felt as they swung the whip, as they created a world with rules and punishments for their charges and the rights reserved for themselves. But that time is over. The only laws here are those of pain and power. 'What crime sentenced me to the pit?'

'The blessed Sisters–'

Lethe's fist finds his face again, opening a wound on his forehead like a wet red eye, then again into his mouth. This time bone shatters against her knuckles and a sharp pain arcs through her hand, but pain is nothing compared to the power coursing through her, the sense of absolute control.

'There was no sin.' She lands another blow, and his breath turns to a raw gurgle, panic in his eyes as he thrashes his head in the attempt to clear the froth of blood blocking his airway. Now he understands the price of his deeds. Now is the reckoning for every touch of the lash, every curse, every gob of spit, every shove and kick and mouthful of dirt, and she has every intention of holding him to account for each one–

A shadow falls across her. A huge figure is standing above her, silhouetted against the flames. Blue-and-bronze armour covers him from the winged helm to his sharpened sabatons, encrusted with spikes and bearing a towering armour rack adorned with rotting heads. One hand is gloved in a razor-tipped power claw, while the other is closed around the grip of a massive power axe. Overseer Yulius draws a rasping breath, but the fight has gone from him, just as it has suddenly left her.

The huge warrior lifts the helmet from his head, revealing a face drawn from the depths of nightmare. The mouth is too wide, the lips stretched back to reveal pointed teeth and a wet, crimson tongue, but it is the eyes that are the worst – the right night-black and bereft of pupil or iris, the left obliterated by a gash from brow to cheekbone, the pulped orb beneath it leaking a steady stream of blood and humour. Terror pins her in place, her blood a rushing river in her ears, her chest too tight to breathe.

'Ave Dominus Nox.'

The warrior's breath smells of long-dead carrion, his voice simultaneously a predator's growl and the shriek of claws on slate. She is shaking uncontrollably, cold sweat breaking out across her skin, but for all his fearful monstrosity there is something fascinating about him, something that speaks of power unconcerned with human notions of righteousness or morality. A smile curves the too-wide lips, the head tilted to the side in amusement.

'There is such hate in you, mortal. Such anger.'

Something thuds into the dirt at her side – a blade as long as her forearm, the bronze hilt fashioned in the shape of a dragon with wings outstretched.

'Take it,' the warrior growls.

A ruby glints in the depths of the dragon's eye as she closes her hand around the metal, cold as the space between the stars. She looks up at the huge warrior, who gestures with his hand like a king granting permission to a particularly lowly subject.

'Go ahead, little mortal.'

Yulius tries to speak, but only a wet red sound bubbles from between his lips. Perhaps it is a plea for mercy.

If so, it comes too late.

The knife in her hand is a promise. Her dark saviour's gaze a palpable force on the back of her neck, Lethe brings the blade to what remains of the overseer's mouth and makes the first cut of many.

X

'All hands, this is your captain.'

Haraquis' voice comes through the ship's vox with perfect clarity. Morvenn's stomach drops. *'We have been boarded and overrun. The* Lux Dominus *is lost. I have given orders to overload the ship's plasma reactors to keep her from the hands of the enemy, and her destruction is now inevitable. You have fought well against insurmountable odds, and there is no shame in this defeat.'*

The ship's passageways are thick with smoke. Winstet is sprinting at full speed, the warsuit thundering in his wake as Morvenn urges it forward to keep his slight figure in her sights as he weaves left and right through the maze of the *Lux Dominus*. The whole vessel is shaking in great rippling waves that set the gravity generators fluctuating wildly, the suit weightless one moment and mag-locked to the deck plating the next.

'This is my final order to you all. All souls, abandon this vessel and throw yourselves on the mercies of the void.' A deafening impact rings through the vox, the sound of a battering ram against an adamantine door.

The captain's voice is serene, a testament to remarkable courage in the face of devastating loss. How must it feel, Morvenn wonders, to be confronted with the loss of your sacred charge, facing the choice between allowing its corruption or becoming the instrument of its destruction?

'The Lux Dominus *has been faithful to me, and I will not abandon her in her final moments. We are all in the God-Emperor's hands. Now go quickly to the salvation pods.'*

A siren begins to wail, the pitch rising and falling in an ululating lament. Footsteps clatter towards them down a side passage, heavy boots beating out a frantic tattoo on the deck plating.

'Voidsmen,' Winstet says, and turns to direct the beam of his flash-lumen at the approaching shadows. Six Naval breachers approach at full speed, skidding to a frantic halt at the sight of the Purgator Mirabilis.

'Abbess Sanctorum!' The breacher sergeant snaps a brisk aquila. She is breathing hard, her long blonde hair slicked to her scalp with sweat. 'The captain has given the order to abandon ship. Will you allow us to escort you to the salvation pods?'

Ignatia's snort is clearly audible through her helmet. 'If the Abbess Sanctorum wills it, we will escort *you* there.'

'Of course, blessed Sister. Forgive me, I intended no offence–'

'Quickly then.' Morvenn urges the warsuit back into motion. 'We have no time to waste.'

'How many salvation pods do these vessels carry?' Hiromi voxes softly through the squad's private channel. 'Enough for all of the crew?'

'They would need tens of thousands for that.' Fionnula's voice is unusually solemn. 'But I fear the Night Lords may have reduced the need for competition amongst the crew by now.'

Fionnula's grim prophecy turns out to be true. Morvenn had expected the compartment containing the salvation pods to be heaving with crew by the time they arrived, but it is eerily silent. The reason for that becomes evident as they draw closer – half of the pods have already deployed, the single lumen over each hatch glowing like a baleful red eye in contrast with the seven green lights of those yet to leave the vessel. The change in the bearing of the armsmen is instantaneous, turning from tension to overwhelming relief in a single moment.

'God-Emperor be praised!' The breacher sergeant motions her squad towards the salvation pods, then stops. 'Blessed Sisters – do you intend to use these salvation pods?' She is trying hard to keep her expression neutral, but the blend of hope and fear is shining through her skin like candlelight through parchment.

'Voidsman Winstet has another solution in mind for us.'

'The cargo-pod,' he says, and the breacher sergeant's face lights up with understanding and relief.

'Of course. God-Emperor protect you, Abbess Sanctorum.' Her squad fan out, each taking their place before a salvation pod and waiting for her instruction before activating the hatches. Winstet ignores them and the seventh green light, and moves to the end of the passageway, to a larger hatch, this one unlit. He places both hands on the opening wheel and moves it to the right, the muscles standing out on his neck as he strains against the rusty metal. Morvenn nods to Zafiya, who steps forward and adds her strength to the voidfarer's own. The wheel makes a squealing sound as it turns, and then a hatch large enough for a Dreadnought opens to reveal another hangar bay beyond.

This one is tiny by comparison to the last, barely large enough to contain the squat cargo container in its centre. Winstet runs to the data-loom mounted on the wall by the airlock control lever and punches a code into the rune panel. Strip lumens overhead blink on, and a faint hum cuts through the ship's wailing siren as the cargo container's hatch swings open. The space inside looks barely large enough to hold the Purgator Mirabilis, let alone her honour guard as well.

'Abbess Sanctorum, may I ask you and your Celestians to step inside the vessel?'

The klaxon is rising in pitch and frequency, and the shuddering of the ship's hull has become a constant earthquake.

'Where will it land?'

'I will enter the coordinates for the Convent Sanctorum, and–'

'Wait.' Morvenn motions her Celestians into the escape pod, but hangs back, towering over the voidsman and the screen of the data-loom. An idea has seized her by the throat and refuses to let go. The Death of Saints has sent his envoys into Imperial territory. Why then should she not do the reverse? 'Change the coordinates to eighty miles north of the convent. Set us down as close to the Cathedrum of Athenasia the Martyr as you can.'

'As you command.' His hands fly across the rune-pad, and the cogitator screen lights up with a map of Ophelia VII's surface. 'But please, Abbess Sanctorum, may I ask you to board the craft?' A small smile crosses his face. 'I would be glad of the time to reach my own salvation pod once you have departed.'

Morvenn nods. 'My thanks.'

'The honour is mine.'

The warsuit only barely fits inside the cargo-pod, almost full already with her armoured Sisters. She watches through the closing entry hatch as Winstet finishes programming their coordinates, then turns with a smile of triumph.

'It is done. God-Emperor willing, I will see you on Ophelia–'

His words are drowned out by a deafening static burst as an armoured figure tears through reality in the passageway behind him. A Heretic Space Marine in Terminator armour rips its way free of the warp, its armour crackling with warp lightning. It raises its enormous autocannon as a second rip in reality opens beside it – Winstet turns at the sound, and Morvenn has just enough time to see the voidsman's eyes go wide. She lunges for the hatch, but Winstet is quicker. His hand snaps out and pulls the airlock lever down in one swift moment, and a gale fills the hangar bay as the doors open. The docking clamps holding the pod in place release, and with a sickening lurch the escape pod careens sideways towards the open airlock doors. A volley of slugs rattle along the vessel's side, the impact propelling it further towards the void. Another dull impact strikes the plating, then Winstet's broken body hurtles past the open door, bloody droplets floating in a trail behind him as atmosphere turns to vacuum – and then the escape pod's hatch slams shut, and they lurch out into space.

God-Emperor, we are in your hands.

Dark spots swim in front of Morvenn's eyes as the acceleration takes hold of her body and squeezes it tight. Her Sisters are praying, each uttering the litany that comforts them most, but for Morvenn there is no comfort to be found in this dizzying descent through void to atmosphere – only a sickening sense of judgement and a growing awareness of what has already been sacrificed for her sake.

On the bridge of the *Lux Dominus*, Captain Haraquis turns his attention inward, communing with his beloved voidship in her final moments. The other control thrones are empty, though his crew had refused to leave at first, before he had ordered them to obey the vows they swore on soul and conscience or else be damned as oathbreakers. That had done the trick in the end. Not all of them will make it to safety, but they have a chance, and that is enough. He owes them that.

The Heretic Space Marines' strike cruiser fills the display screen in front of him, so close he can see the huge spikes on its prow, the glowing crimson lights from the open voidports down its sides, malevolence given physical form. He sends another command through his mind-impulse unit and draws another burst of effort from the voidship's engines. He and the ship have always understood each other, like a knight of ancient Terra and his faithful steed. The God-Emperor has blessed him, and Abram Haraquis is not afraid to die.

'A little further,' he murmurs. 'Only a little further, and then we can rest.'

He spares a last thought for his family. His only son is dead, but his granddaughter is already a voidship captain with a Viper-class scout sloop under her command, a lengthy scroll of heroic deeds in her record and two children of her own. The Haraquis dynasty is in good hands. If the God-Emperor is kind, he will be remembered well.

Haraquis watches the heretic vessel as it fills his viewscreen. He wonders if the Traitor Space Marines on board have realised what he is doing, if even now frantic orders are being issued to alter the strike cruiser's trajectory to avoid impact. This has been his plan since the first instant of the engagement, and his wager that the commander of the heretic vessel would be too distracted by the dogfights and the boarding actions to anticipate the *Lux*'s inexorable approach is about to pay dividends. The strike cruiser opens up with its broadside macrocannons, but that is too little and too late. Even if the shells break the *Lux Dominus* in half, at this speed the impact of even its fragments will still be enough to ensure their mutual destruction.

Through the ship's ventral augur array, he watches the *Lux*'s salvation pods fall like meteorites, haloed in flame as they enter the planet's atmosphere. Some will perish on re-entry, others will succumb to the heretics' spite either in the void or on the surface, but the hope that some will survive is enough to see him through his last moments.

'God-Emperor, may the Abbess Sanctorum live on to bring

death to your enemies,' he murmurs as the *Lux*'s plasma drive ruptures. The explosion spreads from compartment to compartment. Haraquis feels the flames as though in his own body, but there is no fear, only the ardent desire that the last act of the *Lux Dominus* will be to spit in the eye of the Great Enemy one final time.

Darkness fills the viewscreen.

There is a moment of surpassing stillness, then in its final instant of existence the *Lux Dominus* blazes like a supernova.

DREAMS

The dream is always the same.

The boy. The girl. The darkness.

The Death of Saints is not the only one of his warband to dream, but the dreams of which they boast are different. Theirs are shapeless nightmares filled with warp-born slaughter that send them into ecstatic frenzies, or the dark visions of the Ruinous Powers that control and corrupt even as they warn of what is to come – but none dream as he does.

Because his dream is true.

The dream does not come when it is bidden. If he could control it as he controls all other things of his life then it would not haunt him so. He would take it to pieces to examine each raw and bleeding part if he could. Then he would understand the flaw that keeps him from true greatness and cut it from his own flesh – but the dream is a rotting canker embedded in the heart of him, too tangled in his soul to remove.

And it is always the same.

Fear.

Darkness.

The boy and the girl.

He was human once – whatever that means – but no other

memory of that life remains. Reborn as a scion of Konrad Curze, he no longer feels love or sorrow or duty. All those human weaknesses were scourged away with his mortality – but when he dreams he feels the ghost of those forgotten emotions, and wakes with his face smeared in blood and tears.

Because the boy in the dream is him.

He is better, now: stronger, quicker, wise to the universe and its infinite cruelties.

In the dream, the alarm bells are clamouring, echoing at deafening volume through the dormitory. He jolts from sleep into wakefulness in an instant, his hand immediately sliding under his pillow to where he keeps his knife. Moonlight spills through the narrow-arched windows, lighting the cold tiled floor, the rows of beds and the half-sleeping boys in stripes of light and dark.

In the dream, it is long past midnight. Rakhul is fourteen years old, and he hates every living soul in the Imperium except for one.

'Get up!' The matriarch of the orphanarium is standing in the doorway. She wears the same floor-length black robes as always, but in place of her usual elaborate headdress her grey hair is loosely tied under a plain nightcap.

Confused moans rise from the beds around him. The other boys are slow to wake, but Rakhul is already on his feet, pulling his over-tunic and breeches on over his nightclothes, the knife tucked into his sleeve. Emergency drills are a frequent occurrence in the orphanarium, and swift action is the only way to draw the pointless exercise to a close.

'What is it?' he asks.

Matriarch Savra fixes him with a hard stare. 'We must take refuge.'

Rakhul loathes her a little less than the others, for the simple reason that she does nothing to hide her dislike of him behind smiles or false sympathy, but he is no stranger to her hard-handed punishments. Already the voice in his head is waking, telling him to strike her before she takes her belt to him, telling him to draw his knife, to cut the lines of her scowl deeper into her flesh…

He forces the intrusive image from his mind. There will be time to entertain the pleasure of that thought later, when he is back in the darkness he prefers.

'Is this a drill?'

'Do not ask questions. Do as you have done a hundred times before.'

Yawning and stretching, the other boys rise from their beds, those too slow to emerge dragged out at the end of the matriarch's bony arm.

'Quickly.'

Outside in the cloister, the ever-present smells of cleansing unguents, dusty manuscripts and week-old cooking seem twice as strong at night as they did in the day. The other boys mill around in a hopeless mass, and Rakhul finds himself trapped between two lumbering oafs. If they do not hurry, there will be no time to sleep before morning prayers, and he prizes those hours of oblivion beyond any time spent awake.

'Move, you stupid grox.' He shoves the boy again – a lumpen idiot named Drenak whose snores are a perpetual source of night-time torment – and sends him sprawling forwards to bounce off the cloister's stone wall. The voice in his head gives a gleeful laugh, urging him to draw the knife, plunge it into Drenak's doughy flesh, but Rakhul ignores it. The voice is ever-present, but he must not act on it. His sister is the only living soul who knows he hears it – though he keeps the darkest of its urgings from her – and she has been quite clear in her instructions. He must ignore it. He must tell no one. If anyone learns his secret, the matriarchs will punish him and part the two of them forever.

Drenak turns, his cheeks flushing scarlet, small eyes glaring with outrage. 'What did you call me?'

'Grox.' Rakhul tightens his grip on his knife. How sweet would it feel to push it against Drenak's eyeball and press down until the orb yielded beneath his hand? The gush of blood and fluid, the screams – but if he gives in to the voice's secret promise of pleasure, the matriarchs will punish him, send him away from the orphanarium, part him from his sister forever. That he cannot risk. He would rather be dead than live without her.

'Call me grox again. I dare you–'

'Grox. Stupid, slow, lazy–'

The noise that comes from Drenak's throat is halfway between a shriek and a roar. He lunges at Rakhul, fists clenched, but Rakhul steps out of the way and repays the clumsy attempt with a solid punch of his own. Drenak's nose crumples beneath his knuckles, and a fierce thrill of satisfaction runs through him. Blood spills down Drenak's upper lip, and he screams again, throwing himself forward in a frenzy of feet and fists. This time Rakhul is forced to step back, all his attention required to deflect the flailing assault, and his foot catches on something soft, sending him sprawling backwards to the ground. Drenak leaps on top of him and lands a clumsy haymaker on the side of his jaw that rattles Rakhul's teeth in their sockets.

Rakhul's hand steals to the knife in his sleeve and closes around the grip. *Yes,* the voice whispers. *Do it. Forget your sister and do it–*

The dormitory matriarch's thick leather belt snaps through the air, landing between Drenak's shoulders with a sharp smack. He howls in pain, then the matriarch's bony hand closes around his shoulder and drags him back to his feet. Matriarch Savra is not a tall woman, but she has ruled the orphanarium with an iron fist since before Rakhul arrived. She raises the belt again, the buckle glinting in the moonlight as it whips down towards him, and he reacts on instinct, his hand leaving the knife and snapping out to catch the heavy silver aquila before it can strike his shoulder. The silver wings bite into his flesh, but he grips it tightly, enjoying the way the matriarch's face turns scarlet with anger.

'What is the meaning of this?' She heaves at the belt, but Rakhul waits until he gets to his feet before he releases his grip. 'You should be hurrying to the sanctuary, not brawling in the cloister like stray canids!'

'I fell.' Rakhul savours the taste of the lie. The matriarch can punish him all she pleases, but now he has laid hands on her whip, the power dynamic in their relationship has subtly shifted. He is taller than she is, and stronger. Her days of taking the belt to him are numbered. Perhaps he will take it to her. Perhaps he should use the knife instead.

'You are wasting time,' she snaps, and a prickle of unease crawls across Rakhul's skin. 'I would have thought you would hurry for your sister's sake, if not your own.' There is something about the way the matriarch says the words that makes him wonder whether this excursion is a drill after all.

'What do you mean?' he asks the matriarch. 'Is the orphanarium being attacked?'

Savra's thin lips form a bloodless grey line. 'You are to make your way to the sanctuary. Our saviours are already on their way.'

Golden light floods the cloister, brighter than sunrise, brighter than the face of the God-Emperor on the chapel altar. A scalding wind buffets against Rakhul's face, and then the cloister wall crumples inward, stone and dust thundering to the ground in a furious shower. His ears are ringing, the air so thick with smoke and dust that it is impossible to see. He gropes his way along the wall until the smoke clears, and sees that the entire outer wall of the cloister has been blown away to expose a fifty-foot drop to the courtyard below. Drenak is standing next to him, coated in thick grey dust, one hand covering his stupid mouth as he stares at a crumpled heap of black cloth on the ground.

No. Not cloth. Not a curtain. A corpse.

Matriarch Savra is dead. The top of her skull has been caved in like an eggshell, exposing brain matter that glistens with the same dull sheen as her open eyes. Rakhul leans forward, fascinated, then another impact strikes the cloister. This one hits further away, but the explosion is still close enough that it sets the building shaking. Someone is attacking the building, intent on tearing it to the ground. He must find his sister; he must reach the sanctuary–

'Rakhul!' His sister Athenasia's voice cuts across the dusty cloister air as she runs towards him, flanked by a pair of her dormitory-mates, her long black hair loose about her shoulders. She has her outer robe thrown over her nightclothes and looks considerably more awake than anyone should be at this late hour. 'The sanctuary. Hurry.'

He looks back at the dead woman. Hers is the first corpse he has seen since their father was called to the Golden Throne, though the manner of their deaths could hardly have been more different: the matriarch's instantaneous, his father's a tortuous and delirious decline – a fitting punishment for years of beatings and neglect.

But neither will raise a hand to him again.

'I said hurry!' Athenasia – his sister, his twin, the better half of his soul and source of all light in the world – grabs him by the wrist.

They are together, and that is all that matters.

Act II

The Book of War

XI

Two minutes to landfall.

The cargo-pod hurtles towards the surface of Ophelia VII, its thrusters straining in the desperate attempt to control its descent. Flames ripple across the plating of its hull, turning the dimly lit passenger compartment to an oven. Warning runes flicker in the corner of Morvenn's visor display. *Coolant system overloading. Air recyclers deteriorating.* Even through her helmet, the air burns her throat with every breath.

'God-Emperor, we give thanks for the light that guides us through the void.' Sister Ignatia has been praying continuously since the beginning of their descent. The other four are sitting in silence, though Hiromi and Zafiya's gauntlets flash in the grimy lumen-light as they exchange signed words, the dingy illumination catching the silver auditory augmetics implanted above Zafiya's ears. 'We beseech thee, God-Emperor, to guide us to thy enemies that we may bring your swift and holy vengeance upon them.'

One minute to impact.

The *Lux Dominus* is surely gone by now, reduced to an asteroid field of gleaming debris. Captain Haraquis, dead. Voidsman Winstet, dead. Countless dead whose names and faces she does not know, slaughtered by the Heretic Astartes, consumed in the voidship's terminal conflagration or taken by the void. She is in no doubt as to the necessity of their deaths, but that necessity serves only to increase the obligation she carries with her. They are the first casualties of her liberation of Ophelia VII, and like any good commander she must ensure their sacrifices were not in vain.

'Prepare for landing. Ten seconds.'

The automated voice comes as a shock. Ten seconds is nothing at all, and the drop pod has hardly begun its deceleration. If they hit the ground at full speed, the impact will not only kill them all, but wipe out anything and anyone in a generous radius around them. She closes her eyes and forces herself to stay calm. *God-Emperor, have mercy, or at the least ensure we crush our enemies as we land…*

The drop pod decelerates with such force that for a second Morvenn is convinced that they have already struck the ground. Warning runes flash red in her vision, the pod shuddering and shrieking as though shaken by a colossal hand. She tries to address her Celestians, but the pressure of the descent is squeezing the air from her lungs. Black spots dance in her vision, a carillon of bells clamouring in her ears.

The engines cut out. There is a single, giddying moment of freefall, and then the cargo-pod hits the ground like a shell.

They have reached Ophelia VII.

Morvenn opens her eyes, and the oily black spots across her vision slowly recede. Her mouth tastes of blood from her bitten tongue, but she has otherwise escaped serious injury. Tomorrow her bones and muscles will register a painful protest at their mistreatment, but that is a matter for the future.

'God-Emperor.' Ignatia's voice is hoarse. 'We give praise for our deliverance.'

Hiromi rises to her feet and squeezes past the Purgator Mirabilis to reach the cargo-pod's release lever. She pulls hard, a data-rune beside it flashes crimson, and with a deafening hydraulic hiss the hatch opens enough to admit a faint glow – then stops. Hiromi shoves her shoulder into the metal door and pushes with all her strength, but the hatch is wedged tight. By the sounds of gunfire coming through the aperture they have landed close to their target.

'Make room.' Morvenn guides the Purgator Mirabilis to a standing position and leans forward, brushing the warsuit's massive shoulders against the escape pod's overhead. She places Fidelis' gunshield into the gap and twists upward, and with a shriek of tearing metal the hatch gives way at its hinges and clatters to the ground. Instantly the temperature drops. She lifts her visor, takes a grateful breath of cooler air, and steps out onto the cardinal world's broken surface.

'Celestian Kseniya. What can the auspex tell us?'

The sky is darker than she remembers, Ophelia VII's usual light of devotion reduced to a distant fiery glow. The smoke of their descent is clearing, but scattered fires burn along the line of their final approach.

'God-Emperor be thanked,' Morvenn murmurs. If the cargo-pod had struck any of the nearby tower-spires, their descent would have ended in flames. As it is, their landing has punched a crater thirty feet wide in the ground, the crushed remains of a small shrine-chapel scattered around them.

Kseniya's auspex glows green as she joins Morvenn outside the hatch. 'I have triangulated our position to four miles north of the Cathedrum of Athenasia the Martyr.'

Morvenn looks south, but the fog and smoke are too thick for her to make anything out. The auspex gives a gentle chirp, and Kseniya's posture instantly changes. Morvenn understands why without need for explanation.

'How many?'

'Fifty at least.'

'Close?'

'Close, and converging.'

'Celestians, stand ready,' Ignatia says, as the squad move into formation. 'Abbess Sanctorum. We await your orders.'

'Let them come.' The Lance of Illumination blazes into life. Shapes resolve through the smoke: humans dressed in masks and tatters, clubs and knifes and miners' picks clutched in filthy hands. She is the God-Emperor's mailed fist, the instrument of His holy wrath, and she will not be denied. 'If they are so keen for death, we will deliver it unto them.'

'Death to the daughters of the Corpse-Emperor!' a voice screams from the huddle of cultists, and the others raise a ragged cheer in reply. An autogun rattles out a spray of slugs, but rather than seeking shelter Morvenn steps forward to catch them on her gunshield and identifies their source: a man with weeping sores on his jaw and the bridge of his nose. A single bolt-shell from Fidelis obliterates him entirely, leaving nothing but chunks of raw, wet meat, the autogun and the hand that held it describing a bloody arc through the air. She strides forward, lance crackling as more vague silhouettes resolve into enemies – ten, twenty, more – while somewhere in the distance the distinctive thunder of a heavy bolter is delivering death one bolt-shell at a time.

A burst of heat ripples the air to her right as Fionnula's multi-melta discharges a superheated beam of energy into the enemy's front rank. The weapon's effect is instantaneous. Rags ignite; skin chars, blackens and sloughs away before they have a chance to slow, those bearing the brunt of the energy weapon cooked where they stand. Flakes of charred tissues fall away, layer after layer, until there is nothing left but toppling stacks of blackened bone and gristle. The other four Celestians are firing their bolters in perfect unison, destroying rank after rank of heretics, but the sound of battle is drawing more of them in to join the attack without hesitation.

'In the God-Emperor's name!' The Purgator Mirabilis surges forward with such enthusiasm that she almost loses her footing, regaining her equilibrium with a broad, counterbalancing sweep of the lance. The blade traces a brilliant arc through the dark air, and even the most bloodthirsty-looking cultists recoil as it crackles past their faces. The mob answers her charge with a counter-charge of their own, and suddenly she is surrounded by a thrashing mass of bodies, clawing and tearing at each other in their eagerness to reach her.

'Remember what we were promised!' a scrawny woman in an ill-fitting enforcer's tunic shrieks. 'A reward for each head we bring him!'

Morvenn flicks the tip of the spear in a shallow arc that severs the woman's head from her shoulders and sends it bouncing to the ground. The blow continues into the heretic next in line, carving through his torso to meet resistance in his backbone. She pulls the lance free, and the man crumples sideways, hands clawing at the ruined remains of his flank as the light fades from his eyes.

'Death! Death to them all!'

There is no doubting the fervour of the heretics as they run in to attack. Morvenn settles into a rhythm that combines speed and precision – the slash-and-thrust of the power lance interspersed with heavy bolt-shells to clear ground when the press of bodies becomes too great. She is sparing with her ammunition, for no reason other than that she is not sure when she will have an opportunity to replenish her reserves. She cuts a howling woman in half at the waist as her Sisters fan out to lay down a broad arc of covering fire.

'Death to the heretic!' her voice booms through her helmet's vox-amplifiers as she kicks the nearest cultist to the ground and presses the great golden foot of the Purgator Mirabilis down on his chest. 'Where is the Death of Saints?'

To her left, Zafiya is a blur of silver and black, delivering bolter rounds with pinpoint accuracy and smashing the stock of her boltgun into skulls and throats with equal skill. She and Hiromi are fighting back to back, while on her right Fionnula's multi-melta continues to deliver death in a torrent of shimmering heat. Morvenn leans a little more of the Purgator's weight on the man's chest, and he reacts instantly, his eyes growing wide, the muscles in his neck standing out as he strains to breathe.

The cultist hawks a glob of sputum onto Morvenn's gleaming sabaton. 'My lord will come for you,' he says. 'He will take the head from your shoulders and mount it on his armour to rot.'

Morvenn presses the Purgator's foot into the man's chest, hard enough that she feels his ribs snap. He gasps and a froth of blood bubbles at the corner of his mouth.

'Where is he?' She releases the suffocating pressure just enough for the man to draw a breath.

His bloody lips part in a smile. 'The Death of Saints will find you when the time comes. When he has destroyed all that you lo–'

She shifts the warsuit's full weight onto one leg, and the heretic's chest crumples flat. Blood gouts from his mouth and nose, his limbs giving one final convulsive twitch before he falls still. Morvenn pilots the suit forward, leaving bloody footprints as she advances on the remaining heretics. The ground is scarlet with blood, littered with corpses.

But there is more slaughter to come.

'More of them.' Hiromi is fighting with perfect economy of movement, each bolter shell dispatching a heretic with efficient precision.

'For the Death of Saints!' a woman shouts, and the answering howl from her companions sends a shiver of disquiet down Morvenn's back. Individually or in groups, the cultists are no great threat, but the longer this fight continues, the more likely it becomes that one of the Sisters will make a mistake. Errors multiply quickly on the battlefield, and it will take only one misplaced shot or a single blow that fails to kill for this situation to spin out of control.

Sister Fionnula sends another torrent of heat from her multi-melta into the mob. Bodies char and blacken, but the gap in the heretics' ranks lasts only for a moment before it is filled again. A cultist lunges forward, her face soot-marked with black wings across the eyes in a parody of the aquila, a hand flamer held tight in her grip. Morvenn steps inside the woman's reach and knocks the flamer aside with the haft of her spear just as the woman pulls the trigger. A gout of heat washes up Morvenn's armoured wrist. Her anger flares, hotter than burning promethium. These heretics – these wretches – are bogging them down mere yards from their landing site.

But the Death of Saints has demonstrated himself to be too shrewd over the centuries for this to be anything other than deliberate.

'Overhead!' Hiromi shouts. 'Raptors!'

Morvenn looks up and sees a shadow passing behind the cloud. It is human-shaped, dark at the front with the twin tell-tale glow of a jump pack behind and lit a split second later by the brilliant blue-violet glow of a plasma weapon. The bolt of superheated plasma streaks down like a comet to strike Hiromi in the left thigh, igniting her vestments, melting the silver plating on her armour. The Celestian does not scream, but the gasp of pain that fills the squad's vox-system in the injury's wake is a thousand times worse. She stumbles back from the battleline, Zafiya stepping in smoothly to take her place and maintain the squad's arc of fire.

Morvenn spares the swiftest of glances for the downed Celestian. Hiromi's vibro-knife is already in her hand, slicing away smouldering silk-cloth and the bubbling edges of her armour in the vain attempt to slow the plasma's sizzling progress. Black smoke billows around her, and the air smells of roasting meat.

'God… Emperor!' Hiromi's voice is a hoarse rasp. 'Grant me strength… to do thy work.'

The Raptor overhead wheels around, and a second blast of plasma streaks through the sky. Morvenn darts to the side, and only the merest splash spatters her sabaton. She returns fire, Fidelis hammering heavy shells into the obscuring cloud, but there is no explosion to tell her they have found their mark. The cultists surge forward, shrieking, and she catches the merest glimpse of something larger moving at the back of the group, something vast, threatening and dark.

'Take them down. Now!' She lashes out with the Lance of Illumination and bisects a cultist at the waist, bludgeons the next with her gunshield, sends a bolt-shell into a cluster of scrawny men armed with miner's picks and obliterates them entirely.

'More Raptors!' Ignatia shouts from behind her. A staccato burst of gunfire resonates through the thickening smoke. Already it is becoming difficult to tell friend from mortal foe.

A Raptor's screaming chainsword hurtles towards Morvenn's face, and she smashes him from the air with a single strike of her lance. Before he can rise she skewers him through the throat and obliterates his skull with a point-blank bolter shot. Another swoops into range, and she catches him with the side of Fidelis' gunshield, sending him crashing into a ruined wall to vanish in a plume of dust. She turns, searching for her next target, but the Raptors are in retreat, and the last of the cultists lie bloody and dying on the broken ground.

An eerie silence spreads across the ruins. Morvenn clears her throat. 'God-Emperor, we give thanks for this victory.'

But it is a partial victory at best. Over by the cargo-pod, four of her Celestians have regrouped. Zafiya is hauling a grey-faced Hiromi to her feet, while Fionnula and Kseniya stand guard on either side.

'Where is Ignatia?'

'She is not with you?' Kseniya asks. 'I will try the vox–'

'I can do that myself. Celestian Superior, what is your status?' It is unheard of for Ignatia to have deserted the squad, all the more so for her to have left vox-contact. And the answer comes as Morvenn knew it would, in blood and death.

Celestian Superior Ignatia has been laid out on an open patch of ground like a saint in repose, her hands clasped in the aquila across her chest – but the positioning of her corpse is no act of respect. Her severed head is nowhere to be seen, nothing left but an empty, blood-spattered helmet tossed casually to the side.

'What happened?' Morvenn demands, but her Celestians have no answer. What answer is there beyond the obvious? Ignatia fought and fell, and the enemy has desecrated her remains.

Amongst other Orders, the death might be marked with prayers, hymns of devotion, oaths of vengeance against the enemy, but the Order of the Argent Shroud meet death with silence. There will come a time for mourning, but Morvenn cannot allow herself the luxury of grief, not here, not with the enemy so close at hand.

'Celestian Kseniya. Bring up the schematics of the area, find where the enemy is making his base. I will have his head before sunrise.'

'As you command.'

'Abbess Sanctorum!' Fionnula's interruption is laced with

urgency. She has turned to the right, the iridescent barrels of her multi-melta covering a narrow line of approach between two ruined buildings. Even Morvenn's preysight struggles to make out what is moving through the shadows, but the huge shadow she saw before is approaching, rubble and bones crunching beneath heavy boots.

Morvenn steps towards the alleyway and raises the lance.

'Your orders, Abbess Sanctorum.' Fionnula is at her side, weapon aimed. 'Do we engage?'

'Hold your fire.'

The silhouette resolves from out of the smoke, taller than any normal human, dressed in armour so dark that it swallows rather than reflects the light, a sharp contrast to the ember-glow of the helmet's eye-lenses.

And it is not alone. There are three of them now, then four, striding towards the Sisters with heavy steps that shake the earth.

'Declare yourselves, in the God-Emperor's name!' The voice is a peal of thunder, vox-amplified a hundred times over.

She does not hesitate. 'Morvenn Vahl, Abbess Sanctorum of the Adepta Sororitas. Well met, sons of Dorn.'

XII

The Black Templars have made their forward base in the ruins of a shrine to Saint Gerstahl of Cadia, now nothing more than a gutted shell of blackened marble. The gothic arches that once supported the high vaulted ceiling rise into empty air, giving Morvenn the impression that she and her Sisters are standing in the hollowed-out ribcage of a monstrous carcass. The flickering light of heavy pillar candles plays over a scene of furious activity as the sons of Dorn ready themselves for war. A towering Chaplain in a skull-faced helm dispenses benedictions swinging a vast adamantine censer, servitors shuffle and rumble back and forth bearing weapons and ammunition, serfs drape ancient banners on gilded crosspieces and present freshly sanctified weapons to their lords. The details of the rituals are unfamiliar to her, but there is much here she recognises – the reverence and piety, the weight of holy duty, but most of all the sense of purposeful preparation for the great work that is to come.

'Castellan Tancret!' The veteran brother whose squad escorted her here has not removed his helmet, and his amplified voice cuts across the noise like a chainsword through bone. 'I present Morvenn Vahl, High Lord of Terra and Abbess Sanctorum of the Adepta Sororitas!'

The shrine falls silent. A tall Astartes warrior dressed in black power armour strides forward, a snow-white surcoat emblazoned with the barbed cross of his Chapter falling from beneath his chestplate. A black cloak shot with fine adamantine threads hangs from his shoulders, a huge two-handed sword strapped to his back in an ornate silver-chased scabbard. Piercing blue eyes stare out above sharply angled cheekbones, the grey in his hair and beard giving him the appearance of a man in his mid-forties, though the physiology of the Astartes means his age might easily be counted in centuries instead of years.

'Abbess Sanctorum.' The castellan's voice booms across the ruined shrine in a deep, rich baritone. 'You honour us with your presence.'

'As you honour me with your welcome, castellan.' She steps forward. 'You have been assiduous in the defence of Ophelia VII in my absence, and for that you have my sincerest thanks.'

'I have heard the tales of your valour against the forces of the false Witch-Empress on Vastoros. It is to my eternal regret that I was not in the battle when the palace walls came down.'

The name of the accursed world takes Morvenn back to the Jolvos Wilds, fighting a grinding advance with the Sisters of the Argent Shroud and a vast armoured column of Black Templars under the command of Marshal Gheidon. Celestian Superior Ignatia had been at her side that day, her steady presence and wise counsel a constant reassurance as the final confrontation with the heretic psyker had drawn closer. When Morvenn thinks of her old friend she feels oddly adrift, as though some part of her was torn away when Ignatia's head left her shoulders. She forces the memory away. This is no time for weakness.

'There will be other chances to slay the God-Emperor's enemies,' she says, and the castellan inclines his head in agreement.

'Indeed.' He turns and walks back down the aisle to the altar. She follows him to where a detailed schematic of the district etched on heavy parchment has been unrolled, its corners weighted down with palm-sized discs of polished brass. The exquisite penmanship is fit to grace a rogue trader's collection, but this map is no mere decoration. It is as much a tool of war as the power sword on the castellan's back. A tonsured serf with a fine feather quill in his hand looks up at Morvenn's approach, glances to his lord for approval, then marks her position in the chapel with a miniature fleur-de-lys.

'Our time to carry out the God-Emperor's work has already begun,' Tancret says. Morvenn studies the map and with it the castellan's strategy. His plan is a sound one – the enemy is already all but encircled, and with the Black Templars' heavy ordnance positioned on either flank to corral them tightly near the cathedrum. Lines of advance show the orders for each squad, Primaris Sword Brethren leading the advance while squads of veteran Firstborn advance in good order to secure key bottlenecks and vantage points. The battle plays out in her mind's eye, the fighting moving through the streets until they reach the cathedrum and a final confrontation with the Death of Saints. With such allies at her side, victory is surely inevitable.

'What say you, Abbess Sanctorum?' the castellan asks. His pale blue eyes are glittering with anticipation, as though he too has replayed this battle over and over in his mind and longs to set steel to steel at last.

'Your plan is every bit as flawless as I would expect.' There is no idle flattery in her words, merely the approval of an expert in the craft of war to a master. 'Do you know the location of the Death of Saints?'

'I trust once the assault begins he will make his presence known.'

'And where will you be in this, Castellan Tancret?'

The castellan leans forward and places his index finger on the map in the centre of the Black Templars' advance. 'In the thick of the fighting, where the God-Emperor commands. There is a place for you there also, should you wish it.'

'There is nowhere I would rather be.'

The new dawn finds Aleyna stiff and unrested, leaning against the stone wall of what was once a funerary chapel built into the side of the cathedrum. The rest of the building is in ruins after the Heldrake's fiery assault. The roof is gone, the lead melted down to expose the charred and jagged ends of the broken roof beams, the gilded marble floors heaped high with stonework and rubble.

After the miracle – though the word still seems inadequate to describe what occurred – the group covered the last of the distance across open ground without meeting resistance, took shelter in the sole chapel still intact, and barricaded the door to wait for morning. Whether those events too were miracles of the God-Emperor, Aleyna cannot be sure, but as her mind clears and her sense of self returns, the burden of duty weighs only more heavily on her shoulders. The God-Emperor has made her His instrument – He has spared her for a reason – which makes the prospect of failure even more appalling.

'Holy God-Emperor, guide me. Let me understand your divine will.'

Around her the pilgrims are stirring into life, rising from the floor where they had lain down to sleep like corpses in the aftermath of a battle. The novitiate is still sleeping, shielding the reliquary with her body. Seraphim Perdita is already kneeling at prayer, her back to the room and her bowed head to the broken altar.

Aleyna pours a little water from her canteen into a cupped hand, blesses it, and passes it across her face in a token gesture of cleansing. Images of the night before swirl through her head in shades of crimson and black. The great beast that ripped the sky in half. The sound of its screams as it bore down on them. The calm acceptance of her approaching death, and then the miracle. The sense of cool water flowing through her. The knowledge that she was part of something greater, something pure and powerful and eternal, the sense of understanding on a cosmic level that slips away through her hands whenever she tries to recall it, leaving an unendurable sense of loss. For a moment she was one with the divine, and now she understands the meaning of its absence.

But there is work to be done. The chapel has provided sanctuary for a few hours of rest, but they cannot rely on it for long. Her eye falls on the Sisters Retributor, their heads close together in conversation by a shattered glassaic window, and her weary heart leaps. The entrance to the catacombs cannot be so far away nor buried so deep that they cannot find it, not with faith and the God-Emperor's guidance.

The conversation stops at her approach. 'Sister Aleyna.' Rukhsana makes the aquila. 'Did you rest well?'

A new reserve has crept into the Retributor's manner – a mark of respect, Aleyna thinks, but also, perhaps, unease. She can understand that. The God-Emperor's power is terrible and unknowable, and none touched by it remain unchanged. She tries to smile reassuringly.

'As well as can be expected.'

The broken lead of the window frames a stark tableau. The sun has risen over the ruins, but the heavy pall of cloud is so thick that the scant light serves only to deepen the shadows. Smoke rises from the smouldering remains of chapels and shrines, the faint red of the embers' glow the only colour against a world turned black and grey.

Marayd folds her arms across her cuirass. 'We must speak of the work of the day.'

Aleyna nods. 'The flames in the cathedrum have all but died. The entrance to the catacombs must be through its crypts – shifting the rubble will take time, but with the God-Emperor's guidance we will manage.' An idea occurs to her, and her heart fills with fresh hope. 'The stronger pilgrims can help us, while the others keep watch. The more hands turned to the work, the quicker we will be.'

Judging by her frown, Marayd does not share Aleyna's enthusiasm. 'They are already weak, and we have no tools for our search. With the proper equipment, with a full combat patrol of Sisters we might dig out the entrance, but for all we know it has been completely destroyed. We will only waste time. Time that could be put to better use.'

'Time to use doing what?'

'We must leave,' Marayd says simply. 'Our first duty is to the God-Emperor and to our Sisters. We must assume that the heretic is already preparing an assault on the Convent Sanctorum itself. We must bear word of what has happened here to the prioress.'

Aleyna points through the window to the ruined buildings. Some of the roofs still smoulder, once-pristine marble and gleaming gold leaf turned black with soot and sin. 'You cannot propose to take the pilgrims through *that?*'

A rich, savoury scent drifts up through the cold morning air, and her stomach twists with hunger before she realises what she is smelling. There are no livestock pens here, no beasts awaiting slaughter. There is only one source of fresh meat.

'No,' Marayd says. 'I do not.'

'Then you mean to abandon them.'

'We should never have brought them with us.' Marayd keeps her voice low. 'A swift death would have been kinder. I do not wish to leave them any more than you do, but...'

'Sister Superior Kerem has already left. If she has managed to reach help–'

'And what are the chances of that? The district is swarming with heretics.' As if to illustrate Marayd's point, an artillery shell hurtles through the air to demolish a chapel spire a mile or two to the north.

'I like this as little as you do,' Rukhsana says, and Aleyna's last hope of persuading her to side against the other Retributor dies at the note of resolve in her voice. Evidently this course of action was decided upon while Aleyna slept, and this conversation is a courtesy only. 'But we have no other choice.'

'What of the others? Will you take the novitiate?'

Marayd shakes her head. 'This is work for the Militant Orders. If she wishes the reliquary to survive, she will see the sense of entrusting it to our care.'

'And Perdita?'

Marayd rubs at her eyes. 'I cannot rouse her. I have seen Sisters perish of bleeding in the skull before. Without a Hospitaller I fear there is little hope.'

'Then you would have us abandon her, also.'

'She would urge us to do so if she could.' The edge is back in Marayd's voice. 'I would ask the same, if our positions were reversed. As, I think, would you, Aleyna of Our Martyred Lady.'

Aleyna looks back at the huddled pilgrims – the man in tattered velvets, the bold young woman with the blue hair, the father and his grizzling child. Their lives are worth so little compared to everything else at stake, and so many already have perished. What Marayd says echoes everything she has been taught – that her duty is to strive, to suffer, to strike at the God-Emperor's enemies with her final breath. But something has changed. Had Marayd said the same the day before, she might have agreed – but not now. Not after the miracle.

'That is not the God-Emperor's will.'

Marayd's mouth drops open with surprise. 'You are sure of that?'

'Listen to me.' Aleyna leans forward, willing the Retributor to understand. 'The God-Emperor saved them from the daemon engine, just as He saved us all. He would not have done so if His will was that we leave them here to perish.' She turns her gaze to Rukhsana in one final appeal. 'Sister Retributor, please, you must see the truth of this.'

Rukhsana is silent for a long time before she speaks. 'I do not presume to know the God-Emperor's will,' she says at last. 'But I know the teachings of my Order. Only through suffering do we find redemption. In pain and grief we are redeemed. The road to the Convent Sanctorum is perilous, but I cannot cower within these walls while the enemy threatens our world.'

Marayd places her hand on Aleyna's, her former sharpness gone. 'Come with us, Sister. Only a meaningless death awaits you here. And if the God-Emperor truly wishes to preserve these pilgrims, He will do so.'

It would be so easy to agree.

Aleyna bows her head. 'I will not leave them.'

'I understand.' Marayd removes her hand and makes the sign of the aquila. 'We must do as our consciences dictate.'

A shell strikes the ground, closer this time, sending a roost of leathery-winged chiropterae fluttering into the dull grey air. Marayd goes to wake the novitiate. The soft words that pass between them are too quiet to reach Aleyna's ears – but she does not need to hear them to understand. The novitiate touches her fingertips to the reliquary case, closes her eyes, and then nods in acceptance. Marayd takes the silver chest and its precious contents with great solemnity and wraps it in her mantle.

'I will pray for you,' Rukhsana says.

'And I for you.'

Aleyna waits until they are gone, then walks to stand by the dying Seraphim at the altar. Perdita's mouth is moving in silent prayer, but her eyes are fixed and glassy like those of a corpse. Aleyna watches Perdita's lips until she recognises the well-worn prayer as one of the Litanies for Guidance taught in the first days of a novitiate's training – then joins the Seraphim in whispered unison for the final couplet.

'O Light of Terra, shine.' From youngest to oldest, the pilgrims are staring at her in expectation. *'Be thou our beacon for all time.'*

Another shell shakes the chapel's foundations.

'Will you pray for us, blessed Sister?' The man in the velvet tunic has risen to his feet, his filthy hands extended in supplication. She had been ready to hate him after his crude attempts at bribery, but all she feels now is pity at his weakness. What spouse, what children does he have waiting at home for his return? What sorrow he must feel, to know that all his wealth and status cannot buy him a single breath.

'Pray *with* me, brother.'

Aleyna kneels beside the pilgrims on the dusty stone floor. Some pull themselves upright from sleeping positions, others lie with eyes closed, listening, perhaps, or dreaming. She does not begrudge them that either. She has enough grenades to ensure that even if their deaths will not be gentle, they will at least be swift.

'O lord of Terra, from whom all light flows, have mercy.'

Theodosia joins her in the old prayer. *'Great thy vigil, ten thousand years–'*

Aleyna keeps her eyes tightly closed. If they are to die, she thinks, let it be at prayer, and a suffusing warmth passes through her, promising comfort, safety, peace. They are in the God-Emperor's hands, and there is nothing to fear.

XIII

The time of war is at hand.

The Black Templars stand in serried ranks, their ancient banners embroidered with the names of the saints fluttering in the rising air. The thin light of Ophelia's sun picks out gleaming blades, freshly oiled bolters, and golden chains bearing ancient relics cinched tight around snow-white surcoats impossibly bright against the ruins. While at first the helmed Space Marines had seemed indistinguishable from each other, Morvenn is starting to see the differences even in those whose faces are obscured – the taller brothers who have crossed the Rubicon Primaris with their lord, the veterans of the Firstborn who still tower head and shoulders over her Sisters, the Neophytes in gleaming armour who are yet to know slaughter on a planetary scale. They are made for war, to deal death as effortlessly as drawing breath, and all are in the God-Emperor's grace.

'Sons of Dorn!' The Chaplain's voice bellows through his skull-faced helmet, the great spiked censer in his hand billowing smoke as he strides down the ranks. 'Kneel before the God-Emperor!'

With a noise like a thunderclap, the Black Templars drop to one knee, their gauntleted hands bracing their weapons against the ground. Morvenn lowers the Purgator Mirabilis into the same position as her four surviving Celestians kneel around her, Hiromi's soft gasp of pain clearly audible through the vox as she bends her wounded leg. The castellan lifts the visor of his great helm, and Morvenn glimpses sharp blue eyes filled with holy fervour as he hangs on the Chaplain's every word.

'O Emperor!' The Chaplain raises his censer. A gust of wind blows the smoke through the battleline, a harbinger of the fog of war to come. 'In wrath rejoicing at bloody wars, fierce and untamed!'

The Black Templars bellow back the oath in a single voice. 'God-Emperor, lead us to war!'

'Whose mighty power doth make the strongest walls from their foundations shake!'

'God-Emperor, lead us to war!'

'All conquering Master of Mankind, be pleased with this war's tumultuous roar!'

This time Morvenn joins her voice with the cry of the battle-brothers. 'God-Emperor, lead us to war!'

'Delight in swords and fists red with heretic blood, and the dire ruin of savage battle. Rejoice in furious challenge and avenging strife, whose works with woe embitter human life!' Trumpets blare out a fanfare. 'God-Emperor, lead us to slaughter in the name of Dorn!'

War-drums strike in heavy unison. The Black Templars rise with weapons raised.

'For the God-Emperor!'

And the advance on the cathedrum begins.

The Death of Saints has used his time to good advantage, Morvenn thinks, as the Cathedrum of Athenasia the Martyr comes into view. The ruins of the once proud building surmount a hill overlooking the rest of the district, connected to the myriad shrines, places of work, and hab-blocks for the faithful through a warren of broad roadways, bridges and conduits. In normal times, those paths would be swarming with activity, but now they are silent, and each bridge the war-host reaches has been torn down, roads blocked with rubble, walkways cast twisted and broken to the ground below. None of this will stop the Black Templars' advance, but if the enemy's goal is to slow them down, it is certainly succeeding.

An artillery strike hammers into the district to the north, the explosion ripping through a pair of spires, sending them crashing to the ground. For the first time, Morvenn allows herself to wonder what will be left of the district once they have driven the Night Lords from Ophelia VII – if the cathedrum will even be standing – but compared to putting an end to the Death of Saints that hardly seems important. The assault is proceeding according to the letter of the castellan's plan, and by now the perimeter of Dreadnoughts, tanks and heavy artillery should be tightening around the heretic forces like a razor wire garotte.

They meet their first resistance half a mile from the ruined shrine, as the Way of the Saints crosses beneath a great wrought-iron bridge, still standing in miraculous defiance of the devastation around it – but as they approach, it is clear that its preservation is not at the hand of the God-Emperor. An electric charge seems to pass through the Black Templars, their movements quicker and more fluid as the Purgator Mirabilis' sensors register enemy movement around them. She has been expecting an attack as soon as they set foot on open ground, but even so the speed and ferocity of the Night Lords' approach is breath-taking. The Heretic Astartes surge from the shadows, falling from the struts of the bridge overhead, from behind statues where she could have sworn nothing stood a moment before – and the Black Templars surge forward, power swords blazing and boltguns raised.

'For the God-Emperor, Dorn and Holy Terra!' Castellan Tancret bellows, and Morvenn charges forward beside him, caught up in the power and the glory of the moment. This is the pinch in the hourglass, the bolt-shell undetonated in flight, the spear drawn back ready to strike. The faces of the enemy are turned towards her, loathsome and corrupt. The war-drums hammer in time with her surging blood, the trumpets peal out the call to battle. They smash into the enemy like a tidal wave breaking on the shore, and she is consumed utterly in brilliant, bloody war.

Tancret's greatsword flashes with dazzling light as it rises and falls, cleaving through flesh and armour with devastating power. Blood spatters his vestments as a Night Lord topples headless to the ground, but before the corpse has stopped moving he is engaging another with unstoppable skill. The mere sight of him is an inspiration, as though the God-Emperor Himself has descended from the Golden Throne to fight at Morvenn's side.

'For the God-Emperor!' She turns Fidelis in a broad arc, hammering shell after shell into the chests of the oncoming Chaos Space Marines. There is no time to wait to see their effect – she pushes forward, the spear striking with all the force of the Purgator Mirabilis, the pinnacle of the Mechanicus' art. Her own muscles strain with effort as she pushes the mighty warsuit to greater speed and force, striking and stamping, discharging shell after shell until she stands at the heart of a bloody maelstrom of slaughter.

The leering faces of the damned flash into her vision as a five-strong squad of the enemy move in to engage. Plasma bursts against her gunshield, a volley of bolt-shells streak towards her, and the warsuit's energy field flares in a brilliant corona of light. She strides forward, her heart singing with righteous hatred, only for the enemy to press thicker around her. There are cultists moving amongst the heretics now, their faces marked with lines of hatred and livid with fresh scars, but she has wrath to spare for them all.

'In His name shall you burn!' she bellows, and she fires the missiles mounted on the Purgator's shoulders. The warsuit's motors strain against the recoil as a pair of explosives the length of her forearm fly forward at devastating speed, obscuring and obliterating the enemy in a single massive conflagration. One Chaos Space Marine staggers from the smoke, chainglaive raised, but before she can bring the heavy bolter around he stops, the tip of a chainsword protruding from the centre of his chestplate. The heretic staggers and half turns as the chainblade continues to saw downward, falling at last to reveal a Sister of Battle in blood-smeared crimson armour bearing the vestments and insignia of a Sister Superior of the Bloody Rose.

Surprise stops Morvenn in her tracks.

'Abbess Sanctorum! God-Emperor be praised!' The Sister Superior removes her helmet to reveal a sweat-soaked olive face pockmarked with scars, her short dark hair plastered to her scalp. 'I am Sister Superior Kerem of the Bloody Rose. My lady – I dared not hope to find you here.'

As the smoke clears, Morvenn sees the hole the Purgator's missiles have made in the Night Lords' line. The Black Templars are continuing their relentless advance, but the enemy is falling back, those at the rear melting away into the shadows as their brothers lay down covering fire.

'Put them to the sword!' Tancret is bellowing. 'No mercy! No quarter!' He tears the chainglaive from the grip of a dying Night Lord, raises it above his head and snaps it in two. 'So perish all who defy the God-Emperor's will!'

Morvenn returns her attention to the Sister Superior. 'What tidings do you bring?'

'Survivors. Close to the cathedrum. Four Sisters of the Militant Orders, a novitiate of the Order of the Quill, two dozen pilgrims – and the Blessed Skull of Saint Athenasia.'

Of all the news Morvenn was expecting, this was not it. Surprise renders her speechless, and when words return all she can manage is a tight: 'And you *left* them?'

The Sister Superior raises her jaw so that she is meeting Morvenn's eye. 'I went to create a distraction, to buy time for them to reach the cathedrum and enter the catacombs beneath it.'

The distinctive whine of a servitor-guided seeker missile shrieks through the air, and another building vanishes in a plume of smoke. The castellan's plan to retake the district is a sound one, relying on discipline, the martial skill of the men under his command and overwhelming firepower, but no mention was made of civilian casualties for the simple reason that there was no reason to believe that any had survived.

'You believe they are still alive?' Morvenn asks. 'That the reliquary may yet be recovered?'

Kerem nods. 'There is a chance. But if we linger, I fear they are as likely to perish by Imperial artillery as they are at the hands of the enemy.'

'Abbess Vahl!' Castellan Tancret and his Sword Brethren are already a hundred yards ahead of her, his power sword raised to point the way. 'The Death of Saints has been sighted! We shall slay him together, you and I!'

'A moment, castellan!' she calls back.

Kerem's eyes are fixed on hers, ringed in deep grey shadow. 'I beg you, Abbess Sanctorum. Do not leave them to die.'

Lethe breathes in the cool air of morning and looks out over the ruined city. The Death of Saints stands a little distance away with his honour guard, instructing them in preparation for the battle to come. Nothing so large should move with such perfect, predatory grace, but it is clear to her that he is more than mortal, a vengeful god in physical form, come to deliver the vengeance for which she has longed for so many years. The scent of fresh blood ripples from him in heady, sensuous waves, but each time she raises her head to look on his face a profound panic twists in her guts and forces her eyes to the ground.

Mere humans are not meant to look on the face of the divine. But now that Lethe has gazed into that single void-filled eye, she understands the reality of the cosmos, and she would give her soul for another moment in that monstrous, transfiguring gaze. The hilt of her dagger is cold against her palm. It is all that she has in the world, and she will die before she surrenders it.

Others like him move through the flames. Those mortals too slow or too foolish to avoid their progress find themselves skewered on taloned gauntlets or eviscerated by chainglaives, their killers seemingly caring little whether they are former overseers or prisoners. Lethe studies their casual cruelties with a fascinated blend of envy and horror. The thought of wielding such power is intoxicating.

And already their enemies are coming.

In another life she might have found the sight of the ancient knights in their black-and-white panoply inspiring, but now she feels only hatred at their hypocrisy. The transhuman warriors – both those who continue to pay lip service to the Golden Throne and those who follow another path – are built to bring death, to sow fear, to tear down all that human hands have built, and to dress those intentions in piety and honour is meaningless vanity. The truth is as sharp and clean as the edge of a blade. Faith is a lie. All that matters is power, and the willingness to wield it.

Lethe is no tactician, but even she can see that the Death of Saints is holding his power in reserve. While some of his followers have already moved out through the narrow streets to engage the Black Templars, he hangs back, striking from shadows to kill before vanishing again – not out of cowardice, but out of some strategic intent that she cannot begin to imagine.

Two of the lesser demigods – lesser compared to her lord, that is, impossibly exalted by comparison with mere humanity – stride towards the huddle of the former penitents. She presses herself back into the shadows as they draw close. One wears a helmet with a spiked and elongated beak, but the other is bare-headed. His face is scarred and twisted with hatred and contempt, his belt strung with polished human skulls that rattle hollowly with every step of his massive boots.

'Slaves! To battle with you!'

The prisoners begin to move, but their frantic haste is not enough. The helmeted demigod lashes out with the back of a spiked gauntlet and sends a woman crashing to the ground in a spray of blood. The casual cruelty has the desired effect on the rest of the group, and they surge towards the enemy with renewed enthusiasm, a swift death at the Black Templars' hands preferable by far to the wages of disobeying their new masters. Lethe pushes herself further back into the shadows, but the massive warrior moves towards her all the same.

'Wretch,' the bare-headed heretic growls. 'You should know by now that the price of disobedience is death.' He reaches out his hand to take her by the jaw. 'Still. Your skull will make a pleasing addition to my belt–'

Lethe slashes the knife across his gauntleted palm. At first she thinks the blade will simply glance from the ancient ceramite, but its razor-edge scores a narrow channel through gleaming metal into the flesh beneath. Thick crimson blood wells up from the gash. The hideous face creases first in surprise, and then in fury.

'You dare–'

She has nothing to lose. She throws herself forward, her lord's knife pointed at his throat in a final, desperate lunge. If these are to be her final moments, she will spend them drawing blood. The blade's tip touches the skin beneath the warrior's jaw, and then a fist slams her to the ground so quickly she loses all sense of the passage of time. One moment she is lunging towards him, the next she is sprawled her length on the ground, her ears ringing, her mouth full of the taste of iron. She raises herself to her knees and spits blood and teeth on the warrior's armoured boot. A massive hand seizes her by her matted hair and pulls back her head to expose her throat.

'Enough!' The Death of Saint's voice is deafening. 'Leave her.'

'Why, brother?'

'I owe you no explanation, Ostrov Skull-taker.'

The tension between the two Heretic Astartes is a near-tangible force. Ostrov jerks Lethe's head back another inch and presses a jagged-edged blade to her throat.

'This wretch drew blood. I will repay that insult with hers.'

'You will not. She amuses me, which is more than I can say of you.'

The grip on her hair goes slack, and she drops gasping to the ground. A glob of spit hits her cheek.

'This worm is unworthy of the honour of a place on my belt.'

The Death of Saints gives a contemptuous snort. His huge hand closes around Lethe's shoulder and pulls her upright, turning her face to meet his terrible gaze.

'Give me the knife.'

Lethe offers the blade with a shaking hand. Her breath is caught high in her throat, her blood a rushing torrent in her ears. The Death of Saints brings the knife to her face and places the razor-edge in a vertical line across her left eyebrow and cheekbone, so close to her eye that for a moment she is convinced that he means to blind her – and holds her breath as the white line of pain sears down her face.

An eternity passes, until at last the pressure eases and the agony subsides.

'Rise.' The Death of Saints drops the knife at his feet and turns to his followers. 'I have placed my mark upon this one. Her death is mine alone.'

'Aye, lord,' a deep voice rasps, and a mutter of assent passes through the armoured war-host, but already the Death of Saints' attention is elsewhere, issuing orders to advance, retreat, engage and disengage like a master of the regicide board. Lethe snatches up her knife and scuttles crabwise in his wake, the wound in her face a mirror of her lord's, her heart filled with terror and pride in equal measure.

Her lord has put his mark upon her.

She is blessed indeed.

In other times, decision-making has come easily to the Abbess Sanctorum. On the battlefield, she must simply pursue the enemy to their destruction; in all other theatres of conflict she must follow the path of duty as she has always known it – to bring death to the enemies of the God-Emperor by the most direct route, and to lead His faithful by shining example. When her way has been less than clear in the past, she has looked to Ignatia for guidance, but her Celestian Superior is dead, and all that wise counsel is lost forever.

Sister Superior Kerem and the Celestians of Morvenn's honour guard watch her in silence. Two paths stretch ahead of her like a branching road. Along one fork lies the Death of Saints and a battle at the side of the sons of Dorn – along the other, an irreplaceable reliquary and the Sisters who have risked death to protect it. It would have been better, she thinks, if the Sister Superior had never reached her with this news, if she could have continued her part in the assault untroubled by conscience.

'What are your orders, Abbess Sanctorum?' Hiromi is at her side, her voice drawn tight as a bowstring with pain. Morvenn feels a sudden surge of pride and loyalty for her Sisters, and it is that emotion that makes her true path clear. If Hiromi – or any of the rest of her honour guard – were trapped amongst the enemy she would come to their rescue without hesitation, and her position as Abbess Sanctorum means that every Sister of the Adepta Sororitas commands that same loyalty.

'We will relieve the Sisters, and the reliquary of Saint Athenasia. Sister Superior Kerem, lead the way.' She projects her words in the direction of the Black Templars. 'Castellan Tancret, you must continue the hunt without me. My Sisters have need of me elsewhere.'

There is a pause before the castellan replies. 'As you prefer, Abbess Vahl.' The disappointment in his voice is unmistakable.

It seems that all of Ophelia VII is in flames as they push through the ruins towards the necropolis. The smoke is so dense that Morvenn can smell it through her helmet's filters, the heavy particles of soot tickling her nostrils and fogging her lenses. The closer they come to the cathedrum, the thicker the flames become, the shadows of ancient towers and ruined archways set flickering like a warp-spawned nightmare.

The further they travel from the Black Templars force, the greater Morvenn's doubt grows. She has exchanged the surety of holy battle for a task that seems more impossible with each step she takes – to find and preserve a holy reliquary trapped between two clashing armies – but the decision is made, and there is no turning back now.

The necropolis gates loom above them, the ancient metal

warped and twisted by intense heat, the ground beneath fused into a smooth and glassy plane.

'I left them here,' Kerem says softly. 'Amongst the tombs.'

Morvenn looks to Kseniya. 'What does your auspex tell us?'

'The dead are without number, but there is no sign of the living.'

'They took refuge underground.' The worry in Kerem's voice is unmistakable as she moves out of formation to search the featureless ground. 'A crypt by the western wall. Close to a statue of Saint Celestine. But – nothing is as it was here.'

'Enough stone will block the signal.' Celestian Fionnula sounds uneasy.

'What about heat? Power fields?'

'Residual heat in the ground.' Kseniya shakes her head. 'Beyond that I cannot say.'

Morvenn scans the necropolis for any recognisable effigy and finds nothing. Strange protuberances that might once have been statues rise like stalagmites from the undulating plane, but their features have been smoothed away by searing heat.

'I have life signs on the auspex,' Kseniya offers. 'Energy signals. Power armour and weapons.'

'And tracks!' Kerem's voice is an urgent shout, all stealth thrown aside in her urgency. She is kneeling next to a pile of rubble – real, uneven rubble, not the eerie vitrified stone that surrounds them – that was once a tomb. 'Heading towards the cathedrum – perhaps they found refuge there–'

'That will have to wait.' Morvenn focuses her helmet's visual sensors on the space between the tombs as the source of the life signs on the auspex becomes clear. They do not belong to Sisters of the Adepta Sororitas, nor to the lost pilgrims.

They belong to the enemy.

XIV

The Night Lords come as swift as death, driving their heretic cultists before them in a shrieking, capering mass. Morvenn holds her ground and signals to her Sisters to do the same, calculating ranges, arcs of fire and missile trajectories as the enemy move closer, the torrents of burning promethium belching from their heavy flamers turning the necropolis to a hellscape of smoke and fire. She raises her gunshield, counting down the seconds until the first of the enemy reaches bolter range.

This is a battle where the slightest failure will lead to their annihilation.

'Sisters. Hold your fire until I give the order.' She thinks of Castellan Tancret and the effortless charisma with which he inspired his brethren as the battle began. Has he already found the Death of Saints and put the arch-heretic to the sword? She must survive this, else she will never know. 'Hold.'

The cultists close in. Morvenn can feel her Sisters poised to strike, the anticipation building in her own muscles with painful intensity, the Purgator Mirabilis itself straining to unleash holy vengeance upon the foe. Strike too soon and the moment will be lost before it arrives – too late and they will be overrun before she can bring the strongest weapons at her disposal to bear. Slugs chatter from an ancient autogun, the armour's energy field flaring in sparks of light like a meteor shower. Fionnula's prayer whispers through the vox.

'God-Emperor, guide my hand, that I may bring swift and holy vengeance to th–'

The time is now.

'Brace yourselves!' Morvenn fires every remaining missile into the horde at point-blank range, the recoil sending the suit stumbling back with pistons shrieking in protest, filling the air with screams, smoke and rubble. Blurry figures dance in her helmet's thermovision as she advances, skewering and slicing any of the enemy that try to rise from the shattered ground.

'My Sisters! With me!'

A fresh gout of scorching fire billows from a Havoc Marine's heavy flamer; she ignores the searing heat and urges the Purgator towards the source of the flames at a full charge, the Lance of Illumination braced underarm for impact. The strike takes the Heretic Astartes full in the chest and lifts him aloft with flame still belching from his weapon. Morvenn shakes her spear and the body flies through the air, crashes to the ground and lies still. She chooses her next target – a Night Lord bearing a brazen standard in the shape of a fanged and winged skull – and thunders towards him as her Sisters join the fray in earnest, the song of the blessed bolter cutting across the flames.

A human cultist staggers to his feet and fires a green las-bolt through the sleeve of Zafiya's vestments, earning himself a swift death by bolter in return. Kerem's chainsword is a blur as she swings it in a swift upward blow, the impact propelling another cultist backwards with guts unravelling like bloodied banners from his freshly opened belly. Another fills the gap – a burly woman armed with a butcher's cleaver – and Hiromi takes first her arm and then her head, stepping over her falling body to engage the next.

A vivid flash of light splits the sky, bright as lightning but a hundred times more intense. Morvenn's helm-augurs adjust to the brilliant flare, just as its source becomes apparent: a pair of Heretic Astartes, their oil-slick armour glittering in the coruscating light that sizzles from claws, blades, and power mauls. With unearthly grace, the nearer of the two springs into the air, the twin flares of a jump pack billowing thick black smoke, and then both are airborne.

The thrice-cursed Raptors have returned.

Urgency grants additional speed to Morvenn's attacks, and she carves her lance through the haft of the Night Lord's weapon and into the side of his armour, thrusts Fidelis' muzzle into his twisted face and pulls the trigger.

'Celestian Fionnula – hold off the cultists!' Morvenn shouts.

A wash of heat erupts from Fionnula's multi-melta, scorching the nearest cultist to ash and setting the rest aflame.

'Hiro, Zafiya, with me – take this one down!' She gestures with her spear to a descending Raptor and joins Fidelis' fire to the Celestians'. The shells strike home, and the Raptor falls to earth with thick black smoke gouting from his ruined jump pack. The Celestians are on him immediately, firing shell after shell into the helmet's vox-grille until the helmet and the skull within are nothing but a bloody pulp.

But the other Raptor learns from his brother's mistake. The next attack comes from above in the form of a frag grenade dropped directly at Morvenn's feet. It explodes the second it strikes the ground; the shards of metal rebound harmlessly off her warsuit's energy field, but the split second it takes for the field to re-establish itself gives a window for the Raptor to strike.

The tip of a powerblade slices through the Purgator's left pauldron from behind, impaling skin, muscle and bone, and emerges from the other side. A mocking laugh sounds in her ear, and with an overwhelming urgency that is only one step short of panic Morvenn rips her shoulder free of the blade. She turns to face her attacker, but the pain is making her slow, and he has already returned to the air. Someone is shouting, the voice coming in offset chorus through helm-vox and atmosphere, but it takes her a moment to work out who it is and what they are saying.

'Ahead!' The voice is Kseniya's, underscored by her bolter's roar. 'Look!'

The Raptor swoops again. Morvenn deflects his descent with another volley of shells and turns towards the cathedrum to see the unmistakable glow of light through glassaic, and then the Heretic Astartes is swooping again, power sword raised to strike. Fionnula moves to Morvenn's side and unleashes a blast from her multi-melta, sending the heretic twisting away on a tangent. The vox fills with Fionnula's exultant cry.

'Burn, in the God-Emperor's name!'

The blow that kills her comes out of nowhere.

One moment Fionnula is standing, turning as she searches for her next target, the next the brilliant arc of an energy blade opens a rift between her helm and gorget. The glowing eyes of her visor hang in the air, and then they tumble to the ground, the blood spurting from her severed neck turning her vestments to crimson. Zafiya screams in wordless outrage, filling the air with explosive shells that chase the soaring heretic upwards, but more Raptors are descending, made bold by their brother's success.

In moments they will be surrounded.

'Sisters! To the cathedrum!'

Holy light notwithstanding, the cathedrum offers their only chance of respite from an assault that is threatening to overwhelm them at any instant. Morvenn fires Fidelis in a broad arc, shooting to suppress rather than to kill, and leads the charge forward across ground carpeted in severed limbs and ruined torsos. The image of Fionnula's corpse flashes into her mind as Morvenn carves the head from a fleeing cultist. There will be no pyre for her, no funerary rites, no night-long vigil over her body. She will lie unburied, and the heretics will wreak every indignity on her too-corruptible flesh. Morvenn dispatches another pair of cultists with two well-aimed shots, and instantly the gap in the horde is filled by a huge, broad-shouldered figure, smoke billowing from the engine of its damaged jump pack. It has landed in an ungainly crouch, half of its armour scorched and melted from Fionnula's multi-melta, bolts of energy arcing unnaturally from its gauntlet up the melted plastek cables that connect it to its shoulder.

'We are not yet finished,' the Raptor slurs through a mouth filled with too many teeth. He raises his bolter in one hand, sword sparking in the other, and Morvenn closes the distance at a flat-out charge, the wound in her shoulder sending a band of agony down her arm. Zafiya is running alongside her on her left, the white and silver of her armour spattered with scarlet, Kerem's chainsword screaming out its song of death as she spins and slices to Morvenn's right.

The heretic raises his bolter and fires. Morvenn braces herself for impact, but the bolter turns aside with a scream of metal on metal, Kerem's chainsword biting into its barrel. Already the Raptor is bringing his sword around, but Morvenn is quicker, slamming the Lance into the gap in the armour between bevor and chestplate, sawing the blade back and forth until the flesh beneath begins to cook. The hideous face opens impossibly wide, the stench of rotting meat gusting from the open throat as he screams out the last of his hatred.

'You will die for this! The Death of Saints will raze your convent to the ground–'

Zafiya silences him with a bolt-shell.

This close to the cathedrum, Morvenn can make out the details of the sole section of the building still standing – a small side chapel of the sort where a body might be placed to lie in state, or a particularly holy reliquary receive the faithful. There is no glassaic in the arched windows, but warm golden light is streaming through the empty frame to light the ground around it. The faint strains of a familiar hymn fill the air, muting the sounds of gunfire as though they have entered an island of peace in an ocean of war. Morvenn braces herself for another onslaught, but to her surprise she finds that the surviving pair of Raptors are hanging back, reluctant, perhaps, to share the fate of their brothers.

'Do you feel it?' Hiromi asks. Her visor is tipped back, the eyes beneath wide. A fine rain is falling, glittering on her helm and skin like tiny diamonds. 'This is a miracle–'

A servitor-guided seeker missile tears through the air and detonates in the necropolis, obliterating what little remains of the tombs in a plume of fire. A vapour trail hangs heavy in the air behind it, and from the sounds of their engines the Black Templars' rumbling advance cannot be far behind.

Kerem is already moving towards the chapel, her chainsword silenced. 'Sisters? Perdita? Aleyna? Are you here?'

Another missile streaks overhead and strikes the skeleton of the cathedrum's spire, sending it toppling to the ground. Another strike will tear the building apart, and every living soul nearby with it. It would be a bitter irony to have driven away the enemy only to meet her death at the hands of her allies.

She activates her laud-hailers and raises the volume to its maximum. 'Sons of Dorn! My Sisters and I have secured the Cathedrum of Athenasia the Martyr! Hold your fire!'

'Acknowledged, Abbess Vahl.' The booming reply comes from

the Chaplain of the Black Templars. From its volume he and his brethren cannot be far away.

'And the Death of Saints? Is he slain?'

There is a long silence. 'There is no sign of him.'

Before the echo of the Chaplain's voice dies, the chapel door bursts open and a torrent of golden light pours into the gloom. A novitiate dressed in the robes of the Order of the Quill stands in the doorway, her round face transfigured by wonder. Behind her are ragged men and women who can only be Sister Superior Kerem's abandoned pilgrims, while at the chapel's altar two Sisters Militant are kneeling in prayer, one in black armour, the other in silver.

The Battle Sister in black opens her eyes at Morvenn's approach. She is one of the Order of Our Martyred Lady – young, perhaps only twenty Terran standard years, her dark brown skin slick with sweat, her bleached hair dulled to grey by soot and dust. Recognition passes across her face like a dawning sun, and she struggles to her feet, her hands making the aquila.

'Abbess Sanctorum. You came! My thanks–'

'You may thank Sister Superior Kerem for bearing word of your position.' Morvenn scans the chapel, looking for the saint's reliquary. The glow that she saw before has faded, leaving nothing but the flickering light of a few candle stubs. 'Where is the blessed saint?'

'She kept us safe.' A grubby boy of eleven or twelve speaks. Other heads nod in agreement, eyes radiant with faith in their filthy faces.

'Yes, but where *is* she?'

'There, blessed Sister.' The boy is pointing towards the centre of the room. Morvenn lifts her visor, squinting as though the reliquary might be before her in plain sight, but there is only the Battle Sister, staring at the floor in dazed contemplation.

'Forgive me, blessed abbess, but the reliquary is gone with the Sisters of the Valorous Heart,' the novitiate says. '*She* is the saint. The one who preserved us. Saint Aleyna.'

XV

Amrek of Malk is a fortunate man.

When he thinks of the countless worlds on which he might have taken his first breath, the fact that he was born in the shadow of the Convent Sanctorum seems an indisputable sign of divine providence. His late mother had been a sculptor of exquisite skill, and when she died coughing up marble-dust, the Adepta Sororitas had arranged his education in gratitude for her lifetime of service. Though Amrek lacks his mother's artistic talent, he likes to think that he has inherited her affinity for stone, a skill that has served him well through his apprenticeship and the following five years as a journeyman mason.

And as always, there is work to be done.

Amrek secures his work-belt around his waist and climbs the scaffolding, marvelling at the skill of the ancient hands that wrought the shrine-chapel from the black granite of the cliff face. The main entrance is at ground level, flanked by two fifty-foot statues of the God-Emperor, while on the levels above, secondary doorways between Corinthian columns open onto a labyrinth of chambers and passageways that extend for miles beneath the mountainside. It is said that Caelestis is almost as old as the Imperial Faith itself, carved out by the first Ophelians to see the truth of the new-minted creed. Whether that is true or not – and Amrek knows well the value of an inspiring fable – here in the mountains where the bells toll through clear, sweet air is where he feels closest to the God-Emperor.

There was not always peace here – indeed, that is why he and hundreds of other labourers have come here to work. The shrine was badly damaged when the Archenemy attacked after the opening of the Great Rift, but even then he was fortunate. The armies of the God-Emperor answered his prayers and smote the foe, and there is no devastation that faithful hands cannot rebuild. The days are long, and the labour is hard, but he undertakes it with devotion and joy.

'Amrek! Are you ready?'

The voice drifts up from the ground below, where Solana has finished loading the hoist, the floating servo-skull at her shoulder scanning and accounting for each marble tile in the crate.

'Ready!'

Solana takes the pulley-rope and heaves, and the laden platform rises steadily upwards. Amrek's hands guide the rope so that it runs smoothly through the pulley, struggling to tear his eyes from the way that Solana's muscles move beneath her copper skin, or how the sunlight makes fire of her auburn hair. He is so fascinated that he almost fails to catch the hoist in time, and the act of heaving its burden onto the scaffolding almost sends the tiles plummeting back to the ground. Tucked in the crate is a freshly picked sunfruit, its yellow-green peel gleaming like a jewel. He smiles and tucks it inside his pouch to share with Solana later. She is a blessing of the God-Emperor, one for whom he gives thanks with every breath.

'I have it secure!' he calls. Solana waves up at him, then returns to the task of preparing more tiles for the next batch. All around her, the workers attend to their labours – cutting stone to shape, polishing the surface to a perfect shine, carving the script and painting the letters in gold. Servitors lumber between them, bearing the heaviest of the loads, silent and uncomplaining. They too are blessed, Amrek thinks, granted the chance to serve without doubt or question.

He lifts the open crate of tiles onto the waiting suspensor-platform and pushes it along the scaffolding towards the doorway in the stone. Once the ancient mosaics within the cavern are restored to their former glory the faithful will come to marvel at their work, perhaps even the Abbess Sanctorum herself.

The sun is dipping towards the clouds on the far horizon. When the day's work is over, there will be a meal with his fellow labourers, then six hours of unbroken sleep at the side of his betrothed. There can be few in the Imperium who can dream of such a life.

Amrek of Malk is a fortunate man.

The first sign that something is wrong is the cry that comes from the ground below. Solana is standing with her hand over her eyes, squinting into the setting sun. The other labourers are rising from their work, staring at a vast silhouette approaching with wings outstretched. Distracted, Amrek blunders into the suspensor-platform, sending the topmost tiles spilling over the edge of the scaffolding to shatter on the ground below.

'Do not tell me you have dropped another basketful?' A peevish voice echoes from inside the shrine-cavern as the mosaicist shuffles towards the light. 'Foolish boy. I will have sense whipped into you.'

Amrek barely hears him. The shadow is filling the sky, so close now that he can see the segmented armour plating on its underbelly, the metal joints of its wings draped in living flesh, a blasphemous fusion of Neverborn and machine. Two lizard-like heads snap and snarl at the end of elongated necks. One set of jaws opens and blasts a choking cloud of smoke across the ground, while the second unleashes a jet of flame at the scaffolding. He runs for the nearest ladder, the air rippling with a haze so intense that he can barely see a yard in front of him.

Solana. He must reach Solana.

The ladder is on fire by the time he is a third of the way down. His feet catch on the rungs, splinters gouging into his palms as he slides towards the ground. He jumps the last two yards, and the smoke closes in over his head like a suffocating hood. He stumbles towards where he last saw his betrothed, trips on a broken crate and lands with his face inches from the glassy eyes of a dead goldworker. He shoves the body away and scrambles to his feet, only to find himself staring up at a huge man in spiked adamantine armour. A halo of skulls is suspended above his shoulders, the eyes of his faceless helmet blazing with bale-fire.

'God-Emperor!' Amrek turns to run, but his desperate movement sends him slamming into a flaming scaffold pole. With a deafening creak the scaffolding gives way, planks and poles toppling to the ground with flames roaring. He dares not look back, but the hell around him is inescapable. A dozen armoured warriors are stalking through the fire, oblivious to the tongues of flame that lick their armour. A body falls from above, grey robe billowing, and Amrek has a moment to recognise the ancient mosaicist before his wrinkled head hits the ground and ruptures like an overripe sunfruit.

Another huge warrior has a stoneworker by the throat, his feet thrashing empty air three feet off the ground. He watches in horror as the monster in armour punches a long-taloned finger into the man's throat and pulls it slowly downward. The screams turn wet and thick as the breastbone is sliced down its centre, then take on a piercing animal quality as the guts spill from the split abdomen in bloody spools. The warrior holds the dying man up to the light, then casts the body carelessly away.

'Amrek!' Solana's face resolves out of the smoke. She grabs Amrek's arm and drags him with her as a sudden wind buffets his head and shoulders – he looks up into the gleaming underbelly of the two-headed dragon, talons outstretched as it comes in to land. Solana's hand is locked around his wrist, and he sprints with her with no idea of direction other than *away*, the world a maelstrom of fire and suffering.

With a sound like tearing cloth, a spiked chain spins through the air at ankle height with horrifying speed and force. Solana screams and topples forward, her right leg ripped away at the knee. Agony is etched on her face, but she is still clawing at the ground, dragging herself away from the huge warriors and their monster, reaching out for him with broken-nailed hands.

'Help – Amrek!'

He steps back, unable to tear his eyes from the shadow approaching through the smoke.

'Please!'

The two-headed dragon screams, and the last of Amrek's courage shatters. He runs with Solana's pleas turning to curses in his ears. The camp has turned to an abattoir, the choking smoke thick with the smell of roasting human flesh. Was it only moments ago he was gazing over the valley thanking the God-Emperor for his good fortune?

The warlord raises his hand and bellows an order in a language that Amrek does not understand. His followers move forward as though animated by a single will, cutting down fleeing labourers with efficient cruelty. They seem to take pleasure in leaving their victims maimed instead of killing them outright. An image of Solana bleeding on the ground flashes into his mind, and he banishes the thought entirely. She would want him to survive.

One of them has to escape to tell the tale of what has happened here. One of them has to raise the alarm.

Except that is a lie.

Amrek wants to live.

The ground drops away before him, and he skids to a halt with his toes hanging over the edge of a precipitous drop. He searches around him for an alternative route of escape, but it is already too late. The heretic warlord is striding towards him, the skulls leering empty-eyed from his armour rack. Two of the heads are fresher than the others – the rotting face of one is partially obscured by a thick fall of golden hair, but the fleur-de-lys tattooed on the right cheek of the other marks the dead woman out as a Sister of the Adepta Sororitas. If this warrior has slaughtered Sisters of Battle, there can be no hope for anyone else.

'You cannot fly,' the warlord growls in a voice that makes the ground shake. 'Come to me, and I will give you a death of such dark beauty that it would make the saints themselves weep.' He raises an armoured claw, dripping with rivulets of thick, dark blood. 'Your woman is not yet dead. If you beg, I may allow you to see her before you both die. Is that not a kingly gift?'

Some things are worse than death.

'God-Emperor, forgive me.'

Amrek steps back into empty air. The wind buffets his body as he descends, tugging at his tunic and ruffling his hair into wild peaks, until he hits the ground and shatters like a dropped tile.

There is no pain.

Amrek of Malk has always been a fortunate man.

XVI

Pain is a holy sacrament.

Seated in her warsuit in the passenger compartment of the Convent Sanctorum's lander, Morvenn focuses her attention on the wound in her shoulder, still untreated despite the offer of the Black Templars Apothecary. This pain – the white-hot agony of the moment of impact, the dull ache that flares bright with each movement the lander makes – is sent by the God-Emperor. It is a pale shadow of the agony He endures in His perpetual state of sacrifice on the Golden Throne, and whether it is punishment or gift she will endure it in silence.

Her three surviving Celestians sit to her left, Kseniya praying softly for the souls of the dead, Hiromi deeply asleep with her head on Zafiya's shoulder – the result of the morpholox that she had only grudgingly accepted on Morvenn's insistence. Sister Superior Kerem and Novitiate Theodosia of the Order of the Quill are seated opposite in silence, while Sister Aleyna has set herself apart from the rest, her head bent in prayer over the chaplet ecclesiasticus tangled in her fingers.

Morvenn half-closes her eyes and tries to make sense of the last few hours. The chapel, rising from the rubble around it, miraculously intact in the face of all the devastation. The pilgrims. The kneeling Sister at prayer. That strange sense of the numinous, that something transcendent had occurred moments before she arrived. How must it feel, Morvenn wonders, to have felt the God-Emperor's presence? Envy kindles in her, and she does her best to stifle the unworthy emotion. There is little point in dwelling on the fact that she is once again called to bear witness to a miracle rather than to be blessed with a part in it.

The lander shudders like a beast of burden shaking a load from its back. Thick grey cloud ripples across the narrow viewing slit in the passenger chamber as the craft begins its descent towards the Convent Sanctorum. Morvenn presses her shoulder into her seat and focuses on the pain radiating down her arm as the landing lights set the clouds flaring red and white.

'Praise be to the God-Emperor for our deliverance,' the pilot calls back from the flight deck. 'For He hath been our guide through storms and trials, and only through His grace are we brought safe to land.'

The lights of the Convent Sanctorum appear below them like a field of stars, nestled between the spires and domes that rise from the city around it like a mountain amongst foothills. Even now, after all these years, the sight is enough to set the hair prickling on the back of her neck. Signal-fires burn in the watchtowers dotted along the high perimeter walls, braziers lighting the great golden doors to the innermost sanctum and the balcony above it, while its glassaic windows blaze with the light of a thousand candles. It is a vision in adamantine and marble, a testament to the surpassing skill of its ancient architects, a fortress-cathedrum that has withstood millennia of war.

And it is all the home she has ever known.

The lander swoops in a graceful arc around the central dome, and a roost of black-winged avians rise into the air. Wild shadows dance across the inner courtyard, turning the gene-spliced trees that line the approach to the main doors to towering giants crowned with silver laurels.

This close, the Convent Sanctorum's scars are visible: new watchtowers of freshly quarried stone, crude lines of mortar sealing cracks in the walls, buttresses where none were needed before. Proof, she supposes, that the Convent Sanctorum is a living place, capable of healing even as its enemies strive to wound it beyond repair.

Or a reminder that not even stone is eternal.

The pilot clears her throat. 'I have Prioress Illuminata of the Order of Our Martyred Lady on the secure channel for you. Shall I connect you?'

Morvenn lets her eyes close and nods. 'Do so.'

'Abbess Sanctorum!' Illuminata's cracked, acerbic voice comes clearly through her vox-bead, as though the old woman was delivering the words directly into her ear. *'We give thanks for your safe arrival. The Sisters Hospitaller stand ready to attend to your wounds.'*

'Have the pilgrims arrived?'

'Indeed they have.' Morvenn recognises the note of frustration in the prioress' voice. She was on the receiving end of it often enough in her days as a novitiate. *'They are to be accommodated in the western cloister, until more suitable accommodation can be found.'*

'Have the Hospitallers check them for disease. I have no wish to see us weakened further by some foul infection spreading within the convent.'

'It shall be done.'

The lander's engines fall silent, then its landing gear caresses the ground so softly that even Morvenn's wounds fail to register a protest.

'What news of the reliquary?' She pilots the warsuit to a standing position, bracing her injured shoulder against its backplate.

'None, I regret to say.'

'And what of the heretic?' Another question to which she already knows the answer. The silence stretches out so long that she starts to wonder if the vox-connection has been lost.

'His exact location is not yet known to us. But we have some intelligence regarding his movements. With respect, it would be better discussed in person.'

The lander's hatch opens. Morvenn strides out into the convent's central courtyard. Everything is familiar: from the black marble chased in gold beneath her feet, to the stern-faced statues of the saints that line the steps to the inner sanctum, to the huge, circular glassaic window that hangs above the vast golden doors. A cold wind whips colder rain against her face, and that sensation too is familiar. The Convent Sanctorum has never welcomed the weak, but those capable of thriving despite its hardships will be transfigured to greatness.

'Abbess Sanctorum, be welcome!' Prioress Illuminata is waiting by the foot of the steps flanked by a pair of Battle Sisters, clutching a long blackwood staff surmounted with the sigil of the Order of Our Martyred Lady. Four Sisters Hospitaller of the Order of the Eternal Candle stand just behind her, a pair of servitors holding a stretcher a discreet distance away. It seems that Illuminata has prepared for any possible eventuality.

The prioress has aged considerably since the last time Morvenn set eyes on her, but the pale grey eyes in the old woman's face are as sharp as ever. She is more stooped than Morvenn remembers, and the walking staff is new. Illuminata makes no secret of her disdain for rejuvenat and those who use it to stave off the approaches of mortality. The God-Emperor, as she is fond of saying, will call her home in His own good time, though personally Morvenn considers that Illuminata has never quite forgiven herself for failing to find a martyr's end.

'Prioress.' Sister Aleyna is at the foot of the lander's steps, her head bowed, hands clasped at her waist. Behind her, Kseniya and Zafiya are supporting Hiromi as she attempts to walk down to ground level on her ruined leg.

The old woman nods. 'I would speak with you later, Sister Aleyna. Abbess Sanctorum, if you would follow me into the sanctum I will apprise you of the situation as it stands.'

The unease in Illuminata's voice sends a trickle of ice down Morvenn's spine. The prioress' fighting years might be behind her, but she is a skilled and capable strategist devoted to Ophelia's VII's defence, and if the situation is enough to unsettle her then it is graver than Morvenn had thought.

'The Sisterhood is assembled in the Basilikum to mark your arrival–'

'Dismiss them.' The great golden doors swing open, and Morvenn pilots the warsuit inside, the echo of its footsteps reverberating from the high stone walls and vaulted ceiling. 'We have no time for ceremony.'

The old woman's mouth tightens. 'Certainly, my abbess.' She snaps her fingers, and a servant in a high-collared black tunic steps forward. 'Inform Canoness Lucreziana that there will be no need for the Ceremony of Gratitudes today. She may return the Sisters to their duties.'

'Certainly, prioress.'

'And have the war-room made ready.' Illuminata frowns, her hand rising to the micro-bead in her right ear as the servant scurries away. 'Two Thunderhawk gunships are approaching the convent, informing us that they will be landing within the next five minutes. I see they prefer to ask forgiveness than permission.'

Morvenn raises an eyebrow. 'They require neither.'

'And in the meantime, perhaps you will allow Sister Hospitaller Véronique to attend to that wound in your shoulder.' The prioress shoots an uneasy look at the sky. 'Unless I am much mistaken, Ophelia VII will have need of your strength in the days to come.'

'My wounds can wait. Ophelia VII has need of me *now*.'

It takes time and effort, but the Sisters of Battle kneel in the end. Lethe has watched for the last hour from the shadows of a burned-out shrine as the resistance is bled from them, their prayers of defiance silenced, the burning light of faith in their eyes extinguished one knife-wound at a time. Her lord has not bloodied his hands with any of it, allowing his lesser brothers to carry out the work while he stands over the two women in black armour in silent judgement.

Lethe's own hands are clean, but not for want of willingness.

'Enough.' Her lord raises a hand. One of the lesser demigods steps away immediately, but the second – Ostrov Skull-taker, who Lethe is coming to loathe with a hatred that exceeds anything she ever felt for Overseer Yulius and his ilk – continues his bloody work as though he has not heard. The tip of his knife is pressed into the cheek of the older of the two women, a bright bead of blood trickling down her face like a tear.

'Do not make me repeat myself.'

For a moment the world is frozen, then Ostrov turns away, his face twisted with resentment and contempt. 'Weakness,' he growls, though if the Death of Saints hears, he does not react. Instead, he walks to where the Sisters are kneeling and lifts the face of the younger woman – the one whose red hair is now entirely soaked in blood – in his taloned hand.

'Your Corpse-Emperor will not save you.'

The Sister spits a mouthful of blood at him. 'He already has.'

The Death of Saints snaps the Sister's neck with a twist of his wrist and turns his attention to the other woman. Blood is dripping in three slow rivulets from her bowed head to the bloodstained earth. 'Give her to me.'

Lethe cranes her neck to get a better look at the blood-spattered silver case in the woman's lap, the fresh wound down her left brow and cheek burning as the skin around it pulls taut. Nothing whatsoever remains to stop her lord – he must merely extend his hand to take his prize – but there is some complex design at work here, some power in the breaking of the last shard of the woman's will.

'She is not yours to take.' The Sister raises her head and glares defiance with her one remaining eye. 'Blessed Saint Athenasia of the Sorrows, grant me your hatred–'

The Death of Saints moves with the speed and force of a breaking storm. His right gauntlet lashes out and strikes the Sister full in the face, slamming her to the ground in a spray of blood. She draws a rasping breath and struggles to rise, but the last of her strength is leaving her. Lethe would almost pity her, if the bleeding woman were not one of the hated Sisterhood who killed her father, burned her home, consigned her to the torment of the mines. The Sisters deserve nothing but her hatred, and the death they have earned at her lord's hands.

'And still you brought her to me,' the Death of Saints says, and now his voice is dripping with malice. He lifts the reliquary from the dying woman's hands and raises it into the light. One taloned finger traces along the join where the lid meets the body of the box. 'I have sought her for so long.'

The Sister draws a rattling breath. 'Even if you destroy the relic, the saint's truth is eternal–'

'How you cling to your false faith.' The Death of Saints shakes his head. He opens the reliquary case, and light glints on polished bone chased in silver filigree as he lifts it into the air, the box falling discarded to the ground. The skull barely fills his palm. 'I do not intend to destroy that which is most dear to me.

Hers will be the place of honour, where she may witness the destruction of those who parted us. Brother Merthok!'

An ancient Space Marine lumbers forward. He is impossibly old, massive even for one of these warriors. His skin is wrinkled and pockmarked, the vox-grille that must once have formed part of his helm sunken deep in the lower half of his face.

'My lord.'

'You have served me loyally, from our very first battle.' The Death of Saints places the skull in Merthok's outstretched hands, then removes the rotting head of a Battle Sister from the topmost spike of his armour rack and throws it aside. 'This honour falls to you. Place my sister where she belongs.'

Merthok raises the skull above his head. 'Brothers! On your knees!'

And they obey.

The Death of Saints surveys his war-host, the axe glowing in his right hand, then he, too, takes a knee. Merthok stands behind him, the skull and its silver filigree ablaze in the light of the corpse-fires.

'Our lord's sister is returned to us!'

In a smooth downward motion, he skewers the skull on the centremost spike of the Death of Saints' armour rack.

'It is done!'

The war-host roar their approval. The Death of Saints stands and raises his axe high above his head. 'My sister Athenasia is with me once again! And now, we shall punish those who parted us!' He spits in the face of the dying Battle Sister. 'You will not live to see your convent burn.'

Lethe's hand tightens around the grip of her knife. She longs to throw herself forward, to demonstrate to her lord how much she has learned, but Ostrov Skull-taker is already advancing, his blade glinting in his hand.

The dying woman vanishes from Lethe's view, but her screams linger for a long, long time.

The candles are lit in the war-room by the time Morvenn arrives. Many months have passed since she was last here, but even so, walking through the great arched door into the familiar chamber feels like coming home. Blood-red wax dribbles down the pillar candles set upon the wrought iron wall-sconces, their flickering glow warming the faces of the gilded saints in their shallow alcoves. A marble globe five feet wide hangs in a suspensor field in the centre of the room, bas-relief carvings on its surface replicating the peaks and troughs of Ophelia VII's topography. Tiny lumens have been set beneath its surface, shining through in pinpricks of light. Most of the cardinal world is covered in a continuous sprawl of religious buildings and hab-blocks for the people who maintain them, interspersed with manufactoria where parchment, candles, munitions and weaponry are made. Some planets provide food to the people of the Imperium of Man, others machines, soldiers or voidships.

Ophelia VII provides faith.

A large circular table sits at the end of the room, beneath a glowing rose window bearing the image of Saint Celestine in a cloud of rose petals and doves. Eight chairs sit empty around it; Morvenn pilots the Purgator to the far side of the table, where she can clearly see the floating globe, and shoves the chair aside.

'Who speaks for the Orders Majoris?'

The prioress takes her chair. 'I will speak for Our Martyred Lady. Canoness Lucreziana for the Valorous Heart. We have sent word to Canoness Elsvieta of Rheins at the Preceptory of Saint Mina's Hope, but she regrets she is unable to attend.'

'She is unable to attend?' Morvenn leans across the table. 'Did she give a reason?'

'The defence of the preceptory requires her undivided attention.'

'Is the preceptory under attack?'

The old woman looks down at the data-slate in her hand. 'We received reports of an advancing enemy force, but after that vox-contact was lost. A scouting patrol was sent, but they did not return.'

'I see. And there was no one she could spare to send in her stead?'

'It would appear not.'

Morvenn leans forward to watch the globe spin. Elsvieta of Rheins is a formidable warrior and commander, a close friend of the previous Abbess Sanctorum and for a time considered a likely successor. With the Death of Saints and his army spreading across the cardinal world like a cancer, it is hardly a surprise that the defence of the preceptory should be her priority, but her absence is still a very tangible snub.

'Who else?' Morvenn asks.

'The Ebon Chalice and the Sacred Rose maintain only a small presence on Ophelia VII. If you wish I will issue a summons–'

'Issue it.'

'And for the Argent Shroud?'

Celestian Superior Ignatia's name leaps to Morvenn's lips by reflex. She stops herself before she can utter it, the weight of grief settling once again on her shoulders. How long will it be before she accepts the truth of Ignatia's death? She forces herself to think of the empty helmet, the headless corpse lying discarded in the dirt. Ignatia's mortal flesh is gone, her soul ascended to the Golden Throne, and no prayers of Morvenn's can bring her back.

'Celestian Zafiya,' she says instead. Technically Hiromi has seniority by dint of a few months of service in the Celestians, but she is already in the infirmarium undergoing treatment for her injuries. If she is fortunate the Sister-chirurgeons may yet save the leg, but judging by the stench of the wound by the time they reached the convent, Morvenn has her doubts.

The door to the war-room opens again, and Castellan Tancret strides in. His armour is freshly polished, and the bloodstained silkweave vestments in which she last saw him have been replaced by a pristine surcoat. He looks every inch the warlord.

'Abbess Sanctorum. My thanks for your hospitality.'

'As we give thanks to the God-Emperor for the presence of the sons of Dorn.' She extends her arm in welcome. 'Please. Join me.'

Tancret removes his helmet, hands it to the Sword Brother on his left and runs a gauntleted hand through his close-cropped hair. Morvenn studies his face carefully, looking for any trace of the disappointment that she had seen before during the assault on the cathedrum, but the castellan's face is unreadable.

'The Death of Saints lives,' he says, the impact of his armoured feet ringing out on the cold stone of the floor. 'I had hoped to take his treacherous head from his shoulders, but the opportunity was lost. Still.' He joins her at the table. 'My brethren and I shall slay him yet.'

XVII

The other two Sisters arrive together and in silence. Lucreziana of the Valorous Heart wears a simple white robe and surplice, her right hand clad in a blood-red glove. She has changed little since Morvenn last saw her, though her tanned, raw-boned face seems even more gaunt than before, and the mechanical replacement for her right eye is new. Celestian Zafiya is still in her armour, her face grey and her eyes deeply shadowed, her auditory augmetics gleaming on either temple. Both bow their heads and make the sign of the aquila, first to Morvenn and then to the castellan, before taking their places at the table. There is a charge in the air, an electric sense of anticipation that Morvenn knows well. Battle is coming. She is exactly where she needs to be.

'Canoness Lucreziana. My thanks for joining us.'

'I came as soon as word of your journey reached us. I am glad you saw fit to return. There were some amongst my Order who believed that your duty to Terra would keep you from us.'

'While our shrines burn and our Sisters die?' Morvenn snaps out the words with more venom than she means. 'Then they do not know me at all.'

'As I have said.' Lucreziana raises her blood-red glove in placation. 'I doubt neither your commitment nor your faith.'

'Our enemies would do well to remember the same.'

The castellan gestures towards the spinning globe. 'We are here to speak of war. I have little doubt that our combined armies will be a match for any force at the Night Lord's disposal, but the fact remains we must find him.'

Prioress Illuminata creaks to her feet and raps the iron ferrule of her staff on the stone floor. 'With your permission, my lords.'

A pair of cherubim descend from the dark rafters of the chamber, one trailing a six-foot-long scroll of parchment, the other dragging a hovering servo-skull behind it like a kite. The old woman reaches up for the scroll and rolls it into a neat cylinder while the cherub wrestles the skull into a geostationary orbit around the slowly spinning globe.

'Augustus.'

The skull chitters sharply in acknowledgement.

'Begin.'

The room dims, and a series of white lights flare on the globe's surface, projected in flickering beams from the servo-skull's single augmetic eye.

'Each of these lights represents a shrine or chapel from which we have received the *clamor auxilium*.' Illuminata signals the servo-skull. 'Augustus, play the transmission from the shrine at Saint Katherine's Rest.'

The eye glows red, casting the room in a sudden bloody hue as the recording begins. The sound is poor quality, the voice muffled and indistinct, but no one could mistake the crackle of flames in the background, or the distinctive thud of the heavy bolter.

'...stance from the conv–' The broadcast is not loud, but from the rasp in the Sister's voice when it is audible over the sounds of war, it is clear she is shouting. *'–vy assaul... –mon en–'*

'Play that again.'

The prioress shakes her head. 'Your grace, the broadcast is not yet fin–'

'Play it again.'

'Of course. Augustus, repeat the transmission from the start.'

With a grinding of gears, the skull rewinds the audio without turning off its 'casters, the reversed broadcast emerging in a daemonic squawk.

'*...heavy assault...*' There is no mistaking what comes next. '*Daemon engines–*'

Tancret scowls. 'The enemy grows bold in these dark times.'

'We received nothing more from Katherine's Rest,' Illuminata says.

'But there are others?'

'Yes, Abbess Sanctorum. Augustus, play the broadcast from–'

'Tell me in words.'

'Catriana's Fall. The Ossuary at Reykos. The Chantry of the Silver Skull. The reports are all the same. A sudden attack of Heretic Astartes and their cultists, drawing the Sisters out to fight, followed by reports of a devastating aerial assault.'

'And then?'

'Only silence. We have attempted to make contact with them all, but it seems that our enemy has the ability to deny us access to our long-range vox-system whenever they please.'

'Then why allow any broadcasts at all?'

'Because they want us to know what they are doing,' Canoness Lucreziana says. 'They want us to fear them.'

The words fall into the air, heavy with meaning. 'They will earn only our hatred.' A fresh thought sparks in Morvenn's mind. 'Heretics and cultists, you said. I saw their strike cruisers in orbit. How did they make planetfall?'

'We believe the Astartes arrived as you did,' Lucreziana says. 'By drop pods directly from their vessels, small enough to circumvent our orbital defences. The cultists have a more prosaic origin. The penitentia at Galathrix and Oyestra were attacked. Thousands of heretics, unleashed.' Two spots of colour have appeared on Lucreziana's pale cheeks. 'They destroyed Lucia's Ossuary shortly afterwards. I led a mission there, but we arrived too late. We found the flames still burning, the enemy not long departed.' Her mouth twists at the bitterness of the words. 'The enemy had left eight of my Sisters alive, eyeless, tongueless and broken, staked out for us to find.'

Morvenn tries to banish the image from her mind's eye before it can take root, but it is already lodged too tightly. She has seen these sights before, but repetition does nothing to diminish their horror. Cold sweat prickles across her brow, and she rubs it away with her gloved hand, sending a jolt of agony through her injured shoulder. She grits her teeth and counts to ten. This is no time for weakness.

'Abbess Sanctorum, are you well?' The prioress is staring at her, eyes narrowed with concern. 'The Sisters Hospitaller are prepared for you. You will serve the God-Emperor better whole than injured.'

'In time.' Morvenn returns her focus to Lucreziana. 'And you found no trace of the enemy?'

'None.' The canoness' jaw sets. 'Otherwise I would not be at this table. Will you accord my fallen Sisters the honour of listening to their final moments?'

Morvenn nods.

This time there is no voice in the recording, only the endless screams of the dying. She forces herself to listen until the broadcast ends.

'The Death of Saints attacks without warning,' the prioress says, into the silence that comes after. 'There is no pattern to his assaults, only an attack, a conflagration, and once the Sisters are dead, a swift retreat.'

'But his voidship is gone?'

Illuminata nods. 'The orbital auspex detected a massive explosion in the void. We believe that the *Lux Dominus* rammed the heretic's vessel, destroying them both.'

'An act of extraordinary valour,' Lucreziana says, and Morvenn's heart sinks. In some tiny part of her soul she had hoped that the *Lux* and its captain had somehow survived. The stark truth of its obliteration leaves a sour taste in her mouth, a lead weight in the pit of her belly.

'There must be a pattern to his attacks.' Castellan Tancret is studying the globe intently. 'Mark the locations. Show me the elevation of the areas targeted.'

Lights appear on the globe, along with runes highlighting the altitude of each location from chapels at sea level to lofty mountain shrines. There is a piece missing from this puzzle, and Morvenn has no idea where to find it. Her head is swimming, and the chamber is suddenly too warm. The prioress is right – the wound in her shoulder is a distraction she can ill afford. She motions to one of the Sisters Dialogus standing back from the map table.

'Kindly inform Sister-Chirurgeon Véronique that I will be with her shortly.'

'A wise decision, Abbess Sanctorum.' Prioress Illuminata motions to her servo-skull again. 'But we have one further transmission of which you should be aware. Augustus – the shrine of Gudrun of the Broken Blade.'

'...vast...' This time the shouting voice is almost drowned out by the crackle of flames. *'...heads... swooping...'*

The prioress raises a hand for attention. 'And listen.'

The broadcast continues with a sound like a falling curtain. Celestian Zafiya adjusts the sensitivity of her auditory augmetics and inclines her head towards the servo-skull with eyes closed. She frowns. 'That is the sound of wings.'

A daemonic shriek tears through the vox-unit.

'That,' Morvenn says, as the echoes die to silence, 'is a Heldrake.'

The Death of Saints is restless. Lethe can tell from his quick, impatient movements, from the sharpness in his voice whenever he speaks. He has removed the gauntlet from his right hand, and the tips of his elongated fingers are resting on the silver-chased dome of the saint's stolen skull, stroking back and forth with incongruous gentleness.

Daylight is already giving way to evening. This high in the mountains, the air is thin, and the last of the sunlight is painting the stone of the cliffside a bloody red. Ancient chambers extend deep into the rock here, the façade carved by ancient hands and restored by new ones, but what was once a place of worship has become a charnel house. The labourers have joined the tombs' occupants in death, but their bodies have been accorded no gentle burial amongst the ancient graves. Instead, their severed heads have been taken to decorate belts, armour racks, and the rough palisade of metal spikes erected around the camp. Their bodies lie discarded in the midden-heap, crudely dismembered or roasting on spits. The air is heavy with smoke and the smell of charring meat.

The Death of Saints has transformed the tombs at Caelestis to his own dark design, and it is every bit as terrible as Lethe could possibly have imagined. She holds her breath and creeps closer, watching as he reaches above his head to remove the centremost skull from his armour-rack and cradle it in his armoured hands. With a surpassing effort of will she raises her eyes to look at his face, and in the split second before her nerve fails her and she looks away, she catches a glimpse of the single void-dark eye fixed on the skull with unholy intensity. There is something unfamiliar to his expression, something that sits oddly on his inhuman features. Something almost akin to sorrow.

'Look at them.' The soft growl is not intended for Lethe's ears, but the sound still sends a thrill of fear down her spine. 'That these should be my weapons, in this our war of all wars.'

An inhuman warrior with spiked shoulder-armour and a long red scalplock on the top of his head is walking towards them, the claws of his right hand dripping blood, a woman's severed head trailing from his left. When he notices Lethe's interest, his lipless mouth splits open in a broad smile, revealing teeth filed to points beneath. This one is a creature forged for war just as his master is, but while the Death of Saints is a finely wrought blade, this is a blunt instrument, force without grace or finesse. Already others of his kind are approaching to gather in a crowd behind him, predators drawn to the possibility of spilled blood.

'Where next?' The voice from the helmet's vox-grille is a low rasp, the accent thick. She has observed a particular pattern of speech amongst some of the warband, similarities in the clipped consonants and flat vowels that her lord does not share. 'What plans do you have for us, O Death of Saints? Or has your stomach for battle deserted you now you have your prize?'

Lethe holds her breath. Seconds pass before the Death of Saints moves, rising to his feet in a smooth movement like the uncoiling of a predatory serpent.

'You will have your fill of blood in time, Yevgeni.'

'Blood.' Yevgeni spits the word dismissively. 'You have given us blood enough already. The blood of the weak. The blood of labourers and worshippers. Where is the battle we were promised? Where are the daughters of the Corpse-Emperor?'

'You will have all that was promised you. In time.'

Lethe shrinks back into the shadows. The air is darkening around her lord, but the other warrior is oblivious. The other

Heretic Astartes seem to have sensed the gathering storm, hands resting on weapons, muscles tensing ready to strike.

'The Sisters of the false god are in disarray,' Yevgeni continues. 'Strike now, and the world will be covered in an ocean of blood before the sun next rises. And he – he who should lead us to blood and death gives his favour to this filth–'

He stabs a finger in Lethe's direction. Adrenaline floods her veins, every instinct telling her to run – but she knows now that to show a moment's weakness will bring immediate death. Other members of the warband are starting to gather, drawn to the growing conflict. Even the human slaves are pausing in the work of constructing the palisade, turning to watch with mixed curiosity and fear. Lethe sees Ostrov Skull-taker watching from the shadows, his sunken eyes narrowed, a calculating expression on his misshapen face. He has no love for her lord, that much she knows, but he lacks the courage to strike directly against him, at least for now. Yevgeni, it seems, has no such qualms.

'And he will not act!'

'I have already acted.' The Death of Saints raises a hand to point to his armour rack, to its fresh adornments. 'I have slaughtered their faithful. Destroyed their shrines. Killed yet another of their saints. And even now my plan is coming to fruition, though you lack the wit to see it.'

'Your plan. Of course.' Yevgeni turns, sweeping his arms wide, playing to the crowd. 'Tell me, my brothers, who still has faith in our lord's plan? Our lord, who has sacrificed our voidship without concern.'

'Silence,' Merthok growls. 'When Ophelia VII is ours, who will deny us the stars?'

'Ah, Brother Merthok.' Yevgeni spits at the ancient warrior's feet. 'Such loyalty. He promises us the cardinal world, yet he waits while our enemies gather in their fortress and plot our undoing. Let us strike first. Let us bring such fear into their hearts that those who survive will speak our names with horror for a hundred years. Let us remember who we are!'

The Death of Saints points at Yevgeni and opens his hand. Light flashes on a silver blade as it tumbles through the air, then Yevgeni staggers back, blood welling from his throat where the knife has embedded itself hilt-deep. The severed head falls from his grip – he raises a hand to pull the blade free, but the Death of Saints stops him with a single word.

'No.' Firelight glints on the dark enamel of his armour. 'Leave it there. I grow tired of your voice. And as for the rest of you, you will have your slaughter in time. And if any of you have forgotten what it means to bear the blood of Konrad Curze, I will gladly remind you. Face to face. Brother to brother.'

Yevgeni's eyes are bulging like a bullfrog's, his neck smeared with bloody fingerprints, his breath a wet rasp. A lesser human would be on their knees by now, but Lethe knows these beings are made of stronger material than human flesh. She searches the shadows for Ostrov, wondering if this is the moment when the treacherous warrior will strike against his lord, but he is only one of a hundred monstrous shadows.

'And the rest of you.' The Death of Saints turns his gaze to the assembled warriors. 'Answer me this – where does fear grow best?'

'Fear grows in darkness. In silence.' Merthok's chainglaive whirrs into life. 'And in the anticipation.'

In a single smooth movement, Merthok lunges forward, and his chainblade catches Yevgeni across the chest.

The knife falls from his throat, blood gouting in a crimson waterfall to the ground as Merthok strikes again. Yevgeni raises his power claw, but the ancient warrior is too quick for him, and a second blow severs his hand at the wrist. Merthok's blade rises and falls with measured butchery, until the heretic is nothing but a screaming, limbless torso. The armoured warriors press forward, drawn to the violence unfolding before their eyes. Lethe imagines the slaughter escalating, the warriors turning on each other in a cataclysm of whirring blades and glowing power fields, but no one moves, not even Ostrov.

'Enough.' The Death of Saints spits a gob of phlegm on the squirming Yevgeni's face. 'Take this worm and place him in the Dreadnought sarcophagus.'

Yevgeni's screams take on a fresh intensity as Merthok stoops and lifts him by the scalplock. 'No! Kill me! Kill me, you cowards!'

'And as for the rest of you...' The Death of Saints tilts his head upwards and utters a series of harsh syllables in an unfamiliar tongue that sets Lethe's skin crawling as though it were covered in maggots. There is something unclean about the sound, something that sullies the soul of speaker and listener alike.

And the reply is more terrible still.

Unfolding from the cliffside like a vast and malign bat, a fusion of daemonic flesh and blasphemous metalwork throws back its paired heads and shrieks. Its metal scales are the same oily blue as the Night Lords' armour, the teeth in its paired jaws a glittering chrome.

The Death of Saints raises his fist, and the beast takes to the air. Twin arcs of flame tear through the sky, so hot that Lethe's skin burns with pain a hundred feet below. Its wings are a canopy of purest night, covering the sky and any faint glow of the shrouded stars. It is malice given physical form, as abhorrent as it is magnificent, and it answers to her lord alone.

'Challenge me when you command the Heldrake.' High above him, the beast bellows its reply. 'Until then, know your place.'

XVIII

The Convent Sanctorum maintains an infirmarium befitting its status – a sprawling series of interconnected chambers in the west wing where the Sisters Hospitaller tend to their charges. Only their eyes are visible in the gap between their starched veils and the respirators that cover their lower faces as they check the newly arrived pilgrims for the stigmata of disease or corruption. They had been equally thorough in examining Aleyna on her own arrival. The Sister-chirurgeon assigned to her care had discharged her with strict instructions to rest and hydrate before returning to her duties – but she has no duties to which to attend.

The convent has been stirred to frenzy both by the arrival of the Abbess Sanctorum from Holy Terra and by news of the attacks. The prioress is engaged in matters of war, and Aleyna's attempt to seek out a cause to which to devote herself is met with hasty requests to return later once the work already underway is completed. In the end she returns to the infirmarium to pray at Perdita's bedside for a swift recovery, but when she draws back the curtain to the alcove where last she saw the Seraphim, everything has changed. Perdita and her medi-slab have been removed, replaced by a veiled Sister-chirurgeon tending to a

Sister seated with her back to the entrance, her bodyglove rolled down from her right shoulder to expose a full-thickness burn wound in a halo of scarlet inflammation.

'My apologies, Sister-chirurgeon.' Aleyna backs away. 'The Seraphim Sister who was here before, is she–'

The chirurgeon – a tall woman with a high-cheekboned face and cool-toned black skin beneath her veil – waves an irritable hand without turning. 'I left instructions that I was not to be disturbed. Take your question elsewhere. This is delicate work.'

'My apologies.' Aleyna turns to go. 'I did not mean to–'

'Stop.' It is not the Hospitaller, but the Sister to whom she is attending who speaks, the note of command in her voice enough to stop the chirurgeon's hands as well as Aleyna's feet. Aleyna looks up and finds herself staring into a pair of familiar dark green eyes.

'Abbess Sanctorum, forgive me, I–'

'I said, stop.' The abbess scowls at the chirurgeon. 'Not you, unless you intend for us to be here all night. Continue with your work. And you, Sister Aleyna' – she motions to Aleyna to move to the other side of the medi-slab so that they can converse without the need for the abbess to turn – 'we have matters to discuss.'

'Yes, Abbess Sanctorum.'

Even out of her armour with the bare flesh of her shoulder exposed, there is something formidable about Morvenn Vahl – not merely the cords of lean muscle clearly visible beneath her skin, or the way in which she endures the chirurgeon's probing fingers without flinching. There is an intensity to the young abbess that goes beyond normal limits, a sense of latent power waiting to uncoil. In her warsuit she had been a beacon of holy might, but out of it all that power is focused like light through a magnifying lens, burning all the brighter as a result.

'Tell me of what you faced at the cathedrum.'

Aleyna closes her eyes. The memory is still hazy, but the dread she felt returns all too clearly. The horror the creature had invoked had gone beyond the mere fear of her own destruction, as though its presence had weakened the veil that keeps the immaterium at bay. Her mouth is dry at the thought.

'It was a Heldrake. Not one of the true Neverborn, but a daemon engine, breathing fire–'

'Plenty of them breathe fire. Give me details,' the abbess says, as the Sister-chirurgeon sprays a foul-smelling counterseptic across the burn in her shoulder. Instantly the raw flesh sizzles and foams into a thick pinkish froth. The abbess' face twists in a brief grimace before her composure is restored, though her face seems a tone paler than before.

'Yes, abbess. It had two heads–'

'Both with flamers?'

'Yes–'

'Wingspan?'

Aleyna searches her memories. 'Eighty feet? Perhaps more.'

'But not less than that?'

'I do not think so.'

'Larger than those I have faced before, then.' The abbess closes her eyes, pressing her lips into a bloodless line as the six-inch-long hypo-needle attached to the chirurgeon's mechadendrite punches a neat circle of holes around the perimeter of the wound. 'I must congratulate you, Sister-chirurgeon. This hurts considerably more than the wound did when it was inflicted.'

'You were offered an anodyne embrocation for the pain, Abbess Sanctorum.' The chirurgeon seems entirely unconcerned by her abbess' reproach. 'If you have changed your mind–'

'Finish your work.' Abbess Vahl turns her attention back to Aleyna. 'How did you survive?'

Aleyna tries to find suitable words to describe the moment of her transcendence, but in the end it is the simplest that she chooses.

'The God-Emperor saved us.'

'The pilgrims say you were the conduit of His power.' Vahl's eyes narrow, an appraising look on the sharp planes of her face. 'Word has already been sent to the Ecclesiarchs seeking ratification of your miracle. You may yet be declared a saint-potentia. A fair price for a lost reliquary.'

'Two of the Sisters Retributor, they...' Aleyna runs her tongue over dry lips. 'That is to say, we thought they would stand a better chance of taking the relic to safety alone. Has there been word of them?'

'No. We must consider the reliquary lost for now.'

With a final hiss, Sister-Chirurgeon Véronique's mechadendrite dusts the wound in the abbess' shoulder with a cloud of white powder, sealing it in place with a clean linen dressing inscribed with the litanies of healing. The abbess rises to her feet and turns to the Hospitaller.

'My thanks. As always, your hands do the God-Emperor's work.'

The Hospitaller inclines her head. 'I am glad you have returned to Ophelia VII, Abbess Vahl.' Her mouth quirks in the ghost of a smile. 'But I shall pray to the God-Emperor that you do not return to my infirmarium too soon.'

'That is in His hands, not mine.' The abbess pulls her bodyglove back up over her freshly dressed shoulder, slips a cassock and surplice over her head and belts it loosely around her waist. She wears no veil over the short dark regrowth of hair on her scalp, but no one could mistake her for one of the common Sisters. In or out of armour, her every movement marks her out as a superlative athlete. 'And I must prepare for the next steps in this war.'

'I will ensure the Hospitallers are ready for when they are needed.'

Abbess Vahl gives a curt nod. 'They will certainly be needed. As are you, Sister Aleyna.'

Relief washes over Aleyna like cool water. No matter how onerous the duty the Abbess Sanctorum has for her, it can only be better than the weightless, purposeless limbo of the preceding hours. 'How may I serve?'

'You have faced the Heldrake before and survived.' Abbess Vahl's eyes are narrowed in appraisal, and Aleyna once again has the feeling she is being tested. 'The God-Emperor has made a weapon of you. One that I intend to put to good use.'

Morvenn stalks along the cloister towards the war-room with Sister Aleyna in her wake, and wishes she were back in her warsuit. The prioress has given her a solemn assurance that the Purgator Mirabilis will be returned to her once it has been cleansed, sanctified and its energies replenished for the coming battle, but the task of its repair seems to be considerably more involved than her own. There is no doubt that her shoulder feels much improved after the application of Sister-Chirurgeon Véronique's art, but the process has taken valuable time that she would sooner have spent in preparation for war.

Her thoughts are sharper now that the pain has receded and the counterseptics taken hold, but the problem of the Death of Saints remains insoluble. With the Heldrake under his command, he might be anywhere on Ophelia VII, the only mark of his passing a succession of burning shrines and desecrated temples. He is taking the initiative from her, forcing her to react instead of act, a role for which she finds herself desperately ill-suited.

God-Emperor, show me the face of the enemy that I may cleanse this world of his corruption.

But the God-Emperor has no answer for her, and perhaps there is good reason for that. It was her choice to leave Tancret's assault to attempt to recover the relic, and as a result the Death of Saints slipped away in darkness to continue his bloody work. No matter. She will find him soon enough. The war-room doors swing open at her approach, and she strides inside, heading straight for the table at the far end.

'Tell the others I am ready–'

Morvenn stops.

They have continued without her.

On the furthest side of the table, Castellan Tancret is standing haloed in light. He extends an expansive hand to motion Morvenn to the table, covered now with an ancient parchment map.

'Join us, please. Your Sisters and I have made progress in identifying the heretic's location.'

Morvenn walks to the table, banking down the heat of her anger. The matter is pressing, and there is no reason why they should not have continued to plan in her absence – but she had assumed her presence to be integral to the process. 'Celestian Zafiya, I am surprised that you allowed this council to restart without me.'

'Forgive me, blessed abbess. The fault is mine.' Her signing hands tell a different story: *Castellan Tancret would not wait.*

'These are discussions that affect us all. I would not presume to plan in your absence, castellan. Kindly extend me the same courtesy.'

'Time is pressing.' The castellan barely seems to have noticed her indignation, all his attention fixed on the task at hand. 'The longer we wait before slaying the Death of Saints, the more of this world he will destroy.'

His point is valid. If the continuation of the war council in her absence has brought them a step closer to the Death of Saints' destruction, then her pride is a small price to pay.

'And have you found his location?'

'Not yet.' On the other side of the table, Prioress Illuminata raises her head from the map. 'But more information has come to light. Augustus, replay the last animation.'

The servo-skull drifts into position in front of the globe. Its cogitators chirp, and then a series of explosions burst across the miniature planet in a seemingly random pattern.

'Augustus has managed to decipher a data-packet sent from the orbital defences,' Illuminata continues. 'During what we assume was the heretic's initial incursion, his strategy was to overwhelm their augurs with multiple possible targets. While the Mechanicus controlling the defences struggled to distinguish viable targets from decoys, the majority landed successfully, seeding the planet with hostiles.' Another explosion flashes in the illusory stratosphere, bright as daylight in the gloomy chamber. 'The heretics' strike cruiser was destroyed, but before its final engagement with the *Lux Dominus*, a series of orbital strikes obliterated both the defence net and the communications satellites covering one specific area.'

Illuminata signals to the servo-skull again, and a crosshatched pattern of green and black spreads across the globe like oil on the surface of water until it is covering an area to the mountainous west of the convent, easily a hundred miles across.

'Why would he be so selective?' Celestian Zafiya asks. 'From high orbit the Death of Saints could have destroyed Ophelia's entire vox-relay. Did he lack time to complete the task?'

'I do not think so.' Canoness Lucreziana is looking between the globe and the parchment map on the table, her finger tracing out contour lines along its surface. 'He has allowed messages to reach us from almost every location which has been attacked. His methods have been plain from the outset – to sow fear, and to keep us constantly one step behind him.'

'What lies in that area?' Morvenn cranes her neck to look at the map.

'The region is mountainous.' Lucreziana traces out the corresponding area with her index finger. 'It contains several ancient shrine-temples, built in the first days of the planetary settlement. The area is comparatively sparsely populated now.'

'Regardless,' Tancret rumbles, 'if the heretic has taken pains to hide it from our sight, we must lay all its secrets bare.'

'Agreed.' An idea is taking shape in Morvenn's mind, kindling like a candle-flame. 'Prioress, have your servo-skull show us the location of the Death of Saints' attacks.'

'Certainly, Abbess Sanctorum, though there is no pattern to suggest–'

'Exactly. There *is* no pattern.'

'The Heldrake–' Zafiya begins, but Morvenn shakes her head.

'It cannot transport an entire army. The Night Lords are taking a different route.' Morvenn returns her attention to the prioress. 'Map out the catacombs beneath the planet's surface onto the globe.'

Crimson lines spread across the floating world in a tracery of branching veins. The largest run the length of continents, the smallest forming spiderwebs of hair-thin lines between them. Three bright nexuses are visible on this side of the planet, the largest corresponding to the Convent Sanctorum, the second almost as bright beneath the Preceptory of Our Martyred Lady far to the east, and the third glimmering in the black field of the Night Lords' enforced augur-blindness.

'The shrine-temple at Caelestis,' Morvenn says. 'As you say, canoness, the area was settled in antiquity. The caverns beneath it communicate with every cathedrum, shrine and convent on Ophelia VII. He is using them to bypass our defences.'

Castellan Tancret draws himself up to his full height. 'We have the enemy's location. I will make my forces ready.'

Morvenn nods. 'Then we should consider our route of approach–'

'There is no need for that.'

His reply catches her off-guard. 'No need for what?'

'For further consideration. Or discussion.'

'There is *every* need.' Morvenn stabs a finger towards the slowly spinning globe. 'He has a *Heldrake*. Any attempt at assault over-land will be over before it begins.'

'My Thunderhawks will have no difficulty in engaging it.'

'And if they are not enough?' The war-room has fallen silent, all attention fixed on the rapid fire of words passing back and forth. 'He has the advantage of the high ground. Our approach will be obvious to him.'

'We are here to draw him out of the shadows, Abbess Sanctorum, not to hide in them ourselves.'

'We must find another route. He has used the catacombs to evade our defences. Why should we not do the same, and deny him the use of his greatest weapon in the process?'

'My brothers are sworn to uphold the honour of the God-Emperor.' The castellan's lip curls. 'And you would have us creep through the shadows like vermin.' He shakes his head. 'I have said this discussion is at an end, Abbess Sanctorum. I have considered your words. You need not repeat them.'

And realisation dawns. She has approached this discussion as one between the commanders of two allied forces. Tancret, it seems, sees things differently.

'Castellan Tancret.' Morvenn chooses her words with care. 'You and your brethren have been tireless in your defence of Ophelia VII. I am cognisant of the duty that you have shouldered without complaint. But the Adepta Sororitas are not yours to command. They are mine.'

Tancret turns, his broad shoulders blocking the light from the rose window, suddenly less a man and more a living weapon.

'That I do not dispute. But a war cannot be fought by committee. It requires a single voice of command, to be obeyed without question or hesitation.'

'And I take it you intend that voice to be yours?'

'I am a son of Dorn.' He offers no further explanation – but then, no more explanation is needed.

'Then as you say, castellan, this discussion is at an end.'

'I am glad that we agree. Your wisdom and humility do you credit. Sword Brother Balian, ensure that the abbess has all the information and assistance she requires in preparing her mission. I will send word when we are ready to begin our combined assault.'

'You have Thunderhawks. I have no such craft at my command. I want the heretic's head every bit as much as you do – but I will not march my Sisters into the dragon's mouth to take it.'

The castellan's jaw drops in surprise. 'You do not intend to join the assault.'

'Take your brethren by air if you will.' Morvenn meets the ice-blue gaze without flinching. 'I will lead my Sisters through the catacombs and strike from below.'

Tancret's face sets in hard lines of resolve. 'Then keep your oaths as best you can, Abbess Sanctorum, and I shall attend to mine. If the God-Emperor wills it, may we meet again over the corpse of the Death of Saints.'

Act III

The Book of Martyrs

XIX

Aleyna stands at the abbess' side and watches the Sanctorum Guard assemble in the vast stone vault beneath the convent. They are divided into two groups – those who will march beside the Abbess Sanctorum in her magnificent golden warsuit, and those who will remain under the command of Prioress Illuminata. Back-mounted braziers blaze like fiery beacons, while the timeworn effigies of former abbesses regard the warriors with dead-eyed judgement from atop their tombs. History would suggest that most of the sarcophagi are empty, the bones of the martyred dead scattered across the galaxy's warzones, but still the statues keep their solemn vigil in a line unbroken back to Alicia Dominica herself.

A cherub takes flight, parchment streamers trailing from its grip as it soars upwards through beams of coloured light. Though they are hundreds of feet below the ground, the walls are set with glassaic illuminations of the six matriarchs lit from behind by hidden lumen arrays. A vast wall-mounted pipe organ plays the first booming notes of the 'Orisons of War', and a beat later the Sisters join in glorious harmony.

'Be thou my armour, God-of-Terra.'

Aleyna lets the music wash over her, joining her voice to the harmony until the hymn draws to its close. The abbess slams down her visor and activates her laud-hailer.

'Sisters of the Adepta Sororitas!' The vast chamber falls still, silent but for the rebounding echoes of the abbess' vox-amplified words. 'I call upon you to keep your sacred oath. To follow me to war in defence of holy ground. Will you answer the call?'

The answer comes back in full-throated unison. 'Aye!'

'Then heed my words. A heretic has come to Ophelia VII. He has burned our shrines, stolen our relics, slain our Sisters. He thinks to make our world his own.' The echo takes the words and returns them carelessly superimposed. *Shrines. Relics. Sisters. World.* 'This cannot be allowed.' She slams the hilt of the Lance of Illumination into the stone floor. 'We march to war to teach him the error of his ways. To make him pay in blood for the wrongs he has done us. To cleanse this cardinal world of his foulness. Will you march with me?'

'Aye!'

'Will you fight with me!'

'Aye!'

'For the matriarchs, and the God-Emperor!'

'For the God-Emperor!'

With an echoing rumble that vibrates through the granite floor, the vast bronze doors that lead to the catacombs swing open. Trumpets blare out a fanfare, bright as a peal of bells, and the Battle Sisters who must remain part to allow their more fortunate Sisters through. Aleyna falls into step half a pace behind the Abbess Sanctorum, past solemnly bowed heads and hands clasped in the sign of the aquila, her pulse quickening at the thought of what is to come.

God-Emperor, make me worthy of their regard. Else grant me a swift death in your service.

* * *

The day that begins with speeches and trumpets soon settles into the steady march of armoured boots on stone. At first the catacombs are broad, with the same vaulted ceilings and cold granite walls of the tombs, but as Morvenn and her war-host pass beneath the palisade wall the roof lowers and the lumens dim, their amber glow flickering into life ahead of the column and dying to darkness once they have passed.

And then there are the explosives. Lining the tunnels on either side are arrays of fyceline charges, connected with skeins of silver wire – enough to reduce the Convent Sanctorum to rubble at a single word, should the need ever arise.

Her word.

Throne willing, that day will never come.

The two remaining Celestians of Morvenn's honour guard are at her right hand, with Sister Superior Kerem of the Bloody Rose and Sister Aleyna on her left. The war-host around them is different from the last time she marched at the head of the column, the ancient relics borne by Sisters with unfamiliar faces. Those she recognises look ten years older, deep lines of weariness and suffering etched around their eyes and mouths, while others have the faces of young adults, all eager excitement still untempered by war. Half have seen too little, the other half too much.

And then there is the enigma that is Sister Aleyna. Morvenn steals a sidelong glance at the younger Sister, marching in silence. She is not what Morvenn would expect of a Living Saint, even one so early on her journey of transfiguration. Where is the fervour, the holy ardour that should be burning in her eyes? The miracle has left Sister Aleyna more bewildered than transformed.

'What is it, your grace?' Aleyna says.

Morvenn realises how long she has been staring. 'Nothing.' She looks away. 'Merely considering the daemon engine. How you survived its attack at the cathedrum. I pray the God-Emperor sees fit to bless you in such a way again.'

Aleyna nods. 'I pray I am worthy.'

'He has made you an instrument of His divine will. There is no greater proof of worth than that.'

Aleyna looks at her feet, the praise seeming to deflate rather than inspire her. 'My thanks, blessed abbess.'

'Thank Him, not me.'

The first sign of the enemy comes less than a day's march from the brazen gates. They are moving through the deepest level of the catacombs still reliably traversable to avoid the Heldrake's attention when the cries come from above – human in pitch and volume but shrieking with maddening intensity.

'Cultists.' Kseniya projects a schematic of the catacombs above her wrist-mounted auspex, showing the position of their column and the ground above them. 'We are beneath the Sepulchre of the Six Holy Wounds.'

A gibbering shriek drifts down from overhead, and Morvenn's fists tighten on the Purgator's command batons. Lucreziana's voice comes sharply through her helmet-vox.

'Your orders, Abbess Sanctorum?'

'We continue. In silence.'

Lucreziana draws a sharp breath. 'They are desecrating the tombs of the virtuous dead.'

'I am all too aware of that.' Morvenn longs to give the order to advance, longs to cleanse the desecration of the tombs in blood, but she cannot, not while their objective lies ahead. 'We continue with the mission.'

'You would permit this?' Lucreziana's voice is tight.

'We cannot betray our position, not so early. Not even for our dead.'

But all Morvenn's hard-won reserve proves futile. Within a mile, further signs of desecration rear their heads. Unseen hands have daubed the walls with blasphemous sigils, the dusty piety of the air giving way to the smell of human sweat, waste and blood. Morvenn orders the column to advance until the sound of human voices is so loud it seems impossible that they are not already upon them – and then the tunnel turns sharply to the left, and the enemy shows their face at last.

The chamber at the end of the passageway might once have been a natural cavern, the vaulted roof a rough-hewn dome barely visible in the dim light cast by crude torches and smoking campfires. The walls are a honeycomb of alcoves that once held human remains, now sleeping spaces for the living stuffed with filthy blankets and scraps of rotting food – but the occupants are all too awake. They are different to those she faced in the assault on the cathedrum. Those were pallid wretches with crude melee weapons, but these have an unsettling appearance of uniformity, their faces concealed by bronze masks adorned with horns and spikes. Some are starting to show the stigmata of corruption, strange protrusions pushing their way through flesh like embryonic limbs.

Morvenn raises the Lance of Illumination. 'In the God-Emperor's name!' she shouts. 'Charge!'

'Death to the daughters of the False Emperor!' The cry echoes back from the cavern walls, and the cultists surge forward. Their leader is a hulking woman armed with an autopistol and a brutal-looking chain-knife, her mask surmounted by two spiralling horns, the marks of Chaos deeply etched into her flesh. Bolter fire fills the air, and the first of the charging enemy falls in a spray of blood, but momentum carries the second rank over their compatriots' ruined remains. Morvenn urges the warsuit onward, crushing the skulls and femurs of the ossuary's former inhabitants beneath its metal feet, but there is no time to lament their loss. The world flares blue as a bolt-shell slams into her energy field – and then she hits the enemy battleline, and the fight begins in earnest.

The Lance of Illumination blazes like a beacon, cutting brilliant lines through the air as she carves through the flesh of the first heretic. He falls, bisected from shoulder to hip, and she turns to the next, stabbing and slicing with balance and precision. The Lance's range is so great that it is impossible for the enemy to close enough to enter melee, and though the energy field deflects their bullets with ease, they press forward with no thought for self-preservation.

'*Ave Dominus Nox!*' The mindless chant echoes back from the walls.

A group of Celestians Sacresant are singing the Magnificat at her side, their power halberds slicing through flesh and armour in time with her own movements, and she joins her voice to theirs with fervent abandon.

'I am the spear that strikes in holy anger!'

A heretic with a hand flamer dies with his throat impaled on the tip of the Lance.

'I am the shield that turns all blows aside!'

Another falls, carved in half at the waist. Morvenn takes another step forward, and the Sisters close up behind her as a volley of autogun fire rattles down on them from above. Slugs clatter from the Sacresants' shields and vaporise harmlessly on the Purgator's energy field, but this development adds a new dimension to the battle. The cultists may be unafraid to die in their foul master's cause, but they are fighting with order and tactics in a way that their predecessors did not.

'I am the burning brand that lights the darkness!'

A frag grenade flies towards her. She deflects it on her shield and sends it back into the enemy ranks, where it detonates in a spray of bloody shrapnel. Gun smoke is filling the air, and though the cultists' ranks are thinning, the autoguns continue their ceaseless rattle. A woman in a half-breastplate takes a running leap at Morvenn, her momentum lifting her a full four feet from the ground, her knife drawn back to strike. A single shell from Fidelis obliterates her like a Candlemas firework.

'Ave Dominus Nox!'

The words are a desecration, an affront to the High Gothic language, which should be reserved for words of devotion, not praise for heretics and traitors. A volley of autogun slugs activate the Purgator's shields, and she returns fire with one of her newly replenished rockets, turning the wall and its alcoves instantly to smoke and rubble.

'Your masters care nothing for you!' Morvenn slams Fidelis' gunshield into a cultist too bold or foolish to keep his distance, and sends him flying, broken-necked, into the air. Another runs forward, their banner hung with flayed human skin topped with a skull still covered in half-rotten flesh, and Morvenn obliterates both cultist and banner with a single shot. 'They have deceived you!' Another dies on her spear. 'Sold your souls in service to false gods!'

Her furious assault has cleared space around the warsuit, and she uses the time to assess the battlefield. The cultists' ranks are thinning, but the battlelines have lost all cohesion, Adepta Sororitas and heretics locked in bloody hand-to-hand combat. Where is the cultists' champion? She searches the battlefield for the horned mask and sees her with a dozen of her followers, advancing on a pair of Battle Sisters of Our Martyred Lady who have become separated from their unit. Morvenn watches as one Godwyn-De'az bolter runs dry, then charges. She hits the back of the group like a Rhino at full throttle, scattering half-naked cultists in all directions.

'I am a champion of the true gods!' The woman's bronze mask is twisted in a mocking leer, the mouth-hole crafted to distort her voice into an inhuman bellow. She opens fire with her autopistol and closes at speed, slashing out with her chain-knife at the Purgator's heels. Morvenn evades the blow, but the heretic champion is inside her reach, darting back and forward in lightning-quick movements to grind the chain-knife against the back of the warsuit's left knee. The adamantine plating is robust, but behind it lies a vulnerable nest of cables and conduits. Morvenn stabs down with her lance, but the cultist darts back with a pit fighter's dexterity. The surviving heretics are gathering around her, fighting with the same snapping attacks as a pack of canids bringing down a wild grox, and for the first time she feels a flicker of fear. She is not afraid to die, but the thought of meeting death with her duty unfulfilled is enough to spur her into motion.

She spins the Purgator to the left and opens up a circle around herself with a spray of heavy bolter shells. A handful of heretics fall, and the rest are forced back, the leader amongst them. This time she does not hesitate, concentrating her advance on the woman in the leering mask, ignoring the few autopistol slugs that pierce her energy field to lodge in her armour.

'You are no champion! Your gods are false!'

The woman leaps back to avoid the lance, but her foot catches on an ancient skull and she falls backwards, the mask slipping from her face to clatter against the ground. A series of disciplined bolter shots tell Morvenn that her honour guard have joined her to deal with the rest of the cult, and she strides forward until she is towering over the leader.

One blow from the Lance knocks the autopistol to the ground, the second severs the woman's knife-hand at the elbow.

The Lance comes down a third and final time.

Morvenn takes no joy in the woman's death. A moment ago,

she would have hacked the head from the heretic's shoulders with holy joy singing in her heart, but as the battle around her ends, the fierce exultation dies with it. The battlefield that had seemed a glorious maelstrom of gunfire and glory becomes another charnel house littered with the dead and dying – and not all of the bleeding bodies belong to the enemy. Sister Véronique's Hospitallers are already tending to the wounded, dispensing care to those who can be saved and administering the God-Emperor's mercy to those who cannot. Morvenn's own mismatched honour guard is untouched, but one of Canoness Lucreziana's Celestians is amongst the most gravely wounded. Morvenn watches in silence as the canoness removes her helmet to exchange a few words with the dying woman, then ends her suffering with a bolt-round to the skull.

'See to the wounded, then make ready to press on.'

Kerem of the Bloody Rose points her bolt pistol to the far corner of the chamber, where a lanky youth in cultist's rags is creeping crabwise across the rubble towards an exit tunnel. Her shot blows his left knee apart, and he drops screaming to the ground. 'Shall I question him?'

'There is nothing we need from his kind.' What else could the cultist tell them? He was trying to escape. She must assume that others of his false creed have already done so, and the last of her hope that she might advance on the Death of Saints undetected fades.

'As you command.'

Kerem's second shot silences the cultist's screams. Morvenn tries to pray, but the words refuse to take shape. Instead, it is a curse that comes to her lips, bitter as gall, sharp as a penitent's lash.

All of these sins I lay at your feet, Kol Rakhul. Every holy bolt-shell fired. Every drop of blood spilt. Every Battle Sister slain.

And you will pay in blood for them all.

XX

Castellan Aymar Tancret knows the exact position of *Lacessit* without opening his eyes. The Thunderhawk engine's frequency maps reliably to their air speed – though the change is so subtle that only the enhanced hearing of the Adeptus Astartes could identify it – and his finely tuned inner ear detects even the slightest vertical and lateral movements. It has been so long since he became one of the brotherhood that he cannot remember what it was to be mortal, to be uncertain both in terms of position and velocity. Uncertainty is a luxury he is no longer allowed. In all things now, he must be absolute, for to be otherwise is to invite destruction. The brothers of the Adeptus Astartes must stand apart from the common herd, ready to give their all for the mass of humanity to which they can never now return.

If Abbess Vahl holds true to her word – and for all their differences, he is as sure as he can be that she will – the Sanctorum Guard should already be well on their way into the catacombs. His plan is direct to the point of simplicity: his Thunderhawks will deal with the Heldrake, leaving him and his ground troops to encircle the Night Lords force. If the Death of Saints is there then he will meet his death on the point of Tancret's greatsword, and if not, denying him his chosen base of operations will strike the heretic a blow from which he will not recover.

The Thunderhawk changes its bearing four degrees to the right and five aloft. By Tancret's calculations they will be entering the dead zone in a matter of seconds. His battle-brothers shift restlessly, tensing in their harnesses like beasts of war ready to be unleashed. A brassy fanfare peals from the Thunderhawk's vox-casters, and every head turns towards him, awaiting his words of inspiration.

He will not fail them. Not now, and not in the battle to come.

'Sons of Dorn! We ride to war, to drive the heretic Night Lords from this most sacred of cardinal worlds! These false Astartes once called themselves sons of the Master of Mankind. They were given the greatest of gifts, and they have thrown them back in the God-Emperor's face, spurned His every blessing, fallen from the loftiest height to the nadir of existence. They consort with daemonkind and the foulest of heretics. And in return, we will strike them down and drive them from the Imperium's beating heart forever!'

His brethren roar in chorus with the Thunderhawk's screaming engines as it strains to reach the zenith of its approach.

'Fix mag-locks.' The voice of Techmarine Tiberias comes from the pilot's throne. *'Opening rear hatch in five seconds.'*

Tiberias does not trouble himself to give the rest of the countdown. Tancret releases his harness, and mag-locks the soles of his boots to the deck as the rear hatch drops open and the *Lacessit* jerks to the right. A jolt of adrenaline shoots through Tancret's veins, his twin hearts accelerating in response to the sight of the Heldrake trailing black smoke behind them.

'Do you see, my brothers? We have found our enemy!'

High energy las-bolts streak from the Thunderhawk behind them as their own vessel continues its acceleration skyward. The Heldrake has vanished from sight, but Tancret is too experienced a tactician to imagine it is out of range. The vox-trumpets ring out again, sounding out the call to arms.

'Now let him taste our wrath!'

With gut-lurching abruptness, the Thunderhawk's engines cut out. The nose tips downwards, and within seconds they are hurtling from the sky at terminal velocity. The augmented joints of Tancret's power armour brace against the G-force so swiftly that he barely moves.

'Make ready!'

The open rear hatch is pointed at the sky, the shadow of the Thunderhawk behind flitting in and out of view as it follows them on their breakneck descent. Tancret calculates velocity and distance in his head. At these speeds the margin of error grows, but by his estimate they have ten seconds before the *Lacessit* will level off, seven before they jump–

'The God-Emperor is with you, my brothers,' Tiberias says. The angle of bank twists sharply and the Thunderhawk levels out, the grey granite beneath whizzing past mere yards from their undercarriage.

Four seconds to go.

Tancret deactivates the mag-locks on his boots, and strides to the back of the compartment.

Three.

The ground is so close he can almost touch it. Vivid green runes cross his heads-up display, the rapid calculations matching his own mental ones.

Two seconds to deployment.

One.

The Heldrake is above them, eclipsing the sun, casting the whole valley into shadow. Its wings are a hundred feet broad, its two long necks braced back, the mouths of its lizard-like heads open to reveal an unholy light blazing in the rear of its throats.

He has never seen a Heldrake so large, nor a two-headed horror such as this. Unnatural blue lightning arcs along the biomechanical wings, down the spikes that cover its spine and the thrashing barb of its tail – and then there is no time to look any more.

'Deploy!' Techmarine Tiberias voxes. *'God-Emperor speed you!'*

In two long strides, Tancret is over the threshold and falling towards the ground, first into the fray as is his sacred duty and his right. He hits the ground in a warrior's crouch, the impact sending fissures radiating out in the grey stone like the rays of a sun, and his brothers slam down beside him one after another. The Thunderhawk is already rising, vivid las-bolts from its heavy cannon hurtling towards the Heldrake as it flies. The beast screams defiance from one mouth while the other belches flame, but the Thunderhawk is too quick for it, powerful engines and agile thrusters keeping it always one step ahead. Another unit of battle-brothers thuds down fifty yards behind him, as *Dorn's Wrath*, his second Thunderhawk, joins the dogfight, vapour trails spiralling elegantly behind it.

'Let them hunt the beast,' Tancret says. 'And we shall hunt our own quarry.'

The tunnels close in as they leave the ruined ossuary, the roof so low that the Purgator's shoulder-mounted braziers leave twin trails of soot in its wake, so narrow that the column can march no wider than two abreast. Aleyna finds herself walking behind the abbess at Celestian Zafiya's side, Kseniya and Kerem immediately behind them.

These tunnels have fallen from use in recent years, but the painted murals that line the walls – depictions of the God-Emperor's victories over His foes, His ascension to the Golden Throne, the great battle for Holy Terra – have been spared by time, only to be desecrated by the heretics who have made these tunnels their home. Worse, the work has been done by hands with more than a little skill. The God-Emperor's eyes have been painted black, His noble features twisted into lines of cruelty and contempt, even the upturned faces of the faithful reworked to appear foolish and weak. It is as though the artist has held a cursed mirror to the original work and reproduced what they found there.

'This place has been made unholy.' Celestian Zafiya makes the aquila across her chest. 'When the Death of Saints has been brought low, it will be the work of many months to cleanse it again.'

'If it even *can* be cleansed.' Kseniya turns her attention back to the map on her auspex. 'Better for the tunnels to be filled in. Others can be made.'

'And who will do that?' Zafiya's signing hands are moving sharply, adding emphasis to her question in a way that her flat tone of voice does not. 'The penitentia are all but empty.'

'There are always sinners.' Kerem of the Bloody Rose shrugs. 'Or pilgrims ready to earn their place in the Emperor's favour through the sweat of their brow.'

Aleyna looks back at the murals, and a cold shiver runs down her back. The desecrated Emperor's ebon gaze seems to follow her, wicked and knowing. Even if it were hidden behind fresh paint, she thinks, the evil would shine through, corrupting whatever was painted on top of it. The walls would have to be stripped back to bare rock before the sin was expunged – and even that might not be enough.

Kseniya nudges the small of her back. 'Keep moving, Sister. The whole column is behind us.'

'Of course, Celestian.' Aleyna tears her eyes from the blasphemous image and picks up her pace. 'My apologies.'

'Best not to look at such things.' Of all the abbess' honour guard, Kseniya is closest to Aleyna's own age, though she carries herself with unattainable confidence and maturity despite her youth. 'We must move quickly.'

Abbess Vahl has picked up the pace, the golden warsuit drawing away from the front of the column. Aleyna changes her walk to an easy jog-trot, Kseniya keeping pace beside her, and then the whole column is moving forward at a full-paced force-march.

'I see light up ahead.' The abbess' voice comes sharply through the mission's vox-channel.

'That should not be.' Kseniya checks her schematic. 'We have miles ahead of us yet.'

'A wrong turning?' Zafiya asks.

Kseniya shakes her head. 'Impossible.'

'Then what–'

Cold light floods the tunnel as the Purgator Mirabilis strides into the open. Aleyna runs to catch up and steps into an alien landscape. It is as though a massive hand has reached down from the heavens and scooped out a fistful of the earth, leaving only this bleak and empty basin of grey stone and greyer skies.

'There should be an abbey here.' Kerem is looking around in disbelief. 'A mission of fifty Sisters under Palatine Imogene. I was here less than a month ago–'

'It seems there have been other visitors since.' Abbess Vahl's voice is flat.

Aleyna blinks, her helmet's visual sensors struggling to adapt to the sudden change in the light. The stone is blackened with soot and striped with talon-marks from where the daemon engine has toppled the abbey to rubble and gouged out its interior, leaving the roofless foundations beneath it to cradle the broken remains.

'Where do we go?' The abbess is already moving forward into the colourless landscape, the Sanctorum Guard fanning out in formation behind her. The ground shifts as Aleyna moves to follow them – she lurches sideways, bracing herself for a broken ankle or worse, but before she can hit the ground a steadying gauntlet closes around her arm.

'Careful,' Celestian Kseniya murmurs, then says in a louder voice, 'the tunnels should continue to the north.'

Aleyna scans the north face of their crater. Something moves behind the rubble, and she takes aim at a scuttling, spindle-limbed figure, its skin the mottled grey of a day-old corpse. 'What *is* that? Is it human?'

Kseniya slams a fresh magazine into her boltgun. 'Once, perhaps.'

'Accursed Chaos mutants.' The Abbess Sanctorum's voice is grim. More mutant cultists are creeping from the shadows, their bodies twisted and corrupted into grotesque abominations. Horns jut from bulging brows, limbs replaced seemingly at random by lashing tentacles or oversized claws, some still wearing the rags of penitent's robes, some with iron muzzles fused into their faces. One has a set of vestigial wings jutting from its shoulders, flapping furiously as it makes abortive leaps into the air. It turns its head to stare at Aleyna, unhinges its bearded jaw unnaturally wide, and shrieks.

'Stand fast!' Abbess Vahl raises her warsuit's heavy bolter as the horde runs forward, cutting the front rank down with a spray of shells. Aleyna raises her own bolter and fires in time with the Celestians, rupturing corrupted bodies with every shot. Chunks of liquefying meat spatter around her, but the host is undeterred, their bloodlust continuing no matter how many fall.

She fires again. The nearest cultist explodes into crimson pulp, just as a corpse-grey fist slashes across her vision, clutched tight around the grip of a gleaming silver dagger. She deflects the blade with the barrel of her boltgun, but the weight of the cultist's body bears her to the ground with enough force to drive the wind from her lungs. A mouth with too many teeth screams in her face, and a rusty knife stabs down inches from her eye-lenses, scoring the enamel from her helmet's cheek plate. Talons claw at her visor – she tries to raise her bolter, but the cultist is too close, the attack too frenzied to bring the weapon to bear. She grabs the mutant's throat with one gauntlet and shoves it away, but its right arm is so grotesquely elongated that even at her full reach it has no difficulty in continuing its assault. It is trying to tear off her helmet, she realises, as the hinge at the right side of her visor creaks and gives. In a moment it will come free, leaving her eyes naked and helpless against the flashing blade.

God-Emperor, surely you did not spare me only for this?

She raises her bolter, but with a scream of fury the cultist wrenches it from her grip and hurls it aside. Talons lock behind her visor and rip it free, and the stench of the cultist's breath hits her like a fist. She gags, her vision blurring as her mouth fills with the taste of sulphur and rot. Talons slash towards her eyes, the thunder of blood in her ears mixing with the inhuman shrieks and howls. A second heretic with an oversized claw in place of its right arm joins the assault, raking at her gorget and pauldrons, jostling its ally in its haste to crack open her armour and sink its teeth into the soft meat below. She raises her arm to protect her eyes and kicks upward with all her strength. The first mutant lurches back to strike the second in the chest, both sprawling backwards in a tangle of limbs. They hiss and claw at each other in redirected rage, and the distraction is all Aleyna needs.

She pulls her combat knife from her belt and lunges for the nearest cultist's throat. It writhes back at the last moment, and instead of piercing the hollow at the base of its neck, the tip of the knife lodges in the spongy flesh beneath its ragged beard. It opens its mouth to scream and a gout of blood the colour and consistency of an oil-slick geysers over her. She grips her knife tighter and drives it further into the thrashing head, tearing through muscle and flesh until it pierces the roof of the mouth and enters whatever is left of the brain beyond.

There is no time to recover, no time for anything but action. She rolls towards her bolter as the second scrabbles forward. She closes her hands around the grip – *God-Emperor be praised* – and rams the barrel into the bony chest.

'This is the reward of your sin!'

Aleyna pulls the trigger.

The hammer falls on an empty chamber.

The cultist's mouth opens in a mocking leer, the knife in its hand glinting as it brings it down towards her face quicker than she can react – and then a brilliant sweep of golden light takes its head from its shoulders. The knife clatters harmlessly from her gorget and falls to the ground. A vast golden figure stands over her, tearing the enemy apart with bolter fire, skewering and slicing with the blazing spear – and her heart sings with the glory and the rightness of it all. This is the God-Emperor's blessing as much as the miracle at the cathedrum, and she is part of His holy work. The mutants are falling like wheat before the scythe in the face of the Sisters' disciplined fire, and she throws herself into what must surely be the battle's final moments with renewed fervour.

'For the God-Emperor!' She slams another magazine into her bolter. 'For the Convent Sanctorum!' A mutant lurches from the rock face, blood spurting from a severed tentacle, and the Purgator Mirabilis stamps it flat beneath its golden foot. 'And for the Abbess Sanctorum!'

XXI

Bolter smoke clears from the air, and the mist of battle clears from Morvenn's thoughts. The rubble beneath her feet is slick with blood, the air reeking of fyceline. A lone cultist scrambles for the safety of the shadows, and she spares a final shell to blast it to oblivion. The battle is over for now.

She takes a moment to check her armour and weapons. Superficial scratches aside, the Purgator Mirabilis is intact, its energy field still functioning at three-quarters power and her missiles unused – but Fidelis' ammunition reserves are cause for concern. Half of her shells are already spent with greater than half their journey ahead of them. If the intensity of the fighting continues she will have few left by the time they reach Caelestis – an unwelcome development, considering the scale of the threat they face.

Celestian Kseniya has moved away from the rest of the unit, studying her auspex intently, close beside the broken remains of a giant marble face. The devastation is appalling. The abbey has not merely been destroyed – the Heldrake has obliterated it entirely, incinerating wood, turning stone to rubble, gouging out the foundations at their roots as if it might otherwise grow back.

The Heldrake must be destroyed.

'Which way?' Morvenn directs the warsuit towards Kseniya, scanning the rock for any aperture that might signify the continuation of the tunnel.

The Celestian shakes her head. 'Ill news, Abbess Sanctorum.' She points to a heap of broken stone, indistinguishable from the rubble to either side. 'The catacombs to the north have collapsed.'

'Can we tunnel through?'

'I do not believe so.' Kseniya taps the screen of her auspex with an air of finality, and the green schematic vanishes. 'There is a full forty feet of rock before the tunnel opens up again, and no guarantee that it is not blocked beyond.'

'Very well. It seems Castellan Tancret had the right of it after all.' The words taste bitter. 'We will continue overland towards Caelestis, and trust that his Thunderhawks will keep the Heldrake's attention from us.'

Ascending the side of the crater is the worst part. The Sisters move in squads, the Paragons and the Sisters Retributor covering the skies as the others scramble up the sides, before joining them on the crater's edge. In places the slope is shallow – in others, steep mounds of treacherous rubble slip away beneath grasping hands. More than once Morvenn wonders if her warsuit will manage the ascent at all, until at last, with servo-motors straining, she hauls herself over the edge to survey the shattered land around her.

She thinks of the war-room, and the countless tiny red dots scattered across the spinning globe. The ground beneath her feet is one of them, acres of devastation rendered down to a single point of light. The abbey – or rather its absence – is at the centre of a blasted expanse of ruined manufactoria and burned-out hab-blocks.

'There is another option.' Sister Superior Kerem's voice comes through on the squad's private channel. It is strange how quickly she has become one of them, Morvenn thinks, slipping into the place left empty by Fionnula and Ignatia's deaths. Once the battle is over the forthright Sister Superior will most likely return to her own Order, but for now her presence is a welcome one. 'Saint Mina's Hope lies between us and Caelestis by a direct overland route. We can re-enter the catacombs there and continue the rest of our journey beneath the ground.'

'The last I heard of Saint Mina's Hope was when its canoness declined to attend my council of war.'

Kerem meets her gaze without flinching. 'If the canoness had cause to neglect one duty, it will have been in service to a higher one.' She waves a hand across the scorched earth around them. 'I would urge you to consider it, Abbess Sanctorum. The longer we remain on the surface, the greater the risk from above grows.'

'I will consider it. Celestian Kseniya, consult the schematics. Find me the nearest location from which we might re-enter the catacombs.'

There may be places on Ophelia VII's surface where such a vast expanse of sky can be seen, but this should not be one of them. Morvenn keeps a wary eye turned upward as she prowls through the ruins of what was once a munitions manufactorum, now a desolate expanse of broken rockcrete and twisted metal struts. The centre is a featureless void, but as they move through to the far side the remains beneath their feet tell the story of the building's destruction. Melted metal and crystalflex lie in gleaming pools, the last remains of the manufactorum's roof and windows rendered liquid by intense heat. It would not have been long before that heat reached the promethium stores and the stockpiled ammunition awaiting transport, ending the existence of the manufactorum and its workers in a moment of appalling conflagration.

Bodies litter the ground; those nearest the epicentre are little more than ash and fragments of broken bone, but those further out retain more bodily cohesion. Skeletons with a coating of charred flesh lie curled in the foetal position, their muscles contracted by intense heat, while those lying by the outer wall are well enough preserved to be recognised by someone who knew them. A woman lies with her face towards an empty archway, so close that another six feet of crawling would have taken her to freedom. Her hair is a scorched frizz on her head, her one visible eye cooked to grey leather.

'I have a route,' Kseniya voxes. 'The preceptory remains our best option for re-entering the catacombs.'

'Are there no others?'

'Not within thirty miles.'

'And how far to Mina's Hope?'

'Less than half a day.' Even Kseniya is sounding weary now, for all her efforts to hide it. 'If we are fortunate.'

A wasteland of shattered marble stretches in front of them, the last of the day's light fading fast. Far ahead, where the flattened wasteland rises once more into towers, spires and domes, a vivid crimson flash breaks the gloom, followed a moment later by the thunder of the same explosion.

'Sisters of Battle! We make for the Preceptory of Saint Mina's Hope!'

Half a day. Half a day until food, a brief rest and resupply – and perhaps reinforcements.

'If we are to strike, the time is now,' Ostrov Skull-taker says.

Lethe presses herself further into the stone alcove carved into the cliff face, hoping desperately that she has avoided his notice and that of his beak-helmed companion. Their new encampment is alive with activity as they make their preparations for the battle to come, but Lethe finds herself curiously set apart from it all. She occupies a unique space in the Death of Saints' retinue – beneath the notice of the warriors under his command, but spared the duties of the other slaves. Her lord's favour has transfigured her; she has been reborn to a new life in darkness, one where she must move ghost-like through the shadows, for fear of monstrous demigods who would snuff out her existence without a moment's hesitation.

And her lord has set her to watch them.

She fears them all, but she reserves her hate for Ostrov. If the rumours that pass between the mortals of the cult are true, the demigods were once sons of the Corpse-Emperor, wise enough to see the lies behind their creation and turn their backs on their father. It is hard to imagine that any hand shaped Ostrov's lumpen flesh.

'He does not understand,' Ostrov says. 'How could he? He is not Nostraman.'

The word is unfamiliar to Lethe, but it sends a shudder down her spine nonetheless. The other warrior inclines his helmeted head.

'Many of our brothers hail from other worlds, and are our brothers all the same.'

Ostrov snorts. 'But they do not try to lead. With a strong leader the convent would be in flames by now. Instead we are waiting – and for what? He has lost his courage. He is not fit to rule over us.'

'Merthok would say otherwise.'

'Merthok is an idiot!' Ostrov slams his fist into the palm of his hand. 'His mind is addled by time, his body rotting in his armour. It is his fault that Rakhul is one of us, a privilege he should never have been granted. But one fool to stand at his side is nothing for us to fear.'

The beak-helmed warrior shakes his head. 'There are others.'

'And once Rakhul is dead they will fall in line. The sons of Konrad Curze – the true sons – understand the rewards of following a worthy leader.'

'A leader like you, you mean.'

Ostrov preens, a grotesque smile spreading across his scarred face. 'You would follow me, Dmitrev, would you not?' The unsaid threat in the statement is obvious. 'There are others who share my views. Many others, waiting only to be given the word to strike.'

Lethe creeps closer, listening intently.

'He is strong.'

'Is he?' Ostrov shrugs his massive shoulders. 'I see no strength in him. The Dark Gods have granted me gifts already, and promised more, while he acknowledges no greater power than himself.' He tilts his head to the side, revealing the eight-pointed star gouged into the flesh of his neck above the collarbone. 'Do you not question why the Ruinous Powers have turned their faces from us? Why they allow the Corpse-Emperor's daughters to defy us? Rakhul pays lip service to our gods but seeks only to glorify himself. I would bring glory to Chaos Undivided, and we all would reap the rewards.'

Dmitrev shakes his head. 'Now is not the time–'

Ostrov's spiked gauntlet lashes out and locks around Dmitrev's neck, squeezing the soft seal between gorget and jawline in his talons.

'It is past time.' Ostrov shakes the other warrior back and forth as though the bulk of his body and armour weigh nothing at all. 'Do not defy me.'

A panicked rasp hisses from the beaked helmet's vox-grille.

'Now do you understand, Dmitrev? Our foes gather. We must strike while his eye is on them, not us.'

Lethe holds her breath, willing Dmitrev to strike back, to

show his contempt for Ostrov and his loyalty to their lord, but he merely bows his head.

'It is as you say. We deserve a better leader.'

Ostrov smiles. 'And you shall have one.'

Her whole body shaking, Lethe creeps away through the rubble. If Ostrov is telling the truth – if there are others who would see her lord overthrown – then she must warn him before the daggers descend. A tight knot of fear is tangling in her guts – fear for her Death of Saints, but also for herself. If he is slain, her borrowed protection will vanish like water into sand, and she will end her days dismembered by a chainglaive or skewered on the talons of a power claw. She searches for the silhouette of his armour rack, but there is no sign of him amidst the furious preparations for war. She must find him. She must–

A cracked mosaic tile snaps beneath her foot. She stops, her breath caught high in her throat, wondering if now is the moment to throw caution to the wind and run, but there is no movement from behind her, no sound of weapons roaring into life. She lets out a shaky breath of relief, and then the air is torn in half by the whistle of an incoming missile, the firelight from below turning its silver surface to fire. It strikes the rock face with a thunderclap, sending a plume of smoke and dust into the air and hurling her to the ground. The roar of the heretics' anger fills the air, the ground shaking with the thunderous tread of a hundred heavy sabatons, and she rises shakily to her knees, and then her feet.

'You have heard what you should not,' Ostrov Skull-taker says, his voice close to her ear, and her limbs lock in terror. How did he move with such speed and silence?

'My lord – I heard nothing–'

'His favour will not save you now.' Ostrov ignores her helpless protest. Bile floods her mouth. 'But do not fear. He will follow you into death soon enough.'

Lethe casts a desperate eye around her, but her lord is nowhere to be seen. There is no other help for her, no one from whom she can claim protection.

'You will make a poor sacrifice... but I shall offer you nonetheless.'

A second missile strikes, filling the air with fire and dust. The power claw glows through the smoke like a fistful of captive lightning. In the distance a trumpet bellows out the call to war. A third missile streaks through the sky towards them – and Lethe runs.

XXII

Night falls on the Preceptory of Saint Mina's Hope, but darkness does not come. Even from the abandoned chapel four miles away where Morvenn and the Sanctorum Guard have paused before their final approach, the preceptory is clearly visible, the jagged battlements atop its single tower stark black against the crimson glow of the sky.

'At least it is still standing,' Aleyna says softly.

'For now.' Morvenn adjusts her magnoculars, but the few images she can obtain by focusing down the gaps between buildings are blurred and indistinct. Dark figures flit back and forwards through the firelight, some human-sized, others immeasurably larger while a ragged banner surmounted by a rotting human head stirs in the wind of their passing. 'Kseniya. Can you reach them on the vox?'

'Nothing, Abbess Sanctorum.'

'They are under siege,' Sister Superior Kerem says. She has removed her helmet, and her keen amber eyes are narrowed as she gazes towards the distant tower. Her chainsword is across her lap, her hands working automatically to clean scraps of hair and skin from between its metal teeth. 'The whole preceptory is surrounded.'

'It seems Canoness Elsvieta's absence was justified after all,' Morvenn says, more to herself than her Sisters.

'Yes, but surrounded by whom?' Zafiya looks up from her prayer, her pale eyes deeply shadowed. Sister-Chirurgeon Véronique and her fellow Hospitallers are moving through the ranks, checking the dressings of the wounded and offering sacred wafers soaked in invigorating unguents. Such philtres will keep the Sisters on their feet for a few hours more, but there will be a price to pay when the battle is done. There always is.

'The enemy.' Kerem pours sacred machine oil onto her cleansing-cloth, and rubs it into the chainsword's teeth until they are bright and gleaming. 'Does it matter what form they take?'

Canoness Lucreziana is walking towards them, her augmetic eye glowing with brilliant crimson light. 'It matters a great deal in terms of how we engage them.'

'Explain.'

'We have no intelligence of our enemy. We do not know their strengths or the resources they command. With aerial surveillance or contact within the walls we might form a meaningful strategy, but without them we are reduced to undertaking a simple assault. A force capable of keeping Canoness Elsvieta and her Sisters within the walls poses a formidable threat outside it.'

'The closer we come to Caelestis, the greater the danger of the Heldrake becomes.' Morvenn shakes her head. 'Prepare for battle.'

'As you command.' Lucreziana folds her gauntlets across her chest, the left snow-white, the right the colour of clotted blood. 'And I will pray that the God-Emperor grants you guidance.'

Prayer is more than words, Morvenn thinks. Prayer is action. Prayer is sacrifice and pain. And there will be no shortage of any of those in the hours to come.

* * *

As Canoness Lucreziana predicted, there is no subtlety to the assault on the preceptory. Morvenn splits her force into two roughly equal groups, the Sisters of the Valorous Heart with the canoness and those of Our Martyred Lady with Morvenn, with units of the other Orders distributed between the two to shore up areas of deficiency. They move quickly, converging on the preceptory from either side, but the enemy raises the alarm before they are in position to attack and surges forward to meet the Sisters' advance with a counter-assault of their own.

The first wave are humans, and they break like water on the Sisters' armoured prow. Morvenn has chosen her line of attack with care, and the long, straight gap between two Administratum buildings provides an excellent field of fire. The Sisters fire in disciplined volleys, sending row after row of sprinting cultists to the ground in tatters. Those that come within melee range find their lives swiftly curtailed on the halberds and maces of the Celestians Sacresant, or on the tip of the Lance of Illumination itself. The flagstones are coated in gore, blood running freely around the Gothic script embossed on their surface, as though to provide emphasis to the litanies written there.

Abhor the heretic.

It is fitting those words should be haloed in blood.

Another band of cultists runs into the melee, and is cut down in turn. This wasteful series of charges might be nothing more than the enemy's last-ditch attempt to hold them back, leaving only a feeble core of resistance that will shatter in the midst of the Sisters' flanking approach.

Or perhaps there is something else.

A throaty roar bellows from the body of the enemy camp, and Morvenn strides forward, her spear-hand itching with the desire to strike. A shadow the size of the Purgator Mirabilis crosses her path in the space between the two high walls, and she runs forward with exultant joy, all fear and doubt swept aside. Here is a worthy challenge at last. Here is where her duty lies.

'For the God-Emperor!'

The ground shakes as the Traitor Dreadnought turns to face her. It is a blasphemy given physical form, a false and mocking corruption of what was once holy and pure. Crimson light glows from the helmet set beneath the hulking shoulders, one arm ending in a three-pronged siege claw, the other in a siege cannon.

'Grav-weapons!' she voxes, and then the air ripples as a blast of force hurtles towards her. The few cultists still on their feet explode like blood-bags, torn apart by the wave of concussive force surging through the confined space. The Purgator's energy field flares brilliant gold as the grav-weapon's discharge reaches her. Even with the warsuit fully braced, the force propels her backwards, her armoured feet gouging two thick trenches in the ground. With a scream of motors, she urges the Purgator forward, but the Dreadnought is already closing to melee range, its siege claw opening like a set of infernal jaws as it sends a searing melta-blast into her energy field. Before it can fire again she hurls herself forward, the Lance raised over her head like a javelin, and thrusts it directly into the vox-grille below the red-eyed faceplate.

The Dreadnought screams like the damned. Thick black blood wells from around the spear-point – she pushes it deeper and is rewarded by the sensation of her weapon piercing another layer of armour. The arm with the grav-cannon thrashes wildly and she deflects it with Fidelis' gunshield before returning a volley of her own. The same foul liquid oozes from the joint where the gun-arm meets the shoulder, and the corrupted Dreadnought tears itself free of the spear-point and lurches back.

'So perish all who turn from the God-Emperor's light!'

A group of human cultists surge forward to cover the Dreadnought's retreat, but they are no threat. Bolter fire rips through the air around her as she lunges forward, her powerblade cutting through meat and bone as though it were water, carving a route to her enemy. She glimpses the rusting blue armour, the shoulders chased with bronze – and grinds to a halt. The Dreadnought's attention is not on her. It is tearing through its own cultists with a vigour and enthusiasm that exceeds even her own. Bodies press around her, and she kicks the warsuit's legs out to drive them back, rewarded by the haptic pleasure of snapping bone. The Dreadnought has its three-pronged claw around the head of an emaciated man in rags, then with a grinding of gears the claw turns a full three-hundred-and-sixty-degree rotation, ripping the man's head from his shoulders in a spray of blood.

'What is it doing?' Zafiya voxes, her voice tight with apprehension.

The black liquid that serves the monster for blood is flowing in reverse, running back behind the ceramite carapace, the shattered vox-grille re-forming – no, not re-forming, the dread machine is *healing*. It seizes another luckless cultist in its claw and thrusts her directly into the path of its grav-cannon, and she ruptures like overripe fruit.

'It draws strength from their deaths.' Morvenn's mouth floods with acid, and she lunges forward again as it seizes another cultist and cuts him in half at the waist. The man falls in two parts, still screaming in disbelief at the sight of his own severed legs. 'Celestians Sacresant – to me! The rest of you – slay the cultists with all haste!'

The air comes alive with weapons fire. The dull thunder of the bolters echoes from the tall buildings to either side, while flames belch in broad torrents from the heavy weapons of the Sisters Retributor. Ten Celestians Sacresant sprint to flank her, nine with ten-foot-long power halberds, their Superior with a gleaming lance that is her own in miniature. They are fast-moving despite their heavy armour and full-body shields, cutting a clear path through the dead and dying cultists towards the Dreadnought.

'We must be quick! We cannot allow it the chance to heal again!'

The Sacresants advance in formation, the blades of their halberds threshing the air. Morvenn lets them engage its front and rotates to take it in the flank, but the monstrosity seems to have no facing direction, its limbs lashing out wherever they can cause most damage.

A rising hum tells her that the grav-cannon is ready to fire again, and she slams it upwards with the haft of the lance in time for a rippling wave of force to slam into the wall to her left. Stone and plex-glass shatter as the force punches them inward, and she redoubles her assault, firing missiles and shells directly at its centre mass. It staggers back, bright metal craters appearing in the enamel of its armour, the siege claw opening to disgorge another searing blast from its meltagun. The black enamel of the Sacresant Superior's armour blisters like charring flesh, and she falls in silence, her spear clattering to the ground at her side. A booming laugh echoes from the Dreadnought's vox-grille.

'All hail to the Lords of Night!'

There is nothing human in that voice, and nothing sane. The Dreadnought was made to allow a chosen brother of the Legiones Astartes to fight on after his flesh had failed him – and for it to be put to such blasphemous use is something that cannot be tolerated.

'Damn you and your Night Lords!' She plunges the Lance into the join where the dome of the helmet meets the shoulder, and shoves downward. A gush of foul-smelling gas hisses instantly out, the reek of a corpse left rotting for a week in high summer.

She works the Lance deeper, and the Dreadnought recoils, its lashing siege claw smashing a Celestian Sacresant into the wall to her right. She lands badly, one leg bent under her and her helmet knocked askew, and the Dreadnought aims its melta.

'I will feast on your deaths,' it growls, the sound like the grinding of mismatched cogs.

'Press it back!' Morvenn roars. 'No quarter! Back to the warp with you, abomination!' She smashes the melta aside and lunges forward as the claw snaps out again – not for her, but for the Sacresant at her side, tearing through pauldron and chestplate to expose a line of wet red meat beneath. The Sacresant gasps in agony, and Morvenn can feel the numinous connection forming between the wound and the Dreadnought's glowing eye-lenses, sapping the fallen Sister's life force.

'Abbess – I beg you, let my death be at your hands, not his…'

It would be the work of a moment to bring the spear round and take the Sacresant's head from her shoulders – clean, instant and painless, but unthinkable. Her own death is a price she has been ready to pay since first she swore her vows, but this is different.

'You will not die today, my Sister. Véronique! See to the wounded!'

'All shall perish!' the Dreadnought rasps. 'Your souls will sustain me through the night!'

'Not this night.' Morvenn spins the Lance in her hand and brings the tip smashing through the Dreadnought's glowing eye-lenses.

The siege claw convulses shut, the grav-cannon discharging a final burst of power that smashes a granite pillar into dust, and then the strength goes out of one of the huge metal legs and it crashes down on one knee.

'Nor any night.' She adjusts her grip on the Lance and drives it further down, and slick black liquid gushes up from the wound, filling the air with the rancid stench of a freshly opened grave. The siege claw fires its melta in a broad arc, searching, perhaps for enemies or allies from which to draw healing power, but the Sisters are clear and the cultists already dead.

'No,' it grates. 'No, not now–'

'Now.'

Morvenn twists the Lance through a hundred and eighty degrees, the blade shearing through the soft flesh beneath the Dreadnought's carapace. The second leg buckles, and she kicks it to the ground, tugging the Lance free in a spray of ichor. The rounded helmet comes with it, and the face beneath is the stuff of nightmares – rotting flesh fused with cables and metalwork, the lips stretched back in an everlasting rictus, the eyes rotted to empty sockets.

She plunges the Lance through the rotting face and holds it there while the flesh sizzles and blackens, until the grating howls fall silent and the mechanical limbs cease their flailing.

Feet thunder towards her. She looks up, expecting to see Canoness Lucreziana and her Sisters converging on their position, but it is another wave of cultists, driven forward by the warped and misshapen Heretic Astartes behind them.

'Sisters!' She raises her hand. 'Give fire!'

Another torrent of bolter and flame rips the front rank apart, and Morvenn moves out of the alleyway onto open ground. The clearing is packed with bodies – cultists, Heretic Astartes, the armoured figures of Lucreziana's half of the mission making their bloody way towards them – and there is something else pressing at the edge of her consciousness, something that in the moment she cannot quite comprehend.

Singing.

From the rear of the enemy lines, a choral melody is rising, one she recognises.

'Emperor of all, hear thy faithful call...'

Light floods from the preceptory as its heavy wooden drawbridge falls. Metal grinds on metal as the portcullis rises.

'As our song we raise unto thee in praise...'

Torchlight glints on blood-red armour, on bolters and chainswords, on halberds and spears.

'For the God-Emperor!' a woman's voice booms, and the Sisters of the Bloody Rose charge out to join the battle for Saint Mina's Hope.

'No mercy! No respite! Bathe your blade in the blood of your foe!'

Castellan Tancret roars, and his brethren answer the call, their voices mingling in the air with the trumpets' brilliant fanfare. The battle-drums thunder as Tancret and his Sword Brethren run towards their foe. Missiles trace brilliant arcs through the sky as the Devastator squads unleash another coruscating volley overhead, and Tancret runs harder, as though by effort of will alone he can match his speed to theirs.

Runes flash across his helmet's display as a missile finds its target, obliterating a rock face carved with ancient ruins and crushing a cluster of heretic cultists beneath. The approach is the most dangerous part of the battle, through narrow bottlenecks beneath vaulted archways of stone and steel. Already he can hear the sounds of the Traitor Space Marines readying themselves for the attack, and a fierce and furious joy floods through him. Somewhere overhead the Thunderhawks are locked in combat with the Heldrake, but they are so far above the clouds that even his augmetic hearing can no longer make out the sound of their engines.

His Sword Brethren match his pace and the cadence of his step as though they were a single being. The bottleneck widens beneath a broad metal arch, and they surge forward into a battlefield already wreathed in flame, the vast stone décor of the shrine-temple towering upward to his right, the rocky ground sloping away to nothing on his left. His Chaplain is at his side, crozius drawn back to strike and his amplified voice bellowing out the psalms of remorseless persecution, the Crusader squads with pyreblasters and chainswords close on his heels, Terminators and Devastators bringing up the rear. He raises his power sword in his right hand and points his auto-flamer with his left as the first of the Heretic Astartes charge into view.

'Give no quarter! Spare none, in the God-Emperor's name!'

His own distorted reflection charges forward to meet him. The armour is midnight-blue instead of black, the pauldrons surmounted with spikes and embossed with the accursed symbol of the Ruinous Powers, but the heretic moves with the same grace and speed as Tancret's loyal brethren. These Heretic Astartes are the shame of every loyal Space Marine, a living reminder of the price to be paid should their faith and vigilance ever fail.

'Brother!' the heretic shouts. Tancret unleashes a torrent of flame that bathes the blue-and-bronze armour in heat and light. 'Will you not join me?'

Tancret's power sword lashes out, catching on the Traitor Space Marine's chainsword and sending a vivid burst of sparks into the air.

'Leave your False Emperor! Abandon the faith that keeps you in chains!'

Shells spray from the heretic's bolt pistol. Tancret dodges aside and fires his auto-flamer, bathing the heretic in heat and light, a bright, cleansing fury driving him forward.

'Master of Mankind! Grant me your divine wrath!'

The chainsword whines towards him. Tancret steps inside its arc and punches it to the side with the hilt of his broadsword, then cuts a deep gouge across the heretic's plackart. The air fills with the sizzle of searing meat.

'Where is the Death of Saints?' Tancret shoves the blade deeper, enjoying the look of panic crossing the distorted face. 'Tell me, and I may grant you a swift death.'

'Come closer, brother, and I will tell you everything.' The mouth opens, revealing rows of pointed teeth and a forked tongue. 'The secrets that you know in your hearts to be true. Your God-Emperor is a lie. You serve a rotting corpse–'

Tancret slams the crosspiece of his blade into the heretic's lying mouth. Blood sprays from shattered teeth and torn gums, but the Traitor Astartes' smile only widens. The tattered lips draw back in a lascivious smile, and Tancret shoves the heretic away in disgust. One cut with the broadsword's gleaming energy blade severs the Traitor Space Marine's legs at the knee – a second takes the right arm, spraying blood and machine oil. The Chaos Space Marine falls backwards like an upturned borewyrm.

'Filth! The Death of Saints will kill you, and when you are gone he will remake this world in his image!'

'No.' Tancret buries his blade in the heretic's chest. 'He will not.'

The enemy is falling back. Tancret can feel the tide of battle as it turns, the cultists falling and their infernal masters in full retreat. He searches the jagged silhouettes of spiked helms and armour racks for sight of the Death of Saints, but the heretic warlord is not to be found. A Traitor Space Marine – bolder than his comrades, or merely slower to retreat – charges towards him, and Tancret carves his power sword through the haft of the oncoming chainaxe and severs it in two, following up with a devastating strike to the skull, the shoulder, the right arm upraised in defence.

'Where is he? Where is your false lord?' He grabs the heretic by the throat and lifts him upright, but the distorted head falls back, slack-jawed. Tancret hurls the corpse away in disgust. His Sword Brethren are at his side, stepping over their own slain foes, heading towards the retreating heretics as they flee for the shrine-temple and the catacombs beyond – and the vast figure surmounted by its armour rack, standing in the cavern's mouth.

'I have sight of the enemy!' Tancret breaks into a run. 'Sons of Dorn! Advance!'

It seems the heretic hears him despite the battle's roar. The winged helmet turns, and for a fleeting second his gaze meets Tancret's – and then he is gone into the darkness.

No matter. Tancret has the scent of him now, and his blood is up.

He raises his sword. 'Upon my oath, the Death of Saints will die today!'

XXIII

From her place with the Abbess Sanctorum's retinue on the battlements of Saint Mina's Hope, Aleyna takes a long, deep breath that tastes of incense and promethium vapour, and looks out on the devastation below. The shrine is ancient even by the standards of Ophelia VII, and not one she has visited before, its buttressed walls of red granite tipped with polished adamantine spears, a vast statue of Saint Mina gazing sternly across the avenue of approach.

'Abbess Sanctorum. Your arrival is timely, and most welcome.' Canoness Elsvieta of the Order of the Bloody Rose is haloed in light as she strides along the parapet towards them. Black robes billow around her crimson armour, the heart-shaped metal ruff rising from her shoulders casting the reflected glow of the brazier in her right hand onto her face in ripples of silver and gold. She stands a full head higher than Aleyna, so tall that the top of her mitre is level with the bottom of the abbess' helm. She hands her Condemnor boltgun to the Celestian at her side and makes the aquila. 'The God-Emperor has answered our prayers. You have my thanks.'

'No thanks are required.' The Abbess Sanctorum removes her helm, her face glistening with effort, her short hair sculpted into miniature peaks by sweat. 'The fact that the preceptory stands is reward enough.'

Canoness Lucreziana extends her bloody gauntlet and clasps it around Elsvieta's, a smile on her gaunt face. 'I am glad to see you, Sister. When we lost communications, I feared the worst.'

'While I breathe, I will not let Mina's Hope fall.' Elsvieta gestures to the open drawbridge and the light beyond. 'How fares the convent?'

'Well enough for now.'

Elsvieta returns her attention to the Abbess Sanctorum. 'I regret I can offer you little by way of hospitality. We have food and water despite their attempts to contaminate the well, but our ammunition is all but spent.'

The Sisters of the Bloody Rose fan out across the battleground, slitting the throats of those cultists who still possess the spark of life and attending to their own fallen Sisters. There is a weariness to the way they move that attests to the trials they have endured – privation, desperation and a resignation that stops only a fraction short of despair. There has been victory today, but for the Bloody Rose it has been a pyrrhic one.

'Our primary concern was keeping the hellforged leviathan' – Canoness Elsvieta spits at her feet – 'from turning its full attention to our walls. It seemed content enough to wait as we expended our resources. Without resupply the battle would have been over within days. As it stands it will be the work of weeks to cleanse the rest of the heretics from the area – though it will proceed far quicker with your assistance.'

'We are not here to relieve you,' the Abbess Sanctorum says.

Elsvieta raises an eyebrow. 'No?'

'No. Saint Mina's Hope falls on our route to Caelestis. We must re-enter the catacombs and continue our journey to strike at the Death of Saints.' The Abbess Sanctorum pauses. 'Will you and your Sisters join me?'

Silence falls. Aleyna can feel the tension between the abbess and the pair of canonesses, as though they were held at the points of a triangle by invisible sinews.

'Is that your order, Abbess Sanctorum?'

'Why do you ask that?'

'Because I have sworn a holy oath to defend Saint Mina's Hope and the relics within it until my last breath. Until a few hours ago I believed that day had come. Now I am asked to abandon that which I was ready to die to defend.'

'Unless the Death of Saints is slain, all of Ophelia VII will fall. What will become of your relics then?'

'Better I should die protecting them than abandon them to desecration.'

The Abbess Sanctorum shakes her head. 'A wasteful sacrifice serves no one.'

'My life is the God-Emperor's, to give and take as He chooses. We of the Bloody Rose do not fear death in His service–'

'While the Argent Shroud know better than to seek it out.'

'And yet you have taken the Sanctorum Guard when the convent needs it most. If the enemy attacks now, it will fall!'

'Which is why we must strike at him now!'

Canoness Lucreziana raises a hand. 'Abbess Sanctorum, canoness – for us to fight serves only the enemy.'

Elsvieta takes a deep breath. 'Abbess Sanctorum, forgive my rudeness. It has been some days since I slept, and I am ashamed of my words.'

'I would rather hear them than not.'

'Then *I* would speak with you,' Canoness Lucreziana says softly. 'I have been troubled since we left the Convent Sanctorum. I have not spoken out of respect for your rank, but that is a sin that weighs heavy on my heart.'

Abbess Vahl is watching her carefully. 'Speak your mind. I am not afraid to hear it.'

'Very well. Would you prefer we speak in private?'

'Time is short. Say your piece.'

'Your record speaks for itself, Abbess Sanctorum. You are an excellent combatant and exemplary Celestian, but you have not yet learned the skills required to command in a warzone. At every turn you throw yourself into the fray, heedless of consequence. In your haste to engage the enemy you have risked yourself and the Sisters under your command, offended the sons of Dorn oathsworn to defend this world, and left the Convent Sanctorum undefended. These are the sins of inexperience, but they are also the sins of pride. And if they are apparent to me, they will also be apparent to our enemy.'

The tension is back in the air again. The servo-motors of the great warsuit whine as the abbess shifts her position.

'And what would you have me do?'

'Let the Black Templars attend to their duty. If they succeed, the war is over. If they fail, we can use the time to prepare the Convent Sanctorum's defences.'

'You would have us retreat, after all that we have sacrificed?'

'We should never have left.' Lucreziana shakes her head. 'I should have spoken before. That sin is mine to bear.'

A light in the distant sky catches Aleyna's attention, growing like an approaching comet, shifting and resolving into three lights, not one. Lines of autocannon fire paint a tracery of crimson through the night, then a vivid plume of flame silhouettes the distinctive outline of a Thunderhawk gunship and the vast, two-headed shape of the Heldrake. A second gunship hurtles towards it, weaving and diving in an intricate and deadly dance.

'Abbess Sanctorum, canoness...' Aleyna places a hand on the warsuit's skirt in the desperate attempt to catch her commander's attention, but when she looks up she sees that the abbess has already turned her face to the sky. 'God-Emperor protect,' she whispers.

Gravity drags at Techmarine Tiberias as he pushes the Thunderhawk gunship *Lacessit* to speeds that would have killed any normal mortal. Auto-injectors in his power armour flood his system with inotropes and vasopressors to counteract the acceleration's relentless pull, but his body has become an afterthought. He and *Lacessit* are one, and like the cross-and-cog emblazoned on his armour, they are greater together than the sum of their parts.

The Heldrake comes into his sights. He launches the first of his Hellstrike missiles, and the daemon engine darts aside with unnatural speed so that the missile passes harmlessly above it to detonate in empty space. The movement brings it into reach of *Lacessit*'s heavy bolters, and Tiberias delivers a line of fire along its flank, sending the Heldrake shrieking skyward in retreat.

'A worthy blow, my brother!' The voice of Techmarine Sibellian of *Dorn's Wrath* booms through his vox, followed a split second later by a vivid burst of las-fire that paints the Heldrake's underbelly an eerie green.

'As is yours!'

Runes scroll across the display of his augmetic eye, marking the ever-changing trajectories, velocity and coordinates of each of the three combatants. *Dorn's Wrath* peels off in a strafing run along the Heldrake's left flank, and Tiberias mirrors the movement along the right. The manoeuvre has the desired effect: one of the beast's heads tracks *Wrath*, while the other belches blistering flame around *Lacessit*'s armoured hull, but the competing movements are enough to halt the Heldrake's relentless forward momentum long enough for another Hellstrike missile to strike it at the base of its tail.

'A palpable hit!'

The Heldrake's scream of outrage howls through the Thunderhawk's vox, overloading the speakers in a shriek of feedback. Tiberias' augmented ears dampen the signal before it can reach his cogitators, but *Lacessit*'s systems are sluggish to respond, as though stunned by the discharge of sonic energy. The Heldrake streaks across the reinforced armaglass screen in front of him, smoke billowing from the stump of its barbed tail. He punches a line of holes through its lateral armour plating with his lascannons before diving to the side. One head belches a cloud of flame towards him, but the beast is already turning away, gaining altitude with furious beats of its enormous wings.

Directly towards *Dorn's Wrath*.

'Brother! It comes for you!'

'Let it come. We will see who commands the skies when this day is out.'

Tiberias urges *Lacessit*'s engines to their maximal capacity, the G-force pressing him into the pilot's chair like a crushing hand, but even at full speed the Heldrake is pulling away. He fills the space between them with brilliant beams of las-fire, but the beast barely notices, all of its attention fixed on *Dorn's Wrath* as it soars heavenward. It is *separating* them, he realises, just as a huge blast of energy gushes from the Heldrake's paired mouths. His sensor runes flash red at the intense heat even at his current distance, *Dorn's Wrath* nothing but a blackening silhouette at the heart of the flames.

'Brother! Do you read me?'

The vox-channel crackles. *'Engines ablaze. Initiating countermeasures–'*

'Eject! Before–'

Dorn's Wrath explodes. The shockwave radiates out from the dying craft and slams into *Lacessit*. The warning runes beat a crimson tattoo across Tiberias' vision, and he searches the skies in vain for any sign of his brother as the wreckage falls to earth. The Heldrake is closing in at speed, and he fights to bring his Thunderhawk around, both sets of twin-linked heavy bolters opening up in a last-ditch attempt to slow its dreadful advance. Wings spread wide, heads belching flame that turns from orange to crimson to a deep and unnatural purple, the daemon engine fills his viewscreen with wings and talons outstretched. It slams into the Thunderhawk, and for the first time Tiberias feels his control over the craft slip. *Lacessit* lurches backwards – he fires the wing-mounted heavy bolters again only to realise that the guns have already been torn free. The weight of the Heldrake is shoving him down, forcing him from the sky, and he diverts all of the Thunderhawk's power to its engines in a desperate upward thrust without success, then reaches for the activation lever for his ejector seat. Sibellian left his escape a moment too late. Tiberias has no intention of making the same mistake.

A vast talon stabs through the canopy above his head, and he releases the ejector lever a heartbeat before the mechanism would have propelled him directly onto it. The daemon engine is squatting above him, ripping at the Thunderhawk's armour plating with talons and teeth. Tiberias draws his sidearm and fires upward as the canopy tears free, the bolt pistol blasting a crater in the armour-plated neck as the snapping head forces itself inside and bathes him in a wash of blazing heat.

His brothers, he thinks, as the temperature inside his helmet rises. What will become of his brothers? Without *Lacessit* to keep the Heldrake's attention from the ground assault, they are in mortal peril. Too late, he sets the engines to overload, but the reactor is already dying, pierced and torn by monstrous claws.

'God-Emperor, grant me your strength!'

Lacessit lurches downward as the Heldrake casts it aside. This cannot be his death, Tiberias thinks in disbelief. He is a son of Dorn, a scion of the God-Emperor. This is not how his service ends. Blinded and deafened along with his craft, he fights to regain control, slowing the Thunderhawk's reeling flight in one final attempt to bring it safely to earth.

With another second at his disposal, he might have succeeded.

Aleyna holds her breath while the blazing Thunderhawk falls, a trail of thick grey smoke marking its passage through the darkness. Surely it will recover, surely it will right itself – the God-Emperor would not allow otherwise – but her prayers go unanswered. She tries not to think about the craft's final moments, of the conflagration spreading through the compartments, of the pilot tethered by duty, faithful unto death.

'It is over.' The Abbess Sanctorum closes her eyes – praying, perhaps, for the souls of the dead – then opens them again. 'Canoness, I have heard your words. We must continue. Celestians, inform the Sisters Superior to ready their squads for travel within the hour. With the loss of the Thunderhawks the threat the Heldrake poses must be countered with all haste. Canoness Lucreziana, kindly convey the same information to the Valorous Heart.'

Sister Superior Kerem moves for the first time since the conversation began, dropping to one knee at the foot of the Purgator Mirabilis. 'My abbess. I must ask you for a boon.'

'Ask.'

Aleyna's heart sinks. She already knows what Kerem's request will be.

'I beg you to allow me to stay in Saint Mina's Hope. It has been a great honour to serve at your side, but for now my place is with my Order.'

The abbess holds her in her gaze for a long time, then nods. 'I would have none at my side who do not consider their true place to be there. You have served with courage, Sister Superior, and you have my thanks for that.' She turns away. 'Canoness Elsvieta. Have the route to the catacombs opened in preparation for our departure. We have taken enough of your time.'

The catacombs beneath Caelestis reek of death. Even before the Night Lords' arrival they were long-deserted passageways, the murals and mosaics thickly ingrained with the dust of centuries. Signs of their restoration are everywhere, in the labourers' tools, the broken servitors, the rotting bodies of the workers themselves. If their work had been completed then the shrine-chapel and its catacombs might yet have been restored to their former splendour, but the Death of Saints has redecorated them in blood.

But there will be time to think of such things later. Castellan Tancret is at the head of the Black Templars' advance, striding through a morass of cultists like the Emperor's Champion himself. Ragged zealots throw themselves in his way with desperate abandon, heedless of the mighty blade that slashes through flesh and severs limbs with every blow. They throng around him, force of numbers alone sending weapons glancing off his armour and catching in his surcoat, but their deaths achieve nothing. There is something admirable in their dedication, almost enviable. Only those with darkness in their souls could serve such an unworthy master, but their loyalty itself would have been laudable, if only they had chosen to spill their lifeblood as eagerly in a righteous cause.

'Rakhul! Your slaves are dying for your sake! Do you lack even their courage?' He cuffs the next heretic to the side and strides past, ignoring the feeble blows that patter against his armour. Let his Sword Brethren deal with this scum. They are no threat to him, no worthy opponent. The tunnel ahead widens, and he pushes against the tide of squirming flesh as light plays on the familiar silhouette of the Death of Saints' armour rack, tantalisingly beyond his reach.

'Sons of Dorn! Forward!'

A trumpet sounds, and Tancret feels his battle-brothers' energy rise. Righteous fury drives him onward as the passageway opens up into a huge subterranean cathedrum carved of white marble. A shadow flickers across his vision, and his body is in motion before his head has even turned, his mono-edged net erupting from the modified launcher attached to his left gauntlet with explosive force. It catches his assailant – a swooping Raptor in blue and bronze – around the ankles, sending him careering off balance into the rock face. Tancret dispatches him with an overhand stab that pierces his chestplate and ruptures the corrupted flesh beneath.

He glances up, searching for the Raptor's companions, and beholds a sight sent by the God-Emperor Himself. The walls of the cathedrum are filthy, the pillars covered in creeping mould, but where the brazier-light reaches it, the roof is still decorated with the figures of the God-Emperor and His divine sons. It is as though Rogal Dorn himself is gazing down upon him, willing his scion to greatness in his name.

'Heretic!' he bellows, as the Death of Saints retreats once more towards the shadows. 'Face your death!' He is so close now that to reach his target would be a few seconds' sprint, were it not for the cultists – joined now by Heretic Astartes – blocking his way.

The air pressure surges, registered instantly by the vestibular system of his Lyman's ear, and a second later an explosion rips through the tunnels from behind, the force of the blast concentrated and magnified by the confined space. A wave of hot air smashes into his back like a mailed fist as secondary explosions burst through the catacombs, shredding meat and armour, smashing bones and incinerating flesh in a violent conflagration.

'The tunnels are collapsing!' a battle-brother shouts from behind him. Tancret looks up to see the face of Rogal Dorn descending towards him on a Rhino-sized piece of white marble, and the roof of the cathedrum falls upon him like the God-Emperor's judgement.

XXIV

The ancient tunnels north of Saint Mina's Hope are widening again as they approach Caelestis, but these are not the elegant marble catacombs of the Convent Sanctorum, nor the defaced passageways left behind them to the south. These tunnels are deep beneath the high ground, their walls rough-hewn stone, the ground covered in a stinking, ankle-deep soup of water and algae. Side passages lead to what might once have been crypts and ossuaries, but those laid to rest here have long since turned to dust.

Sister Aleyna is at Morvenn's side, wearing her usual serene expression, to all appearances a paragon of serenity and grace. What had she hoped to gain by bringing the young Sister? Morvenn wonders. A last line of defence against the Heldrake? If so, she has erred yet again. The God-Emperor's miracles are not to be compelled. Perhaps the senior Sisters of the Orders perceive her insistence on Aleyna's presence as an attempt to shore up her own authority through reflected glory – a thought that twists her gut uncomfortably. But when she searches her heart, the only grain of truth is something simpler – that the young saint-potentia has been touched by the divine in a way that Morvenn herself never has, and that the chance of witnessing such a miracle – even if she is not its source – would be proof enough of the God-Emperor's favour.

'Was I wrong?' Morvenn asks the question before she has fully considered its ramifications. Aleyna looks up, her brow furrowed.

'Forgive me, Abbess Sanctorum. I do not understand–'

'Was I wrong to act as I did?' She tilts her head over her shoulder, to where Canoness Lucreziana and the Order of the Valorous Heart are marching in silence. 'Speak plainly. I would hear your truth.'

The young Sister's lips purse, her eyes narrowing in thought. 'I cannot answer that,' she says at last. 'That is your burden to bear, not mine.'

Morvenn snorts. The answer is neither a sycophant's agreement nor the vicious condemnation she was half-expecting. 'Very diplomatic.'

Aleyna looks down at her marching feet. 'My apologies.'

'There is no need for those.' Morvenn feels a flicker of frustration. 'As you say. Command is a burden. One I wonder if I am fit to bear.' The act of saying the words seems to break a dam in her, the mere acknowledgement of her deepest fear bringing a tide of bitterness to the surface. 'There were many other Sisters – canonesses and prioresses, the greatest warriors of our Orders – ready to fill Abbess Sabrina's shoes. And yet the High Lords of Terra chose me. I thought it a great honour at first. Now I wonder if what they sought was one they could control, one who would weaken, not strengthen the Adepta Sororitas.'

'I do not think anyone could look at you and see weakness.'

'Nor did I at first.' The passageway turns to the left, with the beginnings of a near-imperceptible upward incline. 'But there is truth in what Canoness Lucreziana says. I was an exemplary Celestian, a living weapon of the God-Emperor. A Celestian needs only know the nature of her enemy and how best to slay them. And now this…' She waves a hand, taking in the catacombs, the mission at her heels, the whole expanse of Ophelia VII. 'I am called upon to know the enemy's weaknesses and my own, and to make decisions that determine the fates of worlds.'

'We do not choose the burdens the God-Emperor places upon our shoulders.' The young Sister flashes her the briefest of smiles, and Morvenn realises that Aleyna is not merely speaking of the difficulties of command. 'He sees strength in us that we do not see in ourselves. We must have faith that all is part of His great plan. No matter how unworthy we may feel.'

'You – unworthy?' Morvenn half-laughs. 'A saint-potentia, a conduit for miracles? There are Sisters who would carve the eyes from their head for such a gift.'

'And I am grateful. I pray only for the God-Emperor's guidance as to what I must do next.'

'Then that we have in common.'

An earthquake shakes the world around them, splashing brackish water up the walls and sending rock-dust falling from the ceiling. Morvenn tries the short-range vox, but there is only the same distant wailing that has come through it since entering the silent zone at Saint Mina's Hope. Another shudder passes through the earth, a distant afterquake of an explosion above and ahead of them. Muffled rhythmic thuds follow – falling rock, or the fire of a heavy bolter. This close to Caelestis, that can only mean one thing.

'God-Emperor, guide us both in what is to come.'

The shockwave alone of the falling debris would have killed a normal man, but Castellan Tancret has left that existence far behind him. If he has been unconscious then it has only been for the merest of moments, but there is a sluggishness to his thoughts, a fog at the edges of his mind that speaks of head trauma, or perhaps simply his bio-augmented systems conserving their energy in response to major trauma. Rocks are pressed close around him, crushing in from all sides as though he were in the grip of a monstrous hand, but as he flexes his shoulders the rubble gives way. He braces against it, unfolds his body upwards and a clamorous torrent of rubble shifts around him. That single movement has brought him a full six feet closer to the surface, close enough that his helmet's sensors can make out moving shapes on the ground above.

'Brothers, to arms!'

He tries his vox-system, but there is no reply. Instead, he turns his energies to clawing up through the last few feet of shattered marble and broken stone, and rises to see the hellscape around him. The air is thick with dust and smoke, the marble cathedrum in ruins with a hole large enough for a drop pod gaping in the domed roof. Before the explosion the enemy had been composed of a handful of Heretic Astartes in a sea of cultists, but the proportions have reversed. Now, the vast majority of the figures stalking through the smoke are larger than human, horns and spikes protruding from the dark metal of their armour, the red flicker of flamers and the blue glow of plasma casting the fog in an unearthly light.

'My brothers! Rally on me! Stand ready to engage the foe!'

Battle-brothers in scarred and dusty armour converge on his position, some tearing themselves free of the rubble that has half-buried them, others pulling themselves through the narrow gaps that are all that remain of the entryway, now entirely blocked. A pair of Raptors take flight from high on the broken dome, descending as their earthbound fellows advance. Do they feel the same electric charge running through them? Tancret wonders. The same anticipation of the battle to come, that sense of being caught at the pinch of the hourglass, the moment where the time before changes to the time after, caught in the inexorable, ever-moving now.

Adrenaline and endorphins flood his system, driving back pain and exhaustion. The blood is singing in his veins, the light through his helmet visor bright and clear, his hearing sharpened to supernatural acuity. The enemy are closing fast – forty yards turn to thirty, then twenty. At fifteen one of the cultists breaks and turns, and a Traitor Space Marine with a pair of vast curling horns on his night-blue helmet lashes his arm out level with the fleeing woman's throat. She hits the armoured gauntlet at speed, rebounds with her head hanging at an impossible angle then crumples to the ground. The heretic brings his boot down on her skull, and after that, there are no more acts of defiance. But the cultists are wrong – the wrath of the Black Templars is a thousand times more terrible than any harm their infernal masters could inflict upon them.

Ten yards. The heretics open fire, and the air becomes a maelstrom of shells and shrapnel. Tancret's augmented physiology kicks itself up another notch, and the world around him slows, the aches in his bones and muscles fading until they are nothing more than a nagging reminder in his hindbrain, the shells like drifting petals that he could reach up and pluck from the air with an idle hand. He pushes himself forward, drawing a pace ahead of the nearest Sword Brother, the clarion call of the trumpets a blessed canticle that sings of holy war in all its glory...

And like a rolling tide, the sons of Dorn crash into the heretics' ranks. The back of Tancret's left fist takes the first cultist in the face, lifts him bodily from the ground and smashes him into the heretic beside him. Bones snap as Tancret storms forward into the gap in the ranks, longsword flashing – another falls, and a fourth, as the entire left flank of the enemy line is torn to shreds in a thunder of heavy bolter fire. He allows himself a moment of satisfaction before his attention is drawn upwards to the crumbling dome overhead. Something is pulling itself through – a vast fusion of flesh and machine, bale-fire glowing from within the segmented plates of its armour as its massive taloned limbs tear through the crumbling stone. The cry goes up from his brothers – 'Heldrake!' – as they fill the air with a volley of fire.

He spares a single thought to mourn his Thunderhawks, and the beast descends.

The world has turned to death and devastation as Lethe stumbles blindly through the catacombs. So far as she can tell, Ostrov is no longer following her, but at each twist and turn of the passageway she finds his jagged silhouette in every shadowy alcove. The battle above her is raging, panic pushing her onwards like a physical force. All that she knows is that she cannot turn, cannot return to her liberator no matter how much she owes him. Ostrov has marked her as a threat, and he and those loyal to him will obliterate her the moment she comes in sight. And even if she could make her way to her lord, what good would it do? He may have changed her life forever, but to him she can only be a momentary diversion. Her word is nothing compared to Ostrov's, or any one of those terrible warriors. She has trespassed amongst gods, and from that there is no returning.

Lights flicker ahead of her. Memory takes her back to the mines, and then further back than that. At first, instead of Ostrov it is Overseer Yulius who is waiting in the shadows to close the muzzle around her face again, and then she is running in terror through the burning hab-block, her father's grip so tight around her wrist that all of her blood feels trapped in her fingers. The tread of heavy feet is all around her, the sound of women's voices barking commands, the appalling smell of incense and burning skin.

She presses herself tightly into a shallow alcove and turns

her face into the shadows. The column of the Adepta Sororitas passes mere inches from her, Sister after Sister following the great golden warrior in the lead, and she holds her breath until her lungs are burning and the rushing of blood in her ears so loud that it seems impossible they have not heard it. She dares to open her eyes a fraction and sees firelight glinting on silver armour. Terror buckles her at the knees. The Sisters have come to finish what they began, to put an end to her sinful and miserable life with fire and the sword as they so nearly did all those years ago.

A trumpet sounds a fanfare, and the Sisters increase their pace. Lethe wraps her arms tighter around herself, closes her eyes and tries to remember her father's face. Instead, it is the Death of Saints in all his cruel majesty that she sees.

And when she opens her eyes, the Sisters have passed, and she is alone again.

Perhaps on some long-forgotten Terran battlefield, Morvenn thinks, enemy commanders would meet to discuss terms of engagement. Hands would be shaken, words exchanged as a mark of respect between equals. But there is no place for civility on the battlefields of the present time. In a galaxy at war, there is only bitter hatred. There will be no mercy and no quarter, the only outcome ahead of her victory or death.

By the time they reach the battlefield – a vast, ruined subterranean cathedrum – the sound of combat is deafening. Their tunnel opens onto a high gallery overlooking the battlefield below, filled already with smoke and slaughter. The Heldrake has landed and is tearing through the ranks of the Black Templars with talons and teeth, the figures packed so tightly that it is almost impossible to make out any single figure.

'Battle Sisters, forward! Relieve the sons of Dorn!'

With the vox-channel full of unearthly shrieking, the Purgator's laud-hailers are the only means she has of issuing orders on the battlefield. Her area of influence will be limited, but from her vantage point on the ledge she has a view of the carnage that will be lost the moment she steps below.

'Squad Aurora! Raptors descending!' She issues the warning as a group of heretics descends towards the left flank, and watches with satisfaction as the Sisters Dominion discharge their meltas upwards. One heretic falls and the rest reverse their trajectory, but she cannot stop to enjoy the sight. Her Sisters need her to be their eyes and ears. Perhaps that is the truth of command after all – always to witness glory, but never to take part in it.

'Any Sisters unengaged, calculate your ranges – fire on the daemon engine!'

A deafening volley of heavy bolter fire fills the air. The Heldrake recoils, hissing steam as it scrambles for higher ground. The Black Templars concentrate their fire, raising bright explosions on its metallic carapace as it falls back out of bolter range, shells exploding uselessly in the air before they can find their mark. A battleline of Bladeguard Veterans and Celestians Sacresant is forming in the front rank, their shields locked together to deflect the oncoming blaze that must surely follow – and there behind the daemon engine is a huge figure in blue and bronze, his armour rack adorned with skulls and helms.

Sabbat-pattern helms.

Morvenn scans the battlefield again. Even her reserves are engaged now, fighting shoulder to shoulder with the sons of Dorn, and in minutes they will all be out of range of her laud-hailer. Tancret and his Sword Brethren are leading the advance, pushing forward through the melee towards the Death of Saints.

She knows what she must do. What Abbess Sabrina would do, or Canoness Lucreziana, were she in a position to command instead of in the fray below. She should seek a position from which she can survey the battlefield and communicate her orders to her Sisters, keep her eyes on the ebb and flow of battle, identify threats as they emerge.

But she is not her predecessor.

'You three. With me.' She is running before Aleyna and the Celestians have a chance to reply, the Purgator's huge feet slamming divots in the crumbling rock.

The Death of Saints has made war on her world.

His death is hers by right.

XXV

Aleyna sprints after the Abbess Sanctorum as she runs along the crumbling ledge above the battlefield. Below them the battle has become a series of loosely interconnected skirmishes, figures moving from fight to fight as though in the steps of an intricate dance. The daemon engine is carving a bloody path through the Sisters and brothers below, and with her eye on the melee she misses her step and almost falls. She rights herself and runs on, her breath rasping in her throat as she strives to match the abbess' punishing pace. She should keep her eyes on her feet, on the path ahead, but the heads on the armour rack draw her gaze with magnetic force.

Light catches on a spill of pale hair. Hair she last saw as the Death of Saints dragged Saint Hestia down to earth and skewered her on his claw. No trace remains of the Living Saint's beauty. Her long golden hair is matted with blood, her once bright eyes sunken in their sockets, her skin already blossoming with decay. Anger and nausea rise in her chest, the blasphemy almost too much to bear. The first scream tears itself from her throat without shape or form – a pure howl of distilled horror and outrage. But by the second, she has recovered enough of herself to spit out her hatred in words.

'Heretic!' Aleyna's furious sprint brings her almost level with the abbess, running until they are within a pistol-shot's distance of the castellan and his bodyguard, a mere bolter's range from the arch-heretic.

'Murderer!'

She thinks of Hestia, of the look of incredulity on her face as the heretic dragged her to earth, the casual cruelty in his eyes as he skewered her on his claws as lightly as the biologis might mount an interesting specimen on a study-loom. Palatine Sujata's head is gone – she is glad of that, at least – but in its place is another trophy, bleached bone chased in silver filigree.

The relic of Saint Athenasia.

'Thief!'

Does the last word attract his attention? The bat-winged helmet turns, but it might just as easily be to regard the castellan, a level below and closing the distance with inexorable speed. She cannot allow him to face the Death of Saints alone. Here at last is her chance – to recover what was lost, to expunge the soul-deep stain of its loss with her death or the enemy's.

'Forward!' the castellan bellows, and the abbess echoes the command.

The sound stops the arch-heretic at last. He raises his axe, lightning flickering down the blade, red eye-lenses glaring as his bodyguard spread out around him – then stops. The Chaos Space Marine to his left pulls a bloody chain-knife from the flank of the Death of Saints before plunging it home again and letting go. The arch-heretic reacts instantly, carving his axe into the traitor's midriff and sending him staggering to the ground. The Heldrake throws back its heads, and screams.

Feedback pierces Aleyna's eardrum like a burning six-inch needle, echoing through her vox into her brain. Hands shaking, she wrenches the vox-bead from her ear and the appalling noise fades. The pain lingers, darkness dancing at the edge of her vision, threatening to drag her down with it into eternal night.

God-Emperor, protect me from this sorcery.

'Aleyna!' The abbess' voice cuts through the fog in her thoughts. 'Charge!'

Morvenn sprints towards the Death of Saints, and her thoughts run red with blood. The Night Lord has desecrated the ancient relic of her Order. He is standing with his lightning claw sparking and axe raised as he meets the Black Templars' charge. Tancret's greatsword burns like a beacon, though his vestments are filthy with dust and his armour is scratched and battered. His right pauldron has been torn free, blood oozing sluggishly from an open wound in his shoulder, but he fights on with unmitigated ferocity. His honour guard move to engage the arch-heretic's companions, and she runs past them to close with their master. The Death of Saints takes a step back, perhaps aware that the odds against him have changed from even to two to one against.

'Well met, Abbess Sanctorum!' There is a clear note of approval in the castellan's voice. She discharges Fidelis at the heretic's centre mass, but he moves aside so elegantly that the shells pass him with inches to spare.

'I would not leave you to face this foe alone, son of Dorn.' Morvenn stabs down with the Lance of Illumination, but the point glances off the blue-and-bronze chestplate without causing damage.

'Your corpse-god has taken enough already.' The skull-faced helmet turns the words to a distorted growl. 'She is mine. You may not have her!'

'She is not yours. She was *never* yours!'

The Death of Saints springs forward, the blood trailing from his side already clotting. Perhaps his treacherous ally thought to fatally weaken him before the battle, but from the look of the twitching remains that lie on the ground, it was a fatal misjudgement. Morvenn catches the lightning claw on her gunshield, and Tancret's sword sweeps round mere inches above Rakhul's winged helm – but it seems the arch-heretic's head was not the lord castellan's target. Instead, his blade slices through the longest skewer in the centre of the armour rack, severing it halfway down its length and sending the topmost skulls – the relic of the saint amongst them – tumbling to the floor.

The Death of Saints staggers back as though the blade has severed limbs instead of merely a piece of metal, roaring with what sounds like agony.

'Take it!' Tancret bellows. He follows the blow with a vicious horizontal lunge that catches the reeling heretic in the plastron, sending him sprawling back.

'Aleyna! The relic!'

The young Sister is on it in an instant, scooping up the silver-chased skull and tucking it into a fold of her vestments. She hesitates for a moment over one of the other severed heads – fresh and rotting, what remains of its golden hair rusting at the roots – and then, with an evident effort of will, tears herself away.

'Abbess Sanctorum?' Aleyna's voice is urgent. 'What must I do?'

A plume of fire descends from above. Morvenn looks up to see the Heldrake swooping down on them. Another terrible polyphonic shriek tears the air in half, shattering her thoughts to fragments – and this time its descent ends with an earth-shaking thud. Four taloned feet find the ground, one head lashing back and forth as it surveys the battlefield, the other raised high, mouth open ready to strike.

'Where is he?' Tancret is bellowing. 'Where is the Death of Saints?'

Morvenn's head feels as though it has been stuffed with parchment. Is this the God-Emperor's design? Perhaps this is the purpose of Aleyna's miracle – that she should be here in this moment to bear the saint to safety.

'Take it. Take the saint and retreat.'

'Abbess Sanctorum, I will not leave you–'

'Do as I command!'

Morvenn does not wait to see Aleyna obey her order. She fills the air with heavy bolter fire, discharging a full volley of missiles into the Heldrake's approaching bulk. They detonate in a single conflagration, but the beast's descent does not slow. Castellan Tancret is still roaring challenges, but once again the Death of Saints is nowhere to be seen.

'With me, Abbess Vahl! We shall slay this beast together!'

Tancret's sword flashes out towards the Heldrake, but one huge steel-toothed mouth comes down with the speed of a striking serpent to lock around his torso. He struggles to tear himself free, but the daemon engine's teeth are lodged tight in the ceramite chestplate. Morvenn hacks at the neck with the Lance of Illumination, but the Heldrake is unyielding, the jaws biting down with unnatural force.

'The God-Emperor's curse...'

It is impossible that the castellan can still have the breath to speak, but he is choking out words through a mouth welling with thick dark blood.

'His curse... upon you...'

There is a wet crack, and Tancret goes limp in the Heldrake's jaws. His blade falls to the ground. The second head comes down to seize his legs between its wickedly sharp teeth, and with a vicious jerk of its armour-plated neck the castellan's body tears apart at the waist, spilling dark blood and strings of purple viscera.

'Abomination!' Morvenn screams. 'You will pay for his death!'

The Heldrake casts the tattered corpse aside and answers her roar with a shriek of its own. Two sets of jaws gape wide above her, descending as if to swallow her whole, but she forces herself not to flinch, to brace the ferrule of the oversized spear firmly in the ground, the tip pointed squarely at the flame burning deep in the daemon engine's throat.

The open mouth slams into the spear-tip with a bone-jarring impact. Morvenn almost falls, only her grip on the Lance's golden shaft keeping her upright. A radiant burst of light erupts from the Lance's blade, setting the serpentine skull glowing from within like a funerary lantern. The daemon engine convulses, the spear-shaft in her hand writhing like a living thing as it tries to tear itself free, but the Lance's barbed tip is lodged deep. Searing black liquid that is half blood and half profane oil gushes over her; the creature's neck tenses, and with a final burst of strength it wrenches its head free, another torrent of scalding liquid catching her full in the face. Half-blinded, she staggers back, and a vast talon catches her below the ribs and lifts her into the air. The Purgator Mirabilis lands with an earth-shaking impact, bolt-shells whizzing past her shoulders so quickly she cannot tell whether they are fired by a Godwyn-De'az or a Mark Vb, and she charges again, the Lance held underarm like a knight of ancient Terra. The Heldrake is still screaming, one head flopping uselessly at the end of a flaccid neck, while the second is drawing back with hatred in its baleful eyes, ready to strike again. She waits for it to descend, waits for the jaws to open and belch flame that breaks on the Purgator's energy field, waits until the great mouth begins to close...

And rams Fidelis shoulder-deep down the gaping throat, pulls the trigger and fires until the ammunition belt runs empty. The Heldrake shrieks and thrashes, claws and talons tearing at the warsuit, wings buffeting the air, and Morvenn drives the Lance deep between the armour plates that cover its chest. With one terminal convulsion it slams the remains of its second head round like a club, and this time Morvenn is not quick enough to avoid it. The blow sends her spiralling through the air, dizzying images flashing across her vision – the Heldrake spurting steam and ichor as it falls at last, the battlefield soaked in the blood of the faithful and heretic alike – and then the warsuit slams into the ground, and there is only darkness.

Aleyna has never run so quickly. The relic cradled against her side, she sprints for the tunnels, her breath coming in rapid, painful gasps. The fighting continues, but by skirting the thick of it she can maintain her pace, leaping across the torn bodies of cultists, the scattered remains of Heretic Astartes, and those of her own Sisters and brothers in faith. The relic's price has been paid in blood a hundred times over. A musician-servitor lies torn almost in half beside its Black Templars master, the trumpet ripped clear of the dead flesh of its face. A figure in a white hood who might be Sister-Chirurgeon Véronique moves like a warp-ghost through the smoke, the mercy-knife in her hand delivering its final benedictions.

The price of the relic. The price of victory.

There is her destination – the aperture that once was a finely carved marble arch, the distinctive silhouette of a Sabbat-pattern helm just visible in the gloom. Hope floods through her like cool water, driving the fatigue from her limbs, filling her lungs with sweet, pure air. The relic of Saint Athenasia is safe at last.

Her trial is over.

'Sister! I have the saint!'

The helm does not turn. Aleyna runs until she is almost at the threshold of the tunnels, and a slow realisation dawns. There is no light in the helmet's eye-lenses – and no neck beneath the dangling aventail, only a trail of blood dribbling down the pole that impales it through its open base. Something hurtles out of the darkness, and she fires her bolter half-blind at the approaching shadow. Shells erupt against flesh, and a figure that is only vaguely human-shaped shrieks and skitters away from the light.

Accursed mutants.

She fires her bolter until it runs dry, then draws her combat knife. The mutants surge forward, each more monstrous, more deformed than the last. She slashes her blade across the chest of a cultist which barely looks human at all, nothing but an empty skin stretched over a hideous latticework of chitinous plates and jutting bone spikes. The blade bites deep between its ribs. She pulls it free and rounds on the next. Taloned hands grab her from behind with inhuman strength, dragging her head back by the hair and exposing her neck. She stabs over her left shoulder, and is rewarded with a shriek as the knife pierces the mutant's eye. Its death buys her a moment's respite, but only a moment. More pour from the shadows, eyes glowing with baleful hate between jagged horns, bony hands clutching razor-sharp knives. As if with a single mind, they spring forward, filling her ears with the flapping of vestigial wings, her vision with mottled grey flesh and glinting teeth.

She hacks down with her blade, and half-clotted ichor sprays in an arc through the air. A dagger screeches across her backplate and plunges into the unarmoured spot behind her right shoulder. Pain lances through her arm – her fingers twitch on her combat knife, and she maintains her grip through a surpassing effort of will, hacking her assailant's arm from its shoulder with a clumsy overhand strike. Another dagger finds her thigh, and she carves her combat knife down to lodge in the top of its wielder's skull. A heavy blow thuds into her shoulder and she reels to the side, kicking out as a hand grabs at her ankle. With the last of her strength, she shakes it free, stamping and slashing and carving in a frenzy of annihilation until she is surrounded by corpses. Her ears are ringing, her mouth full of blood, her vision blurred and shadowed at its edges as though she were already inside the catacombs, already passing from light into darkness. Her shoulder and thigh scream their protest with every movement, the blood from the lacerations on her face clotting into a rigid mask, but she is still on her feet, and the entrance to the catacombs lies open ahead of her.

Aleyna has almost limped over the threshold when something makes her stop. There is no sound – or if there is, it is too soft to be registered by anything other than her subconscious mind – but when she turns, a dark silhouette is close beside her, light glinting on a woman's pale face and the glittering silver blade in her hand.

'Saint Athenasia?'

'No.'

The voice is all too human. Aleyna struggles to focus her vision, picking out the details of matted brown hair and hooded, hungry eyes. How could she have mistaken this scrawny wretch for her saint?

'Give me the skull.'

'Who are you?'

The silver knife plunges down. Aleyna's injuries have made her slow, and the tip of the blade lodges just above her left collarbone. She stumbles back, and her injured leg twists and collapses beneath her, pain skewering her from hip to ankle as she tries to rise on flesh that will no longer obey her will.

'Give it to me,' the woman whispers.

'You have no right to it.'

'So you say.'

Aleyna has nothing left. Nowhere to run, and no strength with which to do it. *God-Emperor,* she thinks, *do not let me die in failure. Surely your plan was not this–*

'There is no right and no wrong.' The ragged woman adjusts her grip on the dagger, then punches it between Aleyna's ribs. 'There is only power, and the strength to wield it.'

Night is falling. Aleyna tries to draw breath for one last prayer, but the air will not come. The knife slides into the soft flesh at the base of her throat, but the pain is nothing compared to the despair.

The last thing she sees before the darkness takes her is the woman lifting the skull of Saint Athenasia in her filthy hands and cradling it to her chest.

XXVI

Morvenn's consciousness returns slowly, the boundary between waking and dreaming fogged by smoke and pain. The air smells of charring meat, promethium and blood. It smells of death.

The vision of the beast-machine comes back to her, the open mouth gaping wide, the golden light gleaming from the point of the Lance. How the great head erupted like a lantern, the eyes sizzling in their sockets, the second head shrieking with pain and rage. Then there had been flames, and weightlessness, then nothing. She is still in the Purgator Mirabilis, lying on her back.

Something sharp prods at her face. She raises a hand to knock it away and finds that her fingers have closed around a gauntleted wrist. Her eyes are sticky with blood, but she forces them open and sees Celestian Zafiya bare-headed in front of her. The Celestian's silver hair has been singed to its roots, and the right side of her face is raw with blisters. Her auditory augmetics are gone, the implants red with traction-marks from where they have been torn free, most likely along with Zafiya's helm.

'Is it–' she begins, then stops as she struggles to remember the correct cant-signs to convey her meaning. The word for daemon will not come, but she settles on the shape for beast. She has allowed herself to become lazy, relying on Hiromi to translate and Zafiya's willingness to use the augmetics she quietly despises. 'The beast. Dead?'

'Dead.' Zafiya answers in words as well as signs.

'The Death of Saints?'

'Unaccounted for.' Zafiya coughs, hacking up a chunk of soot-stained spit on the broken ground. 'My abbess. You must rise.'

It takes both of them to heave the Purgator Mirabilis to its feet, Morvenn at the controls and Zafiya hoisting as much of its weight as she can shoulder from behind. The whole right side of Morvenn's body feels like one continuous bruise, a bone-deep contusion that aches with every movement. The skin of her face feels hot and tight, and when she touches her fingertips to it, they come away sticky with clear exudate that suggests at least a partial thickness burn.

'The saint.' That sign at least she remembers – clasped hands in the aquila, followed by the circle of a halo overhead. 'Aleyna.' She finger-spells the name. 'Did she escape with the relic?'

'I have not seen her body. But we must be quick. The cathedrum roof is coming down.'

'Wait. Where is Kseniya?'

Zafiya does not answer, but her expression says it all.

Another loss. The young Celestian's death is a knife between Morvenn's ribs. She turns her attention to the vox, but instead of the disruption she had expected, the line is clear.

'Sisters. Rally in the tunnel through which we entered.' She looks around her for the Black Templars, but any who have survived have already left the battlefield to rally elsewhere.

Her vox-bead chirps in her ear, and she adjusts the frequency to receive an incoming message.

'Abbess Sanctorum,' Prioress Illuminata says, her voice tinny and distorted. *'This is the Convent Sanctorum. The tech-dominae tell me that they have been able to re-establish a vox-link to you. Can you hear me?'*

'Praise be to the God-Emperor and all His works. I hear you, prioress.'

'How goes the war?'

'The Heldrake is destroyed.'

'The Death of Saints?'

'Vanishes.' Morvenn sighs. 'Once again.'

'And the relic? Did you recover it?'

Morvenn pauses before answering. 'In Sister Aleyna's possession.'

'Excellent news. Will you be returning immediately?'

'As soon as matters permit.'

'That would be for the best.' The deep breath that Illuminata draws is clearly audible despite the physical distance between them. *'I regret to tell you I have further ill tidings.'*

A lead weight drops into the pit of Morvenn's stomach.

'We have reports of increased heretic activity, heading towards the Convent Sanctorum. It is my belief that the Death of Saints is planning an assault on the heart of the faith.'

'How long do we have?'

The silence is palpable. *'I do not know, Abbess Sanctorum. But from the numbers seen amassing, I would advise you to come with all haste.'*

'I should kill you all and have done with your treachery!'

Lightning crackles from the Death of Saints' gauntlet. The mutilated corpse of one of his warriors lies at his feet, but death is no protection against the rage of Lethe's dark lord.

Lethe creeps forward, sticking to the shadows. She has done so since the battle, first dragging the armoured Sister's body into an alcove where she was confident it would not be found, then skirting the side of the ruined cathedrum to the abandoned shrine where her lord's army has regrouped.

'Not all of us are traitors, lord.'

She recognises Merthok's grating voice as she creeps closer, the skull of her lord's lost saint a dead weight in her hands. She is still not entirely sure why she has returned, only that the alternatives – to throw herself on the non-existent mercy of the Adepta Sororitas, or to attempt to strike out on her own – were infinitely worse. Even if things go catastrophically wrong here, she can at least die doing her lord a service.

The Death of Saints drives his clenched fist through a stone pillar, then heaves the broken segment thirty feet through the air into the nearest wall. 'Very well, then, Merthok. Shall we slaughter them one at a time until we find the source of this conspiracy, you and I? Dmitrev was a traitor.' He stamps his boot down on what remains of the dead warrior's skull, and it ruptures in a spray of grey-pink brains. 'A pawn. A weapon in the hand of one of you.'

'My lord!' Lethe steps out of the shadows, the skull held before her like a shield. Every pair of eyes in the shrine turns towards her but one, and that is the only one that matters. All of her lord's attention is fixed on the rapidly disintegrating corpse at his feet.

'The deserter returns.' Ostrov stalks across the broken marble of the shrine's floor. 'Such great favour you were given, only to cast it aside.' He waves a hand to a clump of cultists, who instantly draw their knives and advance on her. 'Show this slave the reward of treachery.'

'My lord! Ostrov cannot be trusted! I heard him plotting to usurp you – with Dmitrev.' A hand grabs her by the throat. She strains against the pressure, but the grip tightens, squeezing her windpipe shut. The skull slips in her hands and she fumbles to keep her grip, nails scrabbling at the eye sockets and sliding over the silver filigree. A cultist's face swims across her vision, a glinting knife raised to strike, and it is the emptiness in the eyes behind the black leather mask that terrifies her most – more awful than rage or hatred. Her death will mean nothing to her killers – nothing more than an additional ration of meat, or a modicum of favour in their overlords' eyes.

'No–' she croaks, but the sound is little more than a wheeze. Black spots dance in front of her eyes as she lifts the skull as high as she can, praying that it will catch the light, praying that her lord will raise his head to look. 'I have... the skull–'

'Stop.' The single word cuts through the roaring in her ears, and the world falls silent. The grip on her neck eases and Lethe drops to her knees, sucking a wheezing breath in through her burning throat.

'Bring it to me.'

The Death of Saints is moving towards her, bearing down on her like a gathering storm. She forces herself upright, the skull outstretched like an offering, and he takes it in his gauntlets and raises it so that he is gazing into the gem-set eye sockets. When he speaks again, the power in his voice drives her back to her knees.

'You have returned what I thought lost to me. And for that there will be a reward.' A gleaming trickle of vitreous humour seeps down his ruined cheek like a tear. 'But first, Brother Ostrov. Explain yourself.'

There is suddenly a space around Ostrov Skull-taker.

'What is there to explain?' He folds his arms, all bluster and defiance. 'You would take the word of a slave–'

The Death of Saints is on him with superhuman speed, his lightning claw opening three parallel weals across Ostrov's face. Ostrov staggers back, and the Death of Saints tears the chain-glaive from Ostrov's hands, spins the haft in his grip and hacks it down hard into the traitor's knee joint. Ostrov and the blade scream together as blood and marrow spray from the wound – he reaches for the chain-knife on his belt, but before he can draw it from its sheath the chainglaive severs his hand at the wrist.

'Brothers!' Ostrov roars. 'We can be free of his tyranny, his madness! Gods of Chaos, grant me strength–'

The skin of Ostrov's face ripples, pushed outwards by the bulging of bone and muscle beneath the surface.

'Yes!' he screams, but as his mouth opens the Death of Saints stabs the chainglaive between his parted lips.

'You might have earned a place on my armour rack, had you proved yourself a worthy foe.'

The skin of Ostrov's lips and cheeks shreds as the Death of Saints pushes the chainblade deeper.

'But you are nothing.'

Ostrov's screams turn wet and ragged, the chainglaive straining against the back of his skull.

'Less than nothing. Less than a slave.'

In a sudden spray of gore Ostrov's skull gives way entirely, and his face comes apart in a shower of blood, bone and marrow. The Death of Saints steps back, leaving the chainglaive standing upright in the shredded face like a grisly grave-marker.

'I trust none of you share Brother Ostrov's views?'

There is no reply.

The Death of Saints raises the skull above his head and places it on an unbroken spike.

'Then know this. I will give you the slaughter you seek. The steps of the Convent Sanctorum will run crimson with blood, and I shall give you war the like of which you have never known in all your years. We will see their convent in flames, their leaders brought low, their holy relics shattered and desecrated.

'And you, child of darkness, arise.' His vast clawed hand caresses Lethe's cheek. 'For your loyalty, for that which you have brought me when all others failed, yours shall be the honour of bearing the tidings of the night that is to come. My Lethe. My Herald of Slaughter.'

VISIONS

The depth of the darkness tells the Death of Saints that he is dreaming.

Since his rebirth he has had no need of light. The shadows are his domain, and they keep no secrets from him even in pitch darkness. His eyes are sensitive to the merest photon, and even in their absence his other senses are more than capable of compensating. Others may fear the terrors in the night. He is the terror that they fear.

But in the dream, the darkness is absolute, and his own fears are growing.

Rakhul has lost track of how long they have hidden in the sanctuary, listening as the thunderous explosions draw closer. From time to time running footsteps echo overhead, accompanied by shouting voices he does not recognise, but no one has come to the door or tried its locks. Some of the other children have managed an uneasy sleep – even Athenasia, after many hours of vigilance – but he cannot. When the door opens – and it will open, of that he is sure – he must be ready to act. If rescue comes, if there is a chance to leave this place, then the two of them must be the first to claim it. And if it is the enemy who comes for them, he has no intention of being caught off-guard.

Someone in the darkness whimpers. Athenasia is asleep by his side, and he considers waking her for the twentieth time in as many minutes. When she is with him the voice is quiet, but it knows when she is sleeping, and takes the opportunity to fill his mind with temptation. There is food in the refuge, enough to sustain them all many weeks – but how much longer would it last if there were only the two of them? Athenasia would never agree to that, of course, but while she sleeps so deeply there might be time to begin. The darkness is his ally. That has always been the way–

Athenasia stirs at his side, and he forces his thoughts back from their dark path. He nudges her awake, desperate to hear her voice in place of the nagging words of temptation in his head.

'No rescue, I take it?' She heaves herself upright. 'Too much to hope for, I suppose.' She stills for a moment. 'Do you hear that? They are getting closer.'

'Whoever it is is here to fight, not rescue orphans. No one wanted us before this began. What makes you think we matter to anyone now?'

'Fine. Wait until the food runs out, is that your plan?'

Rakhul swallows. He has eaten the day's meagre ration already, and it has done nothing to fill the emptiness in his gut. The problem is the others, the voice reminds him again. They are nothing but consumers of precious resources. Once they are dead, all of the food will be his – and why not add fresh meat to their supplies instead of leaving it to rot?

'You're right.' He forces himself to his feet. 'What do we do?'

'We go and look through the door. It's only bolted from the inside.' He can feel her pulling away from him, moving towards the stairs.

'Wait...'

He raises a hand to stop her, but she has already gone. He

gropes his way along the wall to where the stairs rise to the sanctuary door. He counts the steps until he reaches the top where she is waiting, just visible in the sliver of light through the gap in between door and frame. He joins his hand to hers on the corpse-cold metal of the rusty iron bolt, and pulls.

'Now,' Athenasia whispers. Together, they draw back the bolt, and open the door.

There is no one in the cloister beyond, but the sounds of battle are clearer now that the thick oakwood door is open.

'What is it?' Drenak's nasal voice drifts up the stairs. 'Are they here to rescue us?'

'Shut up and let us listen,' Athenasia spits back. 'That idiot's going to get us killed.'

Rakhul feels a sudden rush of love for her in all her determined, sharp-tongued glory. Without her, he would have succumbed to the voice long ago. She is all that keeps him going. All that keeps him good.

'Rakhul?' Athenasia's hand closes around his upper arm.

'What?'

'Look!'

A woman is watching them from the end of the cloister. She is dressed in silver armour from head to toe, a boltgun in her hands – a Battle Sister, one of the God-Emperor's holy daughters who he had half-believed a fiction until now. She raises a gauntleted hand.

'Stop. You two.' Her accent is unfamiliar, the vowels clipped short between staccato consonants. 'I have eyes on them, Sister Superior. These must be the last.'

Rakhul takes a step back into the shadows, but Athenasia stands her ground. 'Are you here to rescue us?'

The Battle Sister's eyes narrow. 'How many of you are there?'

'Twenty.'

The Sister looks from Athenasia to Rakhul, then back again.

'Down there? Take me to them.' Two more armoured women appear in the passageway behind her and take up a covering position to either side as the first moves towards them. She presses an activation stud on the side of her firearm, and a wide lumen-beam pierces the darkness behind the door.

'Move.'

The Battle Sister descends the stairs.

'We should run,' Rakhul whispers to Athenasia, but his sister shakes her head.

'Run where? This is our only chance of escape.'

Her eyes are bright with hope, and for a moment Rakhul feels it too. The orphanarium has met the basic needs of their existence since their father died, but it is as though a set of locked and barred gates are swinging open at last, beckoning them out into the Imperium beyond. No more beatings. No more thin gruel and back-breaking labour. Out there is a future, one they can face together.

The Battle Sister is climbing the stairs again, her helmet under her arm. Her face is that of a young woman, the severely bobbed white hair doing nothing to disguise the fact that she is only a few years older than Rakhul and Athenasia themselves. A string of girls trails along in her wake – Alyx, Verena and Tyla, others whose names he has not bothered to learn – and as she reaches the top of the stairs she shepherds them into the care of an approaching Battle Sister. 'Stay with Sister Priyenta.' She points to Athenasia. 'And you. The rest of you, return to your sanctuary. Help will come–'

An explosion shakes the passageway. The second of the two Battle Sisters raises her visor to reveal eyes narrowed in concern. 'We must hurry.'

'I will not leave.' Athenasia's hand finds Rakhul's and squeezes it. 'Not unless you take my brother.'

'I have said that help will come–'

'Why not him?' Athenasia's jaw is set. She looks around the chosen group, and realisation crosses her face a moment before it dawns on Rakhul.

'Why are you only taking the girls?' he asks.

The white-haired Sister tilts her head, studying his face. 'One of the evacuation transports has been destroyed. The one that remains is almost full, but another is coming. Help will come for the rest of you–' Another explosion sends showers of dust descending from the roof. 'I have my orders. There is little time.'

The Sister of Battle tugs their hands apart, and locks her grip around Athenasia's wrist. She squirms away, but the gauntlet holds her tight.

'Let me go – let me go now!'

Rakhul slides his hand up his sleeve and closes it around the hilt of his knife, imagining how it would feel to press its tip into the hollow below the Battle Sister's throat, the hot gush of blood on his hand, the bubbling sound of her last breaths.

'No more arguments,' the Battle Sister says. 'You, boy. If you love your sister, tell her to come with me now.'

She tugs Athenasia away, and Rakhul's temper flares. His hand slashes out towards the Battle Sister's unarmoured face and opens a six-inch gash across her cheek.

'Little brute!'

'Rakhul! No!' Athenasia's eyes are wide with horror. 'No, no... What have you done?'

'Come on!' He reaches out his hand, but she pulls away, cowering into the Battle Sister's shadow. 'We need to run!'

'No, I–' Athenasia is shaking her head, staring at him as though he were a stranger and not her own flesh. She is seeing him for what he truly is for the first time. She has finally seen the truth of the darkness that he has always tried to conceal.

And she hates him.

The Battle Sister's gauntlet strikes the side of his head, and the world goes dark.

When Rakhul wakes, night has fallen. The door to the sanctuary is open, but there is no noise from within. His hand is still tightly closed around his knife, and standing over him is a colossal warrior in a suit of blue-and-bronze power armour.

Heart thudding, Rakhul scrambles to his feet, the cloister tilting wildly around him. The air smells of blood and gun smoke. This, then, is the enemy that has come to kill them all. He raises his knife in a shaking hand, the blade stained rust-red with the Battle Sister's blood.

'Do it!' he shouts, slashing the blade through empty air. Death is welcome, a thousand times better than living without her – and the gigantic warrior's laugh booms through the vox-grille set into his rotting flesh.

'Are you not afraid?' a deep voice asks. Rakhul throws himself forward, but the giant sweeps the legs out from under him with contemptuous ease. 'Have you never learned the ways of fear?'

Rakhul glares up at him from the marble floor. 'What good does fear do?'

The giant laughs again, the sound like the creaking of ancient timber. 'Fear is a weapon.'

The faint buzzing of corpse-flies rises from the open sanctuary door. When the huge warrior does not move, Rakhul drags himself painfully to his feet, and backs away until his shoulder blades are pressed to the mosaic on the wall.

'I see the hatred in you, boy.'

'Who are you?' Rakhul whispers.

'Merthok of the Eighth Legion. Come with me. Be reborn to darkness.'

'Or?'

The warrior smiles. 'Or stay and die. What is your answer?'

What possible choice does he have?

Death has come for him, to remake him in its image. And when it is over, Kol Rakhul will never fear the darkness again.

Act IV

The Book of Sacrifice

XXVII

The globe of Ophelia VII in the war-room only confirms what Morvenn already knows. The glowing lights that each once represented a shrine under attack have gone dark, replaced by a fresh cluster of flickering blue-grey dots converging on a brighter focus at the head of the valley. There are hundreds of them, new pinpricks of light appearing with every passing moment. How many heretics does each represent? Ten? A hundred? Even with the foe so far away she feels naked without the Purgator Mirabilis, her simple vestments a poor exchange for the magnificent warsuit currently under repair in the convent's armorium.

'They are coming.' Canoness Lucreziana's wounds stand out like quill-strokes on parchment against the pallor of her skin, her hands braced hard against the table to support her weight. They have not spoken together since the retreat from Caelestis – those bloody miles of darkness and pain, and for that Morvenn is grateful. The reckoning has been a bitter one – a decimation and more – and the full extent of the butcher's bill is yet to be tallied.

But the sons of Dorn have lost even more. Their Apothecary returned from the battlefield adorned with gene-seed, but only from a fraction of the lost brothers. The grim-faced

Chaplain survived, and three of the castellan's Sword Brethren, but Tancret himself is gone, torn into shreds by the Heldrake. His loss – all of their losses – will be felt keenly by the Chapter, thousands of years of battlefield experience wiped away in a single disastrous engagement.

And Morvenn knows who is to blame for that.

'Let them come.' She forces confidence she does not feel into her voice. 'The Convent Sanctorum has faced greater foes before and stood.'

'I will pray for the God-Emperor to grant me your confidence.' Lucreziana shakes her head. 'The enemy's numbers are greater than we could have anticipated. With the loss of so many Sisters at Caelestis – to say nothing of the sons of Dorn – this will be a bloody battle indeed.'

'We have reinforcements.' Morvenn turns to Palatine Kharys of the Sacred Rose, newly arrived from the chapterhouse of the Holy Liberator. 'The Sisters of your mission, palatine, and the rest.'

The palatine bows her head, the rich dark brown of her skin a dramatic contrast to the pure white of her armour. 'We are here to serve, Abbess Sanctorum.'

'Another squad of Battle Sisters arrived from the south this morning.' Prioress Illuminata looks up from her data-slate. 'A dozen Crusaders, guarding the shrine at Varanis when the attacks began.'

'Three of them are injured,' Véronique offers. The Sister-chirurgeon has taken Castellan Tancret's seat at the war-table. She brings a different form of expertise to the council, but one that will be needed all the more in his absence. 'Two of those can be made ready to fight.'

Morvenn closes her eyes, trying to make sense of the resources at her disposal – counting individual soldiers in the desperate attempt to mitigate their losses in the face of the approaching enemy. How did it come to this?

'And I take it there is no sign of Sister Aleyna, or the relic?'

Illuminata shakes her head. 'None. The patrols continue to search the catacombs, but the time is coming when we must withdraw them–'

'Then we must consider her lost.' Morvenn speaks the words with deliberate callousness, masking the guilt that has followed her from Caelestis. She should never have made Aleyna a target by sending her alone with the relic, and worse, she should never have presumed to understand the God-Emperor's design. Such a sin deserves a penance of flesh and spirit, but that must wait until the battle is over. 'Sister-chirurgeon, have the infirmarium readied to receive casualties.'

'Of course. When do you expect the battle to begin?'

The tiny dots advance at barely perceptible speed across the globe, but that is an illusion. The real advance is a thousand times quicker, but the answer is still impossible to give. 'We will know more in the coming hours.'

Véronique gets to her feet. 'I take it the preparation of arco-flagellants and penitent engines would be to your liking?' It is unusual for a Sister Hospitaller to involve herself in the creation of the surgically and pharmaceutically altered penitents, but Véronique is a woman of rare talents, her skill almost approaching that of the tech-priests among whom she works.

'How many can you give me?'

The Sister-chirurgeon cocks her head to one side, a smile that holds neither humour nor mockery playing at the corner of her mouth. Perhaps more than any of them, she knows the extent of the carnage that is to come. 'I will have my Sisters assess the sinners in the penitentia for suitability. Ten at the least, perhaps more.'

'I can find use for as many as you can recruit.'

The main door to the war-room opens, admitting a crack of light and the slight robed figure of a lay Sister. A whisper too quiet for Morvenn to make out passes between the newcomer and the Battle Sister to the left of the door, then to a novitiate of Our Martyred Lady, who creeps forward along the wall.

'Either this warrants an interruption or it does not,' Morvenn snaps. 'What do you have to say?'

There is a curious sense of familiarity to the moment. It seems only the space of a breath since Morvenn was standing on Holy Terra, interrupted in a moment of equal solemnity, but in the time between the whole Imperium has changed around her.

The lay Sister drops to her knees. 'Abbess Sanctorum, there is a woman with a reliquary case at the convent steps. She says she will give it only to you–'

Morvenn is on her feet in an instant. 'One of the Sisters Militant?' If it is Aleyna, if the young Battle Sister has returned bearing the relic then surely that is a demonstration of the God-Emperor's favour, a sign that this time of trials is coming to a triumphant end.

The lay Sister opens her hands in helpless apology. 'I have not seen her myself, but I will–'

'No need. I will go.'

Illuminata's eyes go wide. 'Abbess Sanctorum, I must ask–'

'We have time before the enemy reaches us.' Morvenn is already moving towards the door. 'We cannot make ready until we know their route of approach and their full numbers. Have the Sisters instructed to begin their preparations, and I will rejoin you soon.'

And if the God-Emperor wills it, she thinks, I will return with a saint and the tale of another miracle.

Before she even reaches the great golden doors of the Convent Sanctorum, Morvenn can hear the crowd outside. The black marble steps are barely visible beneath the throng of pilgrims and civilians seeking sanctuary ahead of the enemy's relentless advance. Long-dead saints and honoured matriarchs watch her from atop their marble columns as she makes her way towards the crowd. Armed and armoured Battle Sisters are doing their best to keep order, but the desperation in the air is palpable.

'Where is she?'

A tall Sister Superior in the armour of the Valorous Heart turns. 'What is–' She falls silent, her demeanour instantly changing from hostility to deference. 'Abbess Sanctorum. Forgive me. I did not think to see you here. How can I serve?'

'The woman with the reliquary. Where is she?'

'Under guard at the base of the steps. I will have her brought up immediately–'

Morvenn does not wait. She takes the steps two at a time, hope swelling in her like the music of a choir, towards a tightly clustered group of Battle Sisters in black partially obscuring the woman in their midst.

'Aleyna?'

'Abbess Sanctorum!' A Battle Sister steps forward, but Morvenn silences her with an upraised hand. The woman in the centre of the group is robed and hooded, too slight to be Aleyna or a Sister of the Orders Militant, but the reliquary case in her hands is unmistakable. She has seen it a hundred times in the cathedrum, in the saint's procession, even bore it herself once as a novitiate.

It is the silver case that holds the skull of Saint Athenasia.

'Give it to me.'

The woman holds out the box. Two bony wrists extend from the sleeves of her oversized black robe, bracelets of half-healed sores about her wrists. The metal is cold against Morvenn's hands, its weight a familiar comfort.

'How did you come by this?'

'I found it.' The hooded woman's whisper is barely audible, her voice shaking in time with her hands. 'In Caelestis.'

Morvenn thinks of the ruins of the ancient cathedrum there, the shattered shrine-temples, the catacombs running red with blood. She had assumed that the Death of Saints had slaughtered any luckless labourers or worshippers he found there on his arrival, but this trembling creature must have somehow escaped.

'Then you have my thanks for returning it to me. Your journey cannot have been easy.'

The woman tucks her shaking hands into the sleeves of her robe, watching as Morvenn unclasps the reliquary case and lifts the lid.

'God-Emperor protect–' one of the Battle Sisters gasps, but Morvenn barely hears her over the rushing in her ears. Lying inside the gilded case on a stained velvet cushion is the severed head of Sister Aleyna Amarys. Morvenn draws a sharp breath, and the full force of the stench hits her throat – old blood, spoiling meat, damp cloth. Aleyna's mouth and eyes are open, her teeth shockingly white but the sclerae already shrivelled and yellow. A milky film has spread across the warm brown of her irises, granting them a faded, bluish hue. Her neck has been severed just above the shoulders, but a gash gapes like a second mouth just below her slack jaw, a vicious knife-wound severing trachea, carotid arteries and jugular vein in a single brutal swipe.

The dead woman's eyes hold Morvenn in their empty gaze. Fine threads of mould are blossoming across Aleyna's left cheek, spreading out like tiny veins.

A Battle Sister forces the woman to her knees, while a second pushes her boltgun to the side of her head. 'You will die for this!'

The woman does not resist, but her hood falls back, revealing the complexion of an underhiver who has never seen daylight, a scabbed and livid wound across the left side of her face.

'Wait!' Morvenn shoves the bolter aside and grips the snivelling wretch by the throat. 'How did you come by this? Did you know what this contained?'

The woman chokes. Morvenn slackens her grip just enough for her to draw breath, and her mouth opens in a broken-toothed gasp.

'I cut... her throat... myself.'

'Heretic!' She shakes the woman so hard that her head snaps back and forward, longing to crush the scrawny neck to pulp.

'I bring a message...' The woman's voice is a hoarse crackle, filled with depraved fervour. 'From my lord–'

'Abbess Sanctorum,' the Battle Sister says. 'Let me silence this foulness–'

'Her death can wait!' Morvenn throws the woman to the ground and stands over her, trying not to succumb to the temptation of finishing her miserable life. The Death of Saints has been a step ahead of Morvenn since she set foot on Ophelia VII – since she set foot on the *Lux Dominus* – and this is yet another carefully calculated move in his infernal game of regicide. 'What is this message? Speak, if you value your miserable life!'

The woman rubs at her throat with a filthy hand. 'I am his Herald of Slaughter,' she croaks. 'He bade me bring you this gift, as a sign of what is to come. He has taken back that which was stolen from him – not once, but twice – and he is coming to desecrate your convent and kill all who stand in his way. And when Ophelia VII is his dark cardinal world, he will take his great crusade to Holy Terra and the stars beyond, and wipe all trace of your foul Sisterhood from the galaxy forever.'

Morvenn shakes her head, fury coursing through her veins like lava. There are no words harsh enough to condemn this woman's deeds, no censure that can offer atonement for her heresy. 'You are a slave to darkness.' She plants her boot squarely in the woman's ribs, feeling the bone snap against the ball of her foot. 'What could he have promised you to make you betray your own kind – to kill a holy woman who would have laid down her life for you a thousand times over?'

'He gave me my freedom.' The gap-toothed smile fades, and the woman's face sets into lines of bitter hatred. 'And he has promised me revenge. You and your Sisters burned my home, killed my father, destroyed everything I ever knew. You cast me into the darkness without ever saying why – and now he will do the same to you.'

Feet clatter around her. The Sister Superior from the steps has joined them with another unit of Battle Sisters, their sabatons striking sparks from the marble steps. 'Abbess Sanctorum, I beg your permission to grant this heretic the God-Emperor's mercy,' the Superior says.

'I am not afraid to die.' The woman – no, the *cultist* – has propped herself up on one arm, the other curled protectively around her broken ribs. Something moving in the reliquary case catches Morvenn's eye. A glistening maggot the size of Morvenn's thumb is emerging from the tattered stump of Aleyna's neck, its pallid mandibles tearing at the ragged skin. Morvenn swallows down a mouthful of acid and tugs it free between her thumb and forefinger, its fleshy body writhes in blind consternation. She hurls it to the ground and crushes it beneath her boot.

'You do not deserve His mercy,' Morvenn spits. 'There will be no death for you today. Seize her.'

Two Battle Sisters grip the woman by the arms.

'At your command, Abbess Sanctorum.'

A look of abject horror crosses the cultist's pallid face. 'No – where are you taking me? Not the darkness! Not again!' The woman thrashes her limbs in useless panic as the Battle Sisters drag her to her feet. 'I renounce your God-Emperor!'

'Cease your heresy.' Morvenn silences her with a backhanded strike to the mouth. 'The Death of Saints has lied to you. You will live to see the battle for the Convent Sanctorum, and I will grant you the great honour of a part in its defence. Sister Superior, inform Sister-Chirurgeon Véronique that I have found her another arco-flagellant.'

The heretic is still babbling through bloodied teeth. 'The Golden Throne is a lie, the Ecclesiarchs peddlers of empty promises! My soul is promised to the adversary–'

'Throw her in the cells.'

XXVIII

'Why?'

Morvenn kneels at the God-Emperor's feet and waits for an answer that will not come. The private chapel gleams with the purity of white marble, but there is no comfort to be found here. In the common chapel she could drown out the silence with the prayers of her Sisters and the shuffling feet of the pilgrims, but she is learning that rank and solitude go hand in hand.

She has never felt more alone.

So many deaths lie at her feet, and they are nothing but an overture for what is to come.

Her words echo into the empty space. 'I accept your judgement, God-Emperor. Only reveal to me how I have sinned, and I will spend my life in atonement.'

There is only silence.

She is being punished, that is the only explanation. To be offered the mantle of the Abbess Sanctorum was a test, and through the act of prideful vanity that was accepting it, she has failed not only the God-Emperor but her Sisters too. There can be no other reason for the God-Emperor's silence other than His displeasure, and no other reason to explain why her every decision since leaving Holy Terra has ended in failure and destruction. Captain Haraquis and the crew of the *Lux Dominus* sacrificed their lives to bring her to Ophelia VII –and for what? A vainglorious assault that slew the daemon engine at the cost of hundreds of lives, and even then failed to slay the Death of Saints. She has allowed her pride to lead her from one costly battle to another like a grox to the slaughterhouse, the noose which she has allowed the Death of Saints to place around her neck growing tighter at every turn. At the cathedrum she failed them as a warrior and at Caelestis as their commander. Perhaps she deserves to be punished in such a way.

But where was Aleyna's sin?

'Why her?'

She tries to bring the young Sister's living face to memory, but all she can see is the severed head in the reliquary, the clouded eyes, the flesh-eating maggot gnawing at the torn and bloodless skin. What sin had Aleyna committed to fall so far from the God-Emperor's grace and meet such an end? Is her death further punishment for Morvenn's sins? The questions chafe at her skin like a penitent's shirt, and the God-Emperor will not answer.

Ignatia would have told her to look for the God-Emperor's lesson, to see His will in action, not in words. Fionnula would have smiled, offering comfort and a wry observation. Kseniya would simply have walked beside her, a guiding light through the darkness.

And their deaths lie at her feet as surely as if she had wielded the fatal blade herself.

'I did not ask for this. Not for any of this.' Anger is easier to bear than guilt, and she surrenders to it willingly. 'If it was not your will that I be made abbess, then why did you allow it to happen?' She clenches her fists tight in front of her, as though she could coax words from the statue of the divine by force alone. 'Where were your miracles when Aleyna died? You made her a saint – she trusted you – she trusted *me!*'

The candles flicker, and for a moment she wonders if this is the time she has longed for, if this is the moment of her miracle, when all her suffering and doubt will be repaid a thousandfold. But it is no miracle that stirs the air, only the opening and closing of the chapel door, and the soft footsteps of the prioress behind her.

'I accept your punishment, God-Emperor.' Morvenn bows her head in resignation. 'But do not allow the convent to fall. Do not punish my Sisters for my sins. The fault is not theirs.'

The prioress waits until the echoes of Morvenn's voice have faded before she speaks. 'I have ill tidings.'

'More?' Morvenn closes her eyes until the stinging behind them subsides. The last thing Illuminata should see – the last thing any of the Sisters here should see – is weakness.

'Refugees from Gaudeamus Sector have arrived at the convent.'

'That hardly seems surprising.'

'The point is the news they bring with them. The Death of Saints and his warriors draw close – less than a day from the walls at their current rate of progress. Heretic Astartes – far more than we had thought at first. Raptors. Mechanised infantry. Daemon engines.'

'Another Heldrake?'

'No. These are earthbound. A small mercy.'

'Small indeed.'

'We have the Sanctorum Guard, a handful of Crusaders and the sons of Dorn that remain. Any Crusaders within reach have been recalled. Even with every prisoner prepared for arco-flagellation, they will outnumber us two to one.'

Not enough.

The words beat a mocking refrain in Morvenn's skull. She presses her right thumb and forefinger against her eyes, trying to focus her thoughts. Life as a Celestian was simple. Life as Abbess Sanctorum is infinitely, exhaustingly complex.

'We have the void shields, the walls and the artillery,' she says. 'Even outnumbered two to one we can hold them off for many hours.'

'I do not doubt that. Were reinforcements expected that might even prove a winning strategy.' Illuminata shrugs. 'But we must prepare for the very real possibility that the enemy will breach the walls and reach the convent itself.'

Morvenn turns back to the statue of the God-Emperor, to His unchanged expression of stern judgement. 'What must I do, prioress?'

'Pray for His guidance.'

'I have prayed. I have prayed a thousand times over. I prayed at the shrine of Saint Silvana when word of my elevation came, and every moment since. My every breath is a prayer for guidance – and there is never an answer. Am I to believe that it is His will that the Convent Sanctorum should fall into the hands of the enemy?'

'That must not happen.' Illuminata unfastens a small oxblood leather pouch from her belt and places it in Morvenn's hands. 'Destruction is preferable to desecration a thousand times over. You must take this. If all is lost, then the means to deny our enemy the Convent Sanctorum is open to us.'

'The explosive charges in the crypts.'

Prioress Illuminata nods. 'The charges are sufficient to obliterate the Convent Sanctorum and everything within a ten-mile radius. If we cannot have victory in the battle to come, we can at least deny the enemy his.'

Morvenn opens the pouch. The palm-sized golden sphere of a remote detonator catches the light, and she closes the catch again, her stomach churning.

'He will show no mercy,' the prioress continues, her voice as calm as though she were teaching the catechisms of the faith to new novitiates. 'If he enters the convent he will kill everyone within it. Their deaths will not be swift. Some may be weak-willed and join his cause. Better they all should die than to live to embrace corruption.'

'Did you ever speak of such things with Abbess Sabrina?'

'That is a question I will not answer.' Illuminata's face is unreadable. 'I will instruct the tech-dominae to begin the litanies of preparation for the void shields. Will you address the Sisterhood before battle?'

'If I must.'

'You must.'

Morvenn rises to her feet. The Purgator Mirabilis is waiting for her, and it is time to don her armour for what may be the final time. 'Call them to the Basilikum at evening prayers.'

'As you command.'

The chapel door closes behind the prioress. Morvenn can read Illuminata's thoughts as clearly as though she were cursed with telepathy – the battle is futile, their defeat ordained, and all that remains is to destroy the convent and all within it to keep them from the enemy's hands.

But that is a last resort, one that she is not yet willing to accept.

And if the price of the convent's salvation is her pride, she will pay it gladly.

A hush spreads through the convent as Morvenn makes her way from her chapel to the chantry. The cloisters are close-packed with refugees: some of them she recognises as pilgrims from the cathedrum – the father with his babe-in-arms, the exhausted-looking man in tattered red velvet – but there are so many others that are still strangers to her. A steady procession is winding from the outer wall to the marble steps like a fat-bodied serpent: the citizens of Ophelia VII claiming sanctuary. Unless Morvenn can find some way of levelling the odds in her favour, only death awaits them here.

The chantry occupies a chapel of its own a little way from the main house of worship – although all of the convent is holy ground, some areas are naturally holier than others. Even the pilgrims and refugees avoid the narrow corridor that leads to it, either through foreknowledge or simple instinct. What dwells there is dangerous, and the fact that the chantry stands on holy ground is scant protection against what lies within.

Two Battle Sisters of the Argent Shroud stand vigil by the chantry door. Their visors are down, their hands on their bolters. A long silver mercy-knife hangs from each belt, one with a black leather scabbard, the other sheathed in scarlet and gold, their hilts worn smooth by countless years of use.

'Hail, Abbess Sanctorum.' The Sister to the left is the one to speak. 'What service can we offer you in the God-Emperor's name?'

'Open the door.'

The Battle Sister lifts the keys from her belt, places the largest in an ornate golden lock, and turns it. The door opens on frictionless hinges, revealing the flickering candlelight and velvet-draped walls of the sanctified chamber beyond. The blood-red marble of the floor has been inlaid in gold, an intricate pattern of concentric circles and warding runes enclosing what lies at its centre.

'Sister Olycia will accompany you–'

'No.' Morvenn strides through the gap. 'Close the doors. I will speak with them alone.'

'As you command, Abbess Sanctorum.'

The door closes behind her.

But she is not alone.

'Greetings to you, Abbess Sanctorum.'

Standing in the centre of the room are ten men and women in white hooded robes, pale as ghosts in the golden candlelight. Ten heads lift in eerie unison, the hoods falling back with a rustle of silken cloth. They are all blind, some with empty sockets between sunken lids, others with orbs burned milk-white by intense heat, but any appearance of individuality is an illusion. They are the convent's astropathic choir, and the whole has already outlived the sum of its parts.

'We have seen your coming.' The choir speaks in unnerving unity, each voice at a different pitch but with identical speed and inflection. It is composed of sanctioned psykers – those who have stood at the foot of the Golden Throne and emerged from the agonising rite of soul-binding with their minds and bodies intact, their vision burned away by the glory they have witnessed. They are dangerous, their presence a risk to the souls of those around them, but without the choir there would be no way for a message to cross the light-years between here and Holy Terra.

'I am not here for prophecy.'

Ten identical smiles. 'We know that, Morvenn Vahl.'

Morvenn glares back at them, trying to quell her unease. The sheer proximity of such mutation is making her flesh creep, but the choir and their predecessors are a necessary evil and a sanctioned one.

But an evil nonetheless.

'Then you know why I am here?'

'We do.' The rightmost figure – a woman with the tanned and wrinkled skin of a desiccated ploin – speaks alone this time, though her nine companions silently mouth the words along with her. 'But we must hear it with our ears as well as our minds, Abbess Sanctorum.'

'I need you to send a message to Holy Terra. To Cardinal Ritira in the Imperial Palace.' Not for the first time, Morvenn wishes for an Imperium where such evils were not required, where psykers, Navigators and astropaths could be consigned to the cautionary tales where they belong. 'Can you do this?'

'The way is long, and the task arduous.' This time the choir's spokesperson is a man in his prime, his shaven scalp prickling with tightly curled hair a shade darker than his deep brown skin. 'But we will do as we are commanded.'

'The matter is confidential. You understand this?'

'Of course.' The next woman gives the answer in a sweet, child-like voice. 'What would you have us say?'

'Tell her...' Morvenn's mouth is dry. What assurance does she have that the message will even be received, let alone in the form she has sent it? Holy Terra is half a galaxy away, and the warp is a treacherous conduit. 'Tell her the Convent Sanctorum faces an existential threat. Tell her we need reinforcements – whatever she can provide. Any of the Sisterhood. Frateris Militia. The Black Templars, even the guard she promised before. Whatever price is required, I will pay it.'

'Is that all?' The old woman is speaking again, her voice rustling like dead leaves.

Morvenn nods. Even if Cardinal Ritira stood in front of her, she would have no more to say.

Ten pairs of hands make the sign of the aquila across their white-robed chests; ten faces turn skyward, their sightless eyes raised to the ceiling with abject adoration. The song begins low and in unison, a simple melody that tugs at Morvenn's soul before one voice after another peels away from the rest in unearthly polyphony. It is as different to the servitor-choirs of Holy Terra as an augmetic limb is to an arm or leg of living flesh, an act of pure will imprinted on reality. Blood trickles from each useless eye socket, but there is only ecstasy on their faces.

Morvenn's breath hangs silver in the air. A rime of frost creeps across the floor, tipping the velvet drapes in silver. The candles flare blue-white – once, twice – and then die as suddenly as though they have been plunged into a bucket of water, transforming the chantry from a place of sound and light to a dark and silent tomb.

'The Death of Saints comes.' The choir of whispers is different, this time. Before it was concentrated in a single area, but now it comes from every corner of the chantry, a thousand voices rather than ten. 'He will slaughter every soul within. Desecrate every stone.'

Morvenn fumbles at her belt for her lumen-stone, but her fingers are stiff with cold, and the catch on the pouch refuses to open.

'How do I stop him? What must I do?' Every inch of her skin is prickling with static.

'Blade and bolter alone cannot slay him.'

'Then what can?'

Dry laughter reverberates from walls that seem to belong to a far larger space than the chantry.

'Only the past can slay him, Morvenn Vahl. Only the past.'

Her mouth fills with the taste of frozen metal. 'What does that mean?'

A violent report breaks the silence as the door bursts open. Morvenn turns, imagining a bolt-shell streaking through the air towards her, but it is only a vigil-Sister who enters.

'Is all well?'

It is a question Morvenn cannot answer. The light through the doorway is barely enough to reach the far end of the chantry, where the choir sits huddled beneath a thick rime of frost, their hoods pulled so far forward that she cannot tell whether they are facing towards her or away.

'Wait. I...' The brush with the numinous has left her hands shaking. The frost is melting around her in a circle, the radius expanding by the second. Whatever has happened here, it is over.

'If your duty here is done, Abbess Sanctorum, it is best we leave this place.'

'In a moment.' Morvenn waves the protest away. 'What did you mean, the past? How do I defeat him?'

Ten weary whispers speak in unison, so soft that it is near-impossible to tell one voice from another.

'The message is sent, Abbess Sanctorum. Now you must wait for an answer.'

XXIX

Lethe would have preferred darkness. Without the dim brazier-light shining through the bars of her cell, she could have imagined herself beneath a clear night sky, floating in an endless ocean. Even with her eyes closed the amber half-light demands her attention, banishing all hope of peace. It gleams on dripping grey walls, on the thick coating of filth that covers the stone floor, on the manacles that dangle down from the roof, on the desperate faces of her fellow prisoners. Most are slumped against the wall, arms wrapped around themselves to keep out the cold, but one man has been banging repetitively on the bars since the Sisters left for the convent above, protesting his innocence of any crime. There is no one here she recognises. None of them bear the tell-tale facial abrasions of the tunnel miners she knew, but the dead-eyed expressions are the same. These are prisoners beyond hope of escape, and she is one of them once again.

She finds herself wondering what deeds these criminals have committed to condemn them to this – not merely to a lightless existence digging out a purposeless mine but thrown together in stinking cells with not a square yard of clean ground to lie on.

Lethe is not afraid of death. On her journey from Caelestis to the convent she thought of death many times, as her belly grew empty and her mouth dry with dust, the reliquary case with its gruesome burden a dead weight in her hands. There was no terror in those moments, only in the thought of failure. Her lord had entrusted her with a task of surpassing importance, and her death is a price she would willingly have paid for that honour.

But death did not follow. What awaits her is a thousand times worse.

The thought of what lies ahead makes her throat tighten, and she fights down a choking wave of panic. She tries to think of her lord, but his features remain foggy and indistinct. The memory of the Abbess Sanctorum's face is clearer – the look of hope on her face turning to resolve, and then, when the lid of the box was opened, grief, revulsion, confusion, and an anger of such intensity that even the memory of it sends a shiver down Lethe's spine. She lets herself dwell on that moment, and the vicious satisfaction that she had felt. The Sisters had seemed untouchable, but as she had dragged her knife across the black-clad woman's throat she had learned that they were flesh and blood after all. The abbess' reaction made it clear not only that they could be killed, but that they could be hurt far worse in other ways.

'I was going to put it back!' the man at the bars is shouting. 'I wasn't taking it to steal it, it was only to look!'

'No one cares,' a woman says flatly from the corner. 'You're a thief, and they'll punish you as a thief. Same as the cheats and the liars and the forgers. Count yourself lucky you're not thrown in with the *real* criminals.'

'I was going to put it back.'

'Cease your bleating.'

She is one of them, now, Lethe thinks. Imprisoned with petty criminals, awaiting the hour when they are taken from this place and remade in the Sisters' brutal image. But he will come for her before that happens, she tells herself– and if he does not, she will end her own life before she lets the Sisters force her to take up arms against him.

The sound of a door opening echoes down the passageway, followed by the rapping of two pairs of marching feet. Lethe presses her back against the clammy stone and turns her head away from the light. Perhaps the Sisters will take only some now, with a plan to return later for the rest.

But that hope is short-lived.

A Battle Sister in black vestments and armour passes in front of the light, accompanied by a lightly armoured woman wearing what she dimly remembers as a Hospitaller's veil.

'How many?' the Battle Sister asks, and the veiled head turns to scan from one side of the cramped cell to the other.

'All of them.' The Hospitaller's voice is as sharp as a scalpel's edge. 'Sister Véronique wishes to inspect them all. Any found unsuitable can be returned.'

Lethe closes her eyes. A key jingles as it turns in the lock, and suddenly the cell is alive with movement, half of the bodies pressing towards the opening gate and the other half away. The thief is still protesting his innocence – 'I put it back! I swear to the God-Emperor I put it back!' – as other voices add their pathetic wheedling to the clamour. If they knew what the Sisters have come for they would not be so keen to walk towards the light.

'You have sinned against the God-Emperor and against the Imperium of Man,' the Battle Sister says. 'But His forgiveness is infinite, and the Abbess Sanctorum has given me her permission to extend it to you.'

'Grant me forgiveness, blessed Sister,' a woman wheedles.

'All you must do is turn back to the light.'

'I repent!'

Lethe wants to vomit. Is this how the Sisters see her now? A filthy apostate, her soul offered to whichever power is closest? But is that not closer to the truth than she would care to admit? If the Sisters of the God-Emperor had come to free her from the mines, would she not have followed them with the same adoration she had felt for her new lord, the same service, the same joy? Some tiny, traitor part of her soul wishes that had been her lot in life. She might be in the cathedrum above, praying with her fellow devotees, instead of rotting down here in the dark.

Enough.

It is her lord's voice she hears in her head, his rich, contemptuous tones articulating her own thoughts. The Sisters would never have freed her. She is nothing to them. Even this offer of liberty is another falsehood, a trap, a trick, masquerading behind the face of virtue.

A metal gauntlet closes around her arm. Lethe opens her eyes and looks up into an implacable metal visor glinting in the faint orange light, and she is a child again, watching as her life burns to ash around her.

'No!' She pulls away, but the Sister's grip holds her fast. 'No! Let me go!'

With inexorable strength, the Battle Sister drags her forward. 'You have been offered the gift of atonement, and you cling to the path of sin. No matter. You will still serve.'

He is coming, Lethe thinks. My lord will come, and he will take me from this place and burn it to the ground. She keeps her silence as they shove her through the darkness, holding the thought of him close to her heart like treasure.

The abbess' quarters are luxurious by the standards of the Adepta Sororitas, but even the lowliest of the Ecclesiarchy's cardinals would be horrified by the spartan decor: a single bed pushed to the wall, a bas-relief effigy of the God-Emperor frozen in perpetual torment on the Golden Throne, a chair, an ashenwood desk and bookcase, a pair of white candles arranged on either side of a black iron altar. Morvenn had intended only to rest her eyes in preparation for the difficult hours to come, but the temptation of the cool flaxweave sheet lulls her to a shallow slumber, full of shapeless dreams and half-forgotten memories. She is still in the Convent Sanctorum, but it is the place where she spent her youth, built to a grander and more fearful scale than now, its stern-faced drill-abbesses and their tools of discipline the most terrible things in the Imperium. And there is something following her through the cloister, a dark and shapeless horror that vanishes every time she turns.

The knock at her door wakes her with a jolt. The dream takes a moment to fade, the inchoate panic and sense of pursuit by something terrible clinging to her like congealing blood. The knock comes again, and she rises to her feet.

'My abbess.' The door opens, and Zafiya steps in uninvited, her eyes deeply shadowed, fresh auditory augmetics glinting on the newly shaven skin above her ears. 'A reply has come from Holy Terra.'

'From Cardinal Ritira? What does she say?'

Zafiya's eyes drop to the scroll in her hand, but she makes no effort to unroll it. 'The choir will repeat the message to you should you wish–'

'Out with it.' The leaping hope in Morvenn's breast is fading. If her prayer had been granted, the Celestian surely would not look so solemn.

'As you prefer. The cardinal cannot accede to your request. The High Lords have made their position clear, and on this occasion Ophelia VII must stand alone.'

'I see.'

What had she expected? If the High Lords would not accede to her request when she stood before them as an equal, they would hardly have relented to her as a supplicant.

'Did the choir relay anything more?'

'I do not believe so.' Zafiya sets the scroll down on the altar and steps back. 'But I am to inform you that the cardinal did express her great regrets, and suggests a further course of action. There is a Viper-class scout ship within a short warp jump of the Ophelia System. If the Night Lords can be held back from the Convent Sanctorum, she believes it may be possible to evacuate a small number of high-ranking Ecclesiarchal personnel before the main assault begins. Yourself amongst them, of course.'

'No.' Morvenn is surprised by the vehemence of her own response. Ritira must think her a coward, ready to run from battle and leave her Sisters to die, all to save her own miserable skin. That might be acceptable behaviour for a High Lord of Terra, but not for one of the Adepta Sororitas, not even their leader.

'I will tell the prioress.'

'Wait.' Morvenn reaches out a hand to stop her. 'We could send the pilgrims. The lay preachers. The wounded.' The thought of Hiromi and her mangled leg sends a stab of guilt shooting through her. 'If you wish to go with Hiro I would not ask you to stay–'

'Have we displeased you, Abbess Sanctorum? Has our service fallen short of what the God-Emperor demands?'

'Of course not–'

'Then do not speak of sending us away. The Hospitallers have done their work. We are both ready to fight at your side.'

Morvenn studies her Celestian's face, and sees only steady loyalty in the sea-grey eyes. 'I fear for the Convent Sanctorum, and for the Adepta Sororitas,' she says softly.

'As do I. But the God-Emperor protects.'

'And what if He does not?' The anger she felt in the chapel is gone, resignation threatening to consume her in its place. 'Zafiya, I have prayed for a miracle over and over. I have begged the God-Emperor to send us a sign – anything to give us hope – and there is never an answer.'

Zafiya tilts her head to the side, and something in her expression softens. 'My abbess, I fear you have stared so long into the God-Emperor's light that it has blinded you. We live in an age of miracles and Living Saints, and yet you cannot see the truest miracle of all. You are the answered prayer.'

'What do you mean?'

'When the pilgrims of Ophelia VII prayed for deliverance, it was you the God-Emperor sent. When the enemies of the God-Emperor threatened our skies, it was you who slew the Heldrake. And now, with every soul in the Convent Sanctorum praying for victory in the battle to come, it is you who must lead them to it. *You* are the miracle.'

Morvenn shakes her head, the thought too ridiculous to entertain. 'I am no miracle.'

'You need not believe in it for it to be true. We believe, and that is enough.'

'You do not understand. Faith alone cannot win this battle. We are outnumbered, we are not enough. *I* am not enough–'

'Then we shall be proud to die at your side.' Zafiya folds her hands in the aquila. 'Now, my abbess. What message would you have me take to the choir?'

The choice lies ahead of her. Two paths – one into the dark, the other into the light. If only she knew which was which.

'Tell the High Lords we will stand. We will fight for what is ours and die before we see it in the hands of the enemy.'

XXX

Dusk falls like a shroud.

Morvenn stands on the balcony overlooking the wide expanse of ground that surrounds the Convent Sanctorum and tries to banish her fears. A column of light is winding its way through the city around them, marking the passage of Ophelia VII's refugees as they make their way through the gate in the outermost wall. Barricades are being dragged into position, emplacements checked and reinforced, units of gunners taking their place in the inner bastions to ensure that each foot of enemy advance will be paid for in blood. Every Sister in the convent is there, every novitiate capable of wielding a sword, every Crusader. All that she has stands ready to meet the Night Lords' attack.

And it is not enough.

What would you do?

It is not quite a prayer that she shapes in her mind, and not addressed to the God-Emperor. Instead, she thinks of Aleyna, her almost-saint, who she had thought would bring the miracle to save them.

If it were you here instead of me, what would you do?

The desperate column of the lost weaves over bridges and between jagged spires lit by wavering lumens, tiny specks of light in a world turning dark, while behind them, the smoke-cloud on the horizon marks the Night Lords' advance.

They are running out of time.

'We must close the outer gates.' Illuminata's voice is a low rasp. 'The tech-dominae tell me that the perimeter must be sealed in preparation for the raising of the void shields.'

Morvenn studies the column, trying to make out individual shapes from amongst the close-packed bodies. The gate marks the boundary between life and death, and she must be the one to seal it.

'How long do we have until the enemy reaches us?'

'Hours at most.' Illuminata shrugs. 'There is also the issue of how many more refugees we can take. The crypts are already packed with civilians. Better a quick death outside the walls than to starve or be crushed within them.'

That is a lie, of course. If the Night Lords reach them, their deaths will not be quick, but what choice does she have?

'Keep them open until the last possible moment.'

'That moment is now.'

The prioress' robes rustle against the stone floors as she leaves the balcony and descends the spiral stairs to the ground below. Morvenn extends a hand to ask her to wait – even the prioress' cold, critical company is better than nothing – but Illuminata has already gone. The urge to call her back is overwhelming, to beg her to take some small burden of command from Morvenn's shoulders, but she keeps her lips tightly pressed together against the words. She is Abbess Sanctorum. This place, and all those within it, are her responsibility.

She unfastens the oxblood leather pouch from her belt and removes the tiny detonator from inside. It is an elegant enough thing, the metal polished to a fine shine, the crimson rubies set into the eagle's claws gleaming like tiny beads of blood. There is a matching gem set into the right eye socket, but the left is a blinking crimson diode, the home of a tiny slumbering machine spirit. It exists for one purpose only, and if she wakes it, both its purpose and hers will end forever.

What would you do? she asks the dead woman again. But she knows what Aleyna would do, because Aleyna has already done it. Sacrifice is the duty of every Sister, and Morvenn's high rank serves only to add to the solemnity of that duty.

A steady rumble begins beneath her feet as the great iron gates grind shut. The stream of refugees reacts instantly, the procession turning to a crush of bodies as those outside make a desperate dash towards their last hope of safety. Shouts and screams rise with the tolling of the bell – too far away for Morvenn to make out the words, but she can imagine them clearly enough, desperate pleas for salvation that she cannot grant. Through the gap in the gates she watches the outline of a child as its guardian raises them into the air and passes them overhead to the pilgrim before them and then the next, until a human chain is conveying them to the front of the group and through the gate. Other small figures join it, and Morvenn marvels at the sacrifices she is witnessing, these the final desperate acts of hope and love.

Not all are so selfless. Some run forward, holding back the gates through weight of numbers alone, the great motors of the heavy portal shrieking with strain, before the sharp report of a bolt pistol breaks the deadlock. The last and boldest of the refugees surge forward, and then the gates slam shut like a guillotine.

Prioress Illuminata's voice booms out through her laud-hailers.

'The Convent Sanctorum is sealed. Take refuge in the chapels and shrines nearby and pray for deliverance. The God-Emperor protects.'

How many of those turned away will last the night? How many will be torn to bloody shreds for the amusement of a monstrous heretic, and how many will sell their souls to the adversary for a few brief hours of life? Perhaps the Death of Saints will arm them and turn them against the convent that has deserted them, increasing their numbers yet further. The bell tolls, the first chime of six to call the faithful to evening prayer. It is almost time.

'Are the defences ready?' An impossibly deep voice sounds in her ear, and she turns in surprise to find herself staring into the chestplate of a black-armoured warrior. The Black Templar has moved with uncanny stealth for his size, so close that she would be within easy reach of the scabbarded sword hanging between his shoulder blades were she to be fool enough to reach for it. The last rays of the sun are caressing the spires and domes of Ophelia VII, the air suddenly unexpectedly calm. It is as though the world is holding its breath, that sense of the wave pulled back before the tsunami crashes in, the stillness before the avalanche begins.

'As ready as they can be.'

The massive warrior tilts back his helmet, revealing a face that she recognises as belonging to one of the castellan's Sword Brothers. Balian, she thinks, the one who had stood at his right shoulder when they argued in the war-room.

'That is well,' he says. 'I have assumed command of the sons of Dorn who remain here until such time as Marshal Montford relieves me. Our oath binds us to the defence of Ophelia VII, and we will not forswear our solemn duty.'

Morvenn studies his face, looking for anger or contempt. There is nothing there but steady resolve.

'For all the angry words that passed between us, I grieve the loss of your castellan. He was a true warrior of the God-Emperor, and I deeply regret that my actions contributed to his death.'

Balian's heavy brow furrows. 'His blood is not on your hands,

Abbess Sanctorum. Do not indulge in the vanity of believing it to be so. He will be avenged, and he will be remembered for his deeds.'

The last ray of light touches the convent walls, turning the stone to gold.

'I understand you will address your warriors now.'

'So I intend.' Morvenn shakes her head. 'What must I tell them? How do I inspire them when the fight seems hopeless?'

'You know them better than I.'

'Do I? So many are strangers to me. Abbess Sabrina knew them – she knew us all. Had she survived her pilgrimage she would stand here, not I. They would have followed her to victory.'

'As they will follow you.' His tone brooks no disagreement. 'They will fight for the Abbess Sanctorum, for the unbroken line that stretches back to Alicia Dominica herself. You of all people should understand that.'

'And what if I fail? What if I am not worthy of their faith?'

The Sword Brother laughs, a surprisingly rich and pleasant sound. 'Do you think you are the first Abbess Sanctorum to have thought of such things, or to face a foe when she cannot be sure of victory?' He flexes the fingers of his right gauntlet one at a time, as though counting silently inside his head. How many of her predecessors has he fought with in his long life?

She stares at him, searching for the humanity in his dark brown eyes. Something flickers in their depths, and for a fleeting second there is a connection between them, the young abbess and the ageless soldier, a shared humanity born in service to their common god.

'All of the faithful know doubt,' he says.

'Even such as you?'

'"And they shall know no fear." Not "They shall know no doubt." But it is not in our thoughts that we prove our worth,

Sister. It is in our deeds. Tomorrow's battle will go down in the annals of history, whether in victory or defeat. My brothers and I are honoured that our names will be recorded along with yours.'

The last ray of the sun fades to black. Balian replaces his helmet and scans the darkness beyond the convent's walls.

'They are coming,' he says. 'If you would address your warriors, it must be now.'

Lethe fights as the Battle Sister drags her from the cells, fights as she is pushed downstairs into the depths of the catacombs below the cells, through rough-hewn stone passageways into tunnels lined with gleaming black tiles. A waist-high border bears a scrolling design of snakes and staves picked out in red and white, shining as though freshly scrubbed. The smell in the air has changed, too. Now it is neither the soft heaviness of the incense that accosted her senses when she first passed through the convent walls, nor the smell of sweat and human filth ingrained deep in the walls of the penitentium. This passageway smells of disinfectant, machine oil and fresh blood, and the door at the end is open.

'Wait.'

The Hospitaller moves ahead of the group of penitents and enters the chamber beyond. The same gleaming tiles cover the vaulted walls and roof, pillars of black marble dividing the room into interconnected chambers, each with their own medi-slab attended by a pair of robed chirurgeons in surgical vestments and veils. Lethe catches a glimpse of misshapen human bodies, blood trickling around rubber-booted feet that drains sluggishly through the grille in the centre of the chamber's tiled floor.

'Sister-Chirurgeon Véronique, we have the penitents.'

A tall, imposing Sister-chirurgeon turns from her medi-slab and walks towards the door, leaving the twisted lump of bleeding meat on the table behind her. What Lethe can see of it no longer looks remotely human – one arm severed at the shoulder, the other ending in a tangle of articulated metal tentacles, attended by one of the red-robed priests of Mars in the room.

'Bring them in.'

'Why are we here?' one woman asks, and the Battle Sister backhands her across the cheek.

'The Sisters Hospitaller have commanded your presence, penitent. Count yourself lucky to receive their care.'

The miserable group shuffle forward into the chamber. Lethe's muscles are locked rigid, her chest so tight she can barely breathe. The chirurgeon walks along the front rank, her medical mechadendrite hovering at her shoulder, her right hand pointing to each prisoner in turn like a preacher delivering a benediction.

'This one. And this one.'

Hospitallers move to attend to the nominated individuals, pressing a stimm-injector to each dirty neck. The prisoners stand like stunned grox as the drugs take effect, allowing themselves to be led to the medi-slabs with dull-eyed acceptance. The Hospitaller's hand hovers over the man who had protested his innocence with such persistence in the cells, then she shakes her veiled head.

'No. No. These three are unsuitable. Take these two for the penitent engines.'

The chosen pair recoil away at the sound of the fateful words, but the Hospitallers are ready with their sedatives. Lethe fixes her gaze on the floor, as if refusing to meet the Hospitaller's eye will render her somehow invisible.

'And this one.'

Does the Hospitaller mean her? Lethe musters her courage and looks up to see another wretch pushed forward. The Sister-chirurgeon's attention is already turning back to her medi-slab, as the Battle Sisters push the chosen few forwards.

'Take the rest away.'

Lethe sags with relief. They will take her back to the cells to await her lord, and when he comes she will be ready–

'Wait.' The Battle Sister at Lethe's side closes a gauntlet around her shoulder and shoves her into the room. 'The Abbess Sanctorum was clear that this one should be amongst their number.'

Véronique turns, a frown crossing her high-cheekboned face. 'Bring her forward.' She tilts her head downward so that she is staring into Lethe's eyes. 'Ah yes. The one who brought us the head of Sister Aleyna.'

The chirurgeon takes a stimm-injector from the pouch at her belt and moves it towards Lethe's neck. She writhes away in desperation, heedless of the pain as the Battle Sister seizes her by the hair.

'No! Please, no–'

Her struggles buy her a few feet of movement, achieving nothing but a better view of the medi-slab and its gruesome occupant, partially skinned with a pair of twisted metal goads in place of its arms. The face is covered in a dark iron grille from chin to browbone, secured with heavy iron bolts, and the top of the skull has been removed to reveal the gleaming grey matter pulsating slowly beneath, two long hypodermics plunged deep into the cortex.

Panic tightens its grip on her throat. They will muzzle her again. They will open her skull and lay her thoughts bare, flood her with drugs that will strip away all rational thought, then turn her on her lord. Worst of all is the thought that some small part of her might still be conscious within the abomination that they will make of her body, horrified yet powerless to act against the relentless chemical control.

'Please. No.'

She jerks her head to the side as the stimm-injector hisses out its fine mist of drugs so that half of the dose is lost in the air. Even so, half of the dose is enough. Numbness radiates out from the point of contact, first her skin and then the flesh beneath growing cold and thick. She tries to move her left arm, but it feels as though the nerves animating it have been severed, then the strength goes out of her remaining limbs one at a time. She tries to scream, but her mouth will not open. She cannot move, cannot breathe – but her thoughts remain as sharp as ever.

They are going to remake her, and she will be aware of every moment.

The Hospitaller leans forward and props the eyelids of Lethe's left eye open with a device made of silver wire, then applies the same attention to the right.

'Sister Carmine, finish our work. I wish to give this supplicant my full attention.' The chirurgeon points to the medi-slab in the centre of the room. 'Place her on the table.' She moves her face close to Lethe's and lowers her voice to a whisper. 'Let us see if there is anything in you worthy of the God-Emperor's mercy.'

The convent's Basilikum is already full by the time Morvenn arrives at the door, the thin silkweave robe and the bodyglove beneath doing little to keep the chill from the air. Inside, the Sisters of the Militant Orders are moving in squads as though the battle is already underway, replenishing ammunition, sharpening blades and anointing their weapons with sacred oils. One of the Sisters Dogmata – the tall, gaunt Sister Jura of the Sacred Rose – is striding between groups, incense billowing from the head of her anointed mace. The air is alive with prayer and purpose. Novitiates are readying themselves alongside full-fledged Sisters Militant, Crusaders kneeling in prayer in the side chapels. Even the pilgrims have come, packed into every available inch of the transept and the nave. There are children among them, the aged, the wounded and the maimed, but others stand tall, faithful, proud. They are here to receive her blessing, and if the God-Emperor is kind, Morvenn will make of them a blessing of her own.

Through the open door she watches a Mistress of Novitiates blessing autopistol after autopistol, handing them to girls barely old enough to bear arms. Each of them has a simple blade at her side, most already in their carapace corselet, vambraces and greaves. Setting them against the army of heretics approaching their gates feels like sending doves into the talons of hawks, but there is no fear in any of their faces, only resolve.

How many of them will survive the battle that is to come?

The answer could so easily be none at all.

'Kneel for the Abbess Sanctorum!'

Prioress Illuminata's voice booms from the dais, where she stands beside the Purgator Mirabilis. She has donned a suit of battle plate, her white hair a riot of colour in the borrowed light of the glassaic window. Outside the sky is dark, but here in the Basilikum hidden lumen-arrays ensure that all is bathed in sacred colour, the saints and their Sisters gazing down from each vast arched window to their living successors below.

The congregation fall to their knees as Morvenn walks down the transept towards the altar, Sisters, Crusaders and pilgrims all bending in supplication – all but the Black Templars on either side of the altar, their hands at chest height on the pommels of their swords, still as statues. Morvenn kneels before the golden effigy of the God-Emperor. Two cherubim lift the silken robe from her shoulders. Incense billows from the great censer hanging overhead.

A lifetime has passed since the last time she took part in the ceremony of armouring. On Holy Terra she had been restless, eager for physical conflict when all that awaited her was a war of words. If she had won what she had sought from the High Lords of Terra, the battle ahead of her might not be so desperate.

Prioress Illuminata steps forward and slips the gambeson around her shoulders. Celestian Zafiya places the vambrace around her right wrist, while Hiromi – standing a trifle unsteadily on her new augmetic leg but standing all the same – armours her left.

'*Ave Imperator.*'

'Will you accept the burden of this sacred armour?' Illuminata declaims.

'In the God-Emperor's name, I will!'

'Will you wield these weapons – the Lance of Illumination and the thrice-blessed heavy bolter Fidelis – as the God-Emperor ordained, with hatred and fury?'

Every human face in the Basilikum is gazing up at her. Perhaps there is some truth in what Zafiya told her – that they see in her a miracle, an answer to their prayers. If that is so, then it falls to her to be the leader they need.

'In the God-Emperor's name, I will!'

A single voice rises in song, the melody high and pure, the words the unintelligible cant of the Zephyrim. It lacks the complex harmony of Holy Terra's servitor choir, but it is a living sound and all the more precious for that. Morvenn searches for the singer, and her eye falls on a gaunt, pallid Sister of the Argent Shroud with a steel plate bolted to the side of her half-shaven head. Her face is familiar, and a moment's thought brings her name to mind: Perdita, one of Aleyna's companions in the cathedrum. The wounded Seraphim whose death had seemed inevitable has been reborn to holy wisdom. A Zephyrim joins her newest Sister, and then another, until the whole silver-clad squad is singing in unison.

'Will you lead us to Holy War, that all who stand against us shall perish by the bolter and the blade?'

'In the God-Emperor's name, I will!'

'Then don this armour and wield these weapons that you may deal death to all enemies of the faith!'

Morvenn swings herself up into the Purgator's command cradle and closes her hands around the control rods. The soft vibration of its servo-motors soothes the tension from her muscles. The cherubim return, bearing a helm between them on a red velvet cushion, and she takes it in both hands and mag-locks it to her belt. She raises the Lance of Illumination in her right hand and activates the blade.

The congregation falls silent, waiting for her word.

She will not fail them.

'Servants of the God-Emperor!' Her laud-hailer captures and amplifies her voice, sending it echoing back from the cathedrum's vaulted ceiling and overhanging galleries. The sound of her own voice is unfamiliar, more akin to her memory of Abbess Sabrina when last she heard her speak, but perhaps that is all to the good. 'My Sisters. Sons of Dorn. Crusaders of the Holy Ecclesiarchy. We stand on the brink of war. An enemy is coming who intends to tear this convent to the ground.'

A vivid image of the arch-heretic flashes into her mind, his midnight armour with its brazen trim reflecting the blazing fires of the burning shrine-city.

'Kol Rakhul calls himself the Death of Saints, and in truth the name is well earned. He leaves in his wake a trail of bloody footprints across the centuries, seeking revenge for an imagined wrong. He has sent many faithful souls to the Golden Throne, and corrupted countless others to his foul cause. There is none in this world more deserving of our hatred and our wrath. Perhaps none in the Imperium itself.'

A bell tolls in the spire.

'Many of you have fought at my side – some at the Cathedrum

of Athenasia the Martyr, others in the battle for Caelestis, where we slew the Heldrake, and where many lives were lost, Castellan Tancret amongst them. I was proud to fight with you then, just as I am proud to lead you now.'

She had expected the words to ring hollow – she is, after all, no politician and orator – but sincerity grants them power. Heads are nodding in the congregation, a soft murmur of assent rising from a hundred throats. In other times she might have marvelled at how easy the masses are to manipulate, but today all she can feel is a fierce and burning loyalty. They believe in her. Is it not then her duty to believe along with them that this war may yet end in victory?

'And there are those of you who are yet to fight. Some of you saw the miracle at the cathedrum, when the God-Emperor granted Sister Aleyna the power to hold back the Heldrake, and you were blessed indeed. But I believe that each of you who has made the journey through Ophelia VII has made it for a reason. And that reason is to fight.'

A murmur like the rustle of ancient parchment passes through the congregation. The Crusaders are on their feet, but so many of the pilgrims' faces are registering disbelief that she wonders if she has gone too far.

'We are outnumbered. The enemy brings with him a host of the damned – warriors of legend and daemon engines with powers beyond the ken of the righteous. The weak-willed and the corrupt have flocked to his banner, but I see in your faces the courage to stand against him. Every blow we strike against him will rise as a paean of praise to the God-Emperor. And I would have every one of you who can fight at my side as we strike those blows.'

Horrified snippets reach her ears: *Does she mean we should fight? Prayers, surely she means our strength through prayer.* And: *Listen and let her speak!*

'I ask you to take up arms in defence of the Convent Sanctorum. To fight with the Adepta Sororitas, for the God-Emperor, and for Ophelia VII.'

'We are not warriors, Abbess Sanctorum.' A young man's shaking voice drifts from the front row of the congregation. 'And besides, it is forbidden–'

'Forbidden for you, perhaps.' The interruption comes from a rangy woman, her scalp half-covered in white-blonde stubble, half with dyed-blue waves. 'The Decree Passive forbids the Ecclesiarchy to have men under arms, not women.' She rises to her feet. 'Give me a weapon, blessed abbess. I will fight for the convent and her saints.'

'This is madness,' a man in stained velvet robes murmurs.

'They have protected us,' the woman says. 'Do you not remember the cathedrum? How the blessed saint protected us in our hour of need?'

Others amongst them are nodding now. Death might have thwarted any attempt to canonise her, but Aleyna is a saint to them all the same.

'What did she save us for if not for this?'

I know why she saved you, Morvenn wants to say. *She saved you because she saw the worth in you, loved the human soul in you, knew your value was greater than that of a long-dead relic in a gilded box. She should be here in my place, or if not, at my side. She was the best of us, and all that is left is to honour the sacrifice she made.*

Prioress Illuminata raps her stave on the dais. 'Pilgrims! Remember in whose presence you kneel!'

'No more kneeling.' Morvenn pilots the Purgator Mirabilis to the edge of the dais. 'Those who would fight with me, on your feet.'

And they rise.

Some are visibly injured, others too old or young to be fit for the fray, but that does not matter. The Hospitallers will need assistants, the armourers hands to fetch and carry and work the bellows. There are many cogs in the machine of war.

'Any of you who will fight as my zealots, I accept your service. Those of you who cannot fight will be found work in the convent's defence. There will be sanctuary in the crypts for those of you who can only pray. That service, too, is holy.'

Morvenn pauses and surveys her impromptu reinforcements. Even the man in the shabby velvets is on his feet, fists clenched tight as though he is ready to take on the arch-heretic with his bare hands.

'I cannot promise you victory, for only He can do that. But I promise I will fight at your side, and when the battle is over, the God-Emperor will know our names as heroes and martyrs. For the God-Emperor!'

Even the Black Templars join the answering cry. 'For the God-Emperor!'

The echo dies, but the vibration in the stones does not. The lumens dim, and a low-pitched hum that sets the hair prickling on the back of Morvenn's neck tells her that the void shields have risen.

'It is time. Warriors of the Convent Sanctorum, to arms. We are called to holy war.'

XXXI

The Convent Sanctorum is many things.

It is a place of worship and devotion, a shrine for the relics of ten thousand years, a place of refuge for the faithful, but first and foremost it is a fortress. The fortified wall is a six-pointed star standing sixty feet high, the bastion towers at its corners named for the matriarchs. A void shield generator stands at the foot of each tower, the generator coils at its base and the crackling blue orbs above them projecting a shimmering protective dome. It has withstood countless sieges in its long history.

But never the Death of Saints.

Morvenn has been a student of war her entire life, strategy and counter-strategy studied, applied and adapted, and yet the Night Lords defy understanding. The only constant to be relied upon is the perverse satisfaction they take in varying their manner of attack to keep their enemy perpetually off balance, disorientated and vulnerable. It seems their divine father gave them the gift of infinite ingenuity, before they cast aside their filial piety and put those gifts to other, darker ends.

The perimeter wall bears weapons of its own – useless as long as the void shields remain in place, but essential for the convent's defence should they fall. Heavy gun emplacements are built into the top of each bastion, capable of concentrating overlapping fields of fire on the ground on either side of the perimeter, while inside the walls secondary bulwarks have been raised to force any breaching enemy to pass through narrow channels to reach the inner sanctum. Squads of Retributors with heavy bolters stand on the parapets, ready to rain down death in the event of a breach, units of Battle Sisters in position in gun emplacements prepare to deal with any enemy who thinks to clear the kill-zones by speed alone. Half of the new-made zealots stand ready to reinforce them, while the other half remain in reserve inside the convent itself, awaiting the command to join the battle when the time comes. Once the shields and the walls come down, the battle will turn in seconds from order to chaos. Only then will she learn if her preparations have been enough.

'Morvenn Vahl!'

The voice booms over the perimeter wall, the syllables of her name articulated with slow and malicious care. The Death of Saints' army – that which he has chosen to reveal, which means that nine-tenths is still out of sight – has come to a halt a little distance from the walls, just out of bolter range.

'I have come to right the wrong that was done to me! Come out and face me, and those who stand with you need not suffer!'

The Sanctorum Guard falls silent. Any talk of an honour duel to settle the matter is nothing but a distraction to keep her eye elsewhere while he makes his first move. This is a battle to be fought in her mind as much as with her body.

Morvenn sets her vox-amplifiers to full, her voice booming from the steps of the Convent Sanctorum. 'And I have an offer for you, O Death of Saints!'

She flicks rapidly through the pict-feeds in the corner of her visor display, and stops as a series of images transmitted by the vid-skulls on the outer wall catches her eye. A group of ragged figures is making its way towards the point where the nearest void shield touches the ground – no, not one group but two, the larger group unarmed, the smaller prodding the rest forward with whips and goads. There is no possibility of them breaching the shield with such crude weapons.

What is he planning?

'I will listen.' This time Rakhul's voice booms from behind her, as though he were already standing within the convent's grounds. A group of novitiates flinch, their veiled heads turning to follow the sound before their mistress redirects their attention.

'Return the skull of Athenasia the Martyr, and I will grant you the God-Emperor's mercy.'

The shadowy figures have come to a halt near the foot of Mina's Bastion.

'Do you see them?' Illuminata voxes softly from the war-room. *'Cultists. I see three groups. Close to the walls. Moving where the spot-lumens do not reach.'*

'I see them,' Morvenn sub-voxes. 'What are they doing?'

A snarl echoes from every direction. 'Your arrogance will be your undoing, Morvenn Vahl!'

'I have heard those words before. I did not fear them then, and I do not fear them now.'

'See how little your abbess values your lives. Remember, as the blood runs from your veins, that she holds her pride–'

'For the God-Emperor!' Celestian Hiromi's voice cuts across the heretic's words. 'For the God-Emperor!'

Rakhul continues to speak, but the chant grows in volume and power as the rest of the Sanctorum Guard join her, until the walls themselves are trembling with the force of the sound.

'For the God-Emperor!'

'For the God-Emperor!' Morvenn roars.

Silence falls.

'Then see what your pride has bought.'

The screams come next. Through the pict-feeds Morvenn watches the cultists outside the walls turn their attention to their helpless charges, blades and whips descending with meticulous cruelty. Screams of pain drift through the still night air, and the pilgrim warriors inside the walls react instantly, their faces turning ashen.

'How many families did you carve in two with the closing of the gate?'

The screams are growing louder now, the sobbing from beyond the walls mingling with howls of grief from within. Zafiya catches her eye, an expression of unease crossing her face. The pilgrims' morale hangs by a thread already, and it will take little to break them.

'Open the gates, and I will show mercy to those who received none from you.'

'Your deeds prove there is no mercy in you.'

A piercing shriek comes across the wall. He is vox-amplifying them, Morvenn realises in disgust, the better to project the noise of suffering inside.

A middle-aged pilgrim screams, shoving herself forward through the ranks, her face twisted with agony. 'Elodie! Please, I beg you – open the gates!'

'Squad Varna, secure that woman.' Morvenn gestures to a unit of Battle Sisters, who move to surround the pilgrim group. The battle has not yet begun, and already their weapons are turned inward. The woman is still screaming, tears streaking her face, pushing her way through a scene of growing consternation. Another pilgrim runs forward to seize her, but she shakes him off and plunges onward, limbs thrashing wildly in the futile attempt to reach the gates.

'God-Emperor of Terra, our souls we pledge to thee...'

A unit of Sisters Dominion raise their voices, but even in full harmony the song is not enough to drown the sounds of agony from outside the walls. The butt of a Godwyn-De'az boltgun brings the screaming pilgrim woman to the ground, but the chaos is spreading through Morvenn's army like fire through tinder.

A flicker of motion inside the west wall draws Morvenn's attention. She focuses her helm-lenses on a running figure – but he is not heading for the gates, and as he sprints towards Arabella's Bastion, his tattered robes blow back to reveal a crude explosive vest.

He is running for the void shield generator.

She reacts instantly. Fidelis swings upward and discharges a heavy shell through the air. Her aim is true, and the man explodes as the shell ignites his explosives.

'*Ave Dominus Nox!*' The scream is followed by a second explosion, this one in the midst of the pilgrims. The blast sends shards of metal ripping through unarmoured flesh, tearing heads from necks and limbs from torsos. A vast plume of smoke billows upwards, obscuring the dead and dying – and the wall behind them.

'All your defences are worth nothing when my faithful are already inside.' Rakhul's amplified voice drips satisfaction.

'The void shields!' Morvenn shouts. 'Secure the generators!'

But she is already too late.

'It begins, then,' the Sister-chirurgeon says, as the explosion above shakes the roof of the laboratorium. Lethe stares up at her with her pinned-open eyes and waits for the scalpel to descend. If the Archenemy were to appear and offer her the power to slay the Hospitaller with her gaze, she would have sold her soul a thousand times over, but there is no dark miracle, only this endless anticipation filled with cleansing unguents and prayer.

A sharp report echoes into the chamber. Lethe flinches away from the imagined gunshot before logic reasserts itself. The noise is that of an armoured fist on the laboratorium door.

'Sister-chirurgeon! You must come quickly!'

Metal rings on metal as the chirurgeon returns her scalpel to a curved metal dish. Lethe feels an absurd sense of frustration. She has been braced so long for torment that its failure to materialise is almost a disappointment.

'What is it?' Sister-Chirurgeon Véronique motions to the other Hospitaller. 'Open the door. See what it is they want.'

A red-faced novitiate is standing in the doorway, a pair of Battle Sisters a little further behind her in the passageway. 'The assault is underway–'

'So much I understand, yes. Our work here is not yet finished.'

Lethe concentrates all of her strength into her neck, and is rewarded with the merest inclination of her head. The paralytic's iron grip on her is easing – perhaps the fact that she evaded a portion of the dose is limiting its effect – and the urge to blink her eyes is almost irresistible. She tries to ignore the pressure of the clamp against her opened lids. If the Sister-chirurgeons notice that her ability to move is returning they will remove it permanently.

One of the Battle Sisters joins the novitiate at the door. 'One more arco-flagellant will make little difference to the battle. You are required to tend to the wounded.'

'The Abbess Sanctorum was most explicit that this particular specimen should be subjected to arco-flagellation, for what little good it may do her soul. Am I to take it that order has been countermanded?'

'The prioress has ordered that all chirurgeons are required on the battlefield. Especially you, Sister Véronique.'

With a sigh, the chirurgeon removes her heavy surgical gauntlets and casts them to the side. Lethe tracks her movement without moving her head. She tries an experimental flex of her fingers, and is surprised to feel them twitch.

'Very well. Sisters, conclude your work. Carmine, extend the God-Emperor's mercy to this wretch.'

'Certainly, Sister.' The shorter chirurgeon lifts her Superior's discarded scalpel and weighs it thoughtfully in her hand. Lethe tries to bend her knees, but manages only a few useless twitches. If she was free to lift her legs and kick out at the woman, she might manage to buy time to arm herself with one of the dangerous-looking surgical tools on the tray, but the paralytic is wearing off with agonising slowness. She cannot even close her eyes, only watch in horror as the gleaming blade rises and falls–

And stops.

The chirurgeon's eyes fill with horror. 'S-sister Véronique,' she stammers.

'What is it?'

'In the passageway…'

An unearthly blue-violet light is rippling across the dark tiles, the reflection of a brighter light glowing further down the tunnel. A sharp, sulphurous gust joins the acrid odour of the counter-septics, and a fiery ball of light erupts outwards in a flare of indescribable colour. Hellish shrieks blast through the infirmarium – Lethe tries to close her eyes, but the merciless clamps hold her lids open, forcing her to watch as a taloned figure rips an opening into reality.

It is huge – twelve feet tall and half as broad at the shoulders, the helmeted head hanging low below the hulking shoulders, grotesquely elongated lightning claws dangling at the end of its arms. It wears the same blue-and-bronze armour as its fellow Night Lords, but exposure to the warp has altered its proportions, making it more monster than man. The Battle Sister in the corridor fires her boltgun, and the Warp Talon surges forward without hesitation, talons sharp enough to slice through reality carving through armour and flesh in a single vicious slice. She falls in silence, as a second portal to the empyrean flares and another hellish warrior drags itself through.

The surviving Battle Sister shoves the novitiate behind her and opens fire, the priests of Mars and the Sisters Hospitaller raising weapons of their own.

'Carmine!' Sister Véronique says. 'Deal with the criminal. We must retreat!'

'God-Emperor, accept the soul of this penitent, and grant her forgiveness if you see fit.'

The scalpel blade plunges towards Lethe's throat. At the last possible moment, she hurls herself to the side, the clumsy movement enough to topple her to the ground in a heap of useless limbs, the instrument tray and its contents clattering around her as she falls. She tries to rise, but her limbs are still leaden, each convulsive motion requiring a surpassing effort of will. Face down, she drags herself along the base of the medi-slab, waiting for the scalpel-blade to descend on the exposed nape of her neck – but instead there is only a sound like tearing cloth followed by a warm spatter of liquid in her hair. The scalpel falls to the ground in front of her, and she drags herself towards it inch by painful inch as the novitiate's screams end, turning to the tearing of wet meat. A low-pitched growl echoes from the laboratorium's vaulted ceiling, heavy footsteps scraping across the tiled floor.

Lethe pulls the clamps from her eyelids, presses her back to the medi-slab and turns to face the approaching terror.

The Warp Talon fills her vision. Gore is dripping from the blades of its hands, the severed heads and limbs of the dead Sisters littering the ground around it. It hunches forward, the skull-faced helmet like the muzzle of some predatory beast tasting the air.

'The Death of Saints!' The words come out of her mouth thick and slurred. 'I am his herald–'

Flaming plasma gouts through the darkness of the corridor and explodes against the back of the Warp Talon's helmet. It turns, and with speed that distorts the air around it hurls itself back along the passageway to meet its assailant. A chainsword screams as its teeth bite into ceramite, wild shadows dancing on the tiled walls.

'I am his herald,' Lethe repeats to herself. Her hands and feet are burning as though she has thrust them into an open fire, but her muscles are waking from their enforced slumber. She shoves herself up onto her knees, locks one hand around the edge of the medi-slab and drags herself to her feet to search for an exit. A heavy wooden door on the far wall is already open, and she shoves herself through, convinced that it will open onto a storage chamber or a blind-ending alcove, but she finds herself in a narrow passageway that leads to a spiral staircase heading up.

'I am coming, my lord,' she whispers, as the sounds of combat behind her turn to screams. 'I am coming.'

Smoke roils in a plume from the damaged void shield generator. Morvenn urges the Purgator Mirabilis towards its sparking remains, a trinity of Paragons and her Celestians at her side. Two more cultists lie dead, gunned down before reaching their objectives, but the generator at Silvana's Bastion is gone, the coils at its base shredded by the force of the blast along with the hand that detonated the explosives.

Five-sixths of the void shields are still intact, but a segment is missing over the ruined bastion, leaving the wall beneath it exposed. The smoke of the explosion is yet to clear, obscuring the view of the sky, but the roar of jump packs heralds the enemy's first aerial assault.

'Bring forth the angelic hosts!'

A trumpet signals the attack. From their vantage points high on the Convent Sanctorum's dome, Seraphim and Zephyrim soar upward, their banners fluttering in crimson and gold, their braziers streaming flame. The Zephyrim lead the charge, power swords burning like beacons, the Seraphim with their paired pistols close behind. They fly towards the breach in the void shields as the dark silhouettes of Raptors resolve out of the night.

'The augurs are registering a disturbance in the catacombs.' Illuminata sounds distracted, and Morvenn cannot blame her. A flanking attack from below is entirely in keeping with what she would expect of the Death of Saints.

'Images.'

'Transferring them to you now.'

Morvenn divides her attention between the battle unfolding in the sky and the grainy pict-cast in the corner of her visor display, where a squad of Battle Sisters are engaging Warp Talons in the catacombs beneath the convent. The image flares brilliant white, and when the pict-cameras refocus, another monstrosity has hauled itself through a rend in reality to join the fight.

'Dispatch a squad to assist them.'

'Who would you have me send?'

'Mobilise Dominions. Three squads.' A Raptor swoops low over the battlefield, and Morvenn sprays heavy bolter shells to drive him back onto the sword of a silver-clad Zephyrim. The Traitor Space Marine pulls himself free of the crackling blade and redoubles his attack. More Raptors are swooping to join their brethren, their objective becoming more obvious with each assault. Some are aiming for the gate, others for the five remaining void shield generators.

'Celestians, to the gates. Gunners, take aim. Bring them down!'

The angelic hosts surge upward as pintle-mounted autocannons fill the air beneath the dome with a spray of ordnance. A unit of Raptors reacts too slowly to avoid the deadly hail, one of them ripped to shreds before he can fall back, a second hurtling to earth like a flaming meteor as his jump pack ignites. The Zephyrim close on them immediately, their swords ablaze with angelic light, cleaving limbs from torsos and heads from shoulders in mighty blows. Morvenn can hear their wordless song above the thunder of their bolt pistols, high and pure and filled with divine inspiration.

'Dominions dispatched,' Illuminata voxes. *'I recommend we seal the crypt doors as a precaution.'*

'And leave the Sisters there to die?'

'They can be opened again if need be, but we cannot afford to fight a battle on two fronts. If we do not seal the catacombs now then we risk being overrun.' Illuminata pauses. *'And I have more energy signals in the tunnels, approaching from the north.'*

'More Warp Talons?'

'I cannot be sure.'

A flashing light on Morvenn's visor heralds an incoming message. She adjusts the vox-channel, and is rewarded with a deafening burst of static in her right ear. 'What–'

'Abbess Sanctorum!' The woman's voice is a full shout but is still barely audible through the roar of white noise. *'…svieta… Rose!'*

'Repeat yourself!'

Another Raptor swoops within reach, and this time she is quicker, blasting the jump pack from its shoulders with a volley of heavy shells and moving to engage as it drops to the ground. It lands in a deft crouch, bringing the meltagun in its hands around to aim directly at her face, but she lashes out with the Lance of Illumination, the blow sending the Raptor hurtling to the ground. Another shell blasts his right arm into pulp, and she reverses the Purgator's grip on the Lance and drives it vertically downward through his chest. The Raptor shrieks as he dies, the echoes of mortal agony lingering after his corpse has ceased to twitch.

The vox is still hissing in her ear. *'...eft – na's Hope...'* Another deafening crackle. Then: *'...catacombs... close–'*

'Illuminata,' Morvenn voxes, trying to keep the hope from her voice. 'The energy signals in the tunnels. Could they be armoured Sisters?'

A huge shell strikes the void shields close to the destroyed generator at Silvana's Bastion, sending ripples of iridescence spreading across the protective dome.

'I believe so.'

A bright peal of laughter bursts from Morvenn's throat. She takes aim at a swooping Raptor, fires, and watches in satisfaction as the shell blasts him from the air.

'Canoness Elsvieta! Engage the Warp Talons in the catacombs. They must not reach the convent!'

The Sisters of the Bloody Rose have come at last.

And then another shell obliterates the wall at Silvana's Bastion, and all hell surges inside.

XXXII

'Defend the breach!'

Even before the smoke has cleared, the enemy is surging inside. Hundreds of humans in rags and tatters spring forward, as though every penitentium on Ophelia VII has been opened and its inhabitants recruited to blasphemous service. Heavy gunfire rains down from the wall, obliterating the first row of the enemy advance, but the cultists are all but limitless in number. Behind them the vast shadow of a Venomcrawler lurks just beyond the lumens' reach, but it does not join the headlong dash. Instead, its heavy cannons take aim at the gun emplacements on the walls, hammering one after another with meticulous precision.

'Make them pay for every inch of ground!'

Heavy fire from the Retributors hammers the first to climb over the ruins of the wall and the corpses of their own mutilated fellows, careless of their own survival, each rank striving only to cover a yard further than those before them. They press into the narrow kill-boxes, hurling grenades towards the Sisters above them on the secondary emplacements. Most of the explosives are returned before they can detonate, but one explodes at the feet of a Retributor with a heavy flamer, setting her fuel tank ablaze.

'Gunners – destroy the Venomcrawler!'

Streaks of brilliant light sear out from the lascannon on the perimeter wall, and the daemon engine answers in kind. A massive shell slams into the wall, destroying the gun emplacement and gunner in a single brilliant explosion, and a raucous cheer rises from the heretics below. The fire from the Retributor's fuel tank is spreading, sending thick black smoke pluming into the air – other heretics are hurling lit bottles of fuel stuffed with rags to set up smaller blazes of their own.

Chaos unfolds before her, making it impossible to turn her gaze elsewhere...

Which is exactly what she must do.

'Celestians Sacresant! Seal the breach!'

Morvenn steps back as the warriors storm past, shields raised in defence and maces drawn back ready to strike. She turns her attention inward, to the images flashing across her vision from outside the walls – the cultists surging through the breach, the Heretic Astartes massing by the gate at Dominika's Bastion. Another huge shell hammers the void shields from above, the flaring light highlighting a swooping Raptor and the Zephyrim in close pursuit as they hurtle overhead. Squads of Battle Sisters have formed around the base of each shield generator, their boltguns yet to fire.

The first rank of the cultists reaches the Celestians Sacresant, lashing out in impotent fury, clawing at the great golden shields in the vain attempt to drag the Sisters down, even as their skulls are crushed and bones splintered. Another shell takes out the wall-mounted gun emplacement on the other side of the breach, but the Retributors behind their barricades continue to thunder death down on the invaders.

Where are the Chaos Space Marines?

'Elsvieta!' Morvenn tries the canoness' vox-channel. 'Are the catacombs secure?' A combat patrol of Sisters of the Bloody Rose would be a welcome addition to the battlefield, but any reply is drowned out by a whistling roar as a shell skims through the breach and detonates in the centre of the advancing cultists.

Even a hundred yards away the force of the blast sends the Purgator Mirabilis reeling backwards. The heat is unbearable even through her helmet, and she raises her visor on reflex to draw in a breath of equally scalding air. The Paragons are still upright as Hiromi and Zafiya scramble back to their feet, scorched and dirtied but seemingly unharmed – but the kill-zone beneath what remains of Bastion Silvana has been levelled.

He has killed his own, she thinks dully, her ears ringing. Why would he destroy so many of his own followers?

And the second charge begins, and this time they are not cultists.

The earth shakes as the Chaos Space Marines thunder through the breach, crushing the remains of their acolytes and the broken bodies of the defenders beneath armoured boots. The Celestians Sacresant who had dealt such a devastating blow against the enemy a moment before are reduced to metal and meat, the Retributors and their heavy weapons lost in a single sacrificial assault.

'Dominions! Forward!'

Fast-moving shock troops move forward from the reserves. She charges with them, adding the thunder of the heavy bolter to the searing rasp of their meltaguns, but the Heretic Astartes have bolters of their own. They return fire with unexpected discipline. She raises Fidelis' gunshield to cover the Sister to her left, but on her right a bolter shell rips the head from a Dominion's shoulders, the body continuing to run forward for another few steps before toppling forward to the ground. Flames are spreading rapidly across the battlefield, the thick smoke roiling upwards to catch beneath the dome of the void shields, a heavy haze spreading through the air.

'Illuminata! *Fiat Lux!*'

'Upon your order, Abbess Sanctorum.'

Wall-mounted lumens around the inside of the perimeter wall blaze into life, driving out all shadows with their brilliance, and a brief lance of triumph shoots through her. The Death of Saints has come to extinguish the light of Ophelia VII, but she will deny him his darkness. The advancing Chaos Space Marines are no less horrifying in the light, their mutilated faces and blasphemous armour now clearly visible, but something of the terror of the unknown is gone.

The first of the Heretic Astartes is within reach. She smashes the Lance through a spiked blue pauldron and drives him to the ground. The fanged mouth opens, but before he can disgorge his blasphemies she slices through his head just below the eyes. Blood sprays from the open mouth and he topples to the ground, his place instantly taken by another warrior. She slams the ferrule of the Lance into his chest, and as he staggers back gasping for breath she blasts him from his feet with a bolter shell.

There is no time to check the pict-feeds, and strategic control is slipping away. Her task is impossible – one woman alone cannot fight and command.

But she is not alone.

'Prioress Illuminata. You must be my eyes. Describe the battlefield for me.'

A thunderous impact shakes the earth, the air filling with the smell of sulphur and gun smoke, the rattle of hellforged iron chains, the roaring shriek of a damned soul in agony. A colossal figure that towers over even the Purgator Mirabilis stamps forward out of the smoke, chains bolted into its chestplate binding it to Chaos warriors that attend it. One arm ends in a plasma cannon, the other in a double-headed warhammer. Sharpened bone spurs protrude from its armoured back, twin torrents of fire roaring from its shoulder-mounted braziers. Somewhere beneath the spikes the outline of the Dreadnought it once was is visible, but where the helm should be there is only a circular maw ringed with two rows of fangs, a red-eyed skull half-covered in rotting meat screaming in its centre.

'Very well, Abbess Sanctorum,' Illuminata begins, but another scream of rage from the Dreadnought's tormented throat drowns her out. With a convulsive burst of strength it tugs on its chains, sending a heretic attendant flying through the air, and storms towards her.

'Prioress, wait...'

Morvenn urges the Purgator Mirabilis forward to meet the Helbrute's charge. Vivid purple-white plasma washes over her, her energy field rippling as it turns the searing heat aside. The Helbrute stamps its massive foot and screams again as it brings the hammer down in an overhand strike. Morvenn catches the blow on her gunshield and answers with a volley of bolter shells. It slams the hammer down again, the skull's mouth gaping wide as blow follows blow, forcing her on to one knee, her heavy shells ricocheting uselessly from its armour.

'Celestians! Deal with the rest!'

Morvenn activates the missile launchers on the Purgator's shoulders. They have barely left the armour when they detonate, the force of the blast driving her back as much as it does the Helbrute, but it has bought her a moment to recover. This time when she throws herself forward she matches the corrupted Dreadnought's aggression with her own, stabbing the Lance towards its exposed flesh again and again until her muscles are screaming in protest, in unison with the Purgator's servo-motors. The Lance's blade gouges deep furrows through the Helbrute's armoured carapace revealing disturbingly organic-looking flesh beneath, but the injuries serve only to drive it into a wilder rage.

She swings the Lance again, but this time the Helbrute deflects it with a wild haymaker that crashes into her warsuit's shoulder and sends it staggering to the side. The daemonic face screams again, the hammer lashing back and forward, the chains whipping the air in its wake as the plasma cannon belches gout after gout of glowing energy. The Purgator's energy field is straining now, warning runes flashing in her visor in time with her hammering pulse. The Helbrute is not tiring – it cannot tire, trapped in eternal service to its dark masters – and her options are narrowing by the moment.

Another blow slams into her gunshield, the hellforged chain lashing behind it to clatter against the Purgator's forearm. She turns the control rod in her gauntlet through a swift circle, and the warsuit's gun-arm mimics her a split second behind. The movement traps the chain around the mechanical arm in the gap between gunshield and elbow-joint – she flexes her gun-arm and throws the full weight of the Purgator behind it. The Helbrute lurches forward, its momentum embedding the warhammer head-first into the ground, and before it can pull itself free Morvenn strikes again, this time plunging the tip of the Lance into the plasma cannon's glowing energy coils.

Plasma bursts upward in a torrent as she pulls the blade free. The Helbrute screams and thrashes as the fountain of super-heated gas roars from the damaged weapon, then explodes in a blinding flash of heat and light that tears its gun-arm free at the elbow. The glowing red eyes roll in the skull-face, mouth screaming in full-voiced outrage as it staggers back, thick black liquid streaming from the stump of its arm and a jagged-edged hole in its flank. Morvenn presses her attack, concentrating her bolter fire on the newly exposed inner sarcophagus. She carves her blade through the inner layer of metal, revealing the naked, limbless body of a Heretic Astartes. The Helbrute's hammer rises in what surely is intended to be a killing blow, but she steps beneath it to plunge the Lance through the ruined sarcophagus into the meat beneath. The glowing blade rips upward, spilling guts and a torrent of foul-smelling fluid. The hammer blow falls on the warsuit's right shoulder, but the force is gone.

She plants the Purgator's foot in the centre of the Helbrute's chest and kicks it backwards. It staggers and falls, and the crimson light fades from its eyes.

'Abbess Sanctorum?'

'One moment.' Morvenn draws a deep breath and scans her surroundings. The motionless hulk of the Helbrute lies at her feet, those of its attendants who have survived the engagement with her honour guard retreating into the smoke. One of the Dominions is cradling a broken arm, but it seems that this particular engagement has ended at least in temporary victory. 'Prioress. Please continue.'

The barrage of shells against the void shields has become a continual drumbeat, and the smoky air is growing thicker with every passing moment. Morvenn heads towards where the sound of gunfire is loudest, her Lance blazing like a holy beacon.

'Most of the enemy are inside the outer walls.'

Morvenn knows already that this must be true, but even so, to hear it drives away the triumph of the Helbrute's death. 'And outside?'

'Two daemon engines. The Venomcrawler that brought down the wall, advancing through the breach. A Defiler, shelling the void shields.'

Bolts of vivid green las-fire streak through the smoke in front of her, shadows resolving into a group of novitiates and pilgrims, forced back into a tight cluster as a hulking armoured figure advances towards them. For one exhilarating moment she thinks that it is Kol Rakhul – that she has found the Death of Saints at last – but there is no aura of power radiating from this heretic, no dark majesty to chill the blood. This one is nothing but another slave to darkness, and deserves only her ire.

'How do we return heavy fire on the Defiler?'

She closes the distance before the Traitor Space Marine can react and strikes his head with her gunshield, smashing one bronze horn from his helmet and sending him reeling to the ground. Las-bolts fill the air around her as she strides forward and stamps the Purgator's foot onto his chestplate over and over until the ceramite cracks and the flesh beneath is reduced to a bloody pulp.

'Holy abbess! We give thanks for our deliverance!' One of the pilgrim-warriors drops to her knees, but a black-clad novitiate drags her up with a contemptuous glare.

'The best thanks you can give is to fight on,' she says, and Morvenn nods her approval. Two more novitiates are lifting the unconscious body of a Novitiate Superior of the Valorous Heart across their shoulders, while the rest are aiming their all-too-basic weapons into the fog around them.

'Take her to the Hospitallers,' Morvenn says. 'By the convent steps. Go.'

'We cannot return fire with the void shields in place,' Illuminata voxes.

'Not even through the gap at Silvana's Bastion?'

'Not even if the gunnery towers were intact. The enemy have positioned themselves too carefully for that.'

'And if we drop the shields–'

As if in reply a particularly large shell strikes the shimmering dome overhead.

'No need to answer.'

'Indeed, my abbess. The void shields are holding their integrity at a third. They cannot sustain this barrage for long.'

'Very well.'

The Venomcrawler's misshapen bulk is stalking through the smoke, towards a unit of Celestians Sacresant. Sparking mecha-tendrils lash alongside its gnashing mandibles, and as the Sacresant Superior raises her spear to strike, it opens fire with its Excruciator cannon. A blast of warp energy sears across her, stripping first her armour and then the flesh from her bones. Another burst of gunfire from behind her tells Morvenn that her Celestians are engaged again. Her carefully crafted defence is collapsing, and all she can rely on now is the individual courage and prowess of the warriors under her command.

'Very well. Prepare to open the sally port at Dominika's Bastion–'

'For you?'

'Who else?'

'The sons of Dorn.' Illuminata's voice is hoarse and strained. *'I cannot think of any more ideally suited to the task than them.'*

Morvenn bristles at the suggestion. 'I am–' she begins, and then her mouth snaps shut. 'A wise suggestion.' She changes the channel on her vox-unit before her mind does the same. 'Balian! I have need of you and your Sword Brethren!'

The steady pulse of erupting bolt-shells and sword blows comes through her vox-bead. *'What would you have us do, Abbess Sanctorum?'*

'The Defiler at Dominika's Gate. Destroy it before it brings down the void shields.'

A unit of Crusaders charge past her towards the Venomcrawler, their greatswords drawn back ready to banish the abomination from holy ground. They throw themselves into the fray without thought of their own safety, their zealous charge a fitting complement to the discipline of the Sacresants and the power of the three Paragon warsuits – *Alecto, Megaera* and *Tisiphone* – as they engage the daemon engine together. Razor-tipped tendrils lash out, catching a Crusader in a crimson surcoat and dragging him into the monster's waiting jaws. The huge sword of Paragon *Megaera* slices down, severing the tendril close to its base, and as the Venomcrawler recoils, shrieking, the Crusader rolls free and drives his sword into the daemon engine's underbelly.

'It shall be done.'

'Good hunting, brother.'

The prioress' voice cuts across her vox-link. *'My abbess. The enemy has breached the secondary defences. A force of Heretic Astartes is moving towards the convent steps.'*

'How many?'

'At least three dozen. More.'

'And the Death of Saints? Is he amongst them?'

'I cannot say.'

'Sound the retreat.' Morvenn activates her laud-hailers. 'My Sisters! Fall back in good order! Defend the Convent Sanctorum at all costs!'

Morvenn looks back at the daemon engine, thrashing and stamping and spitting out death in fiery torrents. The Paragons have it surrounded, hammer and sword blows opening cracks in its armoured carapace, the Sacresants and Crusaders exploiting its every weakness. The urge to run forward, to bury the Lance between the malign and glowing eyes is almost overwhelming – but that is not where her duty lies.

'Celestians, with me.'

A plume of steam screams from beneath the Venomcrawler's carapace, and Morvenn turns her face to where the Convent

Sanctorum stands shrouded in smoke, to the glow of the lights burning in its windows.

'In the God-Emperor's name, stand fast!' she calls. 'I am coming!'

XXXIII

The outer wall that surrounds the Convent Sanctorum marks a stark dividing line between light and darkness. Beneath the dome all is life and motion, the faithful and the heretic alike moving endlessly through thick smoke stained amber by a thousand blazing fires. A plume of smoke billows through the defect in the void shields, but the overlapping fields of the other generators ensure that the gap is a narrow one. Outside, the darkness is broken only by the infernal fire glowing in the heart of the Defiler, and the bright muzzle flash of its battle cannon. A unit of Havocs prowls back and forward beside its massive, spiked legs, their heavy weapons aimed outward. Balian counts five, including their leader. They have not yet spotted him, or the other sons of Dorn.

There will be no mistaking the moment that they do.

The Defiler launches another shell at the shields, setting the shimmering dome alight. The barrage cannot be intended to strike at the warriors locked in mortal combat within the walls – even if the Death of Saints has no concern for the lives of his human cultists, he cannot squander those of his battle-brothers so readily – but to overload the shields entirely and strip the Convent Sanctorum of its defences.

Balian signals his Sword Brethren to wait. Instinct tells him to throw himself into battle against the hated enemy, but he has not seen so many long centuries without learning the way of caution. Instead, he forces himself to watch the Defiler as it shifts its weight from one spiked leg to another, its crab-like claws snapping at any Chaos Space Marine that comes within reach. It seems the service its masters have ordained for it chafes at the daemon engine's soul, the desire to rend and tear and immolate anything within reach writ large in every restless movement.

If it is so hungry for battle, then Balian will be glad to oblige.

He moves forward through the dark, a huntsman's satisfaction spreading through him, his Sword Brethren's anticipation in perfect harmony with his own.

'We await your command, brother.' Brother Theobalt's voice is soft in his ear.

'Take down the Defiler.' He draws his greatsword, the metal slipping with a whisper from its scabbard. The Heretic Astartes do not react, but something changes in the Defiler's posture, a tension spreading through the abominable fusion of metal and meat. If they are to strike – and strike they must – it must be now.

'Forward, sons of Dorn!'

The Sword Brethren charge forward as one.

'For the God-Emperor! For Rogal Dorn! Death to the heretic, the mutant and the traitor! Let none survive!'

They strike the Traitor Space Marines like a mailed fist. Balian's first strike cleaves through the nearest heretic's armour, opening a wide gash in the metal of the left pauldron. He tears his blade free and brings it round again to clash with the teeth of a whirring chainaxe. A severed head in a horned helm flies through the air, Theobalt's roar of satisfaction awakening a hungry fury of his own. His fallen brothers presume to stand against him, but he will teach them the error of their ways. Balian hammers a second blow into the wound left by the first, driving his blade down through armour to hack deep into the flesh below. The Havoc opens fire with his heavy bolter, but Balian's reflexes are so attuned that he can almost track the shells' passage through the air.

God-Emperor, my eternal thanks for the gifts you have bestowed upon me.

He sidesteps the hammering bolter fire and slices vertically down through the traitor's horned helmet, cleaving the skull into two from top to bottom.

May I put them to use in glorious slaughter.

Behind the surviving Chaos Space Marines, the Defiler screams, raising the bulk of its body back on its four rear legs. The massive claws snip at the air, and twin torrents of flame pour from the heavy flamers above. Balian darts to the side quickly enough that the flame merely blisters the enamel of his armour and chars his surcoat to ash, but the Havoc before him is caught squarely in the blast. He screams as the fires consume him, turning to fire his heavy bolter into the daemon engine even as he burns. The Defiler opens its massive claw and snaps it shut around the Havoc's midriff, slicing him neatly into two halves and throwing the parts aside. A massive taloned leg slams into the ground as it stalks forward, malice glowing in its crimson eyes.

'Forward!'

Another Chaos Space Marine falls, and then the squad reaches the Defiler as it stamps and strikes and discharges flame in a frenzy of bloodlust. Theobalt carves his greatsword through the knee joint of a massive metal foreleg, and the beast recoils, trailing a plume of superheated steam from the ruined limb, before bringing its claw down on Theobalt's helmet. The Space Marine retreats, and as Balian watches the torn metal begins to knit itself together, fresh tendrils of molten metal flowing down to replace what has been damaged. Sword Brother Jehan lunges for the gap between the claws and cannon mount, but as his blade strikes home the Defiler rises up on its rear legs, whipping his body into the air to land in a warrior's crouch twenty feet away.

Swords alone will not suffice.

Balian pulls a krak grenade from his belt and tugs the pin free with his teeth. As in all warfare, timing is critical, but never more so than now. He waits until the Defiler lunges forward and ducks below its metallic undercarriage, searching for a crack in which to wedge the grenade. A narrow gap opens between leg and torso as the daemon engine steps forward, and he rams his fist in elbow-deep, withdrawing it a second before the gap closes around the grenade, and rolling beneath the stamping legs.

A dull explosion shakes the Defiler before he has rolled clear. It howls in a voice like a thousand suffering sinners, and Balian's heart sings in triumph. Smoke is billowing from the joints where legs meet carapace, and he primes another grenade before it has a chance to turn. His Sword Brothers – always swift to learn – are imitating his movements, baiting the beast forward while others attack from behind. He wedges the grenade through the hole the first explosion has created, and is rewarded by a detonation that almost blasts the Defiler from its feet.

'Die, in the God-Emperor's Holy Name!' Theobalt roars, slashing out with his blade – but the wounded Defiler is quicker. Its vast right claw closes around the Sword Brother's helmet and shuts tight. There is a sharp crack, and Theobalt's corpse drops to the ground.

'You will die for that, abomination!'

The Defiler turns on Balian. He reaches for his belt, but the last of his grenades is gone.

No matter. The sword is a more fitting way to send this

abomination back where it belongs. Roaring defiance, he runs forward with his sword raised, the claw snapping shut inches from his neck, flames billowing around him as though he were running through the warp itself, and springs upward. His right foot finds purchase in the Defiler's articulated knee joint, his left mag-locking instantly to the heavy plating of its carapace, and he runs forward along its armoured back to the gun turret that serves it for a head. The cannon rotates through a one-hundred-and-eighty-degree arc, but he is too quick, leaping into the air an instant before it can sweep his feet from under him. He reverses his sword in the air and lands with his full weight on the pommel, driving the blade hilt-deep into the daemon engine's armoured back.

Scalding steam plumes around him. He tears the sword free, opening a yard-long gash in the Defiler's back, then slams it home again. Metal cables coil and thrash beneath the surface, and he takes delight in severing them one by one, his sword's energy field crackling brilliant white in the darkness of the daemon engine's interior. The carapace lurches to the right as the creature's legs collapse; he drives his sword down again, lost in the ecstasy of righteous slaughter. The Defiler has fallen, the convent's void shields made safe, and there is only the heretic warlord to find and slay before their triumph is complete–

The Defiler explodes. The blast sends Balian flying into the air, the last remnants of his surcoat igniting, his skin blistering beneath his bodyglove despite the protection of his armour. Metal shards tear through ceramite and flesh, ripping skin, muscle, bone and the organs beneath. He hits the ground like a drop pod, driving what little air remains in his lungs and all clarity from his skull. Adrenaline and endorphins flood his system, driving away pain, compelling him to rise and fight on in a body too broken to stand.

An armoured foot presses down hard on his throat. Balian

opens his eyes, and looks up at a towering figure in blue and bronze, the winged helm and armour rack with its grisly trophies silhouetted against the light of the convent behind, an executioner's power axe glowing blue in his hand.

'Brothers,' he rasps into his vox, but there is no answer but the hiss of dead air.

'Your brothers are dead,' the Death of Saints says. 'But you will not outlive them by long. And when you are gone, who will stand with the Abbess Sanctorum when I come to cut the treacherous head from her neck?'

'God-Emperor, grant me the strength to smite your enemy–'

'The God-Emperor has forsaken you. He cannot save His saints. What arrogance, to believe yourself more worthy than them.'

The boot grinds down on his throat. Balian's larynx snaps first, and then the bone of his spine.

'But I shall accord you a great privilege.' The Death of Saints lifts his sabaton, but Balian's throat is already crushed to a bloody pulp. 'A place alongside them for all eternity.'

The axe rises and falls, but Balian is dead before his head leaves his shoulders.

Lethe runs through endless catacombs, up spiral stairs and along winding passageways so narrow that to pass through scrapes the skin from her shoulders. The sounds of combat – bolter fire, the whirring of chainswords, Battle Sisters shouting, the crackling of tearing reality – have faded into the distance so that she can no longer tell what is real and what is the product of her terrified imagination. How long has she been running? It can only be minutes at most, but the burning in her lungs and her screaming leg muscles make it feel as though it has been hours already. The further she runs from the laboratorium the dimmer the light becomes, the blazing braziers replaced with cracked lumens at increasingly distant intervals, the smell of counterseptic replaced by ancient dust and damp. Wherever her desperate flight has taken her, she is the first to come this way in many months.

The passageway ahead divides into three, and she forces herself to pause and listen for the sounds of battle above. Surely her lord must be here by now? Perhaps the battle is already over, the Sisters lying bloody by the altars to their false god, their reign of cruelty overthrown at last. Or perhaps it is her lord who has been slain…

No. That thought is not one she is willing to entertain. He has come. He is there above her, beneath open skies, and when she returns he will welcome her with open arms and grant her a place at his side. And when the convent is fallen and all of Ophelia VII is transformed into his dark cardinal world, she will go forth as his chosen herald to spread the message of his cruelty and power.

The last lumen flickers and goes out.

Darkness floods in like a tide, leaving Lethe suspended in a night-black ocean. She stumbles forward, groping for the wall that she knows must be there, but her foot catches on an uneven stone and she falls face-first to the ground. Pain shoots up her wrists from the heels of her hands, her knees throbbing at the sharpness of the impact, but fear drags her to her feet. Something is moving in the darkness, a light scratching noise that brings back memories of mine-rats, of Evania lying like a heap of refuse while yellow teeth gnawed her eyes from their sockets. Her bare foot brushes against something soft, and her nerve shatters completely, sending her blundering through the darkness, rough walls scraping against the skin of her hands, bare feet hammering on hard-packed earth. She runs until she tastes iron in her throat, until her feet are bloodied and bruised, until every muscle is screaming in protest, and she staggers to a halt, hopelessly lost.

Something has changed in the darkness around her. Where before the walls had been close around her, now her rasping breaths echo as though from the roof of a domed chamber. She stretches her hands out and reaches for the walls, but it takes ten halting paces before her palms meet stone. She gropes her way along the rough surface until the wall slopes away into a shallow alcove around six feet in length, deep enough that her outstretched arm cannot feel its furthest extent. There is something in there – something that feels like a dry bundle of sticks and rags. Her fingertips brush against the edge of a piece of metal, and she fumbles it into her grip.

A knife. The blade is rough with rust, the edge dull beneath her hand, but it is metal, and that carries with it the promise of light. She drags it across the rough stone wall, raising a brief cascade of sparks. One burns a pinpoint of agony into the back of her hand, but the pain and the clarity it brings are welcome. She scrapes the knife on stone again, and this time the light is enough to make out her surroundings. The empty eyes of a skull stare back at her from the alcove, the bones of some long-dead Sister still wrapped in a stained linen shroud, and then the darkness closes in again.

A breeze caresses her cheek like the touch of dead fingers, sending a shiver across her skin. There are no ghosts here, only the ancient dead. They cannot hurt her, cannot watch her with their empty eyes, cannot rise and seize her living flesh and tear her apart for her heresy…

Hands shaking, Lethe grabs a handful of linen and tears it into strips, wrapping the rags around a human femur. She grinds the knife along the wall again, placing her makeshift torch in place to catch the shower of sparks. The cloth smoulders at their touch, but the embers die with the torch unlit. She fights down panic, sparks her makeshift flint-and-tinder again and again, until on the third time a tiny shred of fibre catches fire. The flame is miniscule, the light nothing more than a kindling flicker of hope. Lethe holds her breath until she is sure that it has caught, then lifts her makeshift torch to inspect the chamber.

Light reflects from the gilded tiles of what was once an elaborate mosaic, the enamel chipped and the once-vivid colours faded by the years. The walls are lined with alcoves identical to the one she has just emptied, the tunnel behind her an empty mouth leading into darkness.

The torch is burning quickly, thick black smoke roiling from its amber flame as the blaze spreads down the crude wick, and she hastily wraps another to serve as its replacement, trying not to look at the long-dead skull still bearing grey wisps of hair as she plunders its skeleton for bones. She lifts the torch above her head and moves it around the walls, scanning for any aperture or alcove that might show the way out, but finds nothing. The only escape is through the tunnel behind her, back into a labyrinth full of blind ends and false turns – but what choice does she have? Despair settles on her shoulders, and she almost sobs. Even if the Warp Talons are gone and the Battle Sisters with them, she has no great hope of finding her way back to the light. The torch gutters, and she transfers its flame to its replacement. They are burning down so quickly that even if she runs she will barely buy herself more than a few hundred yards before the darkness returns – but it is that or stay here as the crypt fills with the stench of singed bone and thick grey smoke.

The torch flickers again, and a faint gust of air blows against her face. A woman's voice shouts in the distance, followed by the rattle of armoured feet on stone. She has no hope of escape – but she might yet have a few moments with which to hide. Lethe drops the torch and beats out the flame with her bare hands, biting her lip as the skin of her palms singes and crisps, then climbs into the nearest alcove. Bone clatters around her, the dust of the ancient shroud catching in her throat, bringing tears to her eyes.

Vivid blue-white light flares in the darkness of the passageway, and her heart sinks. The Warp Talon is hunting her. She presses herself deeper in the alcove, her back against ancient bricks and mortar as the footsteps draw closer. In a moment it will be upon her. Tears well up in her eyes, stinging their way down the wound in her cheek, her muscles shaking uncontrollably. All of her strength has left her, and she is entirely, wretchedly alone.

Metal grates on stone as the Warp Talon drags its claws along the wall. She can hear the coarse rasp of its breathing as it searches for her hiding place. Will it impale her where she lies, or will it drag her screaming into the chamber before it slices her to bloody chunks? She squeezes her eyes shut, trembling hard enough to rattle the bones around her.

'Help me,' she whispers. 'Please. I will do anything. Only let me live.' She has not prayed since she was a child, since her first dark days in the mine, but helpless as she is, it is all she can think to do. It is a futile act – if the God-Emperor would not answer her when she was innocent, what hope does she have with her soul steeped in sin?

'Open your eyes.'

The voice is so soft she barely hears it, setting her scalp tingling as though someone unseen had breathed suddenly into her ear. The softest of breezes caresses her cheek as she opens her eyes and sees the merest glimmer of light shining through a crack in the back wall of the alcove. She presses her fingers into the gap, and mortar crumbles away at her touch.

The rasp of the Warp Talon's claw grows louder, and she tears at the hole with frantic hands, opening it wide enough to shove her hand through into the space beyond. The ancient partition is crumbling to dust, and she squeezes her shoulders through the widening aperture, scrabbling with her feet to gain purchase on the ground, slithering out of the stifling darkness into open air. The marble floor beneath her is cool against her cheek, and she lies, dust-covered and gasping, as the stone behind her crumbles and blocks the crawlspace. She listens, but it seems that whoever spoke to her before has nothing more to say.

The chamber is nothing extraordinary, nothing but another vaulted columbarium, but here the coffins pressed into the alcoves have not yet crumbled to splinters, the names with their gold leaf still visible on each, and this chamber has something that the last did not.

This chamber has a staircase that leads upward.

To the battle.

To her lord.

XXXIV

A deafening explosion marks the moment of the Venomcrawler's destruction. Smoke and flame billow upwards in a thick column, secondary explosions spreading outwards like ripples across a pond. Visibility is down to yards, and the concentration of promethium vapour is so high that every shot fired risks setting the atmosphere alight. Morvenn runs for the convent steps across a battlefield that has lost any semblance of cohesion, transformed to close-quarters fighting more bloody and chaotic than any she has ever seen.

A body slams to the ground in front of her, and she looks down at the broken corpse of a Zephyrim in silver armour, a shining banner on a snapped pole still clutched in her gauntlet. A novitiate of Our Martyred Lady, her veil gone and her hair wild about her face, stoops and lifts it as a Raptor swoops with bloody claws outstretched to tear the banner from her grasp. Morvenn reacts without thought, firing shell after shell into the midnight chestplate until the heretic explodes, raining chunks of flesh and shattered ceramite on the novitiate in a benediction of blood.

'Fall back!' she shouts. 'Defend the Convent Sanctorum!'

A pack of cultists sprints from the smoke, bearing a Sister in blood-spattered white armour to the ground with the force of their charge. Bare hands tear her visor free as she fires her boltgun, but there are too many of them, their knives glinting like rubies as they stab them down through the gap in her helmet. Morvenn spares a missile to end the Sister's torment and the heretics' miserable lives in a single majestic conflagration.

'My lord is waiting for you,' an inhuman voice growls. A vast shape looms out of the smoke, midnight-black against the blazing flames. The Heretic Astartes wears no helmet, and the exposed flesh on his scalp is mottled and lined with impossible age. Two dark eyes glow in sunken sockets above a vox-grille deeply embedded in the lower half of his face. His armour is draped in human skin, blood and hair tangled in the teeth of the massive chainglaive in his right hand, a bolter adorned with a gilded human skull in his left.

'Where is he?'

Morvenn lunges forward with her spear before the Traitor Space Marine has a chance to answer. He raises his chainglaive to deflect her strike and discharges his bolter across the Purgator's energy field and into the Celestians beyond. One strikes Zafiya squarely in the chestplate, and she falls without a sound.

'Hiromi!' Morvenn steps in front of the downed woman before the heretic can fire again and returns fire. 'Take her to the Hospitallers!' She lashes out with the Lance again, but the vast Space Marine leans out of the way, a raw laugh grating through his vox-grille.

'He is waiting.'

'Kol Rakhul is a coward!' She springs forward, blow after blow slamming against the Chaos Space Marine with force that would have shattered any normal armour, but he barely seems to notice. 'Do you hear me? Come and face me, heretic!'

'He will come. In time.'

'All of this, for what? For his revenge?'

The chainglaive bites into the Purgator's gunshield, gouging a thick furrow in the plating before she can knock it free.

'For him, revenge. For us, service.' He fires his bolter. 'As it has always been.'

Shells burst on the Purgator's energy field like miniature supernovas, each impact striking harder than the last until one breaks through. Most of the force is gone by the time it strikes her armour, but the explosion still drives the breath from her lungs and sends the Purgator spinning backward. Broken ribs grind as she breathes, pain shooting through her chest and shoulder. A unit of Havocs moves to reinforce the ancient Chaos Space Marine, the pilot lights of their flamers casting eerie reflections on their armoured chestplates.

Flame gouts up the warsuit's spear-arm, so hot that blisters rise on her right arm, her shoulder, the side of her face, and for the first time fear creeps into her. There are too many of them. She should never have sent Hiromi away. She should draw back, find reinforcements, regroup before facing the Chaos Space Marine again…

But those are the words of cowardice and its old companion, folly. Retreat is impossible. The Heretic Astartes will run her to the ground and burn her to ash the moment she turns, and who will lead her Sisters then? Instead, she advances through the flames, drives the Lance into the heavy flamer's muzzle and wrenches the barrel open, the blade's energy discharge igniting the fuel-air mixture in its pipes. The Havoc goes up in flames, struggling in vain to release the webbing that holds the burning fuel tank on his back, and staggers into his companion.

Their leader fires his bolter again. Morvenn deflects the shells on Fidelis' gunshield and returns fire in a wide and indiscriminate spray. A second Havoc erupts in flame as a missile strikes his fuel tank. She strides forward into the flames and finishes him with a spear thrust through the chest, but another burst of flame drives her back before she can engage the next.

Two heretics remain along with their monstrous leader. With the deaths of their companions they have fallen back, the heavy flamers spitting short bursts of burning promethium as they move in a wary circle around her. Runes are flashing in the corner of her vision – her missiles almost gone, bolter rounds at less than an eighth of full capacity.

The world glows crimson as two heavy flamers bathe the Purgator in heat and light. Another warning rune flashes. The energy field is moments from overloading. Morvenn hurls herself forward into the flames, ignoring the pain in her broken ribs to strike the nearest Havoc with the back of the Purgator's fist. He staggers sideways, and the torrent of his flamer goes wild, catching the massive Champion full in the face.

A howl erupts through the vox-grille as his face chars and blackens, but Morvenn does not pause. She spends another precious bolter shell to drive the second Havoc back, then pushes her advance, carving through his helmet into the wet meat beneath. The first Havoc is regaining his balance when she reaches him, as the full weight of the Purgator Mirabilis strikes him in the chest. The gunshield smashes the helmet from his head – she kicks him to the ground with one massive golden foot and stamps on his newly exposed face. Bone cracks then shatters as she twists to the right to meet the leader's bolter fire head-on. Her energy field strains and crackles, but she ignores impact after impact, striding forward like a god-engine on a mission of holy destruction.

'Where is he?' she roars.

A bolter shell erupts against the Purgator's chestplate, sending a shard of metal through her armour into the muscle of her shoulder, but she barely feels it. Rage surges through her, and she surrenders to it entirely, the Lance slashing through the chain-glaive's shaft and sending the blade flying from his hands. She reverses her weapon and slams the ferrule into his faceplate, denting it inwards in a gush of blood. The Chaos Space Marine staggers back, and she strikes him over and over until he falls, until his face is a bloody pulp, until she can no longer tell where the skin ends and the metal begins.

'Kol Rakhul!' she screams.

The ground is scorched black underfoot. Soot dances in swirls in the air, the whole world turned to fire and darkness.

'Where is your God-Emperor now, Morvenn Vahl?' There is no mistaking the Death of Saints' voice, echoing from all directions and none. 'Where is your miracle?'

A shadow moves through the smoke, lightning crackling down the blade of a massive axe. She turns, takes aim with one of her few precious remaining rounds, but the shape is gone before she can fire.

'You cannot save your Sisters.' A handful of lightning crackles through the smoke far to her left. 'You cannot save the cardinal world. And you cannot save yourself.'

'The God-Emperor will be the judge of that!'

Where is he? Energy signals trail across her helmet's display, but the searing heat of the flames is making it impossible to tell friend from foe. Deep and mocking laughter reverberates through her micro-bead, deafening and disorientating.

'Your Order took from me that which was most dear. Now I will take the same from you.'

'Come and face me, heretic!'

But there is no reply.

'Illuminata! Where is he?'

'Forgive me, my abbess. I cannot see, the smoke is too thick.'

Morvenn looks up at the clouds of smoke caught beneath the void shields' dome. The damage at Silvana's Bastion is allowing some to escape, but all too little and much too late.

'Is the Defiler destroyed?'

'It is, my abbess.'

'Disable the remaining shields.'

Silence.

'I said, disable them!'

'Abbess Sanctorum, you would leave the convent undefended–'

'The daemon engines are gone. The threat is inside our walls, and we cannot fight what we cannot see.' Morvenn forces conviction into her words. She is gambling with the very future of the Convent Sanctorum. 'I have faith. Our Sisters will not let the enemy reach the convent.'

'Very well, then. It shall be as you command.'

'What reserves remain?'

'Every Sister and Crusader is already on the field. Only the last of the zealots–'

'Mobilise them!'

Morvenn is running before the hum of the shields dies, before the smell of ozone fades, before the choking grey smoke begins to clear, running towards the sound of gunfire, to the last desperate stand on the steps of the Convent Sanctorum.

By the time Lethe reaches the upper level of the crypts, the convent is packed so thickly with bodies that she barely attracts a second glance. Pilgrims huddle in the cloisters, grandparents with grandchildren, brothers clutching sisters, all those too weak or too weary to fight. Her ragged appearance draws little attention. She is not the only one barefoot, not the only one wearing a tunic and little else, not the only one scuffed and scraped and hungry.

But she is the only one moving towards the door.

'Where are you going?' An arm catches her shoulder, and she looks around into the face of a man holding an infant, his brow furrowed with concern. 'Are you with the reserves?'

She shrugs, and the man shakes his head, reaching for her in concern.

'The enemy is out there. They will kill you.'

Lethe jerks her arm out of his reach. His words are truer than he knows. 'I am not afraid.'

'I wish I had your courage.'

She has never met the man before, but there is something in the soft desperation of his voice, in the way he touches his cheek to his child's sleeping head that awakens an old love in her and the old sorrow with it. For a moment she could weep, but then her heart hardens in her like a stone. The Sisters took her father from her, took her freedom, took years of her life that cannot be returned. Her lord has come to make them pay for all their crimes.

'God-Emperor be with you. Be safe.' The man has returned his attention to the child, now stirring drowsily in his arms.

Any borrowed affection she felt for the pair drains away, replaced with jealous contempt. *Be safe.* There is no safety here, no safety anywhere. There is only power, and the law of the weak and strong. She leaves the crypt without looking back, heading to the archway that leads through the cloister to the postern gate where the last of the zealots are assembling. She imagines throwing them open wide, and a thrill of pleasure shoots through her. Her lord will be grateful when she welcomes him into the hated Convent Sanctorum. It will be remade, just as she has been remade, and the world will be reborn to darkness.

The smoke has cleared enough that Morvenn can see almost halfway up the white marble staircase that leads to the Convent

Sanctorum's great golden doors, but the building itself is still wreathed in shadow. The Sanctorum Guard are backed up at the foot of the steps, Celestians Sacresant standing shoulder to shoulder with Crusaders and novitiates while Battle Sisters, Celestians and Retributors deliver volleys of fire from the ranks behind. The outspoken pilgrim with the half-shaven head is there, firing a Godwyn-De'az-pattern boltgun with relentless fervour, despite the bruising recoil against her unarmoured shoulder. Grounded Seraphim fire their pistols from the marble balustrade, while far overhead their Sisters swoop and dive in close combat with the last of the Raptors. Sisters of all Orders are running to reinforce them from all angles – but they are so few, and the advancing Chaos Space Marines are too many.

'Are they all that remain?'

'Not all, but most–'

A scream blasts through Morvenn's vox-bead, piercing like a hot lancet through her eardrum, shattering her thoughts into sharp-edged fragments. The sound grows louder, tearing at her soul, and she drops the Purgator's command rods and tears open her helmet's seals, lifts it off and casts it aside. Her gauntleted hands are shaking as she pulls the vox-bead from her ear, the sound growing fainter, but not vanishing entirely. On the steps, her Sisters are removing their own helmets with quick, panicky movements. A novitiate falls to her knees, blood pouring from her eyes and mouth. A Battle Sister clutches at the side of her helmet then drops, convulsing, to the ground.

'No more tricks, Rakhul!'

Morvenn's ears are ringing, her voice trapped in her own skull. A Traitor Space Marine turns at the sound of her voice and charges towards her, only to be cut down in a hail of bolter fire. She finishes him off with a downward stab then strides forward to smash another Chaos Space Marine in the face with Fidelis' gunshield. A quartet of legionaries rush forward, fanning out as they approach in an attempt to surround her, but before they come within weapons reach two have already fallen, gunned down by a disciplined volley of bolt-shells. She skewers the third through the chest, spinning with the corpse still impaled on the spear shaft to strike his companion with the weight of his armoured body. There is a sickening crunch as skull meets skull, and she casts the dead heretic aside with contempt.

It is then that she realises she is being watched.

The sense of eyes upon her is unmistakable – a heavy, lowering gaze that sets her scalp prickling and the skin crawling at the nape of her neck. She looks up, convinced for one awful moment that the Heldrake has returned from the pit to take its revenge, but there is no monstrous daemon engine, no glowing crimson eyes and throats, only the silver silhouette of a gibbous moon shining through the smoke. She cuts her way through another throng of cultists, pressing forward until the front line of her Sisters opens to meet her, her back to the convent, her spear pointed out at the advancing enemy.

'God-Emperor, be with us now!'

'Your god is deaf to your prayers.'

The whisper is sharp, cutting across the sound of the battlefield. Morvenn turns, and there he is – the Death of Saints, halfway up the steps that lead to the doors of the Convent Sanctorum. Moonlight picks out the details of his armour: the broad wings of his helm, the axe in his right hand and the talons of his left, the armour rack on his shoulders restored to grisly splendour. There is a new head there, larger than the rest.

Balian.

The Death of Saints raises his axe in mocking salute, then turns to ascend the white marble steps.

'Hold the line! For the Convent Sanctorum, do not falter!'

Morvenn steps behind the line, and the Sisters to either side close the gap. 'Kol Rakhul! You have come for me, have you not?'

She forces the warsuit into a run. The Purgator's weight is working against itself, the Lance heavy in her grip as though she is wielding it with her own muscles. They are both weary – but one way or another, the battle will be over soon.

'Why will you not face me?'

The Death of Saints turns. 'Fate has brought us together, Morvenn Vahl–'

She does not wait for him to finish. She fires the last of her bolter shells directly at his chest, but he dodges nimbly aside.

'Your death is ordained,' he says. 'For the sins of your Order–'

'Who are you to speak of sin?'

She stabs with the Lance, but he is too quick for her, and again she strikes empty air. His lightning claw flashes through the space behind the Purgator's left knee, and a hydraulic cable gives way with a hiss.

'Who better than I?' The power axe flashes through the air, carving a gleaming silver line across the Purgator's right pauldron before he is out of reach again. He is impossibly quick, her every blow evaded with consummate ease. 'I who have been wronged. I who was robbed of so much.'

She lunges again, but the damage to the Purgator's left leg steals her momentum. The Death of Saints ducks under the clumsy strike then leaps vertically upwards in a dazzling plyometric display, his beheading axe slashing out towards Morvenn's neck. She raises her left arm to deflect the blow, and instead of taking her head from her shoulders the axe catches the warsuit under the gun-arm, slamming into her armoured chestplate with pile-driver force. The armour buckles into her injured ribs, the pain so intense that stars dance in front of her eyes.

'You took her from me.' The Death of Saints pulls the axe

back. 'You made her hate me. Turned her against me. Sent her to kill me!'

The release of pressure is almost as painful as the strike itself. She sucks in a shuddering breath and forces herself to strike again, but she is too slow, too weak, just as she had feared.

A shout rises from the Convent Sanctorum as the postern gate swings open and the last of the reserves charge out. The Death of Saints turns, hissing in anger, and a tide of pilgrims surges towards him, swords, daggers, maces and laspistols clutched in inexpert hands.

'These wretches will not save you,' he spits, and then they are on him.

'For the God-Emperor, and the Abbess Sanctorum!' The first of the zealots closes the distance between them, the curved combat blade in her hand drawn back to strike. The Death of Saints raises his hand in a gesture of benediction, holds it there, then brings it down on the woman's head, closing it around the dome of her skull with a sickening crunch. His claws tangle in bone and hair until with a violent shake he tosses her still-twitching carcass to the side.

'Nor can you save them.'

Morvenn slashes the blade of the Lance across the hollow of Rakhul's knee and is rewarded by a howl of rage as the power field slices through armour and into skin, but he does not slow. An old man with a shock of white hair above his wrinkled brown face is the next to fall, eviscerated from hip to hip, screaming in agony as his guts spill out over his thighs.

The Death of Saints is right. She cannot save them. She cannot win.

But she can still end this when the time comes.

The heretic punches his claw through the abdomen of a hatchet-wielding woman, lifting her into the air then tossing her forward to strike the zealot behind her with enough force to shatter both of their skulls. Morvenn pushes the suit into a full charge, bringing the Lance around in a broad, round-arm sweep that the heretic evades with ease, stepping inside her guard and carving his axe-blade round. She raises Fidelis' shield, but the force of the blow is still enough to send her staggering back. Another pilgrim in stained velvet robes falls as the axe takes his head from his shoulders; another is impaled on the lightning claw and cast aside. There are no games now, no teasing strike-and-withdraw, merely a brutally efficient fight to the death.

Rakhul knocks the last of the pilgrims aside, and sprints towards her. Sparking claws lock around her gunshield, forcing it down towards the ground. He is impossibly strong, stronger than any mortal has a right to be, stronger even than the Purgator Mirabilis. She tries to bring the Lance down, but he is within her guard and all she can manage is a clumsy blow that glances harmlessly off his pauldron. He draws the axe back to strike, and she parries with the Purgator's metal forearm, his blade gouging deep into the metal. She heaves back, using the warsuit's weight to break the lightning claw's grip, and drives him back with a clumsy slash across the eye-lenses of his glowering helmet. To her surprise, the tip of the blade strikes home, tracing a sparking line across ceramite and armaglass. A split second later he is out of reach again, but the blow has done its work. Crimson eye-lenses flickering wildly, he drags the helmet from his head and casts it aside.

Is it time?

She takes her right hand from the command rod long enough to take the tiny golden detonator from its pouch and wrap the chain around her wrist. The white marble steps are running with blood, the last of the Sanctorum Guard locked in hand-to-hand combat with ancient heretics. The Death of Saints has brought horror to the door of the Convent Sanctorum.

If she does not stop him now he will bring it inside.

Morvenn holds the detonator up to the light. The Death of Saints' one eye widens, and for a moment he is perfectly still. He knows what it is, and what it promises.

'Am I to fear death?' Something in his monstrous face softens. 'I have endured the torment of a thousand years without her.' The softness fades, and once again his mouth twists in a cruel smile. 'Detonate your explosives. Let the Convent Sanctorum fall at the hands of its abbess, and the warp will ring for centuries with the song of your despair!'

The last of the hydraulic fluid bleeds from the Purgator's left leg, and the knee joint buckles forward. Morvenn plants the Lance's ferrule in the earth and tries to keep upright, but the warsuit is too heavy and she drops to one knee. Her mouth is full of blood, her wounds declaring themselves one by one. She has been fighting for hours, and all the adrenaline flooding her veins cannot hold back exhaustion any longer.

God-Emperor, give me the strength to die well.

Her left hand closes around the sphere. Every part of her, every fibre of her being longs to destroy him, even if the price of that destruction is all that she is and all she has. There would be certainty in that act, thousands of years of slaughter brought to an end at her hand. She can feel the crimson gemstone through her gauntlet, tight against the metal as though pressing itself against her skin. It promises an end to all of this. It promises martyrdom. It promises *certainty*.

The Death of Saints walks towards her, the blade of his axe grating a trail of sparks along the white marble steps. 'We will die together, you and I. This is how it ends. How it *must* end.'

Morvenn hangs her head forward, letting a trail of blood drool from between her lips. What was it Aleyna had said? *No one could look at you and see weakness.* But it is so easy to appear weak now, to be nothing more than a broken weapon. Let him draw closer. Only another step. Another step will be enough.

'Detonate your explosives. Or I will take your head and do it myself.' He draws back the headsman's axe, ready to swing.

Close enough.

Morvenn drops the Lance of Illumination and punches the warsuit's hand into his throat. He pulls away, but the heavy metal fingers are locked tight around the gorget of his armour, dragging him near.

'You and I may die today, Kol Rakhul.' They are armour to armour, now, so close that she can feel the unnatural warmth of his flesh, smell the tang of hot metal rising from his skin. She spits in his one good eye. 'But the Convent Sanctorum will not fall.'

Her warsuit's hand locked tight on his armour, she fires the last of her missiles at point-blank range.

A blinding flash sears through the night as a missile explodes, sending a plume of silver smoke pouring upwards into the sky, a wall of heat and force slamming Lethe back into the shadow of the postern gate. There is no sign of her lord, no sign of the false abbess, both obscured entirely by the dust and fumes.

'My lord!'

Lethe runs into the smoke, searching for the Death of Saints, waiting for him to rise. In a moment he will stand, transfigured by the flames. He will rise like a god of war and take revenge on all who have wronged him – all who have wronged *her*. Bodies litter the steps, a scorch-mark radiating out like the rays of a black supernova from the explosion's epicentre, a hand, a head, a limbless torso. There is the abbess in her golden warsuit, lying spreadeagled on the marble steps, her face smeared in blood and the spear lying just beyond her outstretched hand... And there is her lord.

He does not rise.

'My lord?'

The Death of Saints raises his head. The skin has been torn away by the blast, leaving nothing but raw muscle. His one good eye is burned to a milky white, his breastplate torn free, his left arm severed at the shoulder. 'Where is she?' he croaks. 'My sister…'

Half-butchered, he is trying to rise, but his legs are broken like matchwood, bone protruding through the tassets and greaves. His armour rack is warped and twisted, the skulls that once adorned it shattered to fragments of bone and twisted pieces of silver filigree.

'My lord, it is gone…'

His eye closes. He points his one remaining hand towards a tiny golden sphere on a fine chain, lying just outside the abbess' reach. 'Take… the detonator…' he rasps. 'Destroy… the Convent Sanctorum. Kill them… all…'

Lethe takes one step towards it, then stops. The abbess is stirring, one hand fumbling for the command batons of her warsuit, the other wiping blood from her eyes.

'Take it…'

The sound from her lord's throat is no longer remotely human. She looks down at him, at the pathetic ruin of metal and meat who promised so much that in the end he could not deliver.

The hand of the Purgator Mirabilis closes around the Lance. The abbess lifts the glowing blade into the air, plants the end in the ground and starts to lever her warsuit to its feet. Lethe spares the Death of Saints one last look, at the tattered flesh, the stump of his arm, the wildly rolling blind orb of his eye.

Ostrov and the rest were right.

'My Lethe… End… this…'

He is *weak*.

'No,' Lethe says, and turns away.

* * *

Inch by agonising inch, Morvenn drags the warsuit upright. Her head is pounding like a war-drum, her vision hazy, her ears ringing with the echoes of the explosion. She is lucky to be alive – lucky, or blessed, or protected by the last gasp of the suit's energy field, it does not matter. Pain shoots through her broken ribs as she hauls the Purgator back onto its feet. Its left leg is all but useless even with the knee locked, but with the spear for support she manages to get its weight under her and stand upright. Something moves in her peripheral vision, but before she can focus on it the shape is gone, darting away into the last of the smoke.

The Death of Saints is trying to rise. She kicks his axe aside, stamps down on his one remaining hand and drives the Lance point-first through the blackened and twisted remains of his chest.

'Tell me...' His words bubble through a mouthful of black blood. A strange, distant expression crosses his face, as though his blinded eye is looking not at her, but somewhere else across light years and centuries. 'Tell me you forgive me. Sister. Athenasia.'

Only the past can slay him.

A chill breeze passes across her skin, as though the thought had been whispered in her ear by a thousand incorporeal voices. She raises the Lance of Illumination. The past may have brought him here, but her hand will deal the killing blow.

'There is no forgiveness for you. Not now. Not ever.' The spear flashes gold through the air as she brings it down on his bloody neck. 'You chose your own damnation.'

The first blow cuts deep, severing skin, windpipe and arteries, but the bone beneath is unnaturally strong. Morvenn raises the blade and hacks down again and again in great clumsy strikes, her fury and her grief all that remain to give her strength, until at last the head parts from the shoulders and rolls free.

She braces herself on the Lance and draws herself upright, gasping for breath, and through the clearing smoke she sees light glinting on her Sisters' armour – silver, white, crimson and black – hears the sound of their voices, the triumphant clarion call of the trumpets, the hymns of victory filling the air.

It is over, she tells herself. Over at last.

Morvenn turns her face towards the dawn, and the touch of the day's first light on her face is blessing enough.

XXXV

The Basilikum of the Convent Sanctorum is full of the dead. They lie in silent rows, hands folded in the aquila across still chests, their eyes closed for the final time. There are no distinctions in death – battle-brother lies next to Sister, palatine next to novitiate, Crusader next to pilgrim, the Rose and the Chalice and the Shroud all equal in the sight of the Golden Throne.

The time for ceremonies will come. When night falls Morvenn will call her Sisters together in prayer, then each Order will take their dead to bury or burn as ordained by scripture. There will be new saints, new relics, new tales to inspire those that follow after.

But not yet.

She kneels before the tabernacle and touches the lit taper in her hand to a long black candle.

'For the *Lux Dominus*. And for her captain. God-Emperor, grant them a place of honour at your side.'

She brings the taper to the next candle in the row, and then the next, marking each with a spoken name. Ignatia. Kseniya. Fionnula. Aymar Tancret. Véronique. Balian.

And Aleyna.

The Sisters Pronatus have taken the reliquary and its bloody contents into their keeping. Aleyna's skull is to be stripped of flesh, polished, jewelled, filigreed, and returned to the newly cleansed reliquary case that once held the remains of Saint Athenasia. In years to come, novitiates will learn the tales of Saint Aleyna, of her miracle that saved the faithful. There will be processions, triumphs, perhaps even a cathedrum of her own. Her name will be spoken as long as the Adepta Sororitas endure, her death and sacrifice given meaning by the inspiration she leaves behind her.

Morvenn rises to her feet, bracing herself against the tabernacle to spare her freshly strapped ribs. The wound in her shoulder has been washed and stitched, and her burns are gleaming with perfumed unguents. She aches from crown to toe, but she is healing in preparation for battle of a different kind.

She walks between the rows of the dead, committing each face to memory. Their lives were the price of victory, offered up without hesitation for the sake of the Convent Sanctorum and their companions.

The air is cool against her skin as she steps out of the Basilikum into the cloister. Sister Kerem is waiting there, her head bowed in prayer. She looks up as Morvenn approaches and makes the aquila.

'Abbess Sanctorum.'

'Sister Superior.' Morvenn mirrors the gesture. 'I owe you thanks.'

Kerem frowns. 'Why should that be, my abbess?'

'You remained at Saint Mina's Hope. Shortly afterwards Canoness Elsvieta reconsidered her place in the defence of Ophelia VII. I assume I have you to thank for that.'

'The canoness knows her duty.' Kerem looks at her feet, her olive skin flushing a shade darker with embarrassment.

'Nonetheless. I am sure you had some part in convincing her how best she could undertake it. Your arrival was a timely one.'

'I had feared we might not reach you in time.' Kerem looks up, a shy smile crossing her scarred features. 'But the God-Emperor was with us. What will you do now, Abbess Sanctorum?'

'Return to Holy Terra.' Morvenn walks to the window and looks down to the walls below, where the rebuilding of Silvana's Bastion is already underway. 'Face the High Lords. And I find myself in need of a guard. There is a place for you amongst them, should you wish it.'

Kerem looks thoughtful. 'I am honoured, my abbess. Were I to accept, with whom would I be serving?'

'Does that make a difference to you?'

'It does.'

'You have fought with Hiromi and Zafiya before, of course.'

'I am glad to hear their service continues.'

'I am told Zafiya will be fit to travel by the time our voidship arrives.' Morvenn thinks back to the battle's bloody aftermath, the broken ground littered with the wounded and the dying. Canoness Elsvieta ascending the steps, every inch of her vestments soaked in gore. Hiromi cradling Zafiya's head in her lap, crimson-handed Hospitallers working desperately to staunch the lifeblood flowing from her wounds. The solemn procession of the Black Templars bearing their fallen from the battlefield. A golden-haired Zephyrim singing a wordless lament.

'Will there be others?'

'Canoness Lucreziana has already accepted a place within my retinue, on condition that she may speak her mind plainly when we are alone.' Morvenn snorts. 'Prioress Illuminata has declined in favour of remaining to oversee the rebuilding of Ophelia VII, but she has a list of recommendations from Our Martyred Lady long enough to fill a library. I would see representatives of all the Orders Majoris in my honour guard in time.'

'When I lost my squad, I had thought to spend the rest of my life amongst the Repentia, not to be honoured in such a way.'

Kerem pauses. 'I accept, my abbess. On condition that I too may speak my mind, when the need arises.'

'I would expect no less.' Morvenn clasps Kerem's wrist, forearm to forearm. 'Although I warn you that my tenure amongst the High Lords is likely to be short.'

Days pass.

It is easy to vanish in the battle's aftermath. With so many driven from their homes, so many lost, wounded and dead, no one notices one more ragged beggar among the column that trickles from the Convent Sanctorum. Lethe hides in plain sight in the mass of the displaced as they are transported in vast wagons to Ophelia VII's resettlement camps, and is almost offended when no one comes looking for her. She keeps her head low beneath her stolen hood, accepting her daily ration of hot soup and a place to snatch a few hours' sleep. In exchange, she labours in the crematoria, loading the bodies of the dead onto the conveyer belts that will convey them to the furnaces, retrieving the charred remains from the other side and grinding the residual bone and gristle into powder.

If anyone asks – and they rarely do – she tells them she is a quarry-worker from Caelestis, one of the few who escaped the slaughter. She has no fear that some genuine survivor of the massacre will expose her story as a lie, for the simple reason that she knows there are none. She is not the only former prisoner here – from time to time she catches sight of the chafe-marks left by a penitent's muzzle, or long-healed whip-scars on the exposed flesh of neck or back. They do not acknowledge each other, an unspoken agreement passing between them that the past is best left in the grave where it belongs. There is talk of resettlement, of work elsewhere, of a new life in the God-Emperor's service, of second chances. Nothing ever materialises.

No matter.

Lethe has a second chance of her own.

The Death of Saints is gone. She had thought he was her saviour, a god from beyond the stars come to lead her to freedom – but he had proved himself a weakling at the last, a liar and a deceiver.

But she has learned his lessons well. And she has learned to *listen*.

She heaves another rotting carcass onto the furnace-belt and pauses to wipe sweat from her eyes. On her left a gaunt man is heaving a carcass of his own onto the belt, straining against the weight. As she watches, he loses his grip and the body falls to the ground and bursts, spilling rotting guts and faecal fluid across the crematorium's filthy floor.

'Idiot!' An overseer rushes forward, his whip lashing down across the labourer's back. 'Pick it up!'

The labourer drops to his knees, clawing at the rotting viscera spreading out around his feet in the vain attempt to return them to the ruptured belly.

'Quicker!'

Lethe makes sure that none of the other overseers are nearby, then walks to where the overseer is gloating over the grovelling labourer.

'Stop that,' she says.

The overseer's mouth drops open. 'What did you say?'

He raises his whip, and she knocks it aside, grabs a handful of his thinning hair and slams his head face-first into the conveyer belt. He struggles against her, but she is stronger than him, quicker than him, better than him. On the second blow his nose smashes in a bloody fountain. On the third, the skull behind it cracks.

'Help me with this.' She turns to the labourer. 'Into the furnace. Before anyone else sees.'

The man nods, his eyes wide with shock. Between them they haul it onto the conveyer belt with the rest, blood pooling from beneath the overseer's head where he lies face down, making stately progress towards the flames. Firelight catches on the metal hilt of a dagger on the overseer's belt, and Lethe draws it free. He is not quite dead, wet rasping breaths hissing from his mutilated face.

The corpse ahead of him slides into the furnace. With four swift knife-strokes, she cuts a crude eight-pointed star – the same symbol she saw carved into Ostrov's flesh – into the bare skin of the overseer's forearm, then plunges the dagger point-first into the nape of his neck. The overseer gives a rattling sigh and falls silent.

'Accept this offering,' she whispers.

A group of workers are staring at her as she pulls the knife free. Some of them have the distinctive facial scarring that marks them as former prisoners, others bear fresh whip-scars, bruises and grazes. They have all suffered, just as she has, but suffering is not without its rewards. That is what the voice in the darkness has told her, in soft and insidious whispers, promising change, power, followers, a future beyond her wildest imaginings.

'What do we do now?' the labourer asks. The overseer's body falls into the furnace and is gone.

'We wait,' she says. 'We pray to the true gods. And we gather others to our cause.'

'And then?'

Lethe smiles. 'And then we will be free.'

XXXVI

'No?'

'No, Abbess Sanctorum.' The adept looks up at Morvenn, towering over him in her freshly repaired and anointed warsuit. 'Forgive me. The Senatorum Imperialis is already in session.' His eyes flick to the dripping object held in the warsuit's right hand, and his face turns ashen. 'None may enter. Not even you–'

If the two armoured brothers of the Adeptus Custodes had stood in her way, it might be different, but they stand like golden statues. She reaches over the adept's head and shoves the doors open. They fly back with a crash.

'Abbess Sanctorum – I must protest!'

'Adept.' Celestian Kerem takes the shaking man by the collar of his robes and moves him aside. 'Do as you are bidden.'

Morvenn enters the council chamber alone, her eyes straining to adjust as she moves from light into darkness. Figures are rising behind the table, hands moving in desperate gestures towards bodyguards and attendants. Most likely she has already been stripped of her rank, but she has one last gift for the High Lords of Terra before they banish her from their presence.

Grand Master Fadix is on his feet. 'Abbess Sanctorum, this is a closed–'

She hurls the dripping object in the warsuit's right hand onto the table. It hits the wood with a dull thud, and rolls until it is lying face up, the milky eye staring into the shocked face of the Navigator Kadak Mir.

'What is the meaning of–'

'Behold the Death of Saints.' Morvenn's lip curls. 'I have done what you would not. Think twice before you stand in my way again.'

'This is unacceptable!' the Fabricator General rattles.

Kadak Mir's hood falls back, revealing a cadaverous face twisted with outrage. 'My lord, this cannot be allowed–'

'Enough,' an impossibly deep voice booms.

A huge figure unfolds from the darkness. Morvenn blinks as he steps into the light, his armour gleaming ultramarine and gold, the laurels of victory around his brow, the steady blue eyes and the finely carved profile unmistakable. The Purgator Mirabilis falls to one knee almost before Morvenn gives the command.

'My lord regent.'

Awe and wonder fill her soul. She is in the presence of the God-Emperor's risen son, the closest thing to the divine on which she has ever laid her eyes. If he is here to deliver judgement upon her, then she will accept it without question and count herself grateful for the honour.

'Rise, Morvenn Vahl. You have served my father well. You have my thanks for that.'

'I have done my duty, my lord.'

'Indeed you have.' He lifts the rotting head from the table, turns it in his great gauntlets, and places it down again with a sorrowful air. 'The Imperium has need of warriors, but it also has need of leaders. You have proven yourself to be both. I would ask you to retake your seat at this table.'

Morvenn frowns as the warsuit lumbers to its feet. 'My lord.

This council is a place for words. I serve the God-Emperor best in holy war.'

'As do I.' Guilliman leans across the table, fixing her with his ancient steel-blue gaze. 'Which is the very reason I would have your voice heard here before you return to the battlefield.'

Grand Master Fadix sinks back into his seat. 'My lord regent, this is a matter for this council to decide–'

'It is not. I have asked the Abbess Sanctorum, and I await her answer.'

Morvenn hesitates. There she stands, poised on the threshold between two possible futures. Behind her beckons an Imperium at war, a life of battle and conquest in the God-Emperor's name. Ahead is a chamber where wars are fought with words, where her greatest opponents will be those on her own side. She takes a deep breath, closes her eyes, and offers up a prayer for guidance.

There is no answer, but then, there never is. The decision, as always, is hers to make.

'I will serve as you request, lord regent.' Morvenn takes her place at the blood-spattered table. 'Now. Let us speak of holy war.'

ABOUT THE AUTHOR

Jude Reid lives in Glasgow with her husband and two daughters, and writes in the narrow gaps between full-time work as a surgeon, wrangling her kids and failing to tire out a border collie. In what little free time she has, she enjoys tabletop roleplaying, ITF Tae Kwon Do and inadvisably climbing big hills. Her many stories for Black Library include the Warhammer 40,000 novels *Creed: Ashes of Cadia, Morvenn Vahl: Spear of Faith* and *Daemonbreaker.*

YOUR NEXT READ

KRIEG
by Steve Lyons

The Death Korps of Krieg lay siege to a hive city on the outskirts of Warzone Octarius, desperately trying to prevent untold masses of orks and tyranids spilling out into the Imperium. How far will the ruthless Korpsmen go to achieve victory in a seemingly unwinnable war?

An extract from
Krieg
by Steve Lyons

Hive Arathron was lost. In truth, it had been lost from the moment the voidship had crashed into it.

Arathron's doom had come screaming from the heavens without warning, in a ball of vengeful flame. The impact had sundered the hive's walls, collapsing fifty residential levels into one. It had touched off a chain of explosions, ripping through the industrial blocks. Millions had perished, unaware, in those first few fateful seconds.

The ship itself – a ramshackle assembly of armour plates, bolted to the frame of a junked Imperial cruiser – was all but disintegrated. Nothing aboard could have survived; but then, somehow, orks always did.

The planetary governor assumed the crash to be accidental, rather than a deliberate attack: fallout from the war raging through the Octarius System. She may have been right. Where orks were concerned, it was often hard to tell the difference. The result, either way, was the same. The local militia, expecting to find only broken bodies in the wreckage, were taken by surprise and overwhelmed.

A Cadian regiment, diverted from another battlefield, fared better. They fought with their customary skill and precision, in contrast to the feral and disorganised invaders. They kept the orks pinned down for several days.

Just one more, and they might have stood a chance.

Ven Bruin was on the lowest level when he heard the news. He was herding three hundred hopeless stragglers through narrow thoroughfares, towards the exit.

Down here, the hive was more or less structurally sound but creaking under the weight of the devastation above. The greatest threat was other hopeless citizens, driven to panic by the loss of all they knew. Many had allowed the Ruinous Powers into their hearts. They had joined up with the street gangs, whose only aims were to vandalise and terrorise, to satisfy their own gratuitous urges.

For two days, Ven Bruin had fought a running battle with the gangs. His greatest asset in this was his distinctive garb. His black cloak and capotain hat, with the skull motif on their buckles, announced his rank as clearly as did the Inquisitorial seal, which he wore clasped above his heart.

His appearance struck shame and dread into the newly faithless. It reminded them that the Emperor's reach exceeded that of the godless xenos, even now, even still. Many of them melted into the shadows, to cower and weep and regret their impulsive actions. For others, the sight of a witch hunter provoked unreasoning fury. These were the truly damned, and they had had enough of running.

The attack was launched from the steps of a half-demolished church. The gangers used its cracked and crumbling pillars for cover. Perhaps they enjoyed the twisted symbolism. A garbage fire sputtered in the doorway behind them. A few had laid their hands on rusted old percussion rifles. They spat out bullets indiscriminately, into the screaming crowd.

'Everyone, down on the ground!' Ven Bruin yelled, but few of the would-be evacuees obeyed him, and those who did were trampled by the rest. He shouldered his way through them, inferno pistol drawn, looking for a clear shot. He unsheathed his sword and thumbed the activation rune in its hilt, bathing its blade in a field of fierce, bright energy. This had the desired effect of clearing his path somewhat.

Ven Bruin was an old man. Rejuvenat treatments had kept him lean and vital, strong of limb – he took pride in the image he presented, eyes blazing in the shadow of his hat's lowered brim, gritted teeth framed by a silver-streaked beard – but he *felt* old. He would not be around forever, and had begun his search for a successor long ago.

He gained sight of one of the gunners: a straggly haired youth in a ripped vest, bare arms crazed with illiterate tattoos. He steadied his target in his sights as he advanced upon him. The inferno pistol had only a short range, which normally suited Ven Bruin. He did most of his fighting eye to eye.

The youth saw him coming, one old man striding against the tide, and almost dropped his weapon in fright. He loosed off another burst of badly directed fire. Ven Bruin didn't flinch as three civilians were cut down around him. He trusted his body armour – more so, the armour of his faith – to keep him safe. He squeezed his pistol's trigger, and fried a stream of air before him.

The youth's hair erupted into flame and his face blistered. His smouldering corpse broke on the stone steps. What the inferno pistol lacked in range, it gained in power – too much power for so weak a foe, but it made a salutary point.

Three more foes came at Ven Bruin from his left. Three more tattooed heretics, whirling chains above their heads. Immediately, he discerned the weeping pustules on one's neck, the unnatural curvature of another's spine. They were mutants, vermin washed up from the underhive to revel in Arathron's woes.

He holstered his pistol and gripped his sword two-handed. The first mutant leapt at him, screeching, and impaled itself upon the interposed blade. The second accidentally wrapped its chain about its own head. It crumpled with a groan and was stamped to death by a crowd now more disgusted than scared by it.

The third mutant, seeing its fellows' fates, was cautious. Its chain struck like a venomous snake from six feet away, glancing off Ven Bruin's chestplate. He yanked his blade out of the first dead mutant, feeling minimal resistance. The crowd around him had finally thinned out, giving him much-needed elbow room.

The chain lashed out again and he ducked under it, at the same time propelling himself forward. His blade described a brilliant arc of purifying light. It struck the mutant's left side, beneath its ribs, and emerged from its right. The stink of mutant blood assailed his nostrils, but it swiftly boiled away. The blade also cleansed itself.

The sounds of gunfire ceased. The crowd calmed down a little, though some still wailed in fear or mourning. Two of Ven Bruin's acolytes caught up with him. They flanked him, scanning their surroundings for renewed threats, their pistols readied. It was their duty to protect him, their inquisitor. He was well aware how hard he made this for them.

He had brought six with him, just his warriors. The others had been busy too. A second ganger lay dead, slumped against her pillar. The third was on his knees, fumbling with a jammed rifle, as Interrogator Ferran attained the church steps and bore down on him. The ganger, in panic, cast the rifle away and began to raise his hands, tears streaking his crudely inked cheeks. Ferran executed him with a bolt to the temple.

'Keep moving!' Ven Bruin bellowed. He hauled a cringing civilian to his feet, flashed him a contemptuous glare and sent him on his way with a shove. 'No time to lick our wounds or count our dead. Keep heading east – that way – in an orderly fashion. Anyone judged to be impeding others will be shot.'

He reached the steps and marched up them. Someone pressed a laudhailer into his hand, which he raised to his lips. He repeated the instructions, adding directions to the exit. It was likely that no one here had left the hive before. He sent his acolytes back out to guide, protect and motivate them, but signalled to Ferran to hang back.

'There are more of them out there,' said Ferran, once they had a measure of privacy. 'Heretics. Mutants. I saw a shadow behind the church windows. It feels wrong to turn our backs on them, to allow them to profane that holy place.'

'You heard the vox reports?' Ven Bruin asked him.

'I did. The Cadians are pulling out of Arathron today, ceding it to the xenos, Emperor damn them.' The curl of Ferran's lips and the beetling of his dark, bushy eyebrows underlined his disgust at this development.

'It was to be expected,' said Ven Bruin, with greater equanimity. 'Their forces are depleted from their previous engagement. They held out longer than we expected they would.' He allowed himself a sigh. 'Not as long as we had prayed they might.'

'And our mission here, inquisitor? Are we to proceed?'

'If only we were closer, perhaps.'

'It may be days yet before the xenos reach these levels.'

'It may be sooner than we think. If not before we reach our goal, then certainly before we could do anything about it. We could even lead them there ourselves. No, best I feel if Hive Arathron's secrets remain hidden. For as long as they can be.'

'If the xenos don't stumble upon them, the heretics might.'

'If the Emperor is with us, they'll be kept too busy tearing each other apart.'

'We can only pray, again,' the interrogator grumbled.

They spilled out of a broad opening at the hive's base. They were met by the glare of the sun, sitting high in the eastern sky before them. Few of Ven Bruin's charges had seen a light so bright and they flinched from it, complaining that it burnt their eyes.

They joined thousands more evacuees, milling about in confusion. Reservist militiamen, identified by armbands, fought in vain to herd them northwards. Another hive squatted on the distant horizon – at least a hundred miles away, Ven Bruin reckoned.

The barren ground was churned with recent vehicle tracks, but few vehicles were left in evidence. Fights had broken out around a couple of trucks. People clung to their chassis and hammered on their windscreens, imploring, so that while their engines growled and their exhaust pipes spluttered, their tyres could gain no traction.

To their backs, Hive Arathron marinated in a self-created smog. Thicker smoke billowed from its upper levels, miles above, as flyers circled like disoriented insects. Its outer roadways teemed with insects too: the vehicles of the withdrawing Cadians. According to vox chatter, they had pulled back to the bottom hundred levels, collapsing strategic access points to slow down their pursuers.

Ven Bruin took to the hailer again. He ordered the crowd to disperse, to make room for others adding to the crush behind them. He promised that vehicles were being sent back for them, though he knew there would never be enough.

The xenos in the hive had found a cannon. It had only been a matter of time. The Cadians had destroyed artillery emplacements as they left, but orks had a reputation for making the most broken weapons function. Breathless reports squawked over each other in Ven Bruin's earpiece. Explosive shells were landing at the base of the hive to the west, obliterating victims by the hundred.

He knew now that most of the people around him were doomed.

He called for transport, which arrived in less than a minute. Hope swept through the crowd as a shuttle dropped down among them. With some prodding from the reservists, they cleared a space for it to land, almost at Ven Bruin's feet. Hope turned to resentment as they saw that it hadn't come for them. Their objections were swiftly quelled, however, by the witch hunter's fiery glare, along with his warriors' warning shots.

He paused with a foot on the landing ramp. Something drew his gaze upwards, and he saw streaks of light across the cloudless sky. An instant later, the drone of rocket engines reached him. The crowd had seen and heard it too, and wondered what it meant. Ven Bruin knew, as did Ferran. 'Our reinforcements,' murmured the latter, as the streaks converged upon the hive to the north.

'Dead on schedule,' Ven Bruin noted.

Ferran's brow furrowed. 'Already too late,' he added bleakly.

A new command headquarters had been established out on the plain.

It was ten miles east of Arathron, beyond its cannons' range. The Cadians' support staff and fresh-faced, untrained conscripts assembled the last of its prefabricated huts. The first Centaurs and Chimeras rolled up on their tracks, disgorging weary soldiers. Some were helped to the medicae hut. Others headed for the mess hall, where slab was already being served. Tents began to spring up everywhere.

Colonel Drakon, commander of the Cadian 432nd, settled at his new desk. A servitor poured amasec for him and his guests.

The colonel expressed surprise at Ven Bruin's request for quarters for himself and his retinue. 'Am I to infer that you have further business here?' he asked.

'You may infer it, yes,' said Ven Bruin, tight-lipped.

'I heard there was an… issue with the former governor, before he passed away. My people could know nothing of that, of course, but if we can assist in any way…?'

'Not at this present moment.'

Drakon sat back and took a long sip from his glass. Ven Bruin's presence worried him, but he knew better than to push too hard for information. It might have been different had Ven Bruin served the Ordo Xenos. The Ordo Hereticus existed to seek out *human* treachery – and the only humans here now were the colonel's own shock troops.

Ven Bruin could have reassured him, but chose not to. It did no one any harm to be reminded that the Emperor's eyes were always upon them.

'We are to be joined by a Krieg regiment, I hear,' said Interrogator Ferran.

'I believe so,' said Drakon.

'The infamous Death Korps.'

'Exceptional fighters,' Ven Bruin commented, approvingly. 'I have encountered them often. Their world exists on a permanent war footing. Soldiers are their only export, so they are trained from birth, instilled with the highest possible level of commitment.'

'The same was once true of my world,' the Cadian colonel said, a little stiffly.

'You have new orders, presumably,' said Ferran. 'To retake the hive?'

Drakon shook his head. 'To eradicate all trace of xenos from this world – even if it means Hive Arathron is razed in the process.'

Ven Bruin inclined his head, so his eyes fell back into his capotain's shadow.

'This world is a crucial link in the cordon about this system,' the colonel explained. 'It cannot – it must not – fall. The line must be held here.'

Ven Bruin was not surprised to hear it. The Octarius War had been raging for several years. Imperial machinations had set a burgeoning ork empire against a tyranid hive fleet. The hope had been for it to end in mutual destruction. Instead, both sides had thrived on the conflict. The hive fleet had engorged itself on the biomass of billions of foes. The orks had multiplied and grown stronger too, while billions more had flocked to join them from all corners of the galaxy. The war was expanding, the fallout felt on many bordering worlds like this one. Some had already suffered the ultimate sanction.

Those worlds had been destroyed for the sake of keeping the xenos hordes contained.

The approach of the Krieg was first evidenced by a dust cloud on the horizon.

Sergeant Renick saw it as she sat in the dirt outside the medicae hut, waiting for her turn to be seen. Her injuries were less severe than many, just cuts and bruises, but she had taken her last dose of stimm. She had had no choice, after sixteen hours defending a makeshift barricade from wave after wave of ork attacks with no prospect of relief. According to regulations, now she had to be examined for side effects.

She also wanted to replenish her stimms, of course.

At present, all she felt was tired. She lost the battle to keep her eyelids raised, and next she knew, she was woken by a sound like the drone of a million bees. She shook her head and clambered to her feet, reproaching herself for her weakness. She brushed down her khaki fatigues and donned her helmet over her spiky black hair. She fastened the chinstrap so tightly that it cut into her flesh.

The queue ahead of her had dissipated, the temperature had dropped and that dust cloud had drawn closer. Squat, angular shapes were becoming discernible within it, and the insect drone had grown into a roar of heavy-duty engines.

She was in and out of the hut in under three minutes. She gathered with her Cadian fellows outside their tents, beneath the blood-red sky of sunset, as the first armoured vehicles reached the encampment and juddered to a halt.

The rest of the convoy, a mile long and almost as wide, dispersed in search of plots of land to claim. Scores of Gorgon transports were interspersed with smaller Trojans, laden with supplies and towing Earthshaker cannons on platforms. The Leman Russ tank was ubiquitous as always, mainly in its Demolisher siege variant. Renick also saw a pair of massive Baneblades and some vehicles she couldn't identify.

Most of the tanks were customised with trench rails, dozer blades and air filter units, for the harsh environments in which they commonly operated. Their hulls were decorated with cracked and fading decals, depicting grinning skulls with spiked helmets and identifying the Krieg 43rd Siege Regiment.

The most surprising sight of all – the one that had troopers nudging each other and pointing in astonishment – was a phalanx of horses, masked and armoured the same as their straight-backed riders. They had matched the convoy's pace from the northern hive's space port and hardly seemed tired; Renick marvelled at their stamina.

Krieg soldiers poured from the transports and climbed down from their mounts. They set straight to work, unpacking equipment. The sounds of engines died down to be replaced by a